Forgotten Souls

Wes Markin

About the Author

Wes Markin is the bestselling author of The Yorkshire Murders, which stars the compassionate and relentless DCI Emma Gardner. He is also the author of Whitby's Forgotten Victims, the DCI Michael Yorke Thrillers set in Salisbury, and the Jake Pettman Thrillers set in New England. Wes lives in Harrogate with his wife, two children, and his cheeky cockapoo, Rosie, close to the crime scenes in The Yorkshire Murders and Whitby's Forgotten Victims.

You can find out more at:

www.wesmarkinauthor.com

 facebook.com/wesmarkinauthor

By Wes Markin

DCI Yorke Thrillers
One Last Prayer

The Repenting Serpent

The Silence of Severance

Rise of the Rays

Dance with the Reaper

Christmas with the Conduit

The Killing Pit

Fire in Bone

Blue Falls

The Rotten Core

Rock and a Hard Place

Better the Devil

The Secret Diary of Lacey Ray

The Yorkshire Murders
The Viaduct Killings

The Lonely Lake Killings

The Crying Cave Killings

The Graveyard Killings

The Winter Killings

Whitby's Forgotten Victims
Forgotten Bones

Forgotten Lives

Forgotten Souls

Forgotten Graves

Details of how to claim your **FREE** DCI Michael Yorke quick read, **A lesson in Crime**, can be found at the end of this book.

This story is a work of fiction. All names, characters, organizations, places, events and incidents are products of the author's imagination or are used fictitiously. Any resemblance to any persons, alive or dead, events or locals is entirely coincidental.

Text copyright © 2024 Wes Markin

First published 2024

ISBN: 9798343451474

Edited by: Candida Bradford

Published by: WFM Publishing Ltd

Chapter One

This wasn't the first time that the canteen at Scarborough HQ had been kitted out for a birthday party. It was, however, the first time it'd been kitted out for DCI Frank Black.

For very good reason.

Nobody alive wanted to celebrate Frank's birthday, least of all the man of the moment.

DS Reggie Moyes had a lot to answer for. Frank was used to the man's foolish antics, but this one took the biscuit! And it made no sense. Frank and Reggie had been colleagues for over thirty years. At what point did the idea: 'Frank Black may appreciate a surprise sixty-fifth birthday party' set down roots? And how on earth did the daft apeth's idea gestate into the finished event?

He looked around and groaned. How many forced smiles could you cram into one room?

It wasn't dead, *unfortunately,* but Jacob Marley probably had a better turnout at his funeral. This was because most people, unlike Reggie, *got* Frank. They knew what his attitude to such an event would be. It had given them the perfect excuse for non-attendance. They'd be sighing with relief. Most people disliked Frank as much as he loathed parties.

Frank nursed a Coke in a shadowy corner beneath some deflating balloons.

Unfortunately, Wham! was playing full blast. The late sixties and seventies were more Frank's era. Led Zeppelin and Dylan. The DJ was either struggling with maths or just basic human decency. Still, the music was a great excuse for him to lie low. There was as much chance of tickling a great white shark's belly and being pecked affectionately as getting Frank on that dance floor.

Across the room, DC Sean Groves was attempting to flirt with DC Sharon Miller, who looked as unimpressed as she'd been the day she'd ended up on Frank's team. Admittedly, Frank didn't come with the best reputation. Her demeanour had picked up during the last investigation, though, and she'd shown real value. Sharon had even admitted earlier tonight that Frank was different from how she'd thought he'd be. He knew the comments made about him in other departments. Grumpy old Frank Black; it's a Black day; Frank Black as night, etc. His surname had been toyed with many times. Just not, it seemed, in a creative way.

Frank almost felt sorry for Sean's failed attempts at flirtation.

Almost.

He'd been practically sloth-like on their first investigation together, and Frank had been fearing that nothing short of a cattle prod was going to rev him up. However, like Sharon, he'd picked up his game in the second investigation. There was hope, but crashing and burning with Sharon here wouldn't do Sean's confidence much good.

Still, it offered Frank some amusement during this rather drab event.

Donald Oxley, the chief constable, huddled with his cronies in another corner, no doubt discussing important matters like golf handicaps and yacht maintenance. Frank could imagine the conversation: 'We should celebrate Black's sodding retirement, not his bloody birthday.'

Frank chuckled.

Was he clinging to his job just to piss Donald off?

The thought had occurred to him. *Often.*

'Come on Eileen' by Dexys Midnight Runners kicked in. Great. His eardrums were now officially filing for divorce. His phone buzzed in his pocket.

He grimaced at the notification.

It was his weekly update from Paula, a colleague monitoring crime and homelessness in Leeds.

Still no sign of Maddie.

He sighed, his chest tightening. It'd been a good few months since his thirty-three-year-old daughter had disappeared. Apart from three sightings in Leeds, there'd been nothing. The worst thing was she'd returned to him earlier this year after spending many years on the streets, addicted to heroin, and doing God knows what else. He'd broken that dreadful cycle, only to cock it all up at the final hurdle by deceiving her. His own stupidity had pushed her away again, and he'd no idea if she was back in that downward spiral, or even alive.

He rubbed his forehead. Despite loving her with every ounce of his being, he'd failed to be the father she needed at every point in her life.

Now, all he could do was search and monitor these

updates from Paula, hoping against hope that she was out there somewhere, alive and well.

Sensing his distress, Rylan, DI Gerry Carver's therapy dog, nudged Frank's hand. He stroked the Labrador Retriever's head and whispered, 'You get me, don't you, fella? You'd never have organised this grotesque affair.'

Gerry materialised at his side. When he looked up, she made eye contact with him. A rarity. That meant she was here for a confrontation.

'What've I done now? It's my birthday... go easy.'

'Coke.' She pointed at the can of Coke in his hand as if he was holding a live grenade with the pin hanging halfway out.

'Those are some powers of observation—'

'A 330ml can of Coca-Cola contains approximately thirty-five grams of sugar.'

'And?'

'And diet cola doesn't!'

'But diet cola tastes like shite.'

'It also doesn't give you diabetes.'

Frank snorted, shook his head, and sang, 'Happy birthday to me.' He stopped and stared at his watch, willing it to be later. 'You know, Gerry, two months back, this would've been my seventh pint of beer. Wouldn't that have been worse than thirty-five grams of sugar?'

'Yes.'

'Precisely.' He held up the Coke. 'So credit where credit's due?'

Gerry's brow furrowed. 'I don't understand why you should be given credit for drinking cola.'

'Not for the cola then... for knocking alcohol on the head. You know what? Never mind.' Frank sighed. Gerry was brilliant, no doubt about that. Her mind worked in ways that left most people, including Frank, in the dust. But her grasp on social niceties was about as firm as a politician's promise.

'How're things with Tom?' Frank asked, changing tack. 'You two lovebirds planning a Christmas wedding?'

Gerry's face remained impassive. 'Our relationship is progressing satisfactorily. We've hit the 95 per cent threshold for compatibility.'

'Jesus.'

'What?'

'You're still measuring that? After all these months.'

'It could still dip below, Frank. It takes years to stabilise something like that.'

'I see.' Frank took a mouthful of Coke. 'What're the issues then?'

'Well... the sex is still rather frenetic, and he seems a bit too eager to please—'

Frank's Coke went down the wrong way. He spluttered, patting his chest, coughing.

'Are you okay?'

'No. Christ on a bike, Gerry. Do you not remember my special request?'

'Which one?'

'The one about never ever, *ever*, mentioning your sex life to me.'

'Ah, yes. You told me it's an unwritten rule of social interaction.'

'Aye. It bloody well is.'

Gerry looked confused. 'But I've overheard colleagues talking about their sex lives with one another.'

'Were they all female?'

'Yes, but why is gender relevant?'

He sighed. 'Listen. Women and men rarely talk about

5

their sex lives to one another unless they're married. Men might talk about it among themselves, women among themselves.' He made a gesture by crossing his fingers. 'Rarely do those paths cross.'

'It all sounds rather old-fashioned.'

'Aye. Just how I like it. Plus, you're the same age as my daughter.'

'So?'

'So, I'm old enough to be your father. Don't mention sex around me.' Frank shook his head, wondering not for the first time how Gerry functioned in the world. Time to change the subject. 'Listen, give me your read on the room, will you? What do you see?'

Gerry scanned the canteen. Frank sat up, eagerly.

'Donald Oxley is engaged in what appears to be a competitive discussion about golf scores with Superintendent Harrison,' Gerry said. 'Their facial expressions, possibly prompted by elevated cortisol levels, suggest a barely concealed rivalry.'

'Nice.' Frank nodded. 'I like that he's uncomfortable. Go on.'

'Sharon is exhibiting clear signs of discomfort in response to Sean's attempts at flirtation.'

'I'd go for very pissed off like, but I guess discomfort works.'

Gerry nodded. 'I also detect some pity in her micro-expressions.'

Frank snorted. 'Ha. Sympathy. Nice to know she's got a heart.'

'Sean, meanwhile, seems oblivious to her discomfort and disinterest, likely because of a combination of alcohol consumption and misplaced optimism.'

'At least he's roused himself for the challenge. Need to see a bit more of that in the incident room.'

'It might be easier for him if someone made him aware she was homosexual.'

Frank raised an eyebrow. 'She is? How did you figure that out?'

'I didn't. She told me.'

Frank nodded. 'Well, she didn't tell me.'

Gerry stared at him. 'Probably as a result of that unwritten rule of social interaction.'

'Smart-arse. She's okay to tell me she's gay... not what she gets up to in the bedroom.'

Gerry had already moved on. She was tilting her head and regarding the party organiser, Reggie. He was in the middle of the room, attempting what could charitably be called dancing. It looked more like a man trying to swat a swarm of bees. A couple of Reggie's drinking buddies cheered him on, their encouragement fuelled by more than a few pints. 'Reggie's musculature is quite impressive for a man his age. However, his choice of attire seems impractical for the current environment and temperature.'

Reggie, ever the showman, had squeezed himself into a T-shirt at least two sizes too small, the fabric straining against his improbably muscled torso. The words 'Sun's Out, Guns Out' were barely legible across his chest, distorted by his flexing pectorals. At fifty-five, Reggie was in better shape than most men half his age, and he never missed an opportunity to remind everyone of that fact.

Frank snorted. 'Impractical? It's a bloody health hazard. One sneeze and he's going to burst out of it like the sodding Hulk.'

'I mentioned that to him earlier,' Gerry said. 'His words were: "If the guns are too big for the holster then so be it."'

'And you didn't punch him in the face?'

Gerry looked confused.

A chorus of groans and laughter filled the room as Reggie tried to breakdance. Frank pinched the bridge of his nose. 'I had ten minutes left in me. That just slipped to about thirty seconds. I need the loo.'

The quiet of the corridor was a blessed relief after the forced joviality of the canteen. Frank took a moment to lean against the wall, closing his eyes and taking a deep breath. He was getting too old for this nonsense.

After answering nature's call, Frank lingered in the corridor, reluctant to re-join the party. The muffled sounds of conversation and laughter drifted through the closed door. Then, suddenly, the noise died down, replaced by the unmistakable strains of 'Happy Birthday'. They must have thought he was still inside.

Frank's hand hovered over the door handle. The thought of facing that sea of expectant faces, of having to blow out candles and make a speech made his skin crawl.

He took a step back, then another. 'Sod it,' he muttered, turning on his heel.

As Frank made his way out of the station, he felt a twinge of guilt. Reggie had meant well, in his own misguided way. But sometimes, the kindest thing you could do for a friend was to let them be who they were – even if that person was a grumpy old sod who'd rather spend his birthday alone with a takeaway.

The night air was crisp and invigorating after the stuffy confines of the party. Frank breathed deeply, feeling the tension ebb from his shoulders. He'd catch hell for this tomorrow, no doubt. But right now, with the stars twinkling overhead and the promise of some peace and quiet ahead, he couldn't bring himself to care.

On his way home, he stopped by a shop and picked up a litre of coke from the shelf. As he neared the counter to pay, he rolled his eyes. 'Chuffing hell, Gerry!' He returned to the shelf and swapped the Coke for a Diet Coke.

Back home, Frank settled into his favourite armchair, Maddie's photo on the side table next to him, alongside the photo of Mary, his wife, who'd passed away five years earlier.

'Happy birthday to me, love,' he murmured. 'Wish you were both here.'

As he took a sip of Diet Coke, his phone buzzed. A text from Gerry.

> Your absence was noted. Cake was subpar. Reggie's shirt didn't survive. Happy Birthday, Frank.

Frank chuckled, shaking his head. Maybe birthdays weren't so bad after all. At least, not when you had the right people to share them with – even if that sharing happened from a safe distance.

Chapter Two

ASPIRING marine biologist Sarah Chen considered herself a solar-powered creature and so was in no mood for Whitby's gloomy daybreak.

With the annual November goth festival beginning today, however, it felt rather appropriate. Unlike her, Sarah suspected that the arriving dark pilgrims would revel in the mist.

She pulled her jacket tighter against the biting chill and approached Tate Hill Pier. The historic stone structure jutted out into the harbour, its weathered surface slick with sea spray.

She groaned when she spotted Jack's truck at the entrance. She'd been half-hoping they wouldn't show, forcing her to abandon these cold, dismal observations for a quick retreat to her warm guesthouse. Wishful thinking.

Her childhood friends, Jack Pearce and Liam Walsh, were obsessed with magnet fishing and had offered to demonstrate this "art" to her. She was completing a project on the ecological benefits of the practice and really should have been grateful. But seeing her breath cloud in the frigid air was sucking at her enthusiasm now.

She glanced up at the brooding sentinel on East Cliff. The ruins of Whitby Abbey. Even more haunting in the November dawn, silhouetted against the backdrop of gentle, lapping waves. Sarah shivered, wondering if Bram Stoker had stood in this very spot when inspiration struck for 'Dracula'.

Sarah rapped firmly on the truck's window, interrupting the quiet sounds of the sea. Jack cracked the door open, grinning. 'Here she is!'

Sarah eyed their Stanley cups. 'Where's my drink?'

Jack exchanged a glance with Liam. 'Sorry, assumed you'd come prepared.'

Liam nodded. 'It's the first rule of a dawn fish.'

Sarah rolled her eyes. 'Thanks for preparing me.'

'It's all a learning curve.' Jack climbed from the van. 'Besides, it's a mild morn.'

'Is that what you call it?'

'Aye.' Jack's work boots hit the stones with a thump. A religious devotion to weight training and years of construction work had turned him into a brick shithouse. For the once smallest, thinnest kid in their school year, it was quite the transformation.

'Try a Jan fish. Freeze your feckin' bones.'

She grimaced. 'I'll take your word for it. I won't be finding out.'

Liam joined them, his pale face illuminated by the glow of his smartphone, fingers flying over the screen.

Jack grunted. 'Oi Liam, you really know how to kill the atmosphere.'

'I'm telling Lorna I'll be back in time for school drop-off,' Liam replied, not looking up. 'Is that all right, Jack?'

'I'm sure I warned you about having kids.' Jack grinned, revealing a chipped front tooth – a souvenir from a bar fight years ago.

'You did. Over and over. Like a broken record.'

Jack tutted. 'It may have been prudent to heed my advice.'

'Why?' Liam pocketed his phone. 'Life's good.'

Jack guffawed. 'Is it? I've been out here every day this week while you've been on dad duty. Found an old musket the other day. Probably belonged to a pirate. Want to see a photo?'

'You sent me one.' Liam smirked. 'Looked like a rusty air rifle some kid chucked in a long while back. Not like the old handgun I—'

Sarah cleared her throat. 'I'm not here for a pissing contest over magnet fishing. And I'm freezing – can we press on?'

Jack threw an arm around Liam, laughing. 'Pissing contest? Best friends forever, eh?'

The two men led Sarah to the equipment laid out on the pier. Her gaze drifted over coils of rope, heavy-duty gloves, and the stars of the show: three powerful neodymium magnets attached to sturdy lines.

Liam's eyes lit up. 'These beauties can lift over 500 kilos each. You just drop them in, drag them along the bottom, and see what sticks.'

Sarah raised an eyebrow. 'You sound excited...'

Jack clapped his hands and rubbed them together. 'That's an understatement, Sarah. You never know what you're going to drag up. Old bikes, coins, prams...'

'Let's hope you don't catch an old mine from World War II.' Sarah chuckled over her own joke.

No one else laughed.

'It's not unheard of.' Jack's tone was suddenly serious. 'Did you know they found Viking treasure just offshore back in the thirties? I bet this place is teeming with more.'

Liam was already kneeling to ready the gear. 'If that were true, dipstick, we'd be fishing with armed guards, not magnets.'

Sarah sighed, wondering if this cold adventure could really find a place in her dissertation. She took a deep breath, forcing herself to remain positive. Rusted junk was bad for marine life. Magnet fishing came with benefits. She took a few photographs of them prepping on her phone.

Jack posed for a snap. 'Eco-warriors.' He pounded his chest. 'Cleaning up the harbour one bit of rusted junk at a time.'

As her companions continued to set up, Sarah noticed several figures in the distance making their way to the East Cliff and the abbey. Determined goths wanting to make the most of the sunrise. They were in for a disappointment since it was overcast and misty.

Jack sidled up beside her. 'And here they come,' he intoned in a spooky voice. 'The children of the night. Maybe we'll fish a dead one out by their excessive piercings. Or hoist up Gomez Gloomsbury by his silver-plated plat-form boots.'

Sarah didn't laugh.

'Gomez's boots filled with water, see?' Jack said.

'You don't have to explain crap jokes to me. Anyway, stop being judgemental.'

'Look at them taking over my town!' Jack said.

'Did you just say *my* town? Really? Wow,' Sarah said. 'They also bring a tonne of cash into *your* town.'

Liam joined them. 'Sarah's right, Jack, you sound like you're from the dark ages.'

'Piss off.' Jack walked off.

Sarah turned to Liam. 'He's still prone to a tantrum or two, then?'

'Hasn't aged a day since Year Seven.' Liam winked. 'But he's got a truck. And you need a truck for this gig. And to think that you... well, you know.' He closed his eyes, folded his arms and mimed kissing.

She slapped his shoulder. 'Sod off, I was eighteen. Drunk. And that was before his protein breakfasts became big enough to sustain a small family for a year.' She rose an eyebrow. 'And I'm not sure it suits him.'

'What? All that muscle?'

'There's only one muscle I like.' She tapped her temple. 'In here. And he's buggered on that score.'

Jack rubbed his hands together. 'Right then, let's see what treasures Davy Jones' locker has for us today.'

Jack and Liam took turns casting their magnets into the murky water, the splash echoing in the early morning stillness. Sarah found herself oddly mesmerised by the rhythmic motion of casting and retrieving, the gentle tug of the line as it dragged along the harbour bottom.

Twenty uneventful minutes passed. The mist seemed to thicken, and the sunlight struggled to penetrate the gloom, casting everything in a sickly, washed-out hue.

Sarah checked her watch. 'Is it always this slow? I've got ten more minutes in me—'

'Eh up!' Jack said, suddenly tensing. 'The sea has taken offence at your tone, Sarah.' His eyes widened. 'Bloody hell.' His muscles bulged as he tried to haul it in. 'Get here, Liam!'

'Your big guns not enough?' Liam said, rushing to help.

Their combined strength had no impact.

'Now what?' Sarah asked, feeling more intrigued than she'd been all morning.

'Even bigger guns,' Liam said.

The two men edged back towards the truck.

Sarah noticed that a small group of goths had gathered to watch the spectacle. There was a top hat adorned with what appeared to be a stuffed raven, and a woman wearing a corset so tight it seemed to defy the laws of physics.

She usually enjoyed seeing the elaborate costumes around town, but in this moment of tension, with the mist swirling and the abbey looming overhead, it felt unnervingly sinister.

At the truck, Liam and Jack connected a long rope to the winch, while Sarah offered a tentative wave to the curious onlookers. The winch whirred to life, its mechanical groan echoing across the misty harbour.

Jack ran to the edge, shouting, 'Bloody hell. Listen to that *roar*. It's heavy.'

Sarah joined Jack while Liam controlled the winch.

'How is this not exciting?' Jack grinned at Sarah.

'Am I about to see an old Morris Minor pop out of the water?' she asked.

He shrugged. 'But don't get too close. Just in case, you know. We snag a live one...'

She frowned. 'Live what?'

'Live mine.' He gave a goofy grin.

'Piss off.'

A dark mass finally broke the surface, water streaming off its sides. As the object rose higher, Sarah could make out a long rectangular shape, maybe a metre by half a metre, rotating slowly on the rope.

The object bashed against the side of the pier with a hollow thunk. 'Enough, Liam! Halt!'

Liam locked the winch to avoid damaging the pier. They gathered at the edge, peering at their catch.

'What is it?' Sarah asked.

'Old fridge, by the looks of it,' Jack replied. 'Isn't the first time we've snagged one like this.'

'Christ! Are you telling me that people chuck their fridges in the bloody sea?'

Jack shrugged. 'If it doesn't work any more...'

'Then go to the tip,' Sarah muttered. 'Bastards.'

'Maybe we should give them a break. Look at the age of it!' Jack snorted. 'It's probably from an era long before anyone had the foggiest about pollution.'

'Before they had any common sense?' Sarah said, scrunching her face.

Together, they hauled the fridge up over the side of the pier. It scraped against the stones with a teeth-clenching screech.

'How bloody heavy?' Sarah panted. 'We're damaging the pier just doing this. It might be good for the marine life to get it out... but let's not damage the scenery.'

'Why do you think we do this at dawn?' Jack asked. 'No one to come and shut us down.'

'You haven't changed then, Jack, still irresponsible.'

'Ignore his bravado,' Liam said. 'We rarely snag things this heavy. This old thing is a beast.'

Eventually, the fridge lay on its side. Pits and corrosion covered the old rusty unit.

All three backed away, catching their breath.

Jack was already squatting beside it, grinning. 'Let's crack her open, then.'

'Be my guest,' Liam said. 'But let me give you some distance... just in case something's dead in there.'

Jack reached for the corroded door. 'Bet you a fiver that

there's a six-pack of Skol inside. Oh, and by the way, this was my catch.'

Sarah laughed. 'Skol! You're welcome to it.'

Sarah noticed that the goth spectators had moved closer. The sun was a lot higher now, and the mist was clearing. The wet pier shimmered.

Jack yanked at the fridge handle. 'Not budging.'

'You need to up your steroid intake,' Liam said.

Sarah laughed.

Jack grunted. 'Piss off.' The hinges gave way with an ear-splitting shriek. He fell backwards, releasing the handle as the door flew open, and the contents spilled out. Sarah's hand flew to her mouth. Several of the goths gasped.

'Shit! The stink—' Liam said and retched.

It was a body. Partially skeletonised. Strips of leathery flesh still clinging to bones. Empty eye sockets stared accusingly up at the lightening sky; a silent scream frozen on lipless jaws.

Jack turned to his side and threw up.

Hit by the cloying, sweet-sour reek of long-dead flesh preserved in a watery tomb, Sarah stumbled backwards, her mind reeling, bile rising in her throat, until she bumped against the truck.

The small crowd of goths, their elaborate make-up now seeming grotesquely appropriate, stood alongside her, staring in horrified fascination.

One absurd thought cut through the chaos in her mind with crystal clarity as she surveyed the scene, trying not to vomit: *No one could accuse Whitby of not staying true to the gothic theme this weekend.*

Chapter Three

FRANK WOKE FEELING FRESH. The difference since knocking booze on the head was staggering.

Clear-headed, thoughts sharp, he felt like a young man again!

That was until he attempted to hoist himself out of bed. 'For Christ's sake!'

He groaned. *Painkillers for breakfast then.*

After he'd stretched out, he determined to recapture that positive vibe he'd had on first opening his eyes.

No drinking. Tick.

Smoking pending.

I'm rolling back the years!

There it was again… that tingle of optimism.

His phone buzzed. Chief Constable Donald Oxley. Shit.

Did this bastard have a sixth sense for when Frank was in a good mood?

'Morning, sir.'

'Morning, Frank. Enjoy your party?'

Donald expressing an interest in him? That'd be the day. More likely a dig at his early exit.

'Aye,' Frank said. 'Although I left early.'

'Really? I don't think anyone noticed...'

Frank rolled his eyes at the barely-veiled sarcasm. 'Bit of an upset stomach,' he said. 'Must've been something I ate.'

'Right. Well, I'm afraid I've got something that might upset your stomach even more. We've got a body. On Tate Hill Pier.'

Frank took a deep breath. 'Okay.'

'What do you know about magnet fishing, Frank?'

'Eh?'

'Fishing with magnets?'

Frank shook his head, wondering if he was still asleep and this was some kind of surreal dream. 'I know fish aren't made of metal...'

Donald explained magnet fishing.

'And why would anyone do that?' Frank asked.

'For fun, apparently. Like those folk with metal detectors on the beach.'

'Sounds a blast,' Frank said. 'So, what do we have?'

'The magnet fishers pulled up an old fridge this morning. Something from the seventies, I believe. There was a body inside.'

Frank sighed. 'Awful. It was decomposed then?'

'Not completely. The fridge has kept the body partially preserved from the elements.'

Frank rustled through his kitchen drawer for some paracetamol, while keeping the phone pressed between his ear and shoulder. 'Okay, just finishing my breakfast. I'll be straight over—'

'Another thing, Frank.' It was Donald's turn to sigh. 'It looks as if the victim is a child.'

Frank felt his stomach lurch. 'A child?'

'Or a small adult. Forensic pathologist is on the way.'

'Shit... if it's a kid, it won't matter if the body is sixty years old; it'll be big news.'

'You think I'm not aware of that?'

'I know you're aware, sir. I just know how hesitant you are about throwing that kitchen sink when required.' Which meant that if it was a small adult from sixty years ago and not a kid, his investigation would be reduced to fumes. Still, rather a depleted team than a child.

'You try juggling budgets,' Donald said. 'This couldn't have happened at a worse time. The goth festival begins today.'

Frank inwardly groaned and rubbed his temples. *Don't Donald,* he thought. *Please don't go political.*

'Tourism is at its peak,' Donald said. 'We really don't want to disrupt that.'

Frank poured a glass of water for his painkillers. 'I've a thought, sir. How about not letting the tourism disrupt *us*?'

'It would be nice to live in your world, Frank. It really would.'

'What? The one full of morality and decency?'

'The idealistic one. Handle it delicately. The press will be all over it.'

Sod the press, Frank thought, bringing the conversation to a close. *And sod you Donald while we're at it.*

After dressing, Frank left, unable to avoid reflecting on the process of sod's law. Here he was, feeling slightly better, health-wise, than he had in years, only to be confronted with a potential child-killing. His stomach churned, and he immediately felt nauseous. The universe had a sick sense of humour. An especially sick one for him, it seemed.

Outside in the crisp morning air, Frank heard the roar

of an engine. A battered blue Ford Cortina from the early eighties roared past, belching exhaust fumes. He glimpsed two silhouettes inside the car.

Frank slipped his glasses down from his forehead, squinting to make out the number plate, but the car was already round the corner.

As he climbed into Bertha, his faithful but ageing Volvo, he couldn't shake the feeling that the vehicle had left when he'd opened the door to his house.

Is someone watching me?

Chapter Four

As FRANK DROVE towards Tate Hill Pier, the streets of Whitby slowly came to life. Early risers were opening shops, dog walkers were out for their morning strolls, and here and there, groups of gothic revellers were growing in number.

A baker in a flour-dusted apron unlocked his shop next to a group of goths in full Victorian mourning dress, complete with black lace parasols. A jogger in neon Lycra dodged around a man wearing what looked like a full suit of armour spray-painted black.

Under normal circumstances, Frank might have found the mix of the everyday and the extraordinary amusing. Today, with a body waiting for him at the pier, potentially a child's, it felt like a macabre tableau.

Seeing the crowd building around the harbour, Frank opted to park a short distance back and walk the rest of the way.

He spotted an officer struggling to keep some darkly dressed onlookers at bay. Fortunately, they hadn't gone through the yellow cordon, but the young officer's face was flushed; he was clearly putting in a shift to prevent that from happening.

'Ladies and gentlemen,' Frank said to a crowd of about a dozen people. 'The better views are up at the abbey.'

A woman in a Victorian-style black lace dress, complete with a raven-feather fascinator, stepped forward. 'And miss the drama?'

'Aye,' Frank said. 'If you could. What my colleague has neglected to mention is that you risk more drama by interfering with police business.'

'Like what?' some smart-arse called out.

'A criminal charge?'

That should do it.

It didn't. Nobody moved. Frank inwardly sighed and held up his badge. 'DCI Frank Black. Who'd like to be charged first?'

This seemed to work, and they shuffled away.

Frank shook his head. Some people had a warped sense of entertainment. 'Not judging, lad,' Frank said to the struggling young officer. 'We've all been there. But allow me to give you a few tips about crowd control later?'

'Thanks, sir. I appreciate it.' His tone dripped sarcasm. The officer scribbled Frank's name into the logbook.

Frank noticed Samantha Wells from the *Whitby Gazette* lurking nearby. She was in deep conversation with Martin Jeffries, the force press officer. Frank shook his head. Young, ambitious, and with a nose for scandal, Samantha made it her personal mission to report on every detail of Whitby's criminal underbelly. Which, given the town's size, peaceful nature, and lack of any real underbelly, often meant blowing minor incidents out of proportion.

'DCI Black!' Samantha called out, her eyes lighting up at the sight of him. 'Any comment on the body found this morning?'

He approached. She looked eager. She readied her pen.

When he was close enough, he said, 'No comment.'

She looked frustrated. It was usually him on the other side of that response in an interview room. He almost felt sorry for her.

'Will this affect local tourism?'

Bloody hell! She was worse than Donald. This wasn't *Jaws*. There wasn't a great white shark circling the seaside. He gestured at the crowd of eager onlookers in their gothic finery. 'Does it look like tourism is suffering to you? We could probably charge admission.'

Samantha's mouth tightened, but before she could respond, Frank had already moved away and was on the pier.

DI Gerry Carver was waiting for him. Despite the early morn, she was smartly dressed and looked fresh. As was the norm.

'How do, Gerry?'

'Morning, Frank,' she said. She nodded towards a group of pale-faced individuals huddled near a police van.

'Are they the magnet fishers?' Frank asked.

'Two of them,' Gerry said. 'The males.'

Frank grinned. 'Another male-dominated sport, eh?'

Gerry frowned.

'A joke, Gerry, bloody hell... as if this shite is a sport.'

'The lady, Sarah Chen, is studying to be a marine biologist.'

'So why is she here? Aren't those lot more concerned with fish than old shopping trolleys?'

'She's researching. Magnet fishing has ecological benefits. They're removing potentially harmful debris from the water.'

Frank snorted. 'And occasionally, apparently, bodies in fridges. Bet that wasn't in the brochure.' He nodded over to the white-suited SOCOs ahead. 'Let's suit up, Gerry.'

Chapter Five

THE ONCE-WHITE EXTERIOR of the fridge was now a mottled brown, covered in barnacles and sea grime.

It lay on its side, the rusted door hanging open like the jaws of a hideous creature. Beside the appliance, a body was stretched out on the black tarp.

Frank was grateful for the nose plugs. The small, foam-like inserts blocked out the worst of the odours while still allowing for coherent speech and breathing.

He knelt alongside the body, fighting against the discomfort in his protesting back.

The victim's flesh, where it still clung to bone, had taken on a waxy, greenish-grey hue. In places, the skin had sloughed away entirely, revealing patches of discoloured bone and remnants of muscle tissue.

But worst of all was the face. Partially preserved, the victim seemed to grin, while their empty eye sockets stared accusingly at the sky. What remained of the clothes – a T-shirt and jeans – hung off the skeletal frame in shreds, more akin to rotting seaweed than fabric.

Frank's eyes darted between the fridge and the body, his stomach somersaulting. *How long have you been in there?*

He clenched his teeth, pushing away the horrific thought that someone might have crammed the victim in alive before throwing them into the sea. It was a dark possibility he wasn't quite ready to voice aloud.

Where most would recoil, Frank found himself drawn in, leaning closer, the initial revulsion fading to a deep, aching sympathy. If it wouldn't have compromised the scene, Frank might have reached out to offer a comforting touch, a gesture of promise that they weren't alone in the darkness any more.

Dr Nasreen Quereshi, the forensic pathologist, stood nearby, peeling off her gloves with a snap. 'Male,' she stated, 'judging by the pelvic structure and skull shape. Early teens, based on the fusion of growth plates in the long bones and dental development. The fridge's seal preserved the body remarkably well, all things considered. It's possible this body could have been here for decades.'

Despite an age being suggested already, Frank couldn't help but ask, 'So, it is a child?' It was more from general despair than curiosity.

'Some more testing for confirmation, but I suspect so, yes,' Nasreen replied.

How? How could anyone?

But Frank immediately shook off the naivety of his thoughts. He'd been round the block. His reaction was irrational. He knew full well that people capable of such things were out there. 'Any evidence of how they died?'

'There's fracturing.' She knelt beside him and pointed out lines on the skull and facial bones. 'But if the victim was thrown into the water in the fridge, these could be consistent with being jarred around in a small space. We'll know more after a full examination.'

'Could he have been alive... when... it happened?'

Nasreen shrugged. 'I couldn't answer that.'

Frank stood but couldn't tear his eyes from the boy. His mind was already alive with scenarios.

Did he head to the shops for his parents, five-pound notes in hand, never to return? Or did he wave to them at the door on his last journey to school, never to arrive?

He thought of Maddie as a young teenager.

God, he'd so desperately wanted to wrap her in cotton wool, protect her from the world.

Of course, you couldn't, and he'd eventually completely failed in that task, regardless. Yet the parents of this boy had never even seen their child grow, shake off the coils of innocence, become an adult, and make his own journey.

They'd never even had the chance to fail.

Frank looked out over the sea.

Instead, they'd lost him to the depths.

To the darkness.

Where he'd been alone for so long.

Chapter Six

'Frank?'

Frank smiled up at his late wife's closest friend, Chief Forensic Officer Helen Taylor, as she approached. Her sharp green eyes seemed to pierce right through him.

Since Mary had passed, Helen had kept a watchful eye on Frank. She never seemed to like what she saw. She also didn't do subtlety.

Convinced that he was looking fresher since he'd knocked booze on the head, he was curious whether she'd spot it now.

'How do?' he asked her.

'Fine.'

'You look well.'

'Thanks.'

He waited for a simple comment that he, too, was looking well – or at least something better than the usual reflections on his weight.

Blood from a stone.

She held up a plastic bag in her white gloved hand. 'How about this for a blast from the past?'

Inside was a chunky black pager. 'In the victim's pocket.'

'Bloody hell. I had one of them, too. Mid-nineties.' He looked at the body. 'So, the poor lad could have died almost thirty years back?'

'The fridge is from the seventies,' Gerry said, coming up alongside them, tapping away on her phone. 'A Frigidaire FPC12ES6 circa 1975.' She paused, frowning at her screen.

'There were no pagers in 1975,' Frank said.

Gerry nodded. 'I know. These days, the average person holds onto a fridge for ten to fifteen years... so it is possible that whoever did this still had the fridge in the nineties. But it's unlikely. Fridges back then improved at a rapid pace.'

'Aye. And old-fashioned fridges like this with those handles were a deathtrap,' Frank said. 'They wouldn't open from the inside. I'm pretty sure that we'd moved on from them pretty sharpish in the eighties and nineties.'

'We did,' Gerry said.

'Which suggests two things then,' Frank said. 'Whoever did this was still using a bloody old fridge, or they had one stored away?' He looked at the pager in the bag again. 'What're the odds on a pager that's been in the sea for several decades spitting out anything useful, Helen?'

'Good question... I'll let you know as soon as I can. There's also this.' She held up another plastic baggie. 'From around the victim's neck.' The bag contained a pendant on a lanyard. A simple design. Frank leaned closer. A silver circle with strange black blobs on it. 'What's on it?'

'A paw print.'

He leaned in even closer. 'Aye. I can see that now. A dog paw, perhaps? I'd some cufflinks once with my daughter's foot on it...' Frank's throat tightened as he remembered

Maddie's tiny footprint. 'Maybe this was our poor lad's dog? Any serial numbers on the fridge?' Frank asked.

Helen shook her head. 'Too corroded. We might get something once we clean it up back at the lab.'

Frank turned to Gerry, who'd been silently taking notes on her phone.

'Could you get detailed statements from those magnet fishers, Gerry? Reggie can join you when he arrives.'

Gerry nodded and moved towards the huddled group by the van.

Nasreen was examining the body again. Frank went over with Helen alongside him.

He tried to keep his face neutral, but he knew he'd no chance of hiding his true feelings from Helen. She was just like Mary. Both of them had always been able to read him like a book.

She touched his arm. 'This is going to be a tough one.'

'Aye.'

'But remember, it's an investigation, Frank. You're best when you're clear and calm, you know that...'

'Isn't everyone?'

'Yes, but *especially* you.'

Frank stared down at the small, broken form on the mat. The boy's features were distorted by time and the sea, but Frank could still see the ghost of youth in the curve of his jaw, the delicate bones of his hands.

He wanted to see this as just another case. But he couldn't.

This was a child. Robbed of a shot at adulthood.

The sun climbed higher in the sky, its harsh light casting long shadows across the pier. The air was thick with the scent of salt and seaweed. In the distance, he could hear the murmur of a crowd. The goth festival attendees were still watching, their morbid curiosity seemingly insatiable.

As the morning wore on, the pier became a hive of activity. Forensic teams combed every inch of the area while divers prepared to search the waters around the pier in the spot from which the fridge had been hoisted. The crowd of onlookers had grown and were being held back by a line of increasingly frustrated officers.

Frank watched as the shrouded form was lifted onto a stretcher, the white sheet stark against the weathered wood of the pier.

Someone's son.

He thought again of Maddie, his daughter, and of the nights he'd lain awake wondering where she was, and if she was safe.

Who are you?

He observed the body being wheeled towards the waiting van, the wheels clattering.

Who did this to you?

He looked down into the sea. The water lapped at the posts of the pier, dark and secretive.

Chapter Seven

FRANK WAS BYPASSING the cordon off the pier when he heard rapid footsteps echoing on the stones beside him. Expecting Reggie, eager to show off the running prowess of a man half his age, Frank turned, his disinterested expression at the ready.

But it wasn't Reggie. It was John Spears, forensic photographer, jogging towards him, his Canon EOS R5 mirrorless camera bouncing against his chest.

'DCI Black!' He was slightly out of breath. 'I've got something you need to see.'

Frank tilted his head, causing his glasses to slide down from his forehead onto the bridge of his nose. 'Well, if it's worth you breaking a sweat over.'

John fumbled with his camera, pulling up an image on the high-resolution LCD screen. 'It's the lanyard we found with the body.' He held out the camera for Frank to see. 'The pattern has faded, but if you magnify it then...'

The image showed a repeated pattern along the lanyard's length – a stylised depiction of Whitby Abbey.

'If it isn't the heart and soul of our beloved town,' Frank said. 'Good catch, John. Can you email me that image?' He nodded at the looming silhouette of the abbey on the cliff. 'No time like the present.'

As John hurried off, Frank spotted Gerry and Reggie interviewing the magnet fishers. He made his way over to them, glaring at a new group of goths who were pushing their luck by inching closer to the cordon, their elaborate Victorian costumes incongruous against the white suits that came with the gritty modern crime scene.

'Gerry,' he called out. She broke away from the interview. 'Almost done?'

'Yes.'

'Good. I need you to head back to the station and start digging into missing males, early teens, reports from the nineties.'

He didn't need to tell her to cast her net wide into the surrounding areas. Gerry's thoroughness was one of her most valuable traits.

He nodded over at Reggie, who, even from here, looked green around the gills.

'How's George Michael?'

'Sorry?' Gerry asked.

'Wham! singer? Very famous music artist?'

She looked confused. 'I know who he is, but he passed.'

'I was referring to Reggie and his eighties dance moves...' He stifled a sigh. 'Forget about it.'

'He drank too much at your birthday party, so he let me do most of the questioning.'

Frank snorted. 'If I'd known it was that easy to shut him up, I'd have taken him out for a few drinks in the past.'

Gerry's expression remained impassive, Frank's attempt

at humour sailing right over her head. He sighed inwardly and explained about the lanyard.

'Are you going to take the steps?'

He smiled. 'Nah. My hips are almost as weathered as the abbey stones.'

Chapter Eight

FRANK HEADED WESTWARD along Church Street.

Bertha protested against the steep incline, her engine groaning like he would have done if he'd climbed those abbey steps.

He patted the wheel. 'We have to take care of ourselves at this ripe age, haven't we, lass?'

Normally, the bleached curves of the Whalebone Arch off to his right, stark against a grey sky, would inspire awe. But driving Bertha upward, he'd no time for such wonder, because of the anxiety over whether his AA membership was up to date.

Eventually, the 1,500-year-old ruined monastery burst into view.

Gothic arches reached for the skies. Large, empty window frames stared dreamily out over the North Sea.

Frank parked and, feet crunching on the gravel, made his way towards the visitor centre, weaving through a crowd of goths. A woman holding a black lace parasol brushed past him, followed by a man sporting a velvet cloak.

He lowered his head and fought against the racing air,

trying to keep his breathing under control. These days, up here, he really felt the wind. Was that because there was a lot more of him for the wind to pummel these days? Or was it just because he was weary in his later years?

He looked off over Whitby.

'It's quite a sight, isn't it?' Mary's voice echoed in his memory.

When they were younger, they'd come here regularly for the views. She'd rattle off facts about Caedmon and Dracula. If it'd been anyone else, he'd have been bored. Not so with her. He'd been content just to watch her, hypnotised by her enthusiasm.

Frank entered the visitor centre and made a request to speak to a manager. Then he hovered back, looking at a collection of Yorkshire cookbooks, wondering if takeaways should be on his hit list next after the cigarettes.

A few moments later, a middle-aged woman with steel-grey hair and sharp eyes approached. She introduced herself as Maggie Hurst.

Frank presented identification and then pulled out his phone, bringing up the image John Spears had sent him. 'I'm hoping you can help me identify this lanyard. It's part of an ongoing investigation.'

Maggie's eyes widened as she examined the image. 'Oh, yes, I recognise this design. A local artist.' She pointed over to a collection of books in the corner. 'You can find more of his work in his book, over there...' She gazed at the lanyard for a short time. 'As well as buy them, all staff were wearing them at one point – I think I still have mine, somewhere... In fact, it was the second or third year I was here. I know that because lanyard fever hadn't peaked. People just didn't wear them back then like they do now. Just name tags. Some of the staff didn't like the sudden switch. I think several changed their minds with this design, though, because it was rather classy.'

'What year was it you started?'

'In 1997. When I was eighteen, so this would have been around 1998 or 1999. Does that help?'

'Aye.' He handed her his card. 'You couldn't do a little more digging and maybe get us specific dates – when it started and ended.'

She took the card. 'Shouldn't be a problem. Wasn't too long though.'

'Sorry?'

'Wasn't too long it lasted. There was a special Millennium lanyard which had a more traditional design. So, a year or two, tops.'

'And this lanyard was definitely available to the public?'

Maggie nodded. 'We sold them in the gift shop. They were quite popular with school groups, actually. A lot of kids bought them as souvenirs.'

A school group. Kids. The words hit Frank like a punch to the gut.

As he made his way back to Bertha, Frank's mind was racing.

Somewhere out there was a family who'd been waiting since around the turn of the Millennium for their son to come home. They weren't long off finding out that he never would.

Chapter Nine

AFTER THE OBLIGATORY tug of war over resources with Donald Oxley at Scarborough HQ, Frank touched base with Gerry, who was using an office. She had made a start on trawling through missing persons reports, her methodical approach already yielding a fair number of entries on a spreadsheet.

The day was quickly waning, and Frank knew the work would intensify tomorrow when Helen and Nasreen provided more information on the recovered body and items. With a nod to Gerry and a couple of moments on his haunches, allowing Rylan to nuzzle his palm, Frank headed home, determined to keep his energy up for the days ahead, despite the case already sinking its claws into his mind.

The drive home was a blur of streetlights and half-formed theories.

Back home, Frank poured himself a glass of soda water. Considering the day's events, he longed for the taste of beer. He'd already given alcohol-free beer a whirl a month back, but that had only inflamed his taste buds and resulted in him drinking even more of the real thing.

After the soda, he smoked two roll-ups outside. That had been Mary's rule. Since she'd died five years back, he'd sneaked three roll-ups into the living room. But, on each occasion, he'd heard a car outside and flinched, thinking Mary was returning from work and was about to catch him. The sense of pathos that came with realising it couldn't be her, on those occasions, had been so extreme that he'd long since vowed never to smoke in the house again.

Now, the smoke curled around him like the fog of unanswered questions.

He welcomed the sudden distraction of hearing a dog yapping several doors down.

Prior to meeting Gerry and Rylan, he'd had no time for dogs.

Now, since his fondness for the Lab had grown, he wondered if it would make sense to get one.

Dog walks would be a reason to get out of the house each day. They'd also be good for weight loss. Not forgetting that he'd need some company when he finally retired...

Also, with a dog relying on him, he may take his recent healthy living ambition to a new level. It wouldn't be good form to exit the world and leave a new pooch out at sea.

Back inside, his phone suddenly felt heavy in his suit pocket. He considered contacting Paula for an update on Maddie but it'd been less than twenty-four hours, and she'd already warned him off twice about badgering her.

Instead, he went to settle into his armchair, with the remains of last night's takeaway Chinese warmed up.

He thought of the cookbook in the abbey visitor centre. He should have bloody swooped for it...

After eating, Frank closed his eyes and listened to the ticking of the clock on his mantlepiece.

A dream unfolded like a grainy film.

Tate Hill Pier. Dark and quiet. Empty.

The mist rolled in thick.

Up ahead, a fridge was lying on its side.

That fridge.

The magnet fishers' fridge. One man's rubbish is another man's treasure.

This was neither rubbish, nor treasure.

Tragedy, heartbreak, evil.

Frank held the handle and wrenched the door open.

Maddie tumbled out.

Seemingly grinning. Empty eye sockets staring at the sky.

Frank jerked awake. He gasped for air.

His craving kicked in.

He thought about where he could get a drink now. The clock showed ten.

It was possible.

His hands shaking, he gripped the arms of the chair, closed his eyes, willing himself not to move.

Mary. You promised her. At her graveside.

The seconds ticked by, each one a long battle.

Eventually, his breathing steadied, his hands relaxed... the cravings eased—

A faint glow caught his eye, drawing his attention to the window. Frowning, he rose, snatched back the curtain.

There it was again. That same Ford Cortina from earlier, engine idling, headlights blaring.

Who the hell are you?

The car sped away into the night.

Chapter Ten

IT'D BEEN a long time since Frank had arrived at work before five in the morning, but he'd been awake most of the night thinking about that poor boy in the fridge, and knew there was little point in trying for more rest.

Outside, he half-expected to see the Ford Cortina. He didn't. He couldn't decide if that was a good thing or not. After all, he was desperate to know who was spying on him. But at least the day didn't begin with a sudden sharp rise of blood pressure.

The pre-dawn air was crisp and biting as Frank lit up a roll-up in the car park at HQ. He wondered if he'd made it in earlier than Gerry. Now, that would be a feat!

His DI seemed to operate on some unholy combination of efficiency and insomnia, surviving on a mere four hours of sleep per night. It was admirable, if not a little concerning.

Frank's footsteps echoed in the empty corridors on his way to the designated incident room.

When he arrived, there was no sign of Gerry.

Immediately, the blank whiteboard mocked him with its

emptiness, but Frank didn't let it bother him. He knew the board wouldn't stay that way for long.

With a sigh, he set about transforming the blank space into the nerve centre of their investigation. He began by pinning up the few facts they had. A photo of the fridge, the image of the lanyard, the pager, the pendant. He wrote 1998-2000? based on his interview with Maggie Hurst at the abbey. In the centre, he used another question mark to show where the victim's photo should be.

As he worked, Frank couldn't help but think about the seats in the room that would soon be occupied. They were an odd bunch, no doubt about it. Although, anyone outside his team would shrug their shoulders as if it was to be expected. After all, in their eyes, King Odd led the team himself.

Maybe that's why he liked them and had requested them? Maybe he saw himself in them... saw something redeemable, perhaps?

Whatever the reason, they were his. And, despite their quirks – or perhaps because of them – they were gelling into a formidable unit.

The shrill ring of his phone cut through the silence, making Frank jump. Nasreen's name flashed on the screen.

'Dr Quereshi, you're up early too, then?'

'Is it early? Haven't looked. Been at it all night. Dr Glenard lent a hand. And call me Nasreen – this is our second case.'

Frank's eyebrows shot up. Dr Charlie Glenard was a forensic anthropologist, and rumour had it he and Nasreen were more than just colleagues. He recalled Reggie's remark from the last investigation. 'So romantic, eh? Cuddling up over a set of bones.'

Nasreen's voice turned professional as she summarised

their findings: bone development and tooth wear narrowed the age range to twelve to fourteen. Decomposition remained a large issue. Identifying the age of the actual body wasn't easy at the best of times, but when sealed in a container, it muddied the estimates still further.

'However, there's nothing to suggest that it couldn't have occurred between 1997 and 2000, the timeframe you gave us yesterday after visiting the abbey.'

'Good work,' Frank said, scribbling notes.

'We also found a healed fracture on the left arm, possibly from childhood. Could be useful for identification. We've also done a preliminary analysis of height and build based on skeletal measurements.'

He wrote the new information onto the board beneath the large question mark. 'What about the skull? You mentioned the fractures.'

'Yes. But my conclusion is the same. I can't identify if they happened before or after death, or whether they happened inside the fridge while it sank. We've put a facial reconstruction in motion, so if we draw a blank on dental records or other methods later today, you'll be ready to go.'

'Thanks Nasreen. Don't burn yourself out, all right? You sleep tonight.'

She laughed and hung up.

And no more candlelit dinners over decomposing remains, okay? he thought. *It's just not right.*

Chapter Eleven

Hᴜɴᴄʜᴇᴅ ᴏᴠᴇʀ ʜɪꜱ ᴅᴇꜱᴋ, nursing his third coffee of the morning, Frank did a double take when Gerry walked in at nine. 'Bloody hell! What time do you call this?'

Gerry checked her watch. 'Nine.'

'Why are you late?'

She frowned. 'I'm an hour early. Briefing is at ten.'

Frank nodded. 'I meant late by your standards.'

Rylan padded in alongside her and, noticing Frank, sauntered over for some attention, which he promptly received.

'I had to be at the vet's at eight.'

Frank rubbed Rylan's soft, floppy ears. 'Everything all right with this fella?'

'Rylan has developed a case of severe flatulence.'

'Ah-ha.' Frank looked up at Gerry. 'Is that uncommon? Can't you just give him Tums? Usually does the trick for me.'

Gerry shook her head. 'The vet believes it's because of a new brand of treats Tom introduced. There's inflammation now. It may take a period to settle.'

'Bet Tom is on the naughty list.'

'It wasn't Tom's fault. Nothing stood out as offensive on the ingredients. I'll be contacting the company.'

'Well, he smells just fine to me now.'

'He kept us awake most of the evening.'

Frank lifted an eyebrow. 'Rylan sleeps in the room with you both?'

'Yes.'

'And Tom doesn't mind?'

'Not until last night.'

'Ah... don't tell me... just remembered. The 95 per cent compatibility. Out of curiosity, what does he need to do for the remaining 5 per cent? Put the top back on the toothpaste?'

She shook her head. 'Minor differences in our circadian rhythms and dietary preferences account for the 5 per cent.'

'Five per cent is good going. Was that before or after Rylan started farting?'

'Tom may not stay over for a while, but the flatulence is transient. I don't see it being a problem.'

Frank shook his head and resumed playing with Rylan's ears. 'Least you get to spend some quality time just with Rylan. Wouldn't want him getting jealous.'

'He hasn't been. If he was jealous, his behaviours would change. I've noticed no changes.'

'Apart from the gas?'

She nodded. 'Unrelated.'

'Don't worry, Rylan.' Frank rose from his chair and then knelt, his knees creaking in protest. He whispered, 'Better out than in. We've all been there. It'll pass.'

'Would you like to see the missing children for that time period?' Gerry asked, approaching an available computer. 'I was up late.'

Frank nodded. 'Aye.'

While Gerry logged on and brought up a spreadsheet from the cloud, Frank rose to his feet and stretched out his knees and then his back.

'Between 1997 and 2000,' Gerry said, 'there were twenty reported cases of missing male children in North Yorkshire fitting our criteria.'

Frank sighed. 'More than I'd hoped. Any that stand out in particular?'

Before Gerry could answer, Frank's phone rang. 'Sorry...' He looked at the screen. 'It's Helen... could be something...' He answered. 'Helen?'

'Frank, listen. Aiden is a genius,' Helen said.

'And Aiden is *who*?'

'Aiden Foster, our tech specialist.'

'Ah. Good on him. Guess it must be nice to be a genius. What's he know?'

'The pager.'

Frank took a deep breath. 'Brilliant. Go on.'

'Good and bad news though.'

'You know the drill, Hel.'

'Bad first, yes. There were massive problems in accessing the waterlogged pager's memory without damaging it... so we didn't.'

'That's bad,' Frank said. 'I'm struggling to see where the good can come from then...'

'Rein it in. Let me finish. Aiden was able to get hold of a like for like pager, which was no small feat, and then, genius that he is, managed to move the memory over.'

Frank felt a burst of adrenaline. 'Now this sounds good...'

'Unfortunately, most of the messages are too corrupted to read.'

Bloody hell – is there any good news?

'But we lifted one message. Dated 14th October 1998, sent at 7.03 a.m.'

'Bingo,' Frank said, scrambling for a pen, knocking over his coffee mug in the process, which was fortunately, empty. 'Who was it from? What does it say?'

'Temper your expectations, Frank. The sender information is corrupted, and the message is rather cryptic. The message is "losing control" no capitals, full stop at the end. Space. Capital M on "Meet." Space, and then an abbreviation. "WA" Another full stop, and space, capital B on "Bring". Unfortunately the data after Bring is corrupted, and possibly the data before losing.'

Frank looked at what he'd written: *losing control. Meet WA. Bring*

'Nothing else as yet,' she said.

'This is remarkable, though. Let's see what the date brings up. Thanks Helen.'

Frank explained the call to Gerry and she ran the date.

14th October 1998.

'Frank... we've got a match on the date...'

Frank's heart pounded against his ribs.

'Greg Lyle, fourteen years old. Whitby. Reported missing by his mother at 10.06 a.m. on October 14th, 1998.'

Each heart beat echoed in his ears. He moved around the table, and stood behind Gerry and the computer.

A boy's face filled the screen. A boy with sandy hair and a lopsided grin, his arms wrapped tightly around a golden retriever. The dog was looking up at him with unmistakable adoration.

Frank's breath caught in his throat.

Greg Lyle.

He looked down at the message in his hand again. Sent

three hours before Greg went missing: *losing control. Meet WA. Bring*

He looked back up, his eyes tracing the contours of Greg's face.

Who lost control? WA? Where did you meet? Frank's voice was barely above a whisper, thick with emotion. 'And what did you bring with you?'

Chapter Twelve

When it came to the goth festival, Raven Blackstone treated it more like a sprint than a marathon. This made for a rather exhausting weekend. But she was part of a passionate group that didn't take no for an answer, or failure as an option, so even as the dark clouds hovered over the market square, threatening to unleash a storm that would tear to smithereens the concert she was organising, she remained positive and steadfast.

Raven surveyed the square, her eyes lingering on Victorian lampposts adorned with blood-red fairy lights and artificial cobwebs. Around her, black-clad figures swarmed like ravens, their pale faces stark against the dreary backdrop of Whitby's weathered buildings. There was irony here. Victorian architecture spoke of control, and here it was, bearing witness to a celebration of all things dark and rebellious.

Unlike Raven, Damien failed to stay positive. Her close friend and fellow organiser, a wiry man in his fifties with a shock of dyed black hair and a penchant for feathered capes, sidled up to her.

Between the pillars of the old town hall, he pointed at the roiling steel-grey clouds and announced, 'We're buggered.'

Raven raised an eyebrow. 'Unlike you to be so dramatic, Damien.'

'I can complete it with a soliloquy on the futility of organising outdoor festivities in November if you wish?'

'Why? You made your point so eloquently already.'

'How do you always manage to keep such a brave face? Also, you consumed bucket-loads last night... how are you still so bright and breezy?'

'What can I say? The absinthe works in peculiar ways.'

Damien winked. 'Always works particularly well if you don't have to pay for any of it yourself... How was Derek this morning?'

'Don't know what you mean,' Raven said, smiling.

'Well, I imagine that his wallet is as buggered as we are this morning.' He pointed at the sky again, and then gestured at the twelve-foot by twenty-foot wooden stage, elevated three feet off the ground, just in case she didn't get his point.

'It's Whitby, darling.' She squeezed his shoulder. 'The weather is always on the menu. You know that.'

'So bloody stoic,' Damien said.

'Also,' she whispered. 'I checked the forecast. There'll be a downpour within the hour and then it'll clear. Before the concert starts.'

'And you trust the forecast?'

She winked. 'Today, I do. All our gods are smiling down on us.'

Damien snorted. 'All of them? That's a lot of divine intervention for a goth festival.'

She stepped out from beneath the old town hall onto the cobblestones. She felt the first droplets of rain.

At forty-six, Raven cut an impressive figure. Her raven-black hair, shot through with streaks of electric blue, was piled atop her head in an intricate updo that defied gravity. Her porcelain skin, powdered to ghostly perfection, provided a stark canvas for her blood-red lips and heavy eyeliner. She wore a corseted Victorian dress, all black lace and shimmering silk, that hugged her curves before billowing out into a full skirt that swished as she walked.

As she approached the front of the stage, Raven over-heard a group of teenagers whispering excitedly about the upcoming performances. The names 'Morgue Walkers' and 'Crimson Thorns' reached her ears, and she couldn't help but smile. The latter was a band she'd selected after hearing their demo – a decision that had kept her up for nights, second-guessing herself. Now, hearing the anticipation in those youthful voices, she felt a flicker of pride.

She moved out of earshot of the teenagers. 'Mind those lights, darling. We don't want a repeat of last year's fiasco.' She tried to keep her tone light, but she was deadly serious.

'Aye, aye, captain,' Lawrence called back.

She suppressed a shudder at the memory of sparks showering down on the lead singer of 'Grave Whispers', his velvet coat catching fire mid-chorus. The headlines had been less than kind, and Raven had spent months rebuilding the festival's reputation. 'Goth Festival Goes Up in Flames' wasn't exactly the publicity she'd been aiming for.

'Doesn't matter,' Damien said, joining her again. 'The rain will put any flames out.'

Raven rolled her eyes. 'Ah yes, because "Goths

Drenched in Downpour" is such a better headline. Maybe if we sacrifice you to the rain gods, they'll go easy on us.'

He snorted.

Nearby, a street performer had set up shop, his skeletal face paint and tattered ringmaster's costume drawing a small crowd. He juggled what appeared to be human skulls – plastic, Raven hoped – much to the delight of the gathering goths.

As she watched, a family passed by: mother, father, and two young children, all dressed in matching black velvet and lace. The youngest, a boy of around five or six, tugged at his mother's sleeve and pointed at the performer.

Over by the merchandise stalls, a tall, lean figure with a long black coat and silver-tipped cane caught her attention.

Derek.

Not only was Derek handsome, he offered scintillating company.

But life was good at the moment. She didn't want to put her life in any jeopardy over a new relationship.

Even if Derek had soulful eyes that made her weak at the knees.

Even if his smile made her forget, for a second or two, those heavy secrets she carried.

Unbidden, her mind wandered back to the previous night. The Elsinore, Whitby's premier goth pub, packed to the rafters. The air had been thick with the heady scent of patchouli. Derek, who was only in Whitby twice a year, invited her over to share a bottle of absinthe.

As the night had worn on, Raven and Derek had drawn closer together. The man was like a magnet. Still, contrary to what Damien believed, with his coarse language and incessant winking, Raven had fled the pub before eleven. It was better not to open her heart to anyone. And if she slept with him, then you could be sure the floodgates would open.

Some heavier raindrops brought Raven back to the present. She blinked, realising she'd been staring at Derek for far too long. The downpour wasn't long away. People were already moving into the old town hall for shelter.

'Bit harsh on young Lawrence, weren't you?' came a voice from behind her. Raven turned to see Lizzie, one of her regular volunteers, grinning at her. 'I thought we were supposed to nurture young talent, not terrify it into submission.'

Raven smirked. 'Look around you, Lizzie. If they can't handle a little terror, they're in the wrong business.'

Lizzie laughed, her purple-streaked hair bouncing. 'Fair point. After the discovery yesterday, this must all seem like a pantomime.'

'You referring to the body by the pier?'

Lizzie raised an eyebrow. 'Of course.'

'I haven't heard too much about it.'

'Really? Where have you been?'

'Organising the shit out of this festival. The only social-ising I've done was last night.'

Lizzie smirked. 'And that was predominantly with Derek.' She winked. 'Our handsome out-of-towner.'

She glanced over at him again. 'He's handsome. I'll give him that.'

Lizzie laughed. 'Give him *that*, will you?'

'Pack it in... Anyway, this body... any news about who it was? I heard it was old. In a fridge from like sixty years ago or something.'

'There're rumours the body was a child,' Damien said, coming alongside them.

Raven felt a chill that had nothing to do with the rain. She glared at Damien. 'You're joking, right?'

'No. Why would I? Samantha Wells apparently suggested on her website that it was a young kid. Although how she found out is anyone's guess. There's been no announcements. Some people were close when those fishers found it – maybe they saw the body... saw it was small?'

Raven's blood ran cold. The rain grew in weight. Thick, rapid drops pattered against her silk dress, darkening the fabric and plastering stray tendrils of hair to her face.

'Shit...' Lizzie said. 'Let's get under the town hall—'

Raven's hand flew out and grabbed Lizzie. 'Wait.'

She pulled away. 'Why? We're going to get piss wet.'

Raven's stomach was turning over. The world around her seemed to blur, the sound of rain and distant thunder fading into a dull roar in her ears.

Lizzie was already away, streaking towards shelter.

She felt Damien's hand on her shoulder. 'Come on, Raven.'

'Who was the child, Damien?'

'How am I supposed to know that? What's wrong?'

'A child, really? You sure?'

'It's a rumour.'

'But the body was from the sixties or seventies, yes?'

'Again, how could I answer that?'

Raven felt her heart race, a cold sweat breaking out on her forehead.

Get a grip, Raven... this isn't what you think it is...

The world tilted sickeningly, and suddenly she wasn't in the square any more. She was on the floor in a dimly-lit room, the air thick with the acrid stench of fear. She could hear his voice.

'Tell me a story.'

'What about?' she asked.

And then she was back, looking into Damien's concerned eyes. His hair was now plastered to his head. 'Raven? Are you all right?'

She blinked rain from her eyes. 'Yes... yes.'

There was a crack of thunder and the rain intensified.

Chapter Thirteen

Reverend Ray Lawson looked over his congregation from the pulpit. He spoke into the mouthpiece dangling from his ear. 'Second chances. How many are we allowed?' His rich baritone echoed throughout the church. 'One... two... three...' His eyes swept the pews. 'Infinite, perhaps? And what mistakes are we referring to when discussing second chances?' He locked eyes with Kath, his wife, at the organ. 'Are we referring to forgetting to put the rubbish out or paying the TV licence a month late? If so, I'm as guilty as charged.' He raised his hands in mock surrender.

Kath rolled her eyes.

A ripple of laughter spread through the congregation.

'No one is getting struck by lightning for forgetting to put out the rubbish.' Ray put his hands flat on the pulpit. 'In fact, nobody is getting struck down because of any mistake.' He regarded his flock seriously. 'Because whatever the mistake, God offers redemption.'

He allowed the message to sink in while he straightened his aching back. Over the last year, his fifty-five-year-old knees had forced him to give up running. His body could have been more grateful for this sacrifice. Instead, it had shown its appreciation by throwing him several more kilos, and he was aching in places he never used to ache.

If not for his daily walk up to West Cliff to his rather modest St Claude's Church, it could have been a lot worse.

There was a mutter from the back of his church. It wasn't unheard of for his congregation to whisper to one another when he was in full flow, but disruption was a pain in the arse, and he discouraged it every time with a steely look.

He traced the sound to a fidgeting blonde woman, sitting alone on the final pew, at a distance of three empty pews from the next occupied one. He didn't recognise her. That in itself was unusual. A prickle of unease crawled up Ray's spine.

As she wasn't mumbling to anyone in particular, and wasn't causing too much chaos with her fidgeting, he did his best to ignore it and press on. 'But a quick note on redemption. God's redemption isn't just about *forgiveness*.' He intensified the passion in his tone of voice. 'He offers you the opportunity to start anew, to become better versions of yourselves. It's about—'

The woman spoke. Much louder now, no longer a mumble.

He'd no idea what she'd said. He'd been mid-flow.

While he regarded her, several of his congregation looked back.

Had they heard what she'd said?

Right now, the woman had her face lowered and was both fidgeting and mumbling again. He stopped himself short of addressing her directly. Calling her out, embarrassing her, was not the right move. Something wasn't quite right there.

Speaking to her after the service was the correct call.

Clearing his throat, Ray pressed on. 'He gives you the opportunity to recognise your faults and then you must strive to overcome them—'

'Liar,' the woman in the final pew cut him off, trapping his next words dead in his throat.

Ray felt his heart rate quicken. Someone was in his church, questioning his integrity as he preached.

This was uncharted territory.

He'd heard peers, the horror stories. Folk stumbling into their church, drunken, or part-way through some kind of mental breakdown, causing hell. For Ray, though, this one was new.

Out of the corner of his eye, he caught Kath's look. It was a mix of sympathy and concern. She had his back. He looked over at his congregation. Again, in their eyes, he found support.

He used this to soldier on. 'Redemption is also about embracing the love and forgiveness that God offers us, freely and without condition—'

'Liar!' This was much louder, and the feeling of unease that suddenly spread over his congregation became palpable.

Most were looking back at her now. Some were whispering among themselves.

Maybe it was time to speak to her.

If he didn't, then surely someone in his flock would. And that couldn't possibly be the best option.

He reached up to unhook his mouthpiece, preparing to step away from the pulpit, when he noticed Kath rising from her seat at the organ.

She planned to attend to the situation.

Not such a bad thing.

After all, there was no better person than Kath in reassuring and soothing someone in distress. He gave Kath a swift nod when she looked at him. She'd get her outside for some fresh air.

As Kath made her way to the back of the church, Ray took a deep breath, preparing to increase the passion in his voice and eliminate any growth of tension in the room. 'But we remember, no one is beyond redemption. At all costs. No one. Everyone is entitled. If we don't believe this, then we risk overlooking it—'

His wife was alongside the final pew, kneeling, whispering to the woman. He inwardly sighed. His passionate tone had done little to draw the attention of the congregation back. Most were turning in their seats to watch Kath console the mysterious guest.

Real-life drama had upstaged him.

But he had to keep trying. 'No sin is too great, no mistake too terrible, that it cannot be forgiven—'

'LIAR!' Her voice echoed through the church.

There was a gasp from the congregation, and then the woman was on her feet, pointing at him. 'You're a *liar*, Reverend Lawson!'

He felt as if all the blood had drained from his body.

Not because of the confrontation, but because he suddenly recognised her.

That voice... those eyes burning into him... it had to be her!

He gripped the pulpit, his knuckles white, while the church fell into deathly silence.

He swallowed. Now what? How did he stop this getting out of control?

Who am I kidding? This is already out of control...

'Would we be able to talk outside?' His question

sounded strange echoing around the church, so he unhooked his mouthpiece and stepped back from the pulpit. 'Whatever it is' – he moved towards the steps leading down from the platform – 'let's head out to talk about it—'

'Get the fuck off me!' the woman hissed. Kath flew across the aisle and crashed into a pew.

Ray charged down the steps. 'Kath!'

Kath was still standing. She held her hands up. 'I'm fine.'

Now, the congregation was frozen. Unmoving. Stunned into silence. And the woman was on the move. Charging down the aisle. Toward him.

She wore a threadbare jacket over a stained T-shirt, her jeans ripped and frayed. Her appearance was a stark contrast to the neat, Sunday-best attire of the congregation. Her eyes blazed with fury.

As she drew closer, he saw her face clearly for the first time.

It was her. He'd not been mistaken.

Megan.

A cold sweat broke out on his forehead. His heart hammered in his chest.

Before Ray could react, she was upon him with such speed that it threw him off his feet and, with a blinding flash, he felt a searing pain in the back of his head as he hit the floor.

He saw her above, coming again. Then he felt her weight upon him. His skin burned as she raked her nails across his face. She was trying to claw at his eyes. He covered them with the back of his hand.

'Stop—'

'Your eyes,' she said.

He tried to beat her off with his available hand while maintaining a shield with the other.

'I believed you. I looked into your eyes, and I believed you.'

He heard chaos erupting behind her. She was trying to dig her fingers between his hands now to get at his eyes. He could feel them drawing closer... 'My eyes! Stay away from my eyes—'

Someone suddenly lifted the weight.

He looked up and saw Megan being yanked backwards, arms around her.

Ray scurried backwards, tasting blood, trying to figure out what was happening.

It was Brian. One of the younger members of the congregation. The former rugby player had come to his aid. 'That's enough.'

Megan thrashed in Brian's grip.

Ray staggered to his feet, his hand going to his face. He could feel warm blood trickling from the scratches Megan had left, but at least they'd stopped her before she blinded him. His insides felt as if they were melting. His stomach churned.

He stared at the woman writhing in Brian's grip.

He felt complete disbelief.

Megan? Here? Now? How?

'Ray, are you all right?'

He could hear Kath at his side, but wasn't able to respond to her. He was too focused on the woman from his past.

Megan was still for a moment, and their eyes met. He immediately saw past the anger to the deep well of pain beneath.

He started to reach out to her—

But then Brian was pulling her backwards down the aisle, toward the exit.

'Who's that?' Kath asked.

'I... I don't know.' He kept his eyes on Megan as she was taken further and further away. 'I've never seen her before.'

'No,' Kath said. 'She knows you. Did you not see her eyes?'

How could I miss them?

Ray shook his head. 'I'm as confused as you are, dear. Perhaps she's mistaken me for someone else?'

'She knew your name.'

'It's on the front of the church,' Ray said. 'That must be where she got it from.'

Megan and Brian were at the back now. He'd released her. She was catching her breath and looked exhausted.

Brian's tone was gentle now. 'Come outside. Let's go out and calm down.'

Ray felt a surge of adrenaline. *No!*

He couldn't allow that. What would she say?

Ray started down the aisle, hand out. 'Please... allow me... talk to me.'

Megan's eyes widened. 'Liar!' she shouted and then kicked Brian.

Brian wailed and crumpled to the floor, clutching his knee.

Megan bolted outside into the rain.

He approached the door.

Behind him, his congregation, not for the first time today, languished in stunned silence.

As he watched Megan run, he thought about the sermon he'd given his flock today.

There were no sins that couldn't be forgiven.

Suddenly, he wasn't so sure.

63

Chapter Fourteen

THE RAIN HAMMERED against the windows of the Seabreeze Flower Shop. Lilly Petrova didn't mind so much. She had her roses, lilies and carnations. Their colours and fragrances were a riot against the grey day outside. Although, she knew the weather would probably hit this morning's takings.

With no customers yet, Lilly finished preparing a small pot of Zdravets, a traditional Bulgarian geranium. She then displayed it behind the counter. This was her weekly ritual: adding a little piece of home to her shop in Whitby.

The tinkle of the bell drew her eyes from the Zdravets to the front door.

Mrs Hodgson.

Here came the free business advice, served with a side of thinly veiled criticism.

'Good morning, Mrs Hodgson,' she called out, her accent still carrying Bulgarian flavour despite being in England since 1989. 'You're early today. Рано пиле рано пее.'

'Sorry?'

'It means, "the early bird sings early". It is like "the early bird catches the worm".'

Mrs Hodgson shook her umbrella off outside before propping it under the porch. 'Early? My dear, it's nearly eleven. I've been up since dawn, trying to avoid those people.'

Lilly shrugged. 'Who?'

'Who?' Her tone was sharp. 'When I ran my furniture business, dear, I was always acutely aware of what was happening in the local area. Business ebbs and flows depending on weather, season and tourism. How are you not aware of *them*?'

She still felt none the wiser. 'I'm sorry...'

Mrs Hodgson leaned in and whispered as if afraid of being overheard. 'Whitby is overrun with black-clad locusts.'

Lilly shrugged. 'Locusts?'

'Goths.' Mrs Hodgson's tone suggested Lilly should really know better.

Lilly forced back a laugh. Mrs Hodgson's dramatics were always entertaining, even if they were a bit much sometimes. 'The festival? A busy Whitby is good for my business.'

Mrs Hodgson waved a dismissive hand. 'Nonsense. Those gloomy folk wouldn't be interested in your gorgeous, colourful specimens.'

You'd be surprised! 'Ще се изненадаш.'

'What does that mean, dear?'

'I see your point,' Lilly lied. The customer is, after all, always right.

Mrs Hodgson moved to inspect a nearby arrangement. 'These peonies are lovely, but you've paired them with baby's breath. It's a bit... provincial, don't you think?'

Lilly smiled, absorbing the criticism. 'Anything you like?'

'I'll browse, thank you.'

As Mrs Hodgson continued her inspection, Lilly busied herself with arranging a bouquet. Her nimble fingers danced among the blooms, selecting each flower with care and precision.

Lilly's mind wandered as she worked, remembering one of Dimitar's many proverbs. They always involved flowers. **Няма роза без бодли.** Every rose has its thorn.

The proverb reminded Lilly to be patient. Mrs Hodgson had a good heart and meant well, even if she approached it in a rather obtuse manner.

'You know,' Mrs Hodgson said. 'You could really do with larger premises. I think you're ready to be more ambitious.'

Lilly smiled. 'I'll think about it. Anything caught your interest?'

'A few pieces. The flowers are for the Women's Institute meeting. I want something... striking. Something to show those Scarborough ladies that Whitby isn't some backwater. We've culture here, you know. Even if it is currently being overrun by vampire enthusiasts.'

'Actually, I think I've just the thing...' Lilly led the way to a bucket filled with vibrant sunflowers. 'These, with some deep purple irises and white lilies, perhaps? Very elegant, very cultured.'

Mrs Hodgson regarded the flowers with curiosity. It would take a lot for this woman to allow someone else to make a choice for her.

Lilly expected a firm rejection. Something along the lines of *too overpowering* or *too gaudy*.

'Those Scarborough cows won't know what hit them,' Mrs Hodgson said.

Surprised, Lilly gathered the flowers for the arrangement. 'Excellent choice,' Lilly said, handing the credit to the customer.

There was a muffled thump.

Lilly froze, her hand halfway to a sunflower. The thump had come from below their feet.

'Good heavens,' Mrs Hodgson exclaimed, 'what was that?'

Ice spread through Lilly's chest; she felt it constricting her breath.

A second muffled thump followed.

Lilly took a deep breath. *Вземи се в ръце.* Willing herself to get a grip wasn't cutting it though. Mrs Hodgson's eyes were narrowed, which indicated she could sense Lilly's discomfort.

There was a third thump.

'What's down there?' Mrs Hodgson asked.

Lilly forced a smile onto her face. 'It happens. It's the old building settling. These Victorian structures... they have minds of their own.'

Mrs Hodgson didn't look convinced.

Lilly finished the flower arrangement, expecting another thump at any moment. When she'd made it back to the counter with the bouquet with no more disruptions, she felt her heart rate ease slightly, but her eyes continually shifted to the door behind the counter. It was a heavy old thing, solid oak with a sturdy lock, which led down to the basement.

She thought of what lay beyond that door and down those stairs.

The lines that had been crossed.

И от бодил цвете никне.

She shouldn't doubt herself now. It'd been necessary to cross these lines.

Even from a thistle, a flower blooms.

Lilly's hands shook as she handed over the bouquet.

'Are you all right, dear?' Mrs Hodgson asked, peering at her with concern. 'You look peaky.'

Lilly nodded, perhaps a bit too vigorously. 'Yes, yes, I'm fine. Just a little... как се казва... under the weather? But it is nothing, truly.'

She handed over the finished arrangement, a beautiful cascade of sunflowers, irises and lilies.

'This will show those Scarborough ladies a thing or two!' Mrs Hodgson said.

As the older woman made her way to the door, moaning about the awaiting plague of locusts under her breath, Lilly called out, 'Come again soon.'

The moment the door closed behind her last customer, Lilly's cheerful demeanour fell away like a discarded cloak. She rushed to the window, flipping the 'Open' sign to 'Closed' with trembling fingers. Then, she lowered the blinds.

Just as she reached for the last one, a movement outside caught her eye. A young couple, under an umbrella, dressed all in black with elaborate make-up, were peering into the shop. The girl pointed at a bouquet of deep red roses, saying something to her companion.

Lilly's heart raced. She couldn't risk any more customers, not now. Summoning every ounce of her earlier warmth, she opened the door a crack.

'I'm sorry,' she said, trying to keep the tremor out of her voice, 'but we're closed for inventory. Perhaps you can come back later, please?'

The couple looked disappointed but nodded, moving off down the street hand in hand. Lilly watched them go, her fingers white-knuckled on the door frame. Only when they'd turned the corner did she finally close and lock the door, letting out a shaky breath.

For a moment, she stood there, her forehead pressed against the cool glass. The cheerful tinkle of the bell seemed to mock her now, a reminder of the normal life she'd tried so hard to build. A life that was now balanced on a knife's edge.

Another sound from the basement galvanised her into action. Moving swiftly, she crossed to the heavy oak door, her hand hesitating for just a moment before she turned the key in the lock.

The stairs creaked ominously as she descended, each step taking her further from the warm, flower-scented haven above. The air grew cooler, damper, the scent of earth and mildew replacing the sweet perfume of flowers. Lilly's heart pounded in her chest, the sound echoing in the enclosed space.

She unlocked the door with another key, opened it, and regarded the three pale faces in the gloom.

Chapter Fifteen

THE QUESTION MARK Frank had earlier put in place of the victim on the board was no more.

And despite his team being assembled behind him, Frank couldn't take his eyes off the photograph of that smiling, sandy-haired boy with arms wrapped around a golden retriever.

Greg Lyle.

Less than an hour ago, dental records had confirmed it. Thirty minutes back, it'd been rubber stamped with medical records. That fracture in his left arm had been down to a biking accident when he was eight.

Fourteen years old.

He'd seen his fair share of grim cases over the years, but a dead child always hit the hardest. A young life snuffed out before it had really begun.

He took a deep breath, trying to centre himself, before taking a step back and beholding the web of information that Gerry and he had spread over the board.

He nodded and winked at the picture of Greg.

We've got this, son. You can be sure of that.

He turned. Reggie, Sharon and Sean were all browsing documents, re-reading interviews, re-tracing the path of the missing person's investigation from 1998.

They'd been at it for a fair while.

Frank regarded a fresh addition: Clara Jennings, data analyst, sitting at a computer terminal. Her fingers flew over the keyboard, her dark eyes intense behind thick-rimmed glasses. It'd been a while since he'd last had an analyst on a case.

It'd also been a while since he'd investigated the death of someone so young.

Last time, Mary had still been alive. She'd been there to hold him in the early hours of the morning as he'd stared at the ceiling, his thoughts lost to the most despicable of human actions.

This time, he wouldn't have Mary.

And he wouldn't have alcohol.

Frank cleared his throat, drawing everyone's attention. 'Greg Lyle was fourteen. He was reported missing on the morning of Wednesday, October 14th, 1998, at 10.06 a.m., when his parents got word that he'd not arrived at school.' He tried to keep his voice sharp and unwavering. 'As you know, the remains were found inside a Frigidaire from the mid-seventies. Magnet fishers pulled it from the Tate Hill Pier on the morning of November 1st.' He looked down, shuffled some notes on his desk. Then he looked back up at their sad faces. 'Okay, you've access to the reports, so I'll stick to the most relevant details now. You can spend the rest of the day familiarising yourself with them. Greg was diagnosed with autism.' He paused at this point and glanced at Gerry. She was stroking Rylan, who was nuzzling her knee. 'According to his school records and psychological evaluations, he was described as quiet and introverted, but sincere and truthful. He had a deep love for animals, especially his dog, Buddy. A golden retriever, if I remember correctly.' He paused to take a breath. 'Buddy disappeared with Greg.' He gulped. Frank glanced at Gerry again. 'Do we know how old Buddy was?'

'Five,' Gerry said. 'A rescue dog. Healthy, fully immunised.'

Frank nodded, listening to Clara's fingers patter over the keys as she inputted information. Some of these facts were present in the previous missing persons investigation, but he wanted them inputted again. Inconsistencies could often make or break a case of this nature.

'Greg didn't have a social group as such, but he had one very close friend in Terry Kane. They usually walked to school together, but on the morning Greg disappeared, Terry was unwell at home, and didn't attend school.' Frank paused, consulting his notes. 'More information here from his teachers' reports regarding Greg. The lad was highly intelligent, but struggled with social interactions. He had a particular interest in marine biology and could recite facts about sea creatures for hours. His autism manifested in strict adherence to routines and difficulty with unexpected changes.'

Frank moved to the left of the board, where Gerry and he had drawn a relationship map earlier. 'Katie and Simon Lyle. His parents. They were both in their late teens when they had Greg. At the time of their son's disappearance, their marriage was under significant strain.'

Frank's marker squeaked as he drew a line between Simon Lyle and another name on the board: Raven Blackstone. 'The day before Greg went missing, Katie discovered

Simon was having an affair with a young lass called Raven Blackstone, a server at the Harbour Lights Café. She was only twenty years old, twelve years Simon's junior. According to the initial interviews I've just read, Katie had already suspected something was going on. She drove by Raven's house on Church Street, knocked on the door, and found her husband there. Katie admitted to exploding. This was witnessed by Greg. Katie described how Greg then cried all the way home, his hands clamped to his ears.'

'Poor kid,' Sharon said.

Frank directed everyone to shuffle their chairs around so they could view a screen. 'Gerry?'

Gerry stopped stroking Rylan to use her computer. 'We're now going to show you Greg's usual route when walking Buddy. He walked this route daily before returning Buddy home and setting off for school.' A map of Whitby appeared on the screen. 'According to his parents, he never deviated from the route.'

'A creature of habit,' Reggie said, nodding.

'Aye,' Frank said. 'Which makes his route on the day he disappeared interesting. But first, let's look at the usual route.'

Gerry used a graphic drawing tablet to circle the starting point in red. 'He'd start from his home on Esk Terrace at around 7.45 a.m. He'd then head up to St Claude's Church on West Cliff – that's about a twenty-minute walk, covering roughly 1.6 kilometres.'

Gerry weaved a red line through the map of Whitby until it reached the location of St Claude's Church.

'Then, as I pointed out before, he'd retrace his steps home, drop off Buddy around 8.30 a.m. and head to Eskdale School. His parents would have already left for work by this time. As a result, on October 14th, they were none the wiser

73

to him not returning home, and it was only when the school contacted them to say he was absent that they realised that he and Buddy must never have made it back.'

Gerry clicked to the next slide, showing a different route. 'It also came to light that his route had changed on this day according to witnesses. It could be because of his parents' argument the day before outside Raven's home, or it could be this... the recovered message on the pager. The message arrived at 7.03 am.'

Frank tapped the message written on the board with a marker pen, drawing everyone's attention: *losing control. Meet WA. Bring*

'We've speculated that 'WA' could stand for Whitby Abbey,' Frank said. 'But there's no evidence Greg ever made it to the East Cliff – as you'll see from the alternative route, Gerry is about to take you through. Of course, that doesn't mean he didn't go at some point - we just don't have any recorded sightings either way.' He pointed at the route on the screen, guiding his team to refocus on that.

'This was Greg's actual route that morning, as far as we can piece together from CCTV footage and witness state- ments,' Gerry said. 'So, as Frank said, it might not be the pager message that changed his route. It might be the fact that he learned of his father's infidelity the day before. You see, he left home on Esk Terrace with Buddy at his usual time of 7.45 a.m. and went first to Raven Blackstone's house on Church Street. About a ten-minute walk from his home. Raven claimed that she answered the door, but his father, Simon, wasn't there. Greg then continued his walk with Buddy to Seabreeze Flower Shop at Flowergate, about a five-minute walk. He spent about ten to fifteen minutes there, apparently wanting to buy flowers to cheer up his mum – according to the witness statement provided by Lilly

Petrova.' Gerry circled the shop. 'After that, he walked about another fifteen minutes to St Claude's Church on West Cliff. This was the church he regularly attended on Sundays with his family and walked to on his usual route. He was close friends with Reverend Ray Lawson apparently and often stopped in to say hello. On this day, according to Ray's interview, Greg wanted to discuss how he was feeling regarding his father's affair. Finally, after leaving the church, he continued walking along West Cliff. A dog walker, Harold Cross, who also attended St Claude's recognised him. He approximated the time to be 9.15. Harold said he instructed Greg to be more careful as he was straying too close to the cliff edges. He was the last person to see Greg.'

'I assume Harold Cross was thoroughly investigated?' Reggie asked.

Frank nodded. 'Aye. Grilled hard, the report suggests, despite him being a model citizen in his mid-sixties. They searched his premises. The works.'

'Is he still alive?' Reggie said.

'He passed ten years back,' Gerry said.

Reggie nodded, looking disappointed.

'So, to clarify,' Sharon said, looking down at her notes and pointing at the names with a pencil. 'The last four people to see Greg were Raven Blackstone, Lilly Petrova, Ray Lawson and Harold Cross?'

Frank nodded. 'You can see from the files that they were all interviewed... but, remember, the investigators didn't know Greg was dead, and so, apart from with Harold, they didn't push as hard as they could have – strike that – *should* have, done.'

'In my opinion,' Gerry said, 'they pushed too hard with Harold Cross at the expense of others.'

'Yes... it borders on obsession when you read the file back to back... then, when they did finally rule him out, they opted to strike out foul play too. He'd been straying close to the cliff edges, remember? Greg had special educational needs. Considered vulnerable. So they started extensive searches of the shoreline beneath the cliffs. When they yielded no results, they hypothesised that he'd been washed away. The parents accepted the conclusion, but I think they became impatient over the years when the body never materialised.' He sighed. 'Gerry and I are going to inform the mother and father together after this briefing. I've asked them both to be brought to the station in Whitby in light of some recent evidence.'

'Telling them what really happened to that boy... it doesn't get any tougher,' Reggie said.

'Aye.'

'You both need some support, boss?'

'Thanks Reggie, genuinely.' He smiled at his colleague. 'But we'll be fine. Okay, tasks. I don't want anybody talking to anyone until we've spoken to Simon and Katie Lyle. It's getting on already, so I suggest we leave the bulk of those interviews until tomorrow.' Frank looked at Sean. 'But from tomorrow I want you to dig into Greg's school life. Interview his former classmates, teachers, anyone who might have insight into his state of mind or any issues he was facing. Okay, Sean?'

'Yes, sir.'

'Sharon, Reggie...' Frank continued. 'You two will be tracing Greg's movements on the day of his disappearance. Now this is a biggie. I've read the interviews. Apart from the ones with Harold Cross, they're too vague. First thing tomorrow, let's get digging and let's see what we unearth. Gerry and I will support with that.'

Sharon and Reggie nodded.

Frank addressed their new data analyst. 'Clara, I need you to go through all the data from the original investigation with a fine-tooth comb. Compare it with our new findings, see if anything jumps out.'

Clara's fingers flew across her keyboard. Her way of acknowledging the task, he hoped.

He paused, looking around at his team. They were a motley crew, each with their own quirks and foibles, but he trusted them implicitly. 'We'll also be organising community outreach efforts to gather new information. It's been twenty-six years, but memories have a way of surfacing when you least expect them – especially when news of this grim discovery spreads far and wide.' Frank took a deep breath. He could almost feel Greg watching him from the photograph behind him. 'Listen up, this isn't just any case. This is about a vulnerable fourteen-year-old boy who never got to grow up. A kid with a dog who meant everything to him. A son who tried to buy flowers for his mum when she was sad. A child who should be a man now, having found a place in the world, living his life, not...' He broke off and turned away.

He sucked in a deep breath, rubbed his temples and turned. 'He shouldn't be in a bloody fridge at the bottom of the harbour, okay?'

He saw Sharon blink rapidly, Reggie's jaw clench, Sean's eyes widen. Even Gerry dropped her eyes and returned to stroking Rylan.

'Someone out there knows what happened to Greg Lyle. Someone's been carrying that secret for a quarter of a century.' Apart from Gerry, who remained focused on Rylan, he looked each member of his team in the eye, one by one. 'God help us if we can't bring justice for a child.'

He waited for every single one of them to give him a sharp nod.

As the team dispersed to their various tasks, Frank turned back to the board, his eyes once again drawn to Greg's smiling face.

Let's get to know you, lad.

No soul should be forgotten.

Chapter Sixteen

Shivering in her damp clothes, Raven drew her black velvet curtains to block out the fading daylight and sat in the shadowy comfort of her flickering ornate candelabras.

Damien's concerned face swam in her memory. Her flashback – her sudden moment of terror – had shaken him.

She tried to blame it on last night's absinthe binge, but Damien was no fool.

The panic attack had been triggered by the news of the dead child recovered from near Tate Hill Pier.

She'd managed to make it through the opening concert and, fortunately for those she was desperate to entertain, the rain had eventually stopped. However, Damien hadn't once moved his beady eye from her. Eventually, it'd been too much and she'd slipped off home.

Shit, she thought, shaking her head and forcing back the tears. *Soon the questions will come.*

Damien wouldn't let this one lie.

She'd put everything in jeopardy.

She stood and moved over to her large, baroque mirror, whose frame dominated one wall. She looked a state. Make-up smudged over her face, hair out of shape and tangled. She slipped off her dress, so she stood in her underwear and regarded herself. Gone was that lean figure that had come to Whitby thirty years ago. This forty-six-year-old version of herself was barely recognisable.

She was a completely different person.

In the reflection, she spotted the absinthe bottle on a shelf alongside leather-bound books, fake skulls and the favourite few of her large antique doll collection.

The green fairy.

She looked down at the Victorian fainting couch upholstered in deep crimson velvet, looking ready to catch her if she flew with the fairy, and allowed it to numb her racing thoughts.

Her phone buzzed. She read a message from Damien. He mentioned how the second band had been a major hit with the crowd – even better than the first.

His message said:

> Raven, please let me know you're okay. I'm worried about you.

Raven wondered how she'd feel if she told him everything.

But would unburdening herself serve any purpose?

After all, this world of darkness and theatricality had been her reality for so long that pulling back the curtains... well... what purpose would it serve?

Her gaze drifted to the staircase in the hallway. On the way out, she touched the green fairy. 'Wait for me.'

She had to see something first.

Know something.

After all, it'd been such a long time, could she truly rely

on memory? On what lay buried in the shadows of a dark, theatrical world behind the curtains?

She went to the spare room.

A stark contrast to the gothic opulence of the rest of her home. Plain white walls, a simple bed with crisp sheets, and a nondescript dresser.

The stage is behind me now.

What's the truth?

She moved to a chest of drawers, knelt and opened the bottom one. It slid open with a soft hiss. As soon as her fingers took hold of an envelope, she knew the memories were real. That nothing could be truly buried.

And then her mind exploded with them.

Images.

Each of them a sickening thud in the centre of her mind.

Closing her eyes, she fell onto her back.

Screams echoed.

Were they from her now?

Or were they from her memories?

With trembling hands, Raven opened her eyes and emptied four photographs onto the floor from the envelope.

Four sickening thuds.

She shook the envelope again.

A fifth, sickening thud.

She stroked the freckled face, and his gap-toothed smile.

Tell me a story about monsters.

The world of the goth festival, which had seemed so all-consuming just hours ago, now felt distant and unreal.

Like a work of fiction.

Chapter Seventeen

At the station in Whitby, the desk sergeant was happy to keep an eye on Rylan while Frank and Gerry spoke to Greg's parents.

'He follows instructions,' Gerry reassured PS Lucy Kimble. 'He'll stay still and silent if you ask him, too.'

'Well,' Lucy said, 'Hopefully that won't be necessary. Been a quiet day so far, could do with livening it up a little. Rylan and I will get to know each other.' She stroked his ears. 'Won't we, little man?'

Frank noticed Gerry didn't look overly convinced.

'Don't feed him, please,' Gerry said.

'Of course not,' Lucy said, detecting the tone and straightening her posture. 'Wouldn't dream of it.'

'DI Carver is concerned as he's got a bit of a gastric issue at the moment,' Frank said, intending to make the exchange more polite.

'Not that you could feed him on any other occasion,' Gerry said. 'Should you ever see him again.'

'Okay...' Lucy said, nodding. 'I'll remember. And don't worry, unless he likes Mars Bars, I've nothing to offer.'

Gerry widened her eyes. 'Dogs are allergic to chocolate.'

'I know,' Lucy said, exasperation in her tone. 'I've three retrievers.'

Frank smiled. Having failed with politeness, he attempted to inject humour into the situation. 'He may look cute and wonderful, DS Kimble, but feed him after midnight and, well, all hell breaks loose.'

He was glad that the sergeant laughed to prevent him from looking a plonker, because Gerry looked at him in complete bewilderment.

Unsurprisingly, on the way to the interview room, she demanded an explanation.

He told her about the movie *Gremlins*. 'You must have seen it?'

She gave him a look which suggested she hadn't and never would.

'Your loss.'

They reached the interview room.

Chapter Eighteen

It was far too warm in the interview room. It'd attracted a few flies, which were unusual in November. They buzzed and bounced off harsh fluorescent lights.

Simon Lyle paced around the far side of the room in a crisp business suit. Katie Rhodes, who'd since remarried and so possessed a different surname, sat ramrod straight in her chair, her face pale and drawn.

Behind him, Frank heard Gerry closing the door.

Frank kicked it off: 'Mrs Rhodes and Mr Lyle, thank you for being here, I'm—'

'In light of recent evidence?' Simon whirled round, his polished shoes squeaking on the floor. He moved well for a man in his late fifties. 'That was what you said, wasn't it?' He pointed at Frank. 'What new fucking evidence is that, then?'

Frank was left momentarily speechless; he hadn't really been expecting the fury.

'We've been waiting for answers for near on three decades, and now you drag us in here like criminals!' Simon's eyes were wild.

Frank held up a placating hand. 'Sorry, sir. That wasn't our intention. The matter was sensitive, and I didn't think it fair to speak to you both individually at the outset.'

'There're two of you, aren't there?'

Frank gave a swift nod. *We like to do it in pairs*, Frank thought. *After all, who knows what the response will be like... take your response, for example...* 'Duly noted. Anyway, I'm DCI Frank Black, and this is DI Gerry Carver. If you could take a seat, we'll explain everything.'

'I'll stand, thank you.'

Fair enough.

Frank, feeling the heat, peeled off his jacket and put it over the chair.

They both sat, the faint buzzing of the flies a constant backdrop.

Frank looked between the angry eyes of Simon and the sombre eyes of Katie. 'I'm sorry to have to tell you this, but we found Greg's remains yesterday.'

He allowed this to settle for a moment, the silence broken only by the occasional thud of a fly against the light fixture.

Eventually, Simon spoke. 'That body... yesterday... at the pier?'

Frank gave a slow nod. 'I'm so sorry.'

Simon strode forward and placed his hands on the desk between them, leaning over and raising an eyebrow. 'In a fridge?'

Frank swallowed. 'Aye. Mr Lyle, if—'

'In a fucking fridge?' Simon leaned in further.

Frank maintained eye contact with Simon. The man was too confrontational. If he leaned in any further, he'd have to put a stop to it. He gave a swift nod. 'I'm sorry.'

Fortunately, Simon backed off, although his wild eyes

suggested he wasn't quite done. 'Except... Greg fell from a cliff, didn't he?' His voice carried a loud tone of sarcasm.

Shit, Frank thought, *here I am arguing on behalf of my incompetent predecessors.* 'That wasn't the case. I'm sorry. It has turned out that—'

'Turned out... Turned out? You lot were adamant, so what does that suggest?'

'That they were wrong,' Gerry said.

Simon swung his eyes onto Gerry. 'Eh? Wrong? Wrong about my son's death?'

Frank tensed, sensing the situation escalating. He reached out and tapped Gerry's arm beneath the table – she'd clock his instruction not to say anything else.

'I'm sorry, Mr Lyle, for your loss. I understand you're shocked,' Frank said. 'I can only apologise regarding the outcome of the previous investigation.'

'Apologise?'

Is there a chuffing echo in here? Frank thought. 'Aye. On behalf of my predecessors.'

'Well, thank you for that,' Simon said. 'Your apology. On behalf of your predecessors.'

Frank bit back a sigh, his patience wearing thin.

Katie, who'd been silent until now, made a sobbing sound.

Frank looked at her. Remarkably, tears had already soaked her face, and yet no one had heard her till this moment.

'How sure are you?' Her voice was barely above a whisper.

Frank offered her a sympathetic look. 'I'm sorry, Mrs Rhodes. It's been confirmed through dental and medical records.' He reached behind himself and took a packet of

Kleenex from the pocket of his jacket hanging over the chair. He offered her one.

She took it and dried her face. 'How did he die?'

'We don't know for certain as yet,' Frank said.

'You must have some idea,' Simon said. 'He was locked inside a fridge... in the sea... and...'

'Did he suffer?' Katie's eyes pleaded for reassurance.

No doubt the possibility of Greg being alive in that fridge stabbed at the parents like it stabbed at Frank, but he didn't want to open up that debate – not unless they knew for sure. It was a conversation best steered around at this stage. He tried to answer without ruling out the truth. 'We've found nothing to suggest that Greg suffered.'

'When will you know more?' Katie asked.

'I'm not sure,' Frank said. 'But as soon as we do, we will inform you.'

Simon sucked in a deep breath, loudly, letting everyone know he was far from done. Frank looked up at him.

'Someone killed my boy, though, yes?'

Frank also sucked in a deep breath but did so more subtly. He nodded. 'That's what the discovery suggests.'

'Suggests?' Simon put his hands down on the table again. 'In the same way it was suggested that he fell from a cliff?'

Frank fought the urge to fight his own corner. Tell him he wasn't part of that investigation, but playing the blame card would be inappropriate. 'We intend to be as thorough as we can be. We've modern advancement on our side.' It was weak. This case was twenty-six years old and ice cold. If it wasn't solved when it was hot, chances are it wouldn't be solved now that it was cold.

'Would you like some time?' Frank looked between the

parents. 'To process this? We need to ask questions, but I completely understand—'

'Time?' Simon leaned in. 'Time? Is that a fucking joke? We've had bags of that... Twenty-six years.'

Frank had had enough. The situation either needed defusing or wrapping up. The man was unhinged. It was understandable, but that didn't mean Frank should wait around for further escalation. He opened his mouth to tell him to stop leaning in and sit down, or he'd have to call in more support.

'Just sit down, Si,' Katie said.

Simon looked down at his ex-wife in horror. 'What?'

'I said sit the fuck down.' She glared up at him with her swollen eyes. 'You think this is helping?'

Simon's eyes were wilder than ever.

It didn't deter her, though. 'Stop being a dickhead.'

Not good at all. Frank stood. 'Okay, I think we'll take a break—'

Simon turned his eyes back on Frank, pulled out his chair with one foot and slammed himself down into it. 'I'm sitting.' He folded his arms. 'And listening.'

Frank looked down at Katie. *Wow,* he thought. *Did that really just work? Fair play.*

Frank sat back down, coughed, and cleared his throat. 'Now, we're still in the early stages of the investigation, and we will speak to you both individually afterwards, when you feel ready, of course, but there are a few things I could check that would really help now.'

Katie nodded. 'Please ask us anything.'

Simon snorted.

Frank nodded at Gerry, who slid a photograph of the pendant in front of them. 'We found this with Greg.'

Katie's hands shook as she picked up the photo. She

stared at it, her eyes filling with fresh tears. 'It's Buddy's paw print.'

Frank made a note.

'He never took it off... a company took an imprint of Buddy's paw – and then shrunk the image to fit the pendant.' Simon put a fist to his mouth and squeeze his eyes shut.

'There was a lanyard,' Frank said. 'From Whitby Abbey.'

'I remember,' Katie said. 'He got it from a school trip, and he attached the pendant to the lanyard.'

'Shit,' Simon said, lowering his head. The recovered items were obviously making it more real to him.

Frank hesitated, then carefully proceeded. 'There was also a pager with him.'

Katie's gaze remained fixed on the pendant photo as she replied, 'Yes. We gave it to him. He differed from most of the other kids. He was autistic. We wanted him to receive our messages whenever... to call us from payphones, to tell him to come home... that kind of thing. We sent him hundreds of messages after he disappeared.'

This was interesting and something Frank was yet to consider. The last message received was the only one that was decipherable. All the messages before that one had been corrupted. If the parents sent him messages after the school reported him missing, then it meant the pager had never picked them up.

Which meant the pager was immediately switched off by whoever Greg had met; or, Frank swallowed, Greg had already been dead and inside that fridge, cutting the pager's signal off.

Katie looked up, her eyes suddenly distant. 'I just thought of something...'

'Please go on,' Frank said.

'The funeral... Greg's funeral. We already had one. What does that mean, exactly? Does this mean that we need to have another? Arrange another?'

Frank didn't know how to answer that question.

'You're being ridiculous, Katie,' Simon said.

He certainly would never have dreamed of answering it like that.

Katie sobbed again, her shoulders shaking with the force of her grief.

Frank fought back a surge of anger. This man was being a complete dickhead.

'I can't... I can't...' Katie broke off, choking on her sobs. Eventually, she completed her sentence. 'I can't do this with him here.'

Frank nodded. *And who could blame you?*

'Ridiculous, again...' Simon hissed. 'He's our son.'

'Was!' Katie hissed and looked between Frank and Gerry. 'Please. I want nothing to do with him.'

Frank stood.

Simon was glaring at his wife. 'Are you out of your fucking mind? If we're not even together in this... for Greg... then what chance does he have?'

Frank went to open the door and called for two officers to take the couple to different rooms.

Gerry said, 'Mr Lyle, we were planning to speak with you both separately, anyway. I think now would be a good time to ready ourselves for that.'

'Why don't you ready yourself to fuck off?'

Frank swung from the door. Simon was on his feet now. 'Mr Lyle, I'm placing you on a warning. You're not to speak to my colleague like that again.' He looked at Katie, who was sobbing. 'In fact, just say nothing else... for now.'

Simon edged around the table, his body language aggressive. Frank moved alongside Gerry.

Frank narrowed his eyes. 'Did you hear my warning, Mr Lyle? I'm insisting you don't move any further.'

Simon glared at Frank, considered it, and then said, 'Whatever.'

After the officers removed them to different rooms, Frank looked at Gerry. 'Are you okay?'

Gerry nodded. 'Mr Lyle's reaction, while extreme, isn't uncommon in cases like this. The sudden confirmation of a long-held fear often manifests as anger. Although it isn't pleasant, it didn't surprise me, and therefore, I don't feel too unsettled.'

Frank shook his head. *Lucky you*, he thought. He was glad that the adrenaline was ebbing from his system.

'There was one thing that concerned me, though,' Gerry said.

'Oh, and what was that?'

'You, Frank.'

Bloody hell, here we go. Can I do anything right? he thought. 'What was the issue there? I wasn't too macho, was I? Well, if I was, I'm sorry, Gerry, but I was born at a different time. A completely different time.'

'It has nothing to do with your masculinity, Frank. It's more to do with your age. That little standoff with Mr Lyle was risky.'

'So, I'm too old to stand up for you. What if he took a swing for you? I can handle myself. I'll let you know when I'm too old, Gerry. Thank you very much.'

'Have you forgotten what happened the last time you got into a physical altercation? Your face?'

'I was mugged.'

'It still classes as a physical altercation.'

'One I was unprepared for. I was prepared for this one. Believe me.'

'Now you're being too macho. Bravado is dangerous. You're sixty-five.'

He almost corrected her, but then he recalled she was right.

As she always was.

'Bloody hell. Next time someone wants to take a swing, I'll hide behind you! Times have certainly changed.'

'It is nothing to do with times or eras, Frank. I'm more likely to survive a heavy blow than you are.'

'When did I become such an invalid?'

'Not an invalid, but science shows that your bone density won't be as strong and—'

'Enough,' Frank said, thinking, *Sometimes I wish someone would just deliver that final heavy blow and have bloody done with it.*

Chapter Nineteen

Ray stood before the mirror in the vestry of St Claude's Church, dabbing at the angry red lines on his face. He threw the blood-stained cotton ball into a bin near his feet.

Megan.

Her behaviour had been extreme, but understandable.

He'd failed her in the past, and she was responding now to his unconventional approaches.

But did he regret trying?

No.

'Let's not forget,' he muttered to his reflection, 'Jesus himself overturned tables in the temple.'

He looked around his vestry at the polished oak and worn leather.

It was hard not to be concerned with repercussions from Megan's impromptu visit. They felt inevitable. However, he needed to stay positive. His congregation needed that from him.

The vestry door creaked open. Pam Eastwood, the church secretary, poked her head in. Eyes beneath wire-rimmed glasses widened as she took in the state of his face. 'Reverend, are you all right? I heard about the commotion during the service.'

Ray turned. He smiled, trying not to wince over the pain. 'Pam! Nothing to worry about. Overzealous worship.' His chuckle rang hollow in the small room. Her concerned face remained unchanged.

She stepped fully into the vestry, closing the door behind her with a soft click. 'I've been a secretary here for twenty years, and I've never seen "worship" leave marks like that.'

Ray's smile dropped. When it came to positivity, Pam certainly wasn't the right person for the job. 'Okay... the woman clearly needed support, but she left before I could speak to her properly. Please don't worry, Pam, I'll find out who she is and see if I can help.' In a way, he wasn't lying. He was planning to find out where Megan was. After all, what choice did he really have?

He knelt and busied himself with tidying away first aid supplies, which his wife had left out earlier after she'd cleaned his wounds.

The secretary's eyes were burning into his. 'Reverend. The congregation is talking. They're concerned. That woman... she seemed to know you. She knew your name. And she called you a liar.'

Ray's hand stilled for a moment. He took a deep breath and then resumed its task with forced casualness. *This really won't do*, he thought, inwardly sighing.

'You know how it is, Pam. Nature of the job. Sometimes, we become a repository for people's pain, their fears. Sometimes, that manifests in... unexpected ways.'

'But that doesn't explain how she knew your name. The

attack was so personal... so specific. Who was she, Reverend?'

Ray felt a bead of sweat trickle down his back. He stood and faced Pam fully, his mind racing. *Was this going to be a problem?* he thought. *Was Pam going to be a problem?*

He summoned every ounce of pastoral authority he possessed. He went over and put a hand on her upper arm. 'My dear Pam, I really don't know... as yet. As soon as I do, you'll be the first to know. Now, look, I appreciate your concern. I truly do, but I can assure you, there's nothing to worry about. She must have read my name from the door-way, as I told Kath. Now tell me, how are the preparations for the church fete coming along?'

Pam blinked at the sudden change of subject, her mouth opening, but no sound emerging.

'Pam, the fete?' he prompted. 'You were the one insisting that we were behind with the organisation yesterday?'

'Yes, I... well, there's been an improvement, I suppose. Louise is still insisting on manning the cake stall again, despite last year's... incident.'

'Ah, yes, the Great Victoria Sponge Debacle of 2023.' Ray laughed, the sound more genuine this time. He felt some of the tension leave his shoulders as they moved into safer territory. 'Well, perhaps we can station her somewhere less... combustible this year. What about the book stall? She's always had a keen eye for literature.'

As Pam rattled off lists of volunteers and donation pledges, Ray felt a momentary relief. But the weight of his secrets still pressed down on him, threatening to crush him beneath their mass.

When they wrapped up and she turned to leave, she paused at the door and swung back. 'Dreadful business, eh?

That poor child. Makes you wonder what the world's coming to, doesn't it?'

He shook his head, not knowing what she was talking about. 'Child?'

She looked confused. 'I thought you'd have heard. Samantha Wells put something online today about that body at the pier?'

'I didn't talk to anyone in the congregation today... for obvious reasons. Go on, Pam. What did Samantha write?'

'Well...' She lowered her voice. 'Some that witnessed the body in the fridge claim it was a child. That it was far too small to be an adult.'

Ray felt the blood drain from his face. 'Dear God,' he whispered, his voice hoarse. 'How... how horrible. But surely... how would they know that, really? I think they'd be best waiting for news from the police.'

Pam nodded. 'I hope you're right, Reverend. I couldn't bear for it to be a child.'

'Yes,' Ray said, closing his eyes, taking a deep breath. 'It would be awful.'

The colourful light from the stained-glass window suddenly seemed to mock the gravity of the situation. Ray sat in his chair.

'I'll bring you a cup of tea, Reverend, and then we'll look at the flyers for the fete, okay?'

'That would be good, Pam.'

After Pam had closed the vestry door behind her, he touched his damaged cheek and winced.

A child?

Could it be?

He shook off the thought and took a deep breath. Then, for a brief, wild moment, Ray considered taking Megan's hand and leading her to the front of the congregation. He imagined watching her stern face soften as he allowed the truth to pour out.

The idea felt appealing, but then, he thought of his congregation. They needed him. He straightened his collar and squared his shoulders, preparing himself for the day ahead.

Chapter Twenty

KATIE RHODES TWISTED the remains of a tissue between her fingers. Frank offered her another, which she accepted with a grateful nod.

The interview room felt larger without Simon Lyle's stifling presence, but it was still just as hot, and the flies continued to irritate with their kamikaze flights into the light.

Gerry sat beside him with her posture perfect as always, her notepad opened in front of her.

'Mrs Rhodes,' Frank began. 'I know this is difficult, but the more help you can give to us, the more effective we can be. That said, if you *do* need more time, don't hesitate to ask.'

Katie shook her head. A determined look broke out from her red-rimmed eyes. 'No. I'm okay.'

Frank nodded. 'Thank you. Okay, perhaps you could start by telling us a bit more about what Greg was like?'

Katie's eyes softened, and a ghost of a smile crept over her face. 'He was special... unique... I know all parents would say this, but Greg had his own way of looking at the world, of seeing things that others missed.'

Frank smiled, noting to himself how Katie could easily have been describing his colleague beside him.

'By the time he was eight, he could name every species of fish in the North Sea.' The pride in her voice was clear.

Frank's mind turned to Maddie at eight, her passion for drawing covering every wall in their kitchen. He wished he could speak of that with the same pride that Katie had in her voice, but for him, the memory just ached.

'We got Buddy, a rescue dog, for Greg's eleventh birthday. From that day, they were rarely apart.' Katie's gaze was off in the distance. 'Greg would talk to Buddy as if he were one of us. He'd say things like: "Buddy, do you know octopuses have three hearts?" But, you know, Buddy would look at him like he understood every word.'

'Sounds like they were quite the pair.'

'Inseparable. There was this one time, Greg was about twelve, and we took a trip to Robin Hood's Bay. The rock pools fascinated him. He pointed out everything living in them to Buddy. He just stood there, patient as anything, while Greg gave him a full marine biology lecture.' She sighed. 'He was a wonderful dog. Buddy.'

'You've some beautiful memories.'

Katie dabbed her eyes with the fresh tissue, nodding.

'Mrs Rhodes,' Gerry interjected, 'having an autistic child can often come with challenges.' Her tone was neutral, but not unkind. 'Could you tell us about those?'

Katie looked startled by the question at first, and she was silent for a time, while the flies overhead buzzed and butted the light. Eventually, after regarding Gerry for a moment, Katie nodded, and there was acceptance in her expression.

'There were many...' She paused and lowered her head. Frank suspected she'd feel guilty, as if she may somehow be criticising her lost son by voicing the challenges.

Gerry said, 'Please take your time.'

The empathetic side of Gerry was something Frank hadn't often seen. He appreciated this rare glimpse.

'Noises overwhelmed him,' Katie said. 'We noticed when he was really young. He'd sit down, hands over his ears, rocking. It was better after Buddy arrived... You know, he was so curious about the world. So demanding in his need to know about things. Sometimes he was exhausting with his questioning, but it was remarkable to see this fascination grow. And, you know, he was so rule driven. Deviations from rules could cause meltdowns.'

'Neurodiverse individuals are often rule driven,' Gerry said. 'It helps them to cling to identifiable concrete structures in a chaotic world.'

To Frank, it really seemed like Gerry was talking about herself now.

Katie nodded in agreement. 'He'd memorise every school rule, every traffic law. There was this one time, he saw a car parked on double yellow lines. He was so upset, he insisted we wait there until the driver came back so he could explain why it was wrong. He'd have made an excellent police officer. A moral one, anyhow. Although, he may have found it a difficult career path to be accepted into. The world never seemed accepting of my son.'

'The world has taken its time moving on,' Gerry said. 'But improvements have been made. I'm sorry Greg isn't here to see them. I'm certain Greg would have made a wonderful police officer.'

Frank felt a swell of pride at hearing his colleague speak.

Katie pressed the tissue to her eyes and took a moment to compose herself. 'He would have done. And, yes, I can see how society has improved. Even though he was diagnosed, I know that there's more support for children like Greg now. Support in school, an understanding from people around. It was less so then. People turned away. They didn't want to acknowledge anything out of the ordinary. Like you said, I think he'd have thrived in today's world.'

'Aye,' Frank said. 'He would've done.'

She raised an eyebrow at Frank. 'Maybe... who knows... what happened may never have happened?'

Frank's curiosity piqued. 'I'm sorry, Mrs Rhodes, but could you explain what you mean?'

'Nothing in particular... just that a warmer, caring society may have encouraged him to share more of his concerns. Rather than closing himself down and hiding his problems.'

The mention of problems couldn't go unchecked. 'Any in particular... ones that we haven't already discussed?' Frank pressed gently.

'In the months leading up to his disappearance, he seemed more withdrawn. Quieter than usual. I thought it was just him getting older, you know. Hormones. But he'd always been so open with me. Suddenly, he seemed rather closed off. It seemed... jarring.'

'Did you ask him about this?' Frank asked.

'Of course, yes, but he brushed off my paranoia. Greg was unbelievably honest. Had been his entire life. I just couldn't accept that he was hiding anything.'

'Did he mention anyone new in his life?' Gerry asked. 'Any new friends, perhaps?'

Katie shook her head. 'The only friend he ever spoke about was Terry. They had similar personalities. The scoundrels used to hide away in a treehouse in Terry's garden! Thinking back now, Terry was more prone to meltdowns than Greg. My son was definitely more of a brooder. He'd retreat into himself when he was overwhelmed rather than explode...' She paused, gazed off into the distance and then her eyes widened slightly. 'I just remembered something. Martha Higgins, while she was working as a lollipop lady, told me she'd seen Greg talking to a grown man while walking Buddy, during one of his morning walks. This was about three weeks before he disappeared. I didn't know if it was relevant, still don't, *but* I mentioned it to the police back then.'

Frank nodded, recalling the detail from the notes. Despite having a description of a man in dirty overalls, potentially some kind of mechanic, provided by Martha Higgins, the lead had come to nothing. Martha had noted that the man had fallen to his haunches to stroke Buddy. Eventually, the lead had been dismissed as nothing more than a passer-by's interest in Buddy.

'Did you ask him about this passer-by?' Gerry inquired.

'Yes. He said he couldn't remember. He said many people stopped to stroke Buddy, which I guess was true. Still, Martha had said he looked as if he was enjoying the conversation and that it wasn't that brief. Therefore, I thought it was strange he didn't remember. But I didn't push it. I thought if it was important, he'd tell me.' Her face creased. 'Should I have asked more questions?'

Frank offered her a sympathetic look. 'I'm sure you asked enough. Teenagers keep things to themselves. There's only so much—'

'Yes, but Greg was autistic. Should I have paid more attention?'

'From everything you've said,' Frank's voice was gentle but firm, 'I see nothing but an attentive and loving mother.'

She welled up again, but her expression was full of gratitude for the kind words.

'Mrs Rhodes,' Gerry said, 'could you tell us about Greg's relationship with his father?'

Katie's face clouded over. 'Strained... I think you've seen what kind of man Si is. But there was a time when I was blind to his behaviour. I just wanted him and Greg to have a stronger relationship, and I loved Si.' She sighed. 'In a way, I sympathised with Si, because he struggled to understand and come to terms with Greg's diagnosis. If not for his affair, I could still be with him, blinded to what a bastard he can be... Imagine that. He was always pushing Greg to be "normal", whatever that means.' She looked at Gerry. 'Outrageous, eh? Ashamed of his son... embarrassed by him.' Katie's eyes narrowed as she recalled something. 'There was this group fishing trip when Greg was twelve. It was for fathers and sons. But Greg... he couldn't bear the thought of hurting the fish. He spent the first day lecturing Si and the other fathers about marine conservation and the importance of sustainable fishing practices. Si was furious. Dragged Greg home, calling him a "bloody know-it-all" the entire way. Even said he was disappointed to have a son who couldn't even fish properly.' She paused, swallowing hard. 'Greg didn't speak for days after that. Just sat in his room, reading marine biology books to Buddy.'

Frank felt a surge of anger. He'd seen it before. Parents dismissive of their own children.

He thought of his own relationship with Maddie. Had he been similar?

Had he expressed disappointment and shame?

God, forgive me, Maddie, if I ever did that.

'And the day before Greg disappeared,' Gerry prompted gently, 'when Greg found out about the affair? Could you describe what happened?'

Katie's eyes darted before her face crumpled. 'It was just... awful. There are still nights I relive it in my dreams. We went to her house. Greg and I. Raven. She was barely a kid. Disgusting. I still see her about now. She once tried apologising to me. Told her where to take that! Mind you, at least she saw sense in getting shot of Si before it got too serious. She obviously had more of a spine than me... Took the loss of my child to wake me up...'

'What happened at the house?' Frank asked.

'Greg was in the car and he overheard me and Si arguing on Raven's doorstep. Si was shouting... I was crying. I was shocked. So shocked.' She touched her chest and welled up. 'All the way home, Greg rocked in the passenger seat, hands over his ears, saying "Stop, stop, stop" over and over.' Katie lowered her head. 'We did that to our own child.'

'It sounds like Simon is the one responsible,' Frank said. 'Not you.'

'But I shouldn't have exposed him to that. I didn't think. It was a stupid mistake.'

As Frank made notes, his heart fell. Greg, an autistic child, already struggling to make sense of the world, suddenly faced with the shattering of his family unit.

'Greg was gone the next day,' Katie said, her voice barely above a whisper. 'Forever. How could it be a coincidence? That was why I was so quick to believe the narrative behind the cliff... I mean... it didn't seem so hard to believe that he could have taken his own life.'

Frank nodded.

'How did Greg seem the next morning?' Gerry asked. 'Before he left?'

'Not too different,' Katie said, her voice trembling. 'He was quiet most mornings, anyway. He hugged me before he left with Buddy, but then he always did that, so I didn't have any reason to be concerned. Also, he had Buddy to look after him. Buddy. Buddy... was Buddy with him? Have you found him too? Were they together when he died?'

Frank shook his head. 'We haven't found Buddy's remains.'

She lowered her eyes. 'That may have been something. His best friend with him. I wonder what happened to Buddy?'

A good question, and one that the last set of investigators had failed to address properly. After concluding the boy had most likely fallen from a cliff edge, they never thought to wonder what had happened to the dog. Had they just assumed he'd been stolen?

Gerry leaned forward. 'Mrs Rhodes, I know you provided details as to Greg's usual morning routine, but if you could go through it again with us to see if anything was missed?'

Katie nodded. 'Oh yes. He'd wake up at exactly 6.45 every morning, no alarm needed. He'd have his breakfast – always two pieces of toast with strawberry jam, never raspberry – while reading a book about sea life. Then he'd get dressed, always buttoning his shirt from the bottom up, never top down. Then, he'd head out on his walk with Buddy. He'd leave at 7.45, rain or shine, on the dot, take the same route to St Claude's Church, then back home. He'd drop off Buddy and head to school.'

'Did Greg ever deviate from this routine?' Frank asked.

'Not that I was aware of. When the school called to say

he hadn't arrived... I knew something was terribly wrong. Greg would never break his routine like that. Never. I can't believe he went looking for his father at that woman's house...' She buried her face in her hands. 'And then to think he went to buy me flowers to cheer me up... he was such a sweet boy.'

Frank couldn't bear her pain any more. He picked up his chair and went to sit alongside her. He reached out and touched her upper arm. 'Greg sounds like a great lad... and it sounds like he loved you very much.'

She cried for a while, and Frank looked over at Gerry. She had her eyes down as she wrote in her notebook. Her face was impassive, but Frank knew better than to believe this wasn't affecting her, too.

He asked her about the message from the pager, but she merely looked at him, confused. 'As far as I know, only we had his pager number... and I certainly didn't send him that message. What does it even mean?'

Good question, Frank thought.

After a few more questions, Frank returned to his side of the table. When he sat, Katie looked up at him, her eyes wide. 'When can I see him then? Greg, I mean.'

Frank felt his stomach turn. He'd been dreading this question. 'That might not be such a good idea—'

'I need to... I need to say goodbye properly.'

'I understand, Mrs Rhodes, but I'm afraid it wouldn't be possible right now. We're still investigating the cause of death.'

'But he's my son,' Katie pleaded, her voice breaking. 'I need to see him. Hold him one last time.'

'At some point, it may be possible. But, I would advise that it is better to just remember Greg as he was.'

Katie's face crumpled again, fresh tears spilling down

her cheeks. 'I just don't understand. I thought it was suicide. Who'd want to hurt him? He was such a gentle soul. He wouldn't hurt a fly.'

Frank felt his own eyes stinging. He blinked rapidly, trying to maintain his composure. 'We will do everything in our power to find the truth.'

Katie nodded, her grief beyond words now. She clutched at Frank's hand on her upper arm as if it were a lifeline.

Gerry, who'd been silent for a while, spoke up. 'Mrs Rhodes. Is there anything else you can tell us? Any minor detail that might help?'

'I... I don't know. It's all such a blur now. But Greg, he... he always tried to do the right thing. Even when it was hard. Even when other people didn't understand.'

Frank nodded. 'That's good to know, Mrs Rhodes. It helps us understand who Greg was.'

'He was special... unique...' Katie said, burying her face in her hands.

They were the same words she used to describe her son at the beginning of the interview.

A poignant echo that made Frank feel more determined than ever.

Chapter Twenty-One

WHILE SIMON LYLE drummed an impatient rhythm on the table, Frank fought the desire to slam a fist down on the man's fingers. *Remember, he may be a pain in the arse, but don't forget the hell he's lived through, and what he found out today.* 'We know this isn't easy, Mr Lyle.'

Simon puffed out his cheeks and drummed harder.

'However, we could really do with your help,' Frank said.

'What is it you need to know?' There was no enthusiasm in his voice.

Frank exchanged a quick glance with Gerry, who was making notes, probably regarding his demeanour. 'What was your relationship with Greg like at the time?'

'He was my son. We loved each other. What more is there to know?'

Frank inwardly sighed. 'We'd appreciate it... We know there were family problems. The more we can find out about Greg's state of mind on that day, the easier it will be to figure out what really happened.'

Simon snorted. 'You're thinking I'd something to do with it?'

'Why would we think that?' Frank asked.

Simon's face contorted. 'I wasn't the father of the bloody year, but I guess you knew that already, or why would we be going down this line of questioning?'

'Mr Lyle,' Gerry answered. 'We're not here to judge your role as a father. Our goal is to attain the most extensive understanding of those moments leading up to Greg's death. We need to know about the condition of every relationship Greg had around that time.'

Simon took a deep breath, his jaw clenching. 'Okay? Shall we start here?' He waved a finger in the air. 'Scribble this down. I spent thirteen years trying to figure out how to be a father to a boy who... who, well, wasn't like other boys.'

'Did you struggle with Greg's diagnosis of autism?' Gerry asked.

'Struggle with his diagnosis? Listen... I struggled with Greg, full stop!'

'On account of him being autistic?'

'On account of him being not like anyone else. Am I repeating myself? Do you have kids?' He was looking at Gerry directly.

'I do,' Frank replied, trying to take Gerry out of the confrontation. 'A daughter.'

'And?'

Frank was confused. 'And what?'

'Did you completely understand her?'

Frank really had to force back a smile. 'A teenage girl? Well, I had a go. It was challenging to be sure. Not certain I always hit the nail on the head.'

Simon leaned forward, his eyes intense. 'But you had a

go, yes? Because she was a teenage girl. Like other teenage girls. I bet she fit right in, eh?'

Not exactly, no, Frank thought, but he really didn't want to get into that.

'My boy wasn't like any other teenage boy,' Simon continued. 'I tried, but I was fumbling around in the dark.' He looked down at the table for a short time, and Frank realised he was no longer drumming his fingers on it.

'He didn't really want a great deal to do with me, truth be told,' Simon said.

'That may not be true,' Gerry said. 'Greg could have struggled to express what he truly wanted. He may have loved you dearly and not conveyed it in a manner that you'd have understood, or even been comfortable with.'

Simon shook his head. 'Nah. Me and him were chalk and cheese. Greg, he was... he was in his own world half the time. I'd try to connect with him, to do father-son things, but it was like... like trying to communicate with someone I didn't know, nor would ever know. We just weren't cut from the same cloth. I'd have been better off with the teenage girl.' He nodded at Frank.

I don't know, Frank thought, *that hasn't been going swimmingly, either.*

'Everybody is simply unique, Mr Lyle, regardless of any diagnoses,' Gerry said. 'And they all have their challenges. Also, I think things would have been different for you had he been born now with autism. There would have been more support in understanding Greg's needs and reading his behaviours.'

'Great to know, thanks.' Simon's shoulders sagged. 'The reality is I didn't know how to be a father to Greg. Everything I tried seemed to make things worse. And Katie... she made it all look so fucking easy.'

Simon had set himself up as a hard man to sympathise with, but Frank managed some now. There wasn't just frustration in Simon's voice, there was also deep, underlying pain. Here was a man who could really have done with the help Gerry was referring to.

'I bet Katie told you a few stories, eh?' Simon raised an eyebrow. 'The fishing trip, by any chance?'

Frank tried to keep his expression solid.

Simon's sudden snort implied Frank had failed.

'She bloody loves that one!' Simon said. 'My finest hour that fishing trip! Apparently, I told him I was ashamed of him.'

'So you didn't say that?' Gerry asked.

'Not as such. I told him I didn't want to be ashamed of him. That I wanted him to fit in. Desperately. I told him I'd help him in any way I could.'

'You can't force someone to fit in,' Gerry said.

'So Katie often told me.'

'And she was right,' Gerry said.

'Maybe... yes... I see that now. I think it's fairly obvious I fucked up somewhere down the line.'

'What do you mean?' Frank asked.

'I mean, I fucked up.'

'Why do you say that?'

'Well, he's dead, isn't he? So, I obviously fucked something up.'

'So you feel directly responsible for his death?' Gerry asked.

Simon's face crumpled. 'Well, you clearly think I am – why would you be grilling me if not? Look...' He leaned forward and rubbed his temples. 'A father who liked to fix things brought me up. Any problem needed fixing. I viewed autism as a problem that required a solution. Society would baulk at that these days, I know! I tried to fix someone who was unfixable.'

'He wasn't broken,' Gerry said. 'The concept of fixing—'

'Okay...' He cut her off. 'I get that. In a way, that's kind of what I meant. I was trying to do something that didn't need to be done.'

'You said that Katie made it look easy. Could you explain what you meant?' Frank asked.

'She always knew what to do, what to say. Greg would talk to her for hours about his bloody fish and sea creatures. But with me? Nothing. It was like I didn't even exist.'

'Did you ever speak to a professional?' Gerry asked.

'Eh?' Simon snorted. 'So, it was me that needed fixing? Is that what you're suggesting?'

'I didn't mean that,' Gerry said. 'I meant someone who could listen to how you felt.'

'No, I didn't.'

'Okay,' Frank said. 'Let's talk about the day before Greg disappeared. The evening when Katie drove to Raven Blackstone's home.'

Simon closed his eyes and ran both hands through his grey hair. 'Really... I'm sure you've chapter and verse on that one in your notes already.'

'This is a new investigation,' Frank said.

'Well, okay... that evening was a right fucking shit show.' He shook his head. 'You can write that down!'

Frank noticed Gerry was scribbling again, but doubted she was actually recording those words.

'One of Katie's friends had seen me going into Raven's home the day before. Nosy cow filled Katie in almost immediately. You know, I wasn't intending to keep cheating. I was going to tell Katie myself. I was planning to leave her, you see. That was the fair thing to do... I just never got the chance.' He looked between their faces. 'But I can see you judging me.'

Simon was a man consumed with paranoia, guilt and anger, Frank realised.

Simon took a deep breath. 'Anyway, Greg overheard us arguing outside that house. Mainly about Raven's age. Yes, she was young... I get that... but old enough, you know, to know what she wanted? This must have sounded awful to Greg.' He rubbed his temples again. 'The lad was so upset. When I looked over, he was covering his ears, rocking back and forth in the car. I'd seen him bad before, but never as bad as that. Told Katie that if she was any mother at all, she'd get him home. I know, right? A real bastard... after all, this was my fault. I'm not the best at making the right decisions in stressful situations.'

You'd never have guessed, Frank thought.

'Anyway, Katie drove him away from Raven's... and that was that. I never saw my son again.' He stared off into space for a short time. Frank allowed him this moment of reflection. 'I loved him by the way, more than anything, not that anyone seems to believe me. Actually, why not scribble that down in your notebook, too? We may have had communication issues, but I loved him. Get it on record. I. Loved. Him. I'm not sure that it's come across at all yet.'

'I believe you loved your son,' Frank said, and he meant it.

Simon gave him a grateful look. It was the most gentle the bereaved father had looked as yet.

'Now, Greg called at Raven Blackstone's the next morning. She said you were out?' Gerry said.

His eyes lowered. Simon's voice was barely above a whisper now. 'Might as well tell you now... should have done then, really... not that it makes any difference. I was there. Okay. Upstairs in her house. I'd spent the night there.'

Frank nodded. 'So you lied? Both you and Raven?'

Simon looked down, his cheeks reddening with shame. 'I told her to tell Greg that I'd already left for work.'

'Why?'

'Because I couldn't face him,' Simon said, lifting his eyes. 'Because I was spineless.'

'Then why didn't you tell us at the time?'

Simon took a deep breath. 'Because of the fucking shame of it – why else? I was upstairs. If I'd known what was going to happen, obviously, I'd have gone down. But I needed to speak to him properly about Raven, and I didn't want to do that on the doorstep first thing in the morning. At least I'm telling the truth now.'

Twenty-six years later, Frank thought. *Good lord.*

'How did you meet Raven Blackstone?' Gerry asked.

'She was working at the Harbour Lights Café. She was interesting.'

'Twenty years old?' Frank added.

'Well, I was miserable,' Simon said. 'My world was suffocating me. At home, I felt like I was constantly walking on eggshells, never knowing what might set Greg off. With Raven, I could just let go.'

Frank couldn't help but think of his late wife, Mary, and the affair she'd had. Is that why she'd done it, too? Had she felt suffocated? He swallowed and refocused.

Simon sighed. 'But it was wrong. I was wrong. Funny thing was she wasn't even my type. She's a goth. Back then, she wasn't as full on as she is now, but still... dark make-up and black clothes, you get the picture. These days, I can barely recognise her. Bit of a mess, if you ask me. She was pretty as she was.'

'What was the relationship like?' Frank asked.

'Intense. Exciting. I think we were both using each other to escape our own problems. You know about mine. Raven, she'd her own.'

'And what were they?' Frank asked.

He shrugged. 'She never said. She was far more guarded than I was. Whatever it was, it was traumatic. I remember her having horrendous nightmares that made her scream. Still, looking back, we had some fun. We may have had a future if not for what happened to Greg... She couldn't handle me and my trauma, told me straight. Seemed rather unsympathetic but I kind of get it now. If her trauma was anything like mine was after I lost my boy, then I can understand why there'd be no room for anyone else's turmoil.' He stared at Frank.

'How long did the relationship last?'

'About a month before Greg went missing and a month after. Like I said, Raven was unstable. Prone to mood swings. One minute she'd be all over me, the next she'd be pushing me away. Add that to my grief and desperation. It was a volatile mix.'

'Did you notice anything unusual in the weeks leading up to his disappearance?' Gerry asked.

Simon shook his head. 'Greg was all about routine. Same thing, every day. Wake up, breakfast, walk the dog, school. Rinse and repeat.'

'Did he ever mention any new friends? Anyone he was spending time with?' Gerry pressed.

Simon frowned. 'Greg didn't really have friends. Just that Terry kid. And Buddy, of course. That bloody dog was his best mate. Come to think of it, I think he got on with that reverend up at St Claude's.'

'Ray Lawson?' Frank asked.

'Yes. That's the one. I never went to church. That was Katie's thing. And Greg went to Sunday school when she went, which is how he got to know the reverend. Bumped into him a few times. Seemed nice... a little weird, maybe... but pleasant.'

'Weird how?' Frank asked.

'His life's work is the church?' He smirked. 'Isn't that enough?'

'For some, the church is a source of comfort and community,' Gerry said. 'It provides structure and meaning to their lives.'

'For some,' Simon said. 'Certainly not all. Where was God when my son was being stuffed into a fridge?'

Frank interjected before Gerry could respond. 'Did anyone other than you and Katie have his pager number?'

Simon shook his head. 'Of course not.'

Frank wrote down the message that Greg had received at 7.03 a.m. Simon looked at it. 'Odd message.'

'Incomplete... and we don't know who sent it. Does it mean anything?'

Simon shrugged. 'How could it? Could it be a mistake? A fragment from someone else's message. Sometimes, people connect to the wrong phone, don't they... these days? I certainly didn't send it. Maybe his friend, Terry, sent it?'

Frank nodded. 'We'll ask him.'

Now he'd opened up, Frank and Gerry could probe him further, but they struggled for anything new. Frank was on the verge of wrapping the interview up when he noticed Simon's eyes were suddenly glassy, as if he was on the verge of tears. 'You know, the last time I saw him, and I'm not talking about inside the car outside Raven's... I mean really saw him... was a couple of weeks earlier when I caught him sitting on the stairs, listening to me and Katie argue. He looked so... lost. So... scared. I asked him if he was okay, and he just stared at me as if I wasn't even there. I tried to touch him, but there was no response. He just stared right through me as if I was invisible.' The pain in Simon's voice was palpable. Frank could see the man was teetering on the edge.

'Mr Lyle,' Gerry said, her voice surprisingly soft. 'Grief can manifest in a multitude of ways. Looking back on past events to source guilt and self-blame is one way. You should be mindful of this. Memories aren't always productive.'

Simon took a shuddering breath, visibly trying to pull himself together. He looked at Gerry as if he genuinely appreciated her words. 'It feels like yesterday, you know.' He shook his head. 'But, I guess, it always feels like yesterday.'

And it always will do, Frank thought, reflecting on the loss of his wife.

Simon looked up, his eyes meeting Frank's. For the first time since the interview began, there was a desperate, pleading look on his face. 'Please. Make them pay for what they did to my boy.'

Frank thought of Maddie, of the times he'd failed her, of the regrets he carried. In that moment, despite all of Simon's flaws and mistakes, Frank felt a profound connection to the broken man before him.

He gave a swift nod. 'I intend to.'

Chapter Twenty-Two

LILLY'S GAZE drifted to her small pot of delicate pink Zdravets on the counter and she sighed. Bulgaria felt a lifetime away now.

She flipped the 'Open' sign to 'Closed' and locked the front door, then headed to the till to count the day's takings. It hadn't been the best day, but at least there'd been no more dramatic moments.

No more sounds from downstairs.

After recording profits, she picked up a tray of food she'd prepared and headed down to the cellar, the stairs creaking under her weight. At the bottom, she moved the crates and unlocked the wooden door again.

She'd laid out rugs for the children to lie on. A small electric heater hummed softly in the corner, keeping the chill at bay. She placed the tray down on the floor and approached slowly, her hands held out in a gesture of peace. 'Shh, миличък.' *Darlings.* 'скоро. в безопасност си.' *Not long now. You're safe.*

The youngest, a boy of seven, whimpered and buried

his face in the shoulder of the older girl, Ivana. The twelve-year-old met Lilly's gaze with a mix of defiance and fear.

Lilly knelt a short distance away, careful not to crowd them. She smiled gently, her eyes soft with compassion. She informed them she'd brought them food, fresh bread, cheese and fruit, and gestured to the tray she'd set down.

The third child, a boy of ten, eyed the tray hungrily but made no move towards it.

She moved the tray closer to them, but didn't insist they take it. Instead, she whispered, in their tongue, desperate to soothe them in this tense silence. She talked about flowers, and beautiful scenes of nature in their home country.

The children had arrived the previous evening, and she'd made them aware that they'd be here for two or three nights. She pointed to a television and a DVD player and asked them if they'd like to watch Bulgarian cartoons again. Last night, the seven-year-old had laughed, but the older ones had remained stony-faced.

They were scared, and it would be unlikely that they'd ever see Lilly as anything but a threat. And if Lilly had to be seen as the bad guy, then so be it. These three orphaned children were some of the lucky ones, and how they felt about her had no relevance whatsoever.

As they ate, she told them about how the people they'd soon be with were of Bulgarian heritage and were kind. That they'd speak their language and take care of them while they integrated them into society. She omitted the fact that this was illegal and required months of arduous passport forgery and bribery, because they didn't need to know any of that.

When the children seemed more at peace, Ivana asked Lilly what it looked like upstairs.

Lilly spoke of the riot of colours and fragrances upstairs, as well as the fresh flowers and their meanings.

Later, as they watched cartoons again, Lilly's mind drifted back to her first experience of this country. The same age as Ivana. The memory hit her with such force that for a moment she was there again...

Eleven. She huddled in the corner of a damp, dark room, drawing her knees up to her chest. The concrete floor was cold beneath her. A single bare bulb hung from the ceiling, casting harsh shadows that seemed to move and leer at her.

There were eight others.

All girls. All now with the same destiny.

She could hear heavy footsteps approaching, and her heart raced. The door opened, and a large young man with a thick beard and cold eyes stomped in.

Georgi.

He gave them all a piece of stale bread.

She nibbled at the hard bread, her stomach churning with hunger and fear. Georgi stood nearby, his eyes roaming over them.

Her skin crawled.

Lilly blinked, pulling herself back to the present. The cartoons had finished. The children were watching her.

Ivana asked Lilly why she was helping them.

Lilly gave them an abbreviated version in their shared language: *Because long ago, I was like you. Scared, alone. The people who brought me here, who looked after me, weren't kind.*

Ivana nodded. She understood. Her family, who were part of an organised crime outfit before they were murdered, allowed her to understand things that others didn't.

Ivana would have been trafficked into prostitution.

The fate of the other two children would have been similar.

Ivana was curious. She wanted to know how Lilly had survived.

'извадих късмет.' And then she told them how she'd got lucky...

Georgi led them, eight terrified girls, to the minivan parked outside in the dark. Two men stepped out of the vehicle.

Lilly watched Aneta, the eldest among them scream and fight Georgi. She bit his hand and then he struck her. One of the men yanked her up and threw her into the back of the minivan. Another girl, Zora, struggled when they tried to get her in the van. Georgi and the other two took their eyes off the rest of them.

Lilly was at the back of that line. She chose to run.

Having always been the fastest runner at school, she felt confident.

She'd been right to be confident because she'd made it away. However, she reassured them they wouldn't have such experiences. That they were to be taken to kind Bulgarian homes.

The younger boy's stomach growled. Lilly gestured to the remaining food. 'Please, eat. You need your strength.'

She watched the children finish their meal, and as she did, she painted a picture for them of the lives that awaited them. They'd have their own rooms, she explained, with warm beds and plenty of toys. They'd go to school and make friends. Most importantly, they'd be safe and loved. She liked to think she could see the cautious hope in their eyes. That she was helping them in some small way in these terrifying moments.

The older girl asked Lilly if she'd found that after running away.

Lilly nodded. 'I did...'

Lilly ran until her lungs burned and her legs felt like lead. Unfamiliar streets twisted and turned. As she fled, the darkness slowly gave way to the first light of day, revealing a town unlike anything she'd ever seen.

Lilly found herself on a steep street that led down to a harbour. Fishing boats bobbed gently in the water. Perched on a cliff were the ruins of a black, spidery structure.

Most of the shops were shuttered. The windows were dark and uninviting. But one storefront blazed with light and life. A middle-aged man with a bushy moustache and a flat cap was carrying an armful of flowers into the shop. His movements were deliberate and gentle.

*Above the door, a sign proudly displayed the name Seabreeze Flower Shop in elegant gold lettering. Beneath it, in smaller script, was a Bulgarian phrase that made Lilly's heart skip a beat: '**Цветя за всички поводи**' – 'Flowers for all occasions'.*

Lilly stumbled to a stop in front of the shop. The man looked up, his kind eyes widening as he took in her dishevelled appearance and terror-stricken face. She said she was in danger. Without a word, he set down his flowers and held out a weathered hand, beckoning her into the warmth and safety of his shop.

At first, she wasn't sure if she could trust him. But something in the man's gentle gaze gave her courage. With a shaky breath, she stepped forward, crossing the threshold.

'His name was Dimitar.' She smiled. 'And he gave me this home.'

After her story, she told the children that she'd sleep upstairs, on her shop floor. That she'd visit them hourly. But she insisted they mustn't call out. Then she closed the door, turned the key and headed back up to the shop floor.

Midway up the steps, she heard a gentle tapping on the glass.

The shop door.

It would be Nikolai.

She increased her speed. Maybe they were here for the children already? It would be wonderful for them to get to their new homes tonight.

The tapping grew louder and more insistent when she reached the final step.

She didn't like it.

Nikolai was always calm and collected.

Curious, she turned onto the shop floor and regarded the hulking shadow looming behind her front door.

The taps were more like thuds now.

Her blood ran cold. It wasn't Nikolai.

She approached the door.

Georgi Vasilev was close to sixty years of age, with white hair and beard, but he remained the intimidating, cruel giant he'd always been.

In fact, he'd changed in very few ways since that day she'd first met him in 1989 when she was eleven.

'Ah, there you are, момче момиче.' My girl.

'Georgi,' she replied. She always worked on keeping her voice steady when speaking to him. 'What're you doing here? Our appointment is—'

'The last Tuesday of every month. I know... I know...'

He came in and closed the door behind him.

He turned to face her, smiling. He crossed his enormous arms across his chest. 'I've found out something rather... unsettling.'

She felt her stomach somersault. 'What's that?'

He raised a white eyebrow. 'лъгал си ме.'
You've been lying to me.

Chapter Twenty-Three

IMMEDIATELY AFTER THE final briefing of the day, Frank retired to his office to collect his thoughts.

His phone rang. It seemed Helen had other plans for him.

'Hel? How do?'

'Fine, and you?'

He laughed. 'This isn't about the case, is it?'

'How did you know?'

'Because you haven't got straight to the point... which you usually do... so, what've I done now?'

There was a long pause. Never good. Mary used to be queen of the pregnant pause.

'Helen... you still there?'

She sighed. 'Okay, Frank. Here's the thing. I should be facing you with this one, looking you in the eyes.'

Intriguing, Frank thought, raising an eyebrow. 'I must have really messed up this time.'

'I'm such a sodding coward.'

'One thing you're not, Hel, is a coward. However, a

waste of my time, especially at this moment, you most certainly are... Can you just get to the sodding point?'

'It's about Evelyn.'

The name hit Frank like a punch to the gut. He couldn't speak.

'Evelyn Wainwright?' she said.

He took a deep breath, steadying himself. 'I know who she is, Helen.'

Evelyn Wainwright was the widow of Nigel Wainwright. Five years ago, Nigel had been having an affair with Frank's wife, Mary. One night, he'd been driving drunk, and had swerved into oncoming traffic, killing himself, Mary, and a young mother in another car. Frank's world had already been fragile because of the estrangement of their daughter, Maddie. This tragedy had gone and shattered it completely.

'Do you know who she is?' Frank hissed.

'Of course, I—'

'Then why are we even bothering with this conversation?'

'She's not well, Frank.'

'My question remains the same. What's this about, Helen?'

'Very unwell.'

'So?' Frank said. He knew he sounded cold, but he'd no wish to back down. 'What's that got to do with me... or you, for that matter?'

'Before you lose your shit completely, Frank, can I just lay a fact out for you?'

'Lay away.'

'Evelyn Wainwright wasn't the one who had an affair with Mary. '

'Don't be condescending, Helen. You may have more brain cells than me, but I've got more than one.'

'Evelyn, like you, was widowed.'

'Steady on. These concepts may elude my intellectual grasp...'

'I knew this was a bad idea.'

'Aye. So why did you phone? What's the relevancy?'

'It's relevant, Frank, because she's sick, she's sad and she's done nothing wrong. When have people in need been irrelevant to you?'

Frank guffawed. 'This is bullshit. How long have you been friends with her?'

There was a pause on the other end of the line. 'Not friends. But... I've... I've been in touch with her, Frank. Since the accident.'

'You what?' His voice was low. He fought back his anger. 'Why?'

'Because I wanted to understand. Mary was my best friend, too. I needed to ask questions.'

'What questions? Aren't the answers bloody obvious? Her husband killed my wife. And she's a Wainwright.'

He could hear Helen take a deep breath. 'No... I wanted to understand why Mary did what she did. Why she...'

'Why she cheated on me?'

Helen didn't reply.

'Ha. And did you get the answer?'

'Not really.'

'You want the answer?'

'Not now Frank... this isn't why I'm phoning.'

'Take your pick. Fat. Heavy drinker. Work-obsessed. Crap husband. Crap father. I'm pretty sure, being your best friend, she'd have explained this to you before.'

'That's just it, Frank, she didn't. She only ever thought the world of you. Or so it seemed to me.'

'That's got to be bollocks.'

'It's not. And I've never lied to you. I didn't know about Nigel. She never told me and she was like a bloody sister to me.'

'Maybe she was too ashamed to tell you.'

'Probably... but the fact remains – I never thought she'd do that to you. She loved you.'

'She no doubt thought it was all too bloody obvious to all those looking in to bother explaining.'

'Do you ever give up with the self-pity?'

'No. Especially after I find out my wife's best friend has been cosying up with the enemy!'

'Enemy? Grow up, Frank. She's as hurt as you are.'

He sighed and rubbed his temples. 'What does speaking to her even solve?' He gritted his teeth. 'Going behind my back—'

'Again, grow up. I'm a big girl. I can do what I want.'

'Well, good on you. And so what answers did you get from Evelyn?'

'Nothing.'

'Lord have mercy!' He rolled his eyes. 'Let's roll back to the start of the call then. Remember when I suggested this is pointless?'

'It's not.'

Frank stood. 'Look... the only thing we've in common is that her husband ruined everyone's sodding life.'

'It takes two, Frank.'

'I... I...' Frank turned the phone away, growled and rubbed his temples. He turned the phone back. 'Don't, Helen.'

'She doesn't think she drove her husband away.'

'I. Don't. Care.'

'One thing I do know about you is that you care about things. Often, too much. She wants to speak to you.'

'Why? So she can blame Mary again?'

'She doesn't blame Mary!'

'Didn't seem that way when I spoke to her at the cemetery. She seemed to suggest to me that Mary was some great seductress.'

'Yes... she told me about that...'

'And that viewpoint doesn't stick in your teeth?'

'No, because it isn't her view, really. She doesn't believe that. She's sad, angry... confused. Like you. I've been helping her. But you're rather confrontational, Frank... and you were lingering around Nigel's gravestone. That's intimidating.'

He took a deep breath and rubbed the back of his head. *Hopefully, she'd never seen him pissing on the bastard's grave.*

'What're you expecting, Helen?'

'For you to act your age. You're sixty-four.'

'Sixty-five. So how do I act sixty-five?'

'She had a stroke two days ago. She almost died.' The words hung in the air, heavy with implication.

Frank sighed.

'Was that an expression of sympathy?'

'Bloody hell.'

'Was it?'

'No, it was just a sigh. Jesus, Helen, what do you want from me?'

'I don't want anything from you... well, that's not true... I want you to be happy. Healthy. I also want Maddie back where she belongs. I want the same things as you. As what

Mary would have wanted. I'm phoning on behalf of someone else.'

'Christ Almighty! And what would me seeing Evelyn solve?'

'I don't know. Something.'

'Great. That's specific.'

'You and Evelyn have more in common than you realise. She almost died. She wants to let go of the anger.'

'Sounds like therapy.'

'Well, there's never been any doubt from me that that's exactly what you need!'

'I love the way this has been totally turned around. You phone me grovelling, concerned, and now I'm the dickhead.'

'No one has ever called you a dickhead.'

Frank rolled his eyes. 'Well, that's not true, is it?'

'No,' Helen said with a snort. 'That's been fairly regular throughout your career.'

He smirked. 'Piss off.'

'Let me ask you something. Your argument at the cemetery, were you in the right?'

Frank's mind flashed back to that confrontation, to the anger and pain that had radiated from both of them. He'd thought about that day more times than he cared to admit, wondering if he could have handled it differently.

'Frank?' Helen's voice broke through his thoughts. 'She wants to see you. And I'm asking you, as a close friend, as Mary's best friend, please see her. Just once. See if there's anything you can take from it.'

Frank rubbed a hand over his face, feeling the weight of years of anger and grief pressing down on him. 'You shouldn't be asking.'

'No. But Mary would want me to.'

'Are you sure about that?'

'Yes, 100 per cent. And if you think about it, you'd know that too.'

Aye, probably, he thought.

'Just think about it, okay? Take a few days.'

He looked at the picture of Greg again. 'My mind is otherwise occupied.'

'She'll be leaving to stay at her daughter's home in a few days.'

Helen read the address out and he found himself writing it down.

After the call, Frank sat in silence, staring at the ceiling. The case files on Greg lay forgotten on his desk as his mind grappled with this new information. Evelyn Wainwright, the widow of the man who'd taken Mary from him, wanted to see him. To make amends.

He thought of Mary, of her kindness, of her capacity for forgiveness.

Helen had been right. Mary would want him to go.

But the thought of Mary in all her beauty, in her splendour, in everything he adored about her, made him feel the pain and ache of his loss all over again.

The thought of Nigel Wainwright simply made his blood boil too much.

He screwed up the address and threw it in the bin. Then he grabbed his coat and headed for the door.

Chapter Twenty-Four

Before going into the Foleys' stately home, Tom kissed Gerry on the lips and told her, 'You don't have to worry.'

Gerry furrowed her brow. 'I'm not worried—'

'Because I'm certain you'll make a wonderful impression.'

'That would be good,' Gerry said. And she meant it. She wanted to make Tom happy, and she was glad of this, because it showed that her feelings towards him were strengthening.

'They'll love you.'

She nodded, but didn't respond. She understood what he meant, but it still sounded rather extreme to her.

He followed it up with, 'And I love you.'

Again, she didn't respond. She knew he desperately wanted to hear it, but right now, she couldn't confirm that. She knew she cared about him, and that was all.

Within the hour, they were sitting at a mahogany table beneath a crystal chandelier. An elaborate floral centrepiece dominated the table. Silver cloches concealed their meals.

Tom's parents, Reginald and Penelope Foley, sat across from them. Penelope's posture was rigid, mirroring Gerry's. That was where the comparisons ended. Penelope wore an expensive ball gown and had styled her hair upwards, whereas Gerry wore one of her late mother's yellow dresses, and her hair was straightened downwards. Reginald was dressed in a dusty brown tweed suit with longish hair. He slumped slightly, looking more like an academic professor than a rich landowner.

Knowing how easily she strayed from social conventions, Gerry had earlier spent an hour in front of the mirror at home, practising her manners, reminding herself to maintain eye contact, control impulsive comments, and not to offer any reflections on Tom's parents' lifestyle. They were from old money. Tom had warned her that their attitudes and behaviours could be rather archaic and far from liberal.

She wasn't ashamed of who she was, but the whole situation seemed important for Tom, and there had to be give and take in a relationship.

She'd not be willing to compromise on Rylan, though. At her feet, the Lab thumped his tail against the Persian rug.

Penelope cleared her throat. 'So, Gerry, dear, Tom tells us you've a prestigious job in the police force.'

Gerry forced herself to make eye contact and smile. 'Not so prestigious. I'm a detective inspector.'

'An important job,' Tom said. His hand settled on her thigh beneath the table. She didn't like physical contact when focused on something else, so she pushed his hand gently away.

'What does that entail day to day?' Penelope asked.

'Assisting with leading small teams on investigating complex crimes.'

'Murder?' Reginald raised his eyebrows.

'Recently, yes,' Gerry said.

'So, more than a mere policewoman?'

'I consider myself to still be a police officer.'

'But one of more importance?' Reginald asked, gently nodding.

'I'd use the word "responsibility" rather than "importance".'

'Same thing.' Reginald winked.

Not really, Gerry thought. She then realised she was doing okay. That could easily have been an impulsive comment.

'And what drew you to such a challenging profession?' Penelope asked.

Gerry dropped her eyes for a moment. She was finding the process of trying to make a good impression tiring. 'I find the logical puzzles inherent in criminal investigations to be intellectually stimulating. My ability to observe minute details and process information efficiently makes me well-suited for the role.' She lifted her eyes in time to see Tom's parents exchanging glances.

'That sounds fulfilling, dear,' Reginald said.

Gerry, remembering some advice Frank had given her about using humour to lighten the mood, thought of something he might say at this point. 'It pays the bills.'

She could tell the laughter around the table was forced, so she tried again. 'And keeps the bailiffs away.'

The laughter remained forced. 'You know, I always thought Thomas would be more compatible with someone in a more traditional line of work. You know, something fundamental in society. I always thought it might be a teacher or even a nurse. A police officer... a detective inspector, no less. Not just important, but a leader too! How fantastic! I'm happy with that.' Penelope held up her glass and then took a sip.

Gerry sensed Tom shifting uncomfortably in his seat.

Gerry failed to see how a career choice made someone more compatible. Their relationship was based on mutual respect and shared interests, not societal expectations of gender roles. She opened her mouth to speak her thoughts, but steadied herself just in time.

'Personally,' Reginald said, 'I always knew.' He drained his wine glass. The red tinge in his cheeks suggested that this wasn't his first. 'Tom has always been a man that likes to be led, rather than do the leading.'

'Nobody is leading anybody in this relationship, Father,' Tom said.

'Ha!' Reginald leaned forward to refill his glass, nodding sideways at Penelope as he did so. 'Tell your mother that!'

Penelope narrowed her eyes.

An awkward silence fell over the table, broken only by the sound of Rylan scratching behind his ear.

Penelope took a quick sip of wine, and the tightness dropped from her face again. 'Are you sure you won't have some wine, Gerry?'

'Thank you, but no, I don't drink,' Gerry said.

'Ah... is that on account of the autism?'

'Mother,' Tom said.

Penelope looked at Tom. 'I'm sorry...' She raised her eyebrows. 'You said that she preferred people to know.'

'I know, but—'

Gerry interrupted him by touching his arm. It was another convention she'd learned from her parents when she'd witnessed one of them trying to calm the other in a confrontational moment. 'It's okay, Tom.' She looked at Penelope and forced herself to smile. 'Autistic people can drink. Autism isn't a physical condition. It is considered neurodevelopmental. I choose not to drink simply because I don't like it. It makes me feel sick in the morning.'

Reginald winked. 'But it can make you feel good in the evening.' He took another mouthful of wine.

'Tom said that you've this dog because of autism? Is that right?' Penelope asked. 'Rylon?'

'Rylan,' Tom corrected.

'Sorry, Rylan.' She emphasised the *'an'*.

Gerry forced a smile. She wanted to keep all of this polite. 'Rylan helps me navigate social situations and manage sensory overload. His presence allows me to function more effectively in environments that might otherwise be challenging.'

'I see,' Penelope said, nodding, while looking rather unconvinced. 'Shall we eat?' She lifted the cloche closest to her. 'Roast duck with a cherry reduction.'

Gerry lifted her own silver dome. She was relieved to see the duck sitting alone on the plate with no sauce on it. She could sense Penelope watching for her reaction.

'Looks delicious,' Gerry said.

'Tom made us aware that you like your food on different plates.' Penelope pointed out two more cloche-covered dishes close to Gerry's. 'Potatoes and asparagus. Cooked separately. Served separately.' She pointed out a gravy boat. 'The sauce.' She spoke slowly and precisely as if Gerry would somehow struggle to understand. She was used to people who didn't understand her condition doing that, but it didn't make it any less irksome. Still, she kept her thoughts inside.

'Thank you very much,' Gerry said, hoping her gratitude didn't sound too rehearsed and forced.

Reginald was already eating. 'Delicious, dear.' He fixed his son in his stare. 'How are the trees, son?'

He was referring to Tom's job as an arborist.

'I've been busy, but it's been a productive couple of months, we—'

'How many trees?' His father interrupted him before thrusting more duck into his mouth.

'Sorry?'

'How many have you cut down, dear?' Penelope asked, smiling at her husband.

Mouth full, Reginald nodded his gratitude for his wife's follow-up question.

Gerry could hear Tom drawing the air slowly into his lungs. 'I forget.'

'You always did like the outdoors,' Penelope said.

'Yes, I did,' Tom said, cutting his duck.

'Well, as long as you're happy.'

'Thank you.'

It seemed no one was really interested in the answer to the original question.

'I mean, his grandfather is turning in his grave right now.' Reginald winked at Gerry again.

Tom sighed.

'Don't be like that, son.' Again, he spoke directly to Gerry. 'We always have a joke about that.'

'Yes,' Tom said. 'We've a lot of in-jokes.'

'A long line of architects, the Foleys, you see,' Reginald said, sitting up straight for maybe the first time. 'Some of the most important buildings you see are down to us. Has Tom told you about that, dear?'

She considered lying on his behalf, but it was a real anxious struggle for her to do that. 'No.'

'We built cities. And the irony?' He winked. 'He cuts

down the trees to make space for them. Ha! In my day, that was what we paid the uneducated to do.'

'Actually,' Gerry said, 'he doesn't just cut down trees. Tom and his team are responsible for the health and well-being of urban forests.'

Reginald snorted.

'He diagnoses diseases, treats infections and performs surgery on trees that are hundreds of years old. If he didn't, our cities wouldn't be liveable. Our air wouldn't be clear.'

She glanced at Tom. He was smiling in her direction.

She then looked up at Reginald, who nodded and went back to his duck. A moment later, he said, 'Of course, I know all that. It's just the environment, you know. Everybody is obsessed with the sodding environment these days. Sometimes, I just struggle with the idea of saving trees, just to help the wildlife. But I guess if he helps humans too, that's a good thing. Architects, though. That's what the Foleys are.' He shook his fork in Gerry's direction.

It was at this point that Rylan farted.

At first, a stunned silence settled over the table, but then Tom laughed beside her. She, herself, didn't find it amusing, but was pleased to see him looking less uncomfortable.

Across the table, Reginald was eating, having not really noticed, while Penelope's eyes were wide.

Tom was really laughing now, rubbing at his face. He was struggling to get himself together.

Gerry's eyes darted between the three of them – she was learning so much about the family dynamics here this evening.

'So, Gerry,' Reginald said, his voice slurring now, 'Tom tells us you two met through an online dating service. I've heard about them. A new world, eh? When I met Thomas's mother, she was milking cows in her father's farmyard.' He laughed. 'It might not sound that romantic, Gerry, but I knew... the way she moved those hands, I had all sorts—'

Penelope coughed. The way he suddenly jumped suggested she'd kicked him beneath the table. 'So, how did the online dating work then?' she asked, clearly desperate to change the subject.

'It utilises an algorithm to measure compatibility,' Gerry said.

Penelope's expression suggested that this was above her head.

'It finds you a good match,' Tom said. 'And, so far, it seems that the assessment is proving accurate.'

'Yes,' Gerry said. 'There are a few areas that need work. A few incompatibilities. But we're working through them.' She looked at Tom, who smiled at her.

Penelope nodded. 'I see.' She scrunched her brow. 'Incompatibilities. What incompatibilities?'

'It's not considered socially acceptable to discuss such matters at the dinner table,' Gerry replied.

'Exactly right, dear,' Reginald said.

'Especially when they're of a sexual nature,' Gerry said, cutting off a chunk of duck. It was only as she was putting it in her mouth did she realise the awkward silence had returned. After she swallowed it, she took a mouthful of water, worrying that she'd said something wrong.

'Good heavens,' Penelope said, scrunching her face up in disgust.

Gerry caught the odour. 'I do apologise. Rylan has inflammation in his stomach due to his diet. I thought he was over it. He must be getting the last of the trapped wind out and—'

Tom burst into laughter again.

'I wish you'd grow up, Tom,' Penelope said. 'Shouldn't Rylon wait outside?'

'*Rylan*,' Tom said between laughs.

'Yes... well... shouldn't he?' Penelope pressed.

'I'm afraid that's not possible,' Gerry replied. 'Like I said before, Rylan is my therapy dog and provides essential emotional support.'

This was her non-negotiable.

Tom was laughing hard next to her. Sometimes, she wished she could enjoy the humour in situations like he did. He seemed to have a lot of fun.

'Perhaps we could discuss something else?' Tom suggested weakly once he'd regained his composure.

Reginald launched into a detailed explanation of the Foley family tree and every one of their architectural achievements.

The next odour was the most pungent. Even Reginald noticed this time. 'Good heavens, that dog stinks, doesn't it?'

Tom, determined to regain control of himself, blurted out, 'So, Father, how's the golf game coming along?'

Reginald, looking slightly green, latched onto the new topic with obvious relief. 'Ah, yes, well, I've been working on my swing. Broke 80 last week, you know.'

'That's impressive,' Gerry commented. 'Statistically speaking, only about 2 per cent of golfers ever break 80.'

Reginald's eyes widened. 'Yes, that's true...'

'You must have dedicated a significant amount of time and effort to achieve that level of proficiency.'

Reginald puffed up at the praise. 'I suppose I have. It has taken dedication.'

'Don't be modest, dear,' Penelope said. 'It also takes a certain edge!'

'Yes,' he said, looking very pleased with himself. 'Dedication, excellence, I've always tried to instil these things in Thomas.'

'That's good,' Gerry said.

'Tried,' Reginald emphasised. 'Not sure I got it across. He doesn't always listen to me...'

Gerry sensed Tom moving into a slump beside her.

'I think he listened, and I think you got it across,' Gerry said. 'You know your son possesses a high level of dedication and skill in his chosen field. He's been recognised for his innovative techniques in tree preservation.'

She slipped her hand under the table and placed it on his thigh. He smiled and straightened up again. She tried to think of a humorous expression Frank would opt for. 'I bagged a winner.'

Tom's smile broadened.

'In fact.' Gerry nodded. 'While we may not conform to traditional relationship models, our partnership is built on a solid foundation of mutual respect and understanding.'

Tom squeezed Gerry's hand on her leg. She felt her heart rate increase slightly, and felt more excited for sexual intercourse than she had done at any other point in their relationship.

Later, after dessert, and as the evening drew to a close, Tom's parents walked them to the door, their expressions a mixture of relief and lingering bewilderment.

'It was... interesting to meet you, Gerry,' Penelope said, her smile slightly strained. 'And you too, er... Rylon... beg your pardon... Rylan...'

Rylan wagged his tail in response, causing Reginald to take a step back, eyeing the dog warily.

As they walked to the car, Tom let out a long breath. 'Well, that was... something.'

Gerry nodded. 'Indeed. I found the evening to be quite

informative. Your parents' reactions to various topics and situations have provided me with new insights into social expectations and familial relationships.'

'I'm glad you found it educational. I was worried it might have been too... intense for you.'

As they got into the car, Tom reached over and squeezed Gerry's hand. 'Thank you for defending me.'

Gerry smiled. 'I found that rewarding. Also...' She smiled. 'I found it a turn on.'

Chapter Twenty-Five

THE GOTH COMMUNITY's go-to pub, the Elsinore, pulsed with energy.

Raven lost herself in the laughter, the clinking glasses and the pulsing industrial music. Damien held court at his usual corner table, spinning comical anecdotes. 'So, I told him, "Darling, if you're going to dress like a vampire, at least have the courtesy to bite like one!"'

While Damien's companions laughed, Raven raised her glass of absinthe. The green spirit shimmered.

To the green fairy, she toasted. *Your magical powers know no end.*

After knocking it back, she noticed Derek by the bar, his usual long black coat and silver-tipped cane marking him out as one of the more elegant goths in attendance. His eyes held Raven's.

She stood and stumbled over to him, the world growing more and more fuzzy. She really hoped she hadn't peaked too soon.

'Feeling better?' Derek asked, referencing her earlier state.

She leaned in, inhaling his aftershave. 'Better by the second.'

He grinned, no doubt aware of her advances. 'Would it be anything to do with the absinthe?'

'No... but it's everything to do with the company.' She chanced moving another inch closer.

'Who? Damien?' Derek grinned.

'No... He's gay...'

'I see.'

'And not my type, anyway.'

'That's good, because if he's gay, I guess you wouldn't be his.'

'Yes... I mean, no...' She laughed. 'Piss off... you know what I mean. Plus, he's more like a brother to me.'

'Yes, I've seen the bickering.'

She leaned even closer, fixing her eyes fully on his.

'The thing is,' Derek said, starting to look rather surprised. 'Well...' He put an arm around her waist. 'Last night, I thought this was a closed avenue.'

She pressed her finger to his lips. 'I've never been called a closed avenue before.'

'Well, I didn't quite mean it like that.' Her finger muffled his voice.

'Don't worry. Your words. They're sexy.' She pulled her finger away and regarded the black lipstick that was now smeared on it.

She heard him taking a deep breath. 'You seem so different tonight,' he said.

She shrugged and pulled back. 'Just more relaxed. The hardest part of the festival is over.'

'Yes... what was wrong earlier, exactly?'

'It was just the stress of the organisation.'

'Well, it's a shame you didn't hang about for the complete show... It was great. Raven...'

She grinned and leaned back in. 'Yes.'

He sighed. 'I'm afraid I'm off first thing tomorrow.'

'You're missing the last day?'

'Unfortunately, yes. My daughter, Lace, she's at uni.'

'Yes, you said.'

'Well, she's only been gone a couple of months, and she's feeling homesick. Sal is away.'

'Sal, the *ex*-wife?' she asked, purposefully emphasising the 'ex'.

He grinned. 'Yes, the *ex*-wife. I don't lie about things like that! Anyway, I told Lace I'd spend the day with her.'

She pulled back. 'Sounds the right thing to do.'

'But I could come back? Sometime soon, perhaps? Like next weekend?'

She pressed her finger to his lips again. 'Hold that thought... I'm going to smoke. In the meantime, didn't you say you were going to the bar?'

'No,' Derek said. 'Because I'm already standing at it.'

'How fortunate,' she said and winked.

Outside, the cool night air hit Raven like a slap to the face. She leaned against the pub's brick wall, fumbling with her lighter. After several attempts, she lit her cigarette, taking a long drag and exhaling a plume of smoke into the night sky.

As the nicotine hit her system, Raven's gaze drifted across the street. Through the haze of smoke and alcohol, a figure materialised beneath a distant lamp, seemingly staring right at her.

Curious, Raven left the pub garden and went onto the pavement so she could see the person better.

It was a woman. Her long beige trench coat was more

suited to a professional setting than a night out in Whitby, especially during the goth festival. There was something vaguely familiar about her, but Raven's alcohol-addled mind couldn't quite place her. She'd probably need to be closer.

Raven held up a hand to show that she'd noticed her. 'Do I know you?'

The woman didn't respond.

Fine... whatever... Raven finished her cigarette, crushed it underfoot and turned.

'Mrs Blackstone?' the woman called.

Raven turned back as the woman crossed the road.

She finally recognised her as she drew closer.

Samantha Wells. Journalist for the Whitby Gazette.

Raven had spoken to her a few times concerning publicity for the goth festival; however, they'd only met once in person several years back.

'I'm glad I caught you,' Samantha said. 'We met before, Raven.'

'I remember,' Raven said. 'How are you, Samantha?'

'Can't complain. Apart from the torrential rain earlier. I saw that you still got the concert up and running, though?'

'Never in doubt.' Raven smiled. She reached into her pocket for another cigarette. She offered one.

'No, thank you.'

'Are you coming in for a drink?'

'Not sure I'm dressed right.'

'Nobody will care. You had nothing black at home?'

Samantha laughed. 'I save that sort of costume for my husband.'

Raven laughed. 'Lucky boy.'

'About the only way I can get a rise out of him these days,' Samantha said.

Raven laughed again. It was a strange conversation, but mixed with absinthe, a welcome and engaging one.

'What're you doing out at this time, then?' Raven asked.

'Well, I was actually looking for you.'

Raven's intoxicated mind failed to register the oddity of this statement. Instead, she took another long puff of her cigarette. 'You knew I was coming out' – she checked her watch – 'at ten-thirty for a cigarette?'

Samantha shook her head. 'No. But I knew you were at this pub. And I was going to come in to see you. Thank you for stopping me from sticking out like a sore thumb.'

'You're welcome. Is this about the festival? Last day tomorrow, but coverage in the *Gazette* would be great—'

'It's not about the festival.'

'Ah, okay...' Now, this impromptu meeting had her rattled. 'What's it about then?'

Samantha reached into her bag and pulled out a business card. She handed it over. Raven wobbled on her feet, squinting as she tried to read it. She was pissed.

The top of the card displayed 'Shadows of the Past: Unmasking True Crime' in bold lettering.

Raven's blood ran cold.

'I'm branching out,' Samantha said. 'Into podcasting – true crime, specifically. Raven... sorry... but I think your story would make for a fascinating first episode.'

Raven blinked, wondering if she'd misheard. She opened her mouth to speak, but the words caught in her throat.

'And you could tell it. Your transformation from small-town girl to public enemy number one to gothic queen of Whitby.'

Her stomach lurched. 'You've made a mistake.'

'No mistake.' A ghost of a smile appeared on Samantha's face.

Raven edged backwards. She held the card back out. 'Take it.'

'Keep it. No harm done.'

'No. You really have made a mistake.'

'I *really* haven't.'

Samantha pulled out her mobile phone and scrolled through to a photo. The photo showed a fifteen-year-old girl in a plain floral dress, hair pulled back in a simple ponytail – not a hint of the gothic style that now defined her. 'Small-town girl,' Samantha said, her eyes raking over Raven's current appearance, 'to goth queen.'

'Where did you get that?'

'I'm in journalism, I know people, it's—'

'Cut the shit. What do you know?'

'Not enough.' Samantha nodded eagerly, oblivious to Raven's growing distress. 'I don't know your side and ultimately, that's so important...'

'My side?'

'Yes.'

'You shouldn't be here... this isn't fucking allowed. Don't you get that?'

Samantha smiled. 'Let me be your voice.'

Raven screwed the card up and threw it at Samantha. 'Piss off.'

'The podcast is going out, regardless. Better for you that your voice is on it.'

'Makes no difference... You'll destroy me.'

'That's not my intention.'

'Are you insane? What do you think will happen to me?'

'Nothing should hold back the truth... it's nothing personal.'

Raven felt a burning in her fingers. The cigarette had burned down. She winced and chucked it.

Then she felt adrenaline surge through her veins, her vision narrowing to a tunnel focused solely on Samantha. She thrust her hands out, a primal scream building in her throat.

Samantha gasped and stumbled backwards, slamming into the bin close behind her.

'Piss off!' Raven shouted, her fists clenched. 'Piss off before I—'

'Raven?' She felt arms around her, pulling her away. 'Raven, stop it!'

Derek.

She swung in his arms and looked at his serious face and then glanced back. Samantha was already leaving with her hand raised. 'Think about it, Raven,' she said over her shoulder.

'Who's that?' Derek asked.

Raven pressed herself against him, chest heaving with ragged breaths.

The world spun around her, a nauseating blend of alcohol, adrenaline and raw terror. 'Take me home,' she hissed into Derek's ear, her fingers digging into his arms. 'Please, just... take me home.'

Chapter Twenty-Six

THE SOFT TICKING of the grandfather clock filled the hallway as Ray stood motionless, eyes closed, savouring a moment's peace. He'd just hung his coat on the rack, the weight of earlier events still heavy on his shoulders.

'Are you okay?' Kath's voice cut through the momentary respite.

He opened his eyes and watched Kath approach him. When she was close enough, she lifted his chin to examine his cheek. 'It looks sore.'

'I'm fine, dear,' he said, touching her hand. 'It could have been much worse.'

He recalled her words: *I believed you. I looked into your eyes, and I believed you.*

'It's late,' she said.

'It's Sunday service tomorrow. You know how I like to be prepared.'

'I think you should take a day off. It was a shocking experience and...'

'I'll be fine.' He kissed her forehead.

He slipped past her and into the lounge, settling into an armchair. He closed his eyes again and kept them that way.

'Did you tell the police what happened with that woman?' Kath asked from the door.

He didn't open his eyes. 'I'll handle it, Kath.'

Kath's voice sharpened with disbelief. 'Ray, you can't be serious? She attacked you in front of the entire congregation. You must tell the police.'

He opened his eyes, looked at her and sighed. 'The poor woman is troubled, Kath, she needs help, not punishment.'

'But—'

'You know who I am... you know my values.'

Kath edged into the room. 'This isn't just about your values, Ray. This is about safety. What if she comes back? What if she comes here? Puts me in danger, too? Actually, what if she's in danger herself?'

Ray ran a hand through his thinning hair. 'She must be carrying a heavy burden.'

'Ray, she called you a liar, and by name. She scratched your face! How can you be so calm about this?'

Ray's mind flashed back to Megan's face, contorted with anger and pain. It was a look he'd seen too many times before – a soul grappling with an oppressive weight.

I believed you. I looked into your eyes, and I believed you.

And you were right to, Megan. I was genuine. I'm still genuine.

'I'll find her, and I'll help her, Kath. As I've helped others before her. Phoning the police isn't the answer.'

Kath paced the room now. 'How do you intend to find her?'

'Kath, please,' he said, closing his eyes again, leaning back in his chair, and rubbing his temples. 'Trust me.'

Even with his own eyes closed, Ray felt her gaze boring into him. After thirty years of marriage, Kath could read him like one of his well-worn Bibles. She'd know there was more to this.

But some secrets were just too dark, too dangerous to share – even with the woman he loved most in this world.

Discussing lost souls was no straightforward thing.

Finally, she said, 'I hope you know what you're doing, Ray. I really do.'

He opened his eyes as she turned and left the room. He listened to her footsteps echoing in the hallway as she climbed the stairs.

For a while his mind remained locked on Megan, but eventually it turned, as it did most days, to Graham.

With a heavy sigh, Ray pushed himself out of the chair and made his way to his study and his bookshelves. Then, among the theological texts and well-thumbed novels, he drew out one of his photo albums, leather bound, its edges worn smooth.

He locked the office door, settled into his office chair, and opened the album. The first photograph was all he took. He felt his heart clench and took a deep breath.

Two boys smiled up at him from the faded image. The older one, gangly and bespectacled, had his arm slung around the shoulders of a smaller boy with a mischievous grin. Ray traced the face of the older boy with a trembling finger.

Graham. His older brother by three years. His hero.

But he'd been so different from everyone else. Unable to sit still, impulsive and loud. In some people's minds, out of control.

The world had failed to understand Graham and the

weight on his soul. He'd been left vulnerable, and the demons had climbed into his mind.

He'd stopped going to school. He'd swerved the school gates. And if their parents did somehow get him inside, he'd break out and scale the fence.

The therapists tried to identify his vulnerabilities, his learning needs, but the school wouldn't accept them. They were resistant. They were attached to a church and wanted rid of him. He was an inconvenience.

Too disruptive, the reverend had claimed. An animal that couldn't be caged.

The demons would torture his mind with nightmares. Ray would wake to the sound of his brother's screams, before going to him in the corner of their shared bedroom. There Graham would shake, and Ray would hold him.

Towards the end, he'd run away, disappear for days, refusing to tell anyone where he'd been.

Then, one day, he just didn't come back.

Ray traced Graham's face again.

It was Ray that had found him.

Ray remembered the week-long frantic search, the police cars with their flashing lights, the neighbours forming search parties to comb the woods behind their house. He remembered his mother's tear-stained face, his father's grim determination.

Deep down, Ray had known where he was, but had been too scared to go. What if someone followed him? What if they found his brother's secret hiding place?

But, after one week, it was clear to Ray that something wasn't quite right.

So, he went to the old, disused railway line that cut through the forest. And to that ledge, through the broken fence, which sat eight metres or so above the old line.

He'd hoped to see his brother sitting there, as he so often did, sometimes for over a day, desperate not to return to a society that didn't want him.

But he wasn't sitting on that ledge, so Ray sat there instead.

And, on that seventh day, while the village scoured the woods a second time, Ray sat for hours, looking down at the body of his brother.

Eight metres below.

Grey. Staring up into space. Dappled sunlight moving over his face.

Ray had known already what the world would say. Suicide. A tragic result of mental illness.

Society always needed the tidy option.

But on that ledge, looking down, Ray was under no illusions.

It had been caused by that demon inside his brother.

He turned on his computer and searched his files until he found the one labelled 'MP2004'.

He took a deep breath.

Fifteen-year-old Megan Powers stared at the camera from the chair she was sitting in.

I believed you. I looked into your eyes, and I believed you.

He exhaled and said, 'Because I was telling you the truth.'

Then, he listened to his younger self address Megan in the recording.

'Are you ready?'

Chapter Twenty-Seven

GEORGI VASILEV PACED THE SHOP, as he always did, running his hands over flowers, sniffing his fingers afterwards.

He nodded and implied his satisfaction that Lilly was keeping the quality high.

Really, Georgi didn't know the first thing about flowers.

He was knowledgeable and skilful in only one area.

Intimidation.

His usual ritual complete, Georgi halted, his dark eyes piercing Lilly – a stark contrast to his ice-white beard and hair.

The suffocating silence stretched.

She fought the urge to fidget.

He eventually spoke, his voice low and menacing. 'Business good, моето момиче?' The words 'my girl' made her skin crawl. As if he owned her. He genuinely believed that he did.

'The same as usual,' she said.

He nodded. 'I've had someone watching you...'

Her breath caught in her throat.

'And they told me you've been busy.'

Her mind raced, trying to recall what else this person watching her could have seen. Surely, Georgi didn't know. *He couldn't.*

'So, I'm assuming my cheque will be larger this month.'

'It will be accurate... as always...' Her voice trembled slightly, betraying her fear.

'Oh, I don't doubt it.' He cracked his knuckles as he approached her. 'However, I'm not talking about the cut of the fucking flowers.'

Her blood was ice cold. *He did know.*

He drew his hand back, and she closed her eyes, bracing herself. She'd been here before, tasting blood from a broken nose, seeing stars from a backhand. When nothing happened, she drew a deep breath and opened her eyes.

'Relax.' The bastard smiled. 'Okay?'

She gave a swift nod, trying to keep her expression steely, but she felt the tears building.

He chewed his bottom lip for a moment, contemplating something. Then, he said, 'You always were such a good girl...' He reached out and pressed a hand flat and hard against her chest, crushing her breasts against her. 'Such a big heart.' Lilly's skin crawled. She attempted to ease away to the side, along the counter, but found herself trapped.

He was a large man who dedicated time to his strength.

'I can feel it.' He looked upwards and bobbed his head up and down. 'Bang bang. Bang bang. I can hear it, too.'

Bile rose in Lilly's throat. She pulled at his wrist with both hands. 'Please get off me.'

He pulled his hand away and took a step back. He remained within striking distance, though. 'Okay... then. So, what've you got downstairs, Lilly?'

Panic flooded through her. *Shit. He really knew.*

The children were in danger.

'Lilly, I'm waiting,' Georgi said.

She shook her head. 'Stock... Nothing... I...' The way the words fell from her mouth offered no sincerity.

He lifted the palm of his hand again. 'Bang bang... bang bang.' His grin morphed into a predatory sneer as he moved closer. 'Bang bang... bang bang...' He reached out to touch her. 'Bang—'

'Okay... there're some children down there, but please, Georgi. Please. It's...'

He raised an eyebrow. 'It's...?'

'It's not what you think!' The words burst from her in desperation. It was, of course, what he was thinking. The game was up.

Her only goal now had to be to protect the children.

Whether that be through money, or... a chill ran through her body... or doing something about him. About Georgi.

'Ah.' He nodded. 'Okay then. Show me...'

At this stage, resistance seemed futile. Cornered and trapped, she had to manage this somehow. But how? Georgi was a seasoned criminal, hardened by years on the streets. Against him, she felt weak. Pathetic.

She opened the cellar door and led him onto the stairs. How had she been so careless? How had she not noticed she was being watched?

Each step felt like a death knell.

At the bottom, she fumbled with the key, her hands shaking violently.

'Do you need help?'

She took a deep breath. 'I'm fine.' With effort, she steadied her hand enough to unlock the door.

Before opening it, she turned to face him. 'Don't hurt

them.' Her voice was steel, despite the fear churning in her gut. 'They're innocent.'

He grinned. 'Aren't they all?'

'If you must... touch me... I'll give you what you want.'

He ran his fingers down her back. 'Did I ever touch you back then?'

She quivered.

'No.'

'Precisely. Now, open the door.'

She opened the door.

The three children smiled when they saw Lilly, but when they noticed Georgi, they quickly huddled together.

'Здравейте, деца.' Georgi greeted them in Bulgarian.

He looked around the room. At the heater, the rugs on the floor, the television... 'I'm impressed, Lilly.' He turned, grinning up at her. 'It seems you learned well... from me.'

Lilly's jaw clenched. She didn't say what she was thinking. *I learned what not to do. This is different, Georgi, so very different.*

'Ah... I see in your eyes that you disagree?'

'All I know is that I'm helping them.'

'Helping them?' Georgi fixed his gaze on Ivana. 'How so?'

'I'm taking them from danger to safety.'

Georgi nodded. 'How's that any different from what I did?'

She bit her lip. *Sod you, Georgi.*

He turned and smiled at her again. He touched his chest. 'Имаш голямо сърце.' *You've a big heart.* 'But you think what I did was so wrong, Lilly? They've earned money, put food on the table... I mean, look at you now.'

You didn't give me any of this. I ran from you, you prick. Dimitar gave me this.

'How do you think their lives would have been if we'd left them in Bulgaria?'

Lilly's nails dug into her palms. *Better than being sold into slavery, you spineless worm.* She wanted to scream, but she couldn't risk it, not with the children so vulnerable.

'So, who're you working with?' He gestured at the children.

Lilly hesitated. Her mouth was dry.

She was about to say *no one,* but he spoke first. 'Nikolai?'

She flinched. There was no point in lying now.

'Nikolai! He's out of retirement, then? Strange, eh?' He tutted, and winked at Ivana, who drew the young boys tight to her. 'I can't seem to remember Nikolai doing much out of the goodness of his heart back then.'

He was forced, intimidated and controlled by the likes of you. 'He got out when he could. He wants to make amends.' These words tumbled out before she could stop them.

Georgi knelt and reached out towards Ivana's face.

Lilly stiffened. 'Don't.'

Georgi's hand moved closer.

Ivana recoiled. 'Махни се от мен.'

'Feisty one, eh?'

'I told you not to touch them,' Lilly said.

Georgi shrugged.

'Feisty like you, Lilly.' His hand moved towards the girl again.

Lilly couldn't allow it. She lurched and hit him on the back. He barely moved. 'Get away from her. You're making her uncomfortable.'

Georgi stood, laughing, palms out in mock surrender. 'Apologies. I wouldn't want to infringe on her comfort. I know things are different now. With worker's rights and everything.'

'She'll never be a worker. Not like that.' Lilly narrowed her eyes. She took some deep breaths. She needed to regain control. Not antagonise him.

'So, you've found them homes?'

Lilly nodded.

Georgi's stare bored into her. 'How much?'

'How much what?'

'Money?'

'Nothing.'

He threw his head back and laughed, the sound echoing off the cellar walls. After he dropped his head back, he said, 'No, really?'

'It's true. Nothing.'

He looked down at his feet, shaking his head. She saw the anger in his eyes when he looked back up. 'You know, it's that ridiculous I believe you. But you need to put a stop to that voluntary work.'

'I can't.'

'Anyone wishing to take in these children would be rich enough and happy to pay.'

'That's not what this is about.'

Georgi advanced on her. 'But I'm here to tell you the opposite. Remember, you work for me. You've always worked for me.'

Lilly bit her lip.

He looked back at the children and then at her. 'Do you want me to take over? I could find the highest bidder for these children.'

Lilly bit harder, tasting blood.

'Is that how we should do it?'

She shook her head. 'No. I'd rather go to the police.'

'Ha! You would, would you? You do realise that'll put both of us away for a very long time?'

'I'm not sure I care.'

'And then what do you think will happen to these three children? The dregs of their family will want them back. Only for them to sell them on again to the highest bidder. You might as well take the money.'

She wanted to shake her head, scream in his face, but she knew the answer didn't lie here, in this moment. The answer would have to come when she was away from him.

'So the question is, it's going to be you, or it's going to be me. Of course, I'm happy to leave it to you for a suitable compensation… How does that sound? Reasonable?'

She gritted her teeth. She was too angry, and too terrified, to speak.

He smiled, wagging a finger at her. 'Big heart. Too big. I can see you've a lot to think about. You've got until midday tomorrow before I take matters into my own hands. I'll see myself out.' He reached out and stroked her face, and she closed her eyes. When he stood away, she opened her eyes and watched him wave at the children and bid them farewell in Bulgarian.

'Remember, моето момиче, noon tomorrow.'

Lilly sighed, her shoulders sagging under the weight of her predicament. Finding Dimitar had been the best moment of her life. The day Georgi had found her again had been the worst.

She looked at the children, who quivered and huddled together. *I'm sorry,* she thought, her heart aching. *This is all my fault.*

Chapter Twenty-Eight

DEREK'S ARMS encircled Raven's waist, steadying her as she stumbled towards the foot of her staircase.

'I'm sorry,' she said, looking up the stairs. 'I was sold a lie. I was told the green fairy made you fly. You'll have to carry me up.'

'I'd have a go if I wasn't half-pissed myself.'

Raven turned in Derek's embrace, her eyes searching his face. She saw the desire there, but she also detected his concern. She stroked his cheek. 'Thanks.'

He creased his brow. 'For what?'

'For stopping me from doing something I would've regretted.'

'To that woman?'

She nodded.

'How about telling me who she was?'

The mere thought of talking about Samantha Wells made Raven's head spin even harder. This was why Derek was here. To take her mind away from Samantha. From the fear, if only temporarily.

'It's not important,' she lied, pressing her lips against Derek's.

The kiss quickly intensified.

But then he broke off. 'You're drunk.'

'So are you... Let's both take advantage.'

Their kisses grew more passionate as they made their way to the bedroom, shedding clothes along the way. Raven desperately tried to keep a complete focus on the experience now, but her mind was a cauldron of contrasting emotions: fear, desire, shame, and a desperate need for connection.

Until Derek figured out how to caress her skin, and an indescribable sensation settled on her, quickly anchoring her to the moment.

In the soft, ethereal glow of a Himalayan salt lamp, shadows danced on the walls of Raven's bedroom. Ornate mirrors reflected their entwined forms as they fell onto the bed, a tangle of limbs and breathless anticipation. Raven closed her eyes, losing herself in the rhythm of their love-making, in the tenderness of Derek's touch.

She clung to him, digging her nails into his back, desperate to stay out of the dark waters of her past. With each movement, each kiss, she pushed away the image of Samantha Wells, and her fear of drowning subsided.

As they reached their climax together, Raven felt a moment of perfect clarity. It was little more than a fleeting heartbeat away from the storm.

But it was powerful. Singular.

Still, as her breathing slowed, her haunting emotions returned. She turned on her side away from Derek, afraid that if he looked into her eyes, he'd see the truth lurking there, behind her tears.

'Raven.' Derek's voice was soft, tentative. 'Who was that woman?'

Raven closed her eyes. 'I told you, it's not important,' she whispered. *And unless I can stop her,* she thought, *you'll know soon enough, anyway.*

Derek persisted. 'I've never seen that look on your face before. You were terrified. I'm not just a pretty face... I'm actually a good listener, too.'

A laugh escaped Raven's lips. She turned to face him and kissed him on the nose. 'Thank you,' she said. 'But I don't want to talk about it.'

He smiled at the affection, but then must have noticed her tears, because his face fell again. Derek reached out, cupping her cheek in his hand. 'Raven, whatever happened in your past, I want you—'

'No,' she cut him off. 'Please. I'm asking you to stop... just... hold me, Derek. That's all I want right now. It's what I need.'

Derek nodded, pulling her close. Raven buried her face in his chest, inhaling his scent, trying to ground herself in the present as she had done during sex, and in the immediate aftermath.

Raven allowed the world to fade, and she slept...

The sparse furnishings of the dining room bathed in weak daylight. A yellowed curtain billowing by a half-open window. Some of the curtain's rings had come free of the runner and pattered against the glass. The oak table beside her was bare, its surface marred by years of use.

Raven turned to face the corner of the room, her heart pounding. As she watched, the daylight faded. The room darkened. She wept and shivered, desperate to leave.

Behind her, she heard his voice calling her. *Tell me a story.*

It grew darker.

Of course. About pirates?

She started to turn.

No. Tell me a story about monsters.

A solitary candle cast the table in an ethereal glow. A small figure slumped over.

She couldn't stop herself going to him. This dream had never been hers to control. In the same way that the reality had never been hers to control either.

His left cheek was pressed against the oak. He looked like he was still smiling that same gap-toothed smile; still staring with those same wide eyes. There was a spoon in his hand, and an overturned bowl.

But he was so cold, and still.

The only movement was from the steady drip of the soup running off the table.

Drip. Drip.

Just a child.

A voice behind her: *Let me touch your wings, little bird.* Cold hands gripped her wrists, their touch sending icy tendrils of fear through her body. *Fly, little bird, fly.*

Screaming, she stared up into Derek's eyes.

He was gripping her wrists, and she was down on the floor.

'Raven. You're safe. You're safe!'

She took deep breaths.

'It was just a dream,' he said.

She threw her head from side to side. She tried to pull her wrists free. *Let me touch your wings, little—*

'I'm not a little bird,' she screamed up in Derek's face.

I'm a raven.

Derek slipped down beside her, pulling her tight against him. 'I know... I know...'

Fly, little bird—

'I'll fly when I bloody well want to.'

'Yes, of course,' Derek soothed. 'Whenever you want.'

Then she cried, muttering the same words over and over, 'When I want to. When I want to.'

Finally, when she was calmer, and her mind was clearer, she looked up at him. 'I don't want to ever forget.'

He looked confused. 'Forget what, Raven?'

She took a shaky breath. 'Everything.' She paused, her voice dropping to a whisper. 'Hold me.'

'Yes,' Derek said.

It gave her a tiny moment of hope, but Raven knew, deep down, that he couldn't be there for her.

No one could be.

And when she woke in the morning, he was gone.

And she was again, another lonely soul.

Chapter Twenty-Nine

LILLY STARED down into the empty cash register, unsurprised by Georgi's raid on his way out of the shop. She sighed and closed it, her mind drifting back to when she was sixteen.

It'd been just over four years since she'd run from Georgi into the arms of Dimitar Petrova. At that point, her kind benefactor had broken the law to organise her residency in order to offer her the new life she needed. It'd been a time of promise.

If only Natasha hadn't shown up that day...

Lilly knew she was being watched from across the street as she arranged the Easter display at the front of Seabreeze. As always, she kept her eyes forward. Her background, who she was and where she came from, made her vulnerable.

'If anyone ever comes looking for you,' Dimitar told her time and time again. 'You must turn away and come and speak to me.'

'Lilly?'

The voice was familiar, catapulting her mind back to

dark compartments on boats and claustrophobic rooms in grimy English buildings.

Her instinct was to deny she was Lilly and then flee inside, but when she looked at the young woman alongside her, a name flew to her lips. 'Natasha?'

Natasha had been the eldest of the trafficked children in 1989.

At first, they embraced, excited conversation ensuing, but after the emotion of reconciliation died down, bitterness and resentment emerged. Natasha became curious why Lilly had never spoken to anyone, sought help for the rest of them. Natasha then wept, and Lilly listened to some of Natasha's stories.

It was devastating. Lilly, also tearful now, apologised over and over. She emphasised that she'd only been twelve. That she'd been confused and terrified, and that an older, kind man had looked after her and told her to stay quiet.

She begged Natasha for forgiveness, but deep down, Lilly knew this would be impossible. How could Natasha not be envious of what Lilly had found for herself? And how could she not have been bitter about being left to suffer?

A few times, Natasha looked at the shop, shaking her head, and stroked the flowers, looking forlorn.

Then, she showed Lilly her wedding ring. In order to escape slavery, Natasha, at seventeen, had married one of her exploiters.

It was in this moment that Lilly realised she was now in a perilous situation. Even though Natasha assured her that her secret was safe, she knew deep down that it wasn't, really. It was obvious now that her world was about to come crashing down.

Before the week was out, Georgi was standing in Dimitar's shop. The sneaky pig had waited until Dimitar was running an errand. When inside, the large man locked the front door and flipped the sign to 'Closed'.

He turned and said, 'моето момиче.' My girl.

Initially, he showed restraint while expressing his deep sadness at losing her, emphasising that he'd always held such high hopes for her. He acted surprised at how near she'd been. He'd expected her to have run to another part of the country, not take refuge in a local shop. It was his conclusion that they were always meant to be reunited.

'беше писано в звездите.'

Written in the stars.

When Dimitar returned, he tried to protect her. He demanded Georgi leave. But the old man was no match for the ruthless trafficker. Going to the police was a no-go, because Dimitar had also broken the law, and Lilly was, of course, here illegally. In the end, Georgi took advantage. Regular payments to keep Lilly's past a secret, to prevent her deportation back to Bulgaria where she had no one and nothing.

...Lilly looked at a picture of Dimitar on her phone, captured a month before his death. There wasn't a day that she didn't miss him. Dimitar had adored Lilly. He'd paid a percentage of the shop's takings to Georgi until the day he died, and Lilly had been paying ever since.

To think that Georgi would never cause another problem again had been foolish on Lilly's part. Yes, he only visited once a month to collect money, and they were several weeks from his next arranged visit, but she really should have known better. She should have suspected he might send people to check up on her every now and again. She'd put those poor children in danger—

There was a knock on the glass. Her heart skipped a beat, but she sighed in relief when she saw Nikolai peering through the glass door. She'd called him and he'd arrived within minutes.

Nikolai was a tall, lean man in his early fifties, with salt-and-pepper hair. He'd once been part of the same world as Georgi and had been one of the group that had brought Lilly into the country. He'd only been sixteen years old and, in her opinion, had also been a victim of exploitation. She'd forgiven him. Now, he too committed himself to trying to do what was right.

Once Nikolai was inside the shop, and the door locked again, she collapsed into his arms. 'He knows... the bastard knows...'

Over tea, Nikolai kept reassuring her.

'I don't think Georgi will be stupid enough to get involved,' Nikolai said. 'People from his era are dinosaurs.' He tapped his chest. 'Myself included.'

She smiled. His steady demeanour had always been a stark contrast to the chaos Georgi brought into her life.

'Who can he call on for support? No one will be interested. Think of the people we have on our side, back home. Powerful people. Good people, who want to do right by these children. Georgi would be a fool to ruffle feathers.'

'But he is a fool,' Lilly said. 'What if he destroys me out of spite?'

'That would be the icing on the cake of his idiocy! If he destroys you, he destroys part of his income. For all we know, you could be his sole source these days. His pension!'

She sighed. 'He takes so much.' She looked at Nikolai. 'But it's worth it if he stays away.' She gestured to the cellar with a nod of her head. 'This matters to me.'

He reached out and took her arm. 'I've made a phone call. I've tried to speed up the process. It could be tonight...

at the very latest, tomorrow night. We will deal with Georgi when they're safe.'

'He wants to know by noon tomorrow.'

Nikolai nodded. 'Then text him at noon. Tell him that this doesn't concern him, and he's better leaving it alone if he wants to continue to be paid.'

'And you think it will work?'

He sighed. 'I think so. Look, call his bluff. He gets something or nothing. I'm betting he'll back down.'

'He's greedy.'

'He's a thug, and one that's way past it. He'll back down.'

She grinned. 'Sometimes, I wonder if it's best to just... you know... kill him?'

Nikolai's expression darkened.

'I was joking,' she said.

'I know, but don't even discuss it in humour.'

'Okay.'

He then leaned in and kissed her, and she suddenly felt lighter than she'd felt in days.

Afterwards, Nikolai looked at Lilly and stroked her fringe from her eyes. 'You know about that body they found down by the pier?'

'Yeah, I heard.'

He nodded. 'They're saying it was a child... from the late nineties.'

'Sorry?'

'A child.'

'No, when?'

'Late nineties.'

She did some calculations in her head, and her stomach dropped. She'd been on a rollercoaster of anxiety for days, but this drop felt steep.

'Late nineties... you don't think... well...' Lilly broke off, unable to give words to her fears.

She watched the colour drain from his face as he cottoned on. 'Oh... I didn't realise that the police had confirmed a date... Could it be a rumour? Look...' He put his tea down on the counter and clutched her hand. 'I—'

'I still see his face, every day, when I wake up, Nikolai.' She gulped. 'Standing at that door, wide eyed. He was just a child, not much older than me when I was lost... alone with no one.'

Nikolai stroked her face with his other hand. 'Try not to let everything bring it all back.'

'Greg was my friend. If it's him, then it's my fault.'

'It wouldn't be your fault, and it probably won't be him.'

She paused and looked off into space. A smile spread across her face. 'Reading about sea creatures.'

Lilly closed her eyes, memories of Greg flooding her mind, as vivid and clear as if they'd happened yesterday. She'd been a much younger woman, barely into her twenties. He'd come into the shop most mornings, drawn like a bee to their flowers.

She recalled his gentle, sweet tone the first time he'd ever walked through that door. 'I like smells. Flowers are one of my favourite things. I could smell them all day.' It seemed he was telling the truth. He returned daily, for months on end, with his dog, Buddy. Dimitar didn't like dogs in the shop, but he made an exception for Buddy because he was so well behaved, and he could see that Lilly liked to talk to Greg.

'What else do you like, other than smells?' she'd asked him one day.

He pulled a little sketch book out. On the first page, a detailed pencil sketch of a seahorse, its curled tail and intricate patterns captured with surprising skill. Then, the next page – a majestic whale, breaching the surface of the water. Each page had a different sea creature, drawn with the same careful attention to detail.

'Sea creatures,' he said. 'Yes. Three favourite things.'

'You've only told me two.'

'And Buddy, too, of course. Buddy is number one.'

She recalled stroking Buddy. 'I can see why.'

Greg then asked her, 'What's your name?'

'Lilly.'

'Well, Lilly, what're your favourite things?'

She told him the truth, her voice soft. 'Children... children who are happy.'

Chapter Thirty

THE MORNING SUN filtered through the stained-glass windows of St Claude's Church, casting a kaleidoscope of colours across the worn wooden pews.

Reverend Ray Lawson stood at the pulpit, his fingers gripping the edges. The usually full pews were half-empty.

This was the smallest turnout for a Sunday service in as long as he could remember.

Today's topic suddenly seemed very appropriate. 'Good morning. Today, we'll be discussing the power of faith in times of adversity.'

Parishioners shifted in their seats.

'In Psalms 46:1, we are reminded that "God is our refuge and strength, an ever-present help in trouble." These words ring especially true in times of uncertainty and fear.'

He caught indecipherable whispers in the air.

Ray pressed on, determined to maintain an air of normality. 'We remember that our faith is tested not in times of peace, but in moments of tribulation.'

His eyes hunted for familiar faces. Mrs Hodgson, who'd attended every Sunday for the past thirty years, was nowhere to be seen. The entire Thompson family, usually occupying most of the third pew on the left, had also failed to appear.

And he was certain that every time he caught someone's eye, they flinched and looked away.

This is my time of tribulation.

He took deep breaths, steeled himself, focused... His mind was telling him he was done, finished. His heart beating faster, he looked over at his wife, Kath, sitting at the organ. He needed her reassuring gaze, but she wouldn't make eye contact.

She, too, felt betrayed by him.

He fought on. 'It is easy to believe when all is well, but true faith shines brightest in the darkness.'

He reached up to touch his sore cheek. The memory of Megan's anger and bitterness intertwined with his words about faith and adversity. He'd tried desperately with her. So long ago now, while he was in another church in North Yorkshire. Knaresborough. Last he'd heard, she'd been piecing herself together. But Megan had always been his most challenging case.

His biggest failure.

But should he be judged only on that?

Realising he was sweating, and losing himself to his own thoughts, Ray announced a hymn. 'We'll sing "Abide with me".'

He stood back from the pulpit but sang with his congregation. His mind raced back to the image of his brother's body. Graham's death had set him on this path, a path that had led him to the priesthood and to the darker, hidden aspects of faith that the Church rarely acknowledged. Helping those who found themselves caught in the crossfire of a battle between good and evil that they couldn't comprehend. He sang instinctually while his mind dwelled in the past. He thought of the children he'd helped, and the children he'd failed. All so long ago now. Almost three decades! But still so vivid in his memory.

And sometimes he'd succeeded, and sometimes he'd failed.

Couldn't that just be accepted?

Midway through the hymn, Ray noticed the two church doors opening.

A man and a woman, both dressed in smart suits, slipped into the back pew. Unfamiliar faces. The woman held a golden Lab on a lead.

The man was older, heavyset, in his sixties, perhaps, with greying hair and a stern expression. The woman was younger, her posture rigid and alert. They didn't join in the singing.

Their presence was surely official and out of place among the regular parishioners.

Police? Was this it? Was this the end?

And why was the dog here? Was it a guide dog? Did the woman have vision problems?

His thoughts were in turmoil. Images of Megan as a young girl in Knaresborough flashed through his mind, followed by so many other faces.

How many more of those he tried to help would emerge to turn against him?

When the hymn ended, Ray returned to the pulpit, his legs feeling unsteady beneath him. 'Let us pray.' He closed his eyes as he recited the prayer, desperate to keep himself focused. In the darkness behind his eyelids, he saw Megan's accusing face, heard the echo of her screams:

I believed you. I looked into your eyes, and I believed you.

He felt her nails in his cheek again, trying to get up to his eyes.

'Lord. Grant us the strength to face our trials with courage and faith.' Was he praying for his congregation, or for himself?

Opening his eyes, he found his gaze drawn once again to the two strangers at the back of the church. The man had his eyes fixed on Ray. The woman's eyes were down.

With a supreme act of will, Ray pulled his attention back to his sermon. 'In times of darkness.' He raised his voice in the hope it would refocus him and draw him from his panic. 'We must cling to our faith all the more fiercely. For it is through faith that we find the light to guide us home.'

Almost three decades! Back then, the world had changed so quickly. Spending time alone with children was becoming frowned upon, a clear sign of suspicion that everyone would cling to. He'd no choice but to stop.

Greg Lyle had been the last.

His fundraising... his outreach programmes... for so long that had been the force with which he'd battled the evil that had taken his brother and would take others. No, it hadn't been enough, but goodness was goodness, and it'd been better than nothing.

Now, it seemed that over a quarter of a century later, his sacrifice hadn't been worth it. He should have carried on... Saved more if he could have done...

And now, he wondered what his judgement would be... and his sermon took a sharp turn that wasn't part of his planning. 'We are all sinners. All of us have fallen short of the glory of God. But it is in acknowledging our sins, in facing them head-on, that we find the path to redemption.'

And if I'm redeemed, then I can carry on helping.

The service concluded in a haze of confusion and whispered conversations. The congregation filed out, quickly, most not wanting to wait around and shake his hand as was custom. Ray found himself rooted to the spot, unable to move from the pulpit.

He watched as the two strangers rose from their seats and made their way towards him. With each step they took, Ray felt himself moving further and further away from redemption.

Chapter Thirty-One

REVEREND RAY LAWSON's vestry smelled of old books and beeswax candles. Frank settled into the worn sofa alongside Gerry. Rylan, as instructed, sat calmly at Gerry's feet. Across from them, Ray sank into an old leather chair, which squeaked with every movement. He interlaced his fingers tightly in his lap. 'Beautiful dog. My father kept Labs. That one is a stunner.'

'His name is Rylan,' Gerry said.

'Well, Rylan.' Ray winked at him. 'You fancy joining my congregation?'

Having interviewed his fair share of ecclesiastics over the years, Frank found him typically personable and bubbly.

'Are you sure I can't get you both a cup of tea?' Ray asked.

'No, thank you. We'll be fine.' Frank glanced at Gerry, concerned she may have disliked him answering on her behalf. But if she did, she didn't show it. At this moment, she was getting her notebook ready.

Frank regarded the angry red marks on Ray's cheek.

They looked fresh, the surrounding skin still swollen. 'Nasty scratches you've got there, Reverend. Everything all right? What happened?'

Ray regarded Frank as if he'd not been expecting the question. After a moment's silence, he shook his head, smiling. 'You heard, then?'

'Sorry?' Frank said. 'Heard what?'

'A woman came into the service the other day. In front of everyone. She lost her temper and attacked me. No reason.'

'Who was this?' Frank asked.

Ray shrugged. 'Never seen her before. She was about late thirties, early forties. I tried to talk to her afterwards, but she ran.'

Frank nodded. 'I see. I wasn't aware. Funny. I assume you've reported it?'

He shook his head.

'Why not?'

He sighed. 'I wanted to see if she came back first, so I could talk to her. Help her. Rather than get her into trouble.'

Frank shook his head. 'Better you report it. She could be in trouble now. *You* could be in trouble if she comes back. Does anyone in your congregation know her?'

Ray shook his head. 'If they did, no one said anything. I'll report it.'

'I think that's wise,' Frank said.

'Reverend,' Frank began, 'we're here about a body recently recovered from the water near Tate Hill Pier.'

Ray leaned forward. He maintained his composure, but Frank noticed his hands tightening their grip on each other. 'Awful. I heard about it. Terrible business...' He sat back, nodding. 'Awful.' He paused and frowned. 'What's my relevance to that?'

Frank had watched the reverend intently while he was delivering his sermon. He was a performer, that much was clear. He'd be able to deliver lies under pressure.

Frank had already briefed Gerry not to go straight to the point. He wanted to get a detailed feel of the reverend before throwing him completely under the spotlight. 'We'll get to that. First, though, I'd like to confirm a few details about your background, if you don't mind. DI Carver?'

'Our records show you've been the reverend here at St Claude's for twenty-seven years, since September 1997. Is that correct?' Gerry said.

'It is.'

'And before that, you were in Knaresborough for ten years?'

'Also true. Time flies, doesn't it?'

'Aye, it does,' Frank agreed.

'It hardly seems possible that I've been here for nearly three decades.'

'I also see from my notes that you're very well-regarded in the community,' Gerry said.

Ray attempted a modest smile. 'Well, if you say so.'

Gerry read from her notes. 'Several commendations from the Diocese of York for your community work, including the Bishop's Award for Excellence in Ministry in 2015. The Order of St Mellitus in 2018 for your outstanding contributions to pastoral care and community outreach.'

Ray nodded. 'I'm honoured by all the recognition, of course, but I assure you, I'm just doing God's work. These awards belong to many in my congregation. They're the ones who make all our initiatives possible.'

Gerry nodded. Frank noticed her make eye contact with him for the first time. 'Could you tell us about your charitable work, Reverend?'

'It's a big subject. Where would you like to start?'

Gerry held his stare. 'You seem to focus on people with extreme learning needs. Can you start there?'

Ray shifted in his seat, and the old leather squeaked. 'Well, I've always felt called to help those who might struggle to integrate into society. We've established several programmes over the years.' He listed them off, counting on his fingers. 'There's the "Sensory-Friendly Worship" service we hold monthly, designed for individuals with autism or sensory processing disorders. We dim the lights, keep the music soft, and provide fidget toys to help people feel comfortable.'

Frank nodded encouragingly, while Gerry looked down and made notes.

Ray continued, his voice growing more animated. 'We also run a weekly support group for adults with learning disabilities, focusing on life skills and social interaction. Our "Buddy Reading" programme pairs volunteers with children who've dyslexia or other reading difficulties. And we've recently started a music therapy programme for individuals with severe cognitive impairments.'

'That's very impressive,' Gerry remarked, looking back up. 'And what about your outreach programmes? I understand you're involved in work beyond the church walls as well.'

His face brightened further. 'We've a mobile soup kitchen that serves homeless individuals with mental health issues in Leeds. It's not just about providing food, but also offering a listening ear and connecting people with resources.' He paused, taking a breath before continuing.

'Our "Art for All" workshops provide a creative outlet for people with various disabilities. We've seen remarkable progress in participants' self-expression and confidence. And then there's our "Inclusive Sports Day" event, which brings together people with and without disabilities for a day of fun and friendly competition.'

Frank observed Ray as he spoke. There was a softness in his eyes, a slight smile playing at the corners of his mouth as he described the impact of his work. He also heard the genuine passion in his voice. It told the story of a good man, rather than a murderer.

Altruistic behaviour as a front was not something Frank was inexperienced in. Although, if that was the case here, Frank would have to concede it was at a level he'd never seen before.

Ray looked at his watch. 'With all that on the go, I can get rather busy. I've a fete to organise. I'm sorry to sound rude, but are you able to tell me why you're here? You mentioned that body? Awful business.'

'Almost there, Reverend, just one more thing... DI Carver?'

Gerry looked up again. 'Reverend, an accusation was made against you during your time in Knaresborough.' She paused.

Frank had asked her to do this, and it worked a treat at unsettling him. Ray's brow furrowed, a flicker of unease passing across his features. 'Knaresborough? As we established, that's a fair while back!'

Gerry continued, her voice neutral. 'You were accused of intimidating two boys with severe educational needs.'

Ray gave a brief shake of his head. 'It was a misunderstanding.'

'The parents of Ethan Wilkins, who had Down

syndrome, and Philip Foster, who was non-verbal autistic, lodged a complaint against you. They complained that their children became more withdrawn after spending time with you.'

'I remember the details.' He shook his head harder now. 'And like I said, it was a misunderstanding, and they quickly dropped the case.'

Gerry said, 'Sorry, could I confirm the accusations with you?'

'Is it necessary?' Ray asked, widening his eyes.

Gerry went ahead anyway. 'The boys became nervous at the mere mention of your name. Ethan referred to you shouting and having frightening outbursts. Philip wrote his concerns: "using strange words, saying things I don't understand, continuing even when I was crying".'

Ray shook his head. 'A misunderstanding. The boys faced significant challenges. They had many issues, bless them. I only ever tried to help them. I think communication was an issue. I might have spoken more softly, used less complex vocabulary when communicating. That kind of thing. I've learned a lot over the years.'

'Still,' Frank said, 'why continue if one of them was crying?'

'Continue what? Talking? I don't know... I simply didn't notice. Anyway... I don't want to be rude or disrespectful.' He flashed his eyes between them. 'But someone inspected this. They found that their changes in behaviour were related to their conditions, and not necessarily to my interactions with them. I was trying to help those boys, to give them a safe space to be themselves. Yes, I could have adapted my approach to them. I learned from it all.'

'Except you didn't need to adapt your approach to them,' Gerry said. 'They left the church.'

Ray nodded and looked down. 'Yes. It was all very unfortunate.'

'The complaint was also about you spending time alone with them, individually?' Gerry's voice was calm but insistent.

'It was a different time then. We didn't have the same... awareness... that we do now about boundaries. Being alone with children.' He leaned forward, his eyes moving between Frank and Gerry. 'Now, I'm very careful to ensure I'm never alone with children. The world has changed, and we must adapt to it. All our programmes have strict safe-guarding policies in place... Now, look, am I being investigated for this again?' Ray raised an eyebrow.

Frank shook his head. 'We just need to cover every possibility.'

'Why? You still haven't told me what this is about.'

'The body by the pier,' Frank said. 'Sorry, one more thing before that... In several articles we looked at, you cited your brother as an inspiration for your work with children with special educational needs. Can you tell us a bit about that?'

Ray sighed and looked away. Frank thought he was about to lose his temper, but then his expression softened. 'Graham was different. Brilliant, intelligent, funny, but the world didn't understand him. He struggled in school, couldn't sit still, was always getting into trouble. Today, doctors would have diagnosed him with autism and ADHD, I'm certain. But back then, he was just labelled as difficult, disruptive.' Ray paused, his eyes distant, lost in memory. 'He took his own life when he was fifteen.'

He lowered his face.

'I'm sorry,' Frank said. 'And you found him, is that right?'

'Yes... I was thirteen.'

'It must have been hard.'

'Very... It set me on my path, though. I knew I had to help children like him. Children who didn't fit into the world's narrow definition of "normal". That, combined with my calling from God... well, it kind of slotted into place, I suppose.'

Frank nodded sympathetically, noting the raw pain still clear in Ray's voice. 'I'm sure your brother would be proud that his memory has driven much of your work.'

Ray nodded. 'I hope so. I want to make sure no other child feels as lost and misunderstood as he did.'

Frank exchanged a glance with Gerry before continuing, his voice gentle but firm. 'Now, Reverend, I'm sorry to inform you that the body recovered belonged to Greg Lyle.'

Ray looked straight at Frank.

Frank waited for him to speak, but he didn't.

'You knew Greg, didn't you?'

Ray still didn't speak. He was pale, and his face was rigid.

'Reverend?' Frank pressed.

'Greg?' Ray said.

'Yes... I'm sorry if this has shocked you.'

Ray turned his head from side to side, his complexion completely ashen. 'He died from a fall... from a cliff. I heard about the child by the pier... it wasn't a fall.'

'No, it wasn't,' Frank said.

'The fall was the conclusion from the missing person's report,' Gerry said. 'But they never found the body. It never should have been concluded, really.'

He looked like he was going to vomit. 'How do you know it's him?'

'Dental records,' Frank said. 'I'm sorry to have to tell you this way.'

'Weren't they in... a fridge?' His eyes were widening.

'Aye,' Frank said.

'Then it just can't be him!' His eyes were filling with tears.

'What makes you say that?'

He rubbed at his eyes. 'Because he was such a good boy... such a good, good boy... Who could do such a thing?'

'We hope to find out,' Frank said. 'So, now you understand the importance of us being here, maybe you could tell us about your relationship with Greg?'

'He was part of this church. He came to Sunday school.' He broke off, shaking his head. Ray leaned forward, rubbing his temples. 'So bright, so curious...'

'And were you two close?' Gerry asked.

'Yes... but I can't believe this. Don't get me wrong, I knew he was *already* gone. I knew he was never coming back. I mourned him. But I thought it may have been suicide, like Graham.'

'I'm sorry that this has hit you so hard,' Frank said. 'You said you were close. Are you able to go into more detail about your relationship with Greg?'

Ray dropped his fingers from his temples and his head snapped up with a flash of defensiveness in his eyes. 'I try to be close to all my parishioners, within the realm of respectability.'

'So your relationship with Greg was no different to your relationship to any of your parishioners?' Frank asked.

Ray gave a sharp nod. 'Nothing out of the ordinary.'

'I see... so you were never alone together,' Frank pressed.

Ray sighed. He looked frustrated. 'Look... we spoke a

187

lot. He came to me for support, trying to understand the world. For friendship, too, I guess. He was misunderstood, autistic...'

'So, you were alone with him?' Gerry asked.

Ray flinched and then nodded. 'Yes. But this was what, the end of the nineties? After that, after being investigated by the police when he went missing, I changed. I've been more careful ever since. As I said before, I make very sure that I'm never alone with children now. I should have been more careful then!'

You should have learned your lesson after Knaresborough, Frank thought, but he didn't say so. The man seemed rattled enough just now. 'Okay, so what were your interactions like?'

Ray took a deep breath. 'Greg needed someone who understood him, who could listen without judgement. His parents were struggling, and he had few friends his own age.' Ray's eyes took on a faraway look, a small smile touching his lips. 'Greg reminded me so much of Graham in some ways. Brilliant, but misunderstood. He had such a passion for marine life, could recite facts about sea creatures for hours. But he struggled with social interactions, with changes to his routine.' He paused, shaking his head. 'People often underestimated Greg because of his autism. He struggled to articulate himself properly. His language skills developed at a slower pace. People would speak to him like he was a small child or ignore him altogether. But he was so intelligent, so observant. He just needed someone to listen, to take him seriously.'

Frank leaned forward. 'You told the investigators in 1998 that Greg visited you often when walking his dog, Buddy. Is that right?'

Ray nodded. 'Yes... admittedly, every day at one point.

He was routine driven.' He looked down at Rylan and smiled. 'Buddy. That dog was a godsend to Greg. Nothing was ever better for that boy than Buddy. You understand that, don't you?' He looked at Gerry.

'Therapy dogs can be incredibly beneficial for individuals with autism. They provide emotional support, reduce anxiety and can help with social interactions,' Gerry said.

'The bond between them was... beautiful,' Ray continued. 'Buddy seemed to understand Greg in a way that his parents or I couldn't.'

'Did Greg's parents know about your friendship with Greg?' Frank asked.

He nodded. 'Of course. Like I said, they were parishioners.'

'So, they knew you were alone with him?'

'Yes...'

Such trust, Frank thought, but then he seemed very trustworthy, and society back then had been so much less vigilant.

Ray sighed. 'After Greg disappeared, Katie and Simon never returned... Katie lost her faith.'

'Did you stay in touch?'

'I tried, for a time. But Katie had completely lost her faith. And Simon, well, Simon always seemed aggressive. He came by several times to interrogate me because I'd seen Greg on that last day. I could see a wildness in his eyes. A suggestion that he was going to stop at nothing. Eventually, I must have convinced him I was nothing to do with it. I've never really seen him since.'

I've seen that same wildness in his eyes, Frank thought.

'How did you try to help Greg?' Gerry asked, her pen scratching across the paper.

'I tried to create a safe space for him, where he could be

himself without fear of judgement. We'd talk about his interests, work through his anxieties. I encouraged him to write and draw, to express himself in ways that felt comfortable to him.'

Frank nodded. 'October 14th, 1998 was the day that Greg disappeared. Can you walk us through what happened that morning?'

'I remember it, and it helps that I told this story on several occasions to the investigators. I'm assuming you have it?'

'We do,' Frank said.

'I apologise for any inconsistencies then. It's been twenty-five years.'

'Twenty-six,' Gerry said.

Ray nodded. 'Greg was agitated. Confused. Even Buddy was struggling to keep him calm. He'd found out about his father's affair the day before. He couldn't understand why his father would do something like that. It had shaken his entire world. Routine was so important to Greg, you see. This... this was a massive disruption. He kept saying, "It doesn't make sense. Why would Dad do that? It's not right."'

'What did you do?' Gerry asked.

Ray sighed, running a hand through his hair. 'I listened. Tried to comfort him as best I could. I explained that sometimes adults make mistakes, that it didn't mean his father loved him any less. But Greg was struggling to process it all. There was something else bothering him, too.'

Frank leaned forward. 'What was that?'

'He wouldn't say, which was unlike him. Usually, he'd tell me everything. It was something other than this affair, though, I'm certain. He mentioned rules. Broken rules. I remember him clutching his dog tightly to him as he said it.

As if he might suddenly run away or disappear. I guess he must have been desperate for that comfort. That was all that really happened. At least, all I can remember right now.'

'We've been told that Greg was rule driven.'

'Yes. Something had caused him great anxiety.'

Frank showed Ray the message they'd recovered from Greg's pager.

'Does this mean anything to you?'

He thought about it. 'I'm sorry. No. WA could mean Whitby Abbey, perhaps?'

'Yes, we considered that. Did he ever mention Whitby Abbey to you?'

He shook his head. 'Look, he didn't mention meeting anyone. I remember suggesting he take Buddy for a long walk along the beach to clear his head. That always seemed to calm him down. For years, I wished he'd done what I'd asked. I knew that he continued walking along West Cliff, and this was where I thought he fell. Now I know that this may not have been the case. So sad...' Ray looked up, his eyes filled with regret. 'I told him to come back if he needed to talk later. Of course, he didn't. That was the last time I saw him.'

Frank observed Ray, noting the genuine grief in his eyes. 'Reverend, I know this is difficult, but is there anything else you can remember about that day? Anything at all that might help us understand what happened to Greg?'

Ray shook his head, tears spilling down his cheeks. 'I've gone over it a thousand times in my head. If only I'd done something differently, said something else... maybe he'd still be alive. Maybe I should have kept him here, called his mother... When I thought it may have been suicide, like Graham, I felt like I'd failed him, just like I failed my brother. It took me a long time to come to terms with that.'

Frank and Gerry continued for a while, trying to prompt Ray into remembering something else from that day, that time, that may have shed light on where Greg had gone after the church, but just like the investigators from twenty-six years ago, they came up blank.

Eventually, Frank stood, signalling the end of the interview. 'Thank you for your time, Reverend. We may need to speak with you again as our investigation progresses.'

Ray nodded, his shoulders slumped. 'Such an awful thing.'

On the way out, Frank turned back. 'I'd also get those scratches looked at. They look sore.'

Chapter Thirty-Two

AFTER SHARING NOTES, Frank eased the Audi they'd checked out from the carpool at HQ onto the main road. Gerry sat quietly, her notebook open on her lap, still considering.

'Okay, that's it for you, Gerry. I'm dropping you off.'

'I don't mind—'

'No, you've already gone above and beyond. It's Sunday. You need to rest.'

'Okay... take me home. Tom will still be in bed.'

'Please, Gerry, we've had this discussion.'

She frowned. 'Sorry?'

'About sex.' He felt his cheeks warm as he said it.

'I didn't mean that,' Gerry said. 'I meant he'll still be there so I can arrange something with him.'

'Ah... how were his parents, by the way? Did you follow my advice?'

'Some of it.'

Frank raised an eyebrow. 'Good. Then it probably went better than when I met Mary's parents.'

'What happened with Mary's parents?'

'Her father took one look at me and told me straight out I wasn't good enough for his little girl.'

'How did you respond?'

'By proving him right...' Frank said.

'I think you need to be kinder to yourself.'

Frank glanced at her. 'Heard... considered...' He looked back at the road. 'And dismissed. So, it went well?'

'I don't know,' Gerry said.

'Do tell,' Frank said, indicating to change lanes.

Gerry's brow furrowed. 'Well, Tom's father seemed fixated on the fact that Tom chose to become an arborist instead of following the family tradition of architecture.'

'Thought you were the one they were supposed to be focusing their attention on.'

'They struggled with that. Especially the mother. She kept offering me wine, even after I explained I don't drink. Then she asked if it was because of my autism, as if autism and alcohol were medically incompatible.'

Frank winced. 'Ouch. I could just imagine your detailed explanation of neurodevelopmental conditions and their non-correlation with alcohol tolerance.'

'I didn't want to overwhelm her.'

'Eh?' He regarded her. 'Do you only reserve that for me? What did I ever do so wrong?'

'I mainly do it with people I'm fond of.'

'Fond of me!' He laughed. 'Wow... if only the other 99 per cent of people I've ever worked with could hear this now. I can give them the Vs and tell them how misunderstood I was.'

'I practised etiquette in front of the mirror before the meal, and that worked out well.'

Frank nodded and grinned. 'Any other highlights?'

Gerry nodded seriously. 'Rylan's gastrointestinal issues are ongoing.'

Frank glanced in his rear-view mirror at Rylan in the back seat. 'Poor lad.'

'He passed wind rather loudly during dinner. Tom found it hilarious.'

Frank laughed. 'I bet he did.'

'His parents... less so,' Gerry said.

Frank laughed harder. 'Oh, like that are they? To have been a fly on *that* wall.' He pulled to a halt outside her house.

Gerry glanced at him, her expression thoughtful. 'You know, Frank, I think I'm getting better at these social situations. A few months ago, I might have lectured them on the statistical improbability of their son following the exact career path they'd chosen. Progress, don't you think?'

Frank couldn't help but smile. 'Aye, that's progress all right.'

You'll be a regular social butterfly in no time.

'What're you doing this afternoon, Frank?'

'Bits and bobs.'

'Involving this case?'

He smiled. 'Haven't decided yet.' But, of course, she was right. 'I'll drop the car off and then I might check out one or two things.' *Or ten or eleven things...*

'You need to rest too.'

'Why?' Frank shrugged. 'I don't drink. What's there to do when at rest?'

'Just because you're not drinking doesn't mean you can't relax. Have you considered taking up a hobby?'

Frank snorted. 'What, like stamp collecting? I'll pass, thanks.'

'You know,' Gerry said carefully, 'there are support

groups for people who've given up drinking. It might be helpful to talk to others who understand how challenging an alternative lifestyle can be.'

'I'm fine, Gerry. I don't need to sit in a circle to talk about my feelings.'

Gerry nodded, but Frank could see she wasn't convinced. 'You should speak to Evelyn Wainwright.' She'd said it matter-of-factly, as if it was a natural part of the conversation, which it so wasn't.

Gerry cracked open the door.

'Wait a sec. Where did that come from?'

Gerry didn't respond. She'd realised that she shouldn't have let that slip. She'd be admonishing herself for the impulsive slip.

'When did you speak to Helen?'

Gerry said, 'Last night. Also, twice last week—'

'I didn't realise you'd become close?'

Gerry shook her head. 'We haven't. She just phones to talk about you.'

For crying out loud!

Ironic really. They should be happy he'd knocked booze on the head, and here they were, driving him back to it! 'So you two are, what? Comparing notes? Gossiping won't help matters.'

Gerry shook her head. 'Not gossiping, Frank. We're concerned about you. Helen thinks – and I agree – that talking to Evelyn might help you with—'

'Gerry, stop!' He closed his eyes, feeling exhausted. 'I appreciate the concern, but meeting Evelyn... it's not that simple.'

'Why?'

'For a start, it reminds me of everything I've lost.'

Gerry was quiet for a moment. 'Maybe that's exactly

why you should see her, Frank. To view Evelyn as someone like you, someone also suffering... not just an extension of your own loss.'

Frank sighed. 'Does Helen ask you to badger me like this?' he asked.

'Badger?'

'Pester?'

'I know what the expression means. I just didn't think I was.'

He grunted. 'Evelyn Wainwright! Of all the conversations I never thought I'd ever have with you, this ranks highly. Last thing on the matter. A cosy chat with the widow of the man who killed my wife isn't something I'm entertaining.'

'In my experience, avoiding painful things makes them more painful.'

Give me strength! 'Thank you, Auntie Sue.' Frank sat there for a moment, then sighed heavily. 'See you tomorrow, Gerry.'

Gerry collected Rylan from the back seat. 'See you tomorrow, Frank.'

As Gerry walked away, Frank called out, 'Gerry?'

She turned back, eyebrows raised.

'Thanks,' he said gruffly. 'For caring. Even if you've got a bloody odd way of showing it sometimes.'

Gerry smiled. 'You're welcome, Frank.'

Back at HQ, he wondered if he should take the rest of Sunday too. But then his eyes caught the photograph of Greg and Buddy on the board, and he realised that wouldn't happen.

He went over the interview notes with Ray again and again.

The reverend had painted a similar picture of Greg as

his mother had done. A gentle, curious child who saw the world differently. Struggling to fit in, but with a kind nature. Ray spoke of Greg with genuine fondness.

He thought of Katie, Greg's mother, breaking down in front of him as she recalled her son's adoration of sea creatures and Buddy. She recalled her comments regarding Simon and his inability to connect with his son.

Frank shook his head.

He didn't want Greg to remind him of Gerry, but he felt it happen in his head.

Greg, like Gerry, had struggled to fit in.

The difference?

Gerry had been given the chance to find her way and look at how she'd flourished.

Greg, on the other hand, had been thrown away as if he didn't matter.

Someone was going to pay for that.

Chapter Thirty-Three

Frank sat at his desk Monday morning, willing his tired eyes to stay open.

He looked over at the bin full of empty Coke cans.

He'd emptied the vending machine the day before. Every sip had been a silent rebellion against Helen and Gerry's attempts to micromanage his life. *Overloading on this shite is on you two!* His silent rebellion had severely backfired, and he'd been left tossing and turning all night from a caffeine overdose.

There was a knock at his office door. He gave the word and he was pleased to see Gerry and Rylan.

'Over here, fella,' he said, wheeling his chair around the side of the desk, so he could take the Lab's head in both his hands and rub his ears.

He looked up at Gerry. 'How do?'

'What's wrong?'

'Eh?' He furrowed his brow. 'Just tired.'

'Okay...' She didn't sound convinced. 'Anyway, I've discovered something.'

'Fantastic.'

'But I'll warn you, you'll have to speak to Donald.'

'Ah shit... really not in the mood for that.' And that was the truth. 'Maybe it's best you just don't tell me?'

She stood there, regarding him.

'That was a joke, Gerry. Sit... please.'

Gerry sat and pulled out her notebook. 'While digging into Raven Blackstone's background, I found inconsistencies...'

'Okay.' Frank leaned forward. 'Go on.'

'Raven moved to Whitby in 1997, one year before her affair with Simon Lyle. She would've been nineteen years old. Over this time, her employment history shows she worked in admin for various companies.' She consulted her notes. 'Whitby Maritime Services, Endeavour Accounting, and Bram's Bytes IT Solutions. She also worked at the Harbour Lights café evenings and weekends. She's been involved with the goth festival organisation since 1999. Prior to Whitby, she supposedly lived in Scarborough. She graduated from college with A levels at eighteen in 1995. This was the inconsistency I was referring to. She should have graduated in 1996 as she was nineteen in 1997, remember?'

Frank's head rattled with the onslaught of information, but he managed to see the point. He raised an eyebrow. 'Well spotted, Gerry. What could it mean? Maybe she retook them?'

'I thought that, so I spoke to Scarborough College to confirm it. Raven Blackstone didn't graduate in 1995, or 1996, for that matter. The information is bogus. I tried to contact her listed parents... and they don't exist either.'

'Jesus.' Frank could feel his pulse in his temples. 'Weird.'

'It's almost like she only started existing in 1997. Three

years ago, Raven was arrested for drink driving. They fingerprinted her and put her in the system. It seemed like a long shot, but given the issues I mentioned, I went ahead and ran those fingerprints.'

Frank leaned forward. This was a typical Gerry trail. And typically, it always ended with a bang. 'And?'

'I got two hits, Frank. I got two separate identities.'

Frank's breath caught in his throat. 'Impossible.'

'The first hit was for Raven Blackstone – the identity I just presented to you. But there's a second identity linked to those same prints.'

Frank shook his head, struggling to process this. 'What do we know about this second identity?'

'I've got nothing for the second identity.'

Frank shook his head. 'A mistake, obviously. Has the system added a second record with no information? A bug?'

Gerry shook her head. 'The record exists. It is denying me access. It is locked down.'

Frank sucked in a deep breath and nodded as the truth sank in. 'An identity change? Witness protection? I've seen it before. I suppose she could be a spy! Okay, well nothing else for it, we need access.' He stood. 'You were right, all along. Don Corleone it is.'

'Don Corleone?' Gerry said.

'The Godfather... from the movie... the head honcho. Solves all problems. I mean Donald Oxley, of course. Ironically, he's a man who rarely solves problems. Merely creates them. But today, he's solving this one for us... as I'm in no mood for his bullshit.'

'I've something else,' Gerry said.

'Bloody hell, I was the one here all day yesterday, and you're the one producing the goods!'

'It's about Lilly Petrova.'

'Remind me again what we know about Lilly Petrova?'

Gerry consulted her notes. 'Lilly Petrova, age forty-six. Born in Bulgaria. She's the niece of the original proprietor, Dimitar Petrova. He was a legal immigrant who opened the shop in the late 1970s. Dimitar brought Lilly over in 1990 when she was twelve. The records said she'd been orphaned in Bulgaria, but there wasn't a significant amount of detail. Processes weren't as stringent as they are now. Lilly has been running the shop since Dimitar passed in 2015. She's unmarried. No children. Greg stopped by the shop on the morning he disappeared to buy some flowers for his mother. Lilly claimed she didn't notice anything unusual about his behaviour, and that she didn't know Greg. Had never seen him before.'

'Okay,' Frank said. 'And what do you have?'

Gerry offered her phone. Frank slipped his glasses down his nose and squinted at the screen. The image showed a delicate pencil sketch of a flower, its petals unfurling with remarkable detail. Beneath the drawing was a word in Cyrillic script that Frank couldn't decipher. 'What's that?'

Gerry said. 'That's from one of Greg's sketchbooks photographed into evidence for the investigation in 1998. The flower is a Bulgarian species – Silene thracica, or Balkan catchfly. The name beneath is written in Bulgarian. There was a date. September 2nd, 1998.'

'Jesus. So this suggests he was there a month earlier... sketching the flower in her shop? How many sketch books have you looked through, Gerry?'

'He had fifteen.'

Frank looked at her. *Wow. I really am lucky to have you.*

'Okay.' Frank stood. 'Amazing work, Gerry. Your reward is to lead the briefing while I talk with Donald. No one is to go near Raven Blackstone until we know who she is. Is that clear?'

Gerry nodded.

'Assignments are pinned, but just in case. First thing, you and I are taking a run at Lilly Petrova. Reggie and Sharon need to speak to Terry Kane, Greg's best friend. Oh, and get Sean to pop down to see Kath Lawson... I'm interested to see how she feels about those scratch marks down her husband's face.'

And then Frank left, steeling himself en route for a showdown with Oxley.

A hidden identity?

It'd been a very long time since he'd seen anything of this nature.

Could it be about to blow the case wide open?

Chapter Thirty-Four

OUT OF RESPECT FOR GERRY, Frank didn't smoke while she was in the car, but God, after his meeting with Donald, he didn't half need one!

'Anyone would think I was asking for the code to activate our nuclear deterrent,' he said.

Gerry said, 'Did you explain clearly to Donald that we need the background on Raven Blackstone? She was one of the last people who saw Greg alive.'

Frank glanced at her. 'I'm going to pretend you didn't say that... I explained in *numerous* ways, Gerry, with varying degrees of aggression. You can be sure he understands how important this is now! But he's delaying access because he doesn't want to ruffle any bloody feathers! Typical.'

'So what did you say?'

'I told him to get bloody ruffling! Pronto!'

'And?'

'He told me that he'd be taking a more measured, methodical and *professional* approach to accessing the information.'

'He's right to follow procedure,' Gerry offered.

Frank glared at her with a raised eyebrow. 'Are you deliberately trying to send my nicotine craving through the roof?' He turned back, tightening his grip on the steering wheel. 'We need that information now, not after it's been through a committee and had all the useful bits redacted. Anyway, he's had his ultimatum.'

'What was that?'

'Twenty-four hours to get me that information, or I'll find an alternative route to it. This case is too important to let bureaucracy slow us down.'

'And what did he say?'

'Not much.'

'He may not have believed you.'

A grim smile crossed Frank's face. He flashed her a look. 'That would be a grave misjudgement.'

They lapsed into silence as Frank navigated the last turn onto Church Street. The Seabreeze Flower Shop came into view. The building was a charming mix of old and new: stone walls and bright signage. Colourful bouquets and potted plants lined the storefront, giving it a fresh, inviting appearance.

Frank pulled to a stop across the street from the shop.

Chapter Thirty-Five

FRANK SCANNED the quaint storefront for a sign in the window. *'Well-behaved dogs welcome.'* He pointed it out. 'We're good to go.'

Frank pushed open the door, and a tinkling bell announced their arrival. He immediately felt overwhelmed by colour and fragrance.

I'm going to need sunglasses and a hay fever tablet, he thought.

Frank observed a smartly dressed tall woman serving a customer. She'd dark hair cut into a bob, a slight figure and kind eyes that crinkled at the corners when she smiled. Her hands moved deftly, wrapping a bouquet in brown paper and tying it off with a flourish of ribbon. Frank could only imagine the mess he'd cause if he attempted something like that.

In the rear corner of the shop, close to the counter, a large worktable was covered in ribbons, wrapping paper and half-finished bouquets. The two detectives and Rylan waited beside it.

'There you are, Mrs Lane,' the server said, her accent

carrying just a hint of Bulgarian. 'I hope your sister enjoys them. The freesias should last at least a week if you change the water daily.'

After the customer had left, the woman's eyes fell on the two detectives. Her smile faltered slightly, a flicker of uncertainty crossing her face. Frank watched as her gaze darted to Rylan, then back to them.

Frank stepped forward, pulling out his warrant card. 'Ms Petrova?'

'Yes. Can I help?'

'I'm DCI Frank Black, and this is DI Gerry Carver. We were hoping for ten minutes of your time.'

'Is there a reason?'

Frank looked down and then up. 'You may have heard about some remains that have been recovered from the sea near Tate Hill Pier.'

The colour drained from Lilly's face so quickly that Frank wondered if she might faint. This was a reaction which was getting very common.

'Are you okay, Ms Petrova?' Frank asked.

She steadied herself against the counter. She took a deep breath and seemed to regain some control of herself. 'Ужасно е... просто ужасно е.'

'I don't understand,' Frank said.

'Oh sorry... yes... I said it was awful, just awful... one moment.'

She shifted around the counter and hurried to the door, flipping the sign to 'Closed' and turning the lock. Frank saw Gerry making a note in her book. *Was she noting Lilly's extreme reaction?* Frank wondered. *Had Lilly already surmised it may be Greg? The boy she'd seen on his last journey twenty-six years ago. And, in that case, why so horrified over a boy she barely knew?*

Lilly returned to the counter, gesturing for them to join her. Her movements were jerky, almost robotic.

Frank noticed a small framed photo behind the till on the wall. A younger Lilly standing next to an older man, both smiling proudly in front of the shop. Her uncle Dimitar, he presumed.

'I'm sorry...' she said. 'But was it that boy? The one I was asked about a long time ago. He came in here to buy flowers for his mother on the day he disappeared?'

'Aye,' Frank said. 'I'm afraid so.'

'Greg Lyle?' Lilly touched her chest.

Frank nodded. 'You've an excellent memory. It was a long time ago.'

'I remember it well. I spoke to the police then, you know?'

Frank nodded. 'We know.'

'They came back and told me he fell from a cliff.' She put a hand to her mouth and paused. Frank let the silence linger for a time. 'I heard about the refrigerator... How awful... how awful... What happened to him?'

'We're trying to find that out,' Frank said. 'You told the investigators back in 1998 that you didn't know Greg. That you'd never seen him before?'

Lilly nodded, avoiding eye contact. Her movements remained jerky. 'Yes. That's right. He came in that morning, wanting to buy flowers for his mother. Carnations, I remember. Pink ones. He said that she was sad. That his father had been unpleasant to her.'

He glanced at Gerry, who was clearly looking at the original statement in her notebook. She gave a swift nod to show that the report was the same. Lilly had recalled her script well. 'Ms Petrova, the investigation back in 1998 was for a missing person. This investigation is for a murder. Is there anything you wish to add to your story from back then?'

She looked away. 'I'm not sure what you mean.'

Frank took a deep breath. 'Really? Because, honestly, Ms Petrova, I think there's more to this story.'

She looked back at him. 'Why do you say that?'

'Well, to begin with, you seemed very shocked when we mentioned the body.'

'Yes. Hearing about anybody's death is shocking, isn't it?'

'DI Carver?' Frank prompted.

Gerry showed Lilly the sketch of the Bulgarian flower on her phone.

'Балканско плюскавиче.' She put a hand to her mouth.

'Sorry?' Frank asked.

'Balkan catchfly,' she translated.

'Aye,' Frank said. 'And not the sort of thing a young boy from Whitby would typically know about.'

She sighed.

'Unless he'd some connection to Bulgaria. Or someone from Bulgaria. But we've no evidence of that,' Frank said. 'Do you sell this flower here, Ms Petrova?'

Lilly closed her eyes, took a deep breath and nodded. 'I'm sorry... I'm *so* sorry. I didn't think I could help you back then... I should have told you more... **Прости ми**... forgive me.' Lilly's hands trembled slightly as she smoothed down her apron. Frank noticed a small stain on the fabric – pollen, perhaps, or just the wear and tear of daily work with flowers.

'Aye,' Frank said. 'The date suggests he drew that a month before he disappeared. Did you see him on that day, too?'

She nodded. 'Greg first came in when he was twelve. He wanted to buy flowers for his mum's birthday, but he didn't have enough money. He was so earnest, so determined. I helped him pick out a few carnations that he could afford. I gave him a few extra, too...' A small smile played at the corners of her mouth.

Frank ignored the creases around her eyes, and, for a moment, he imagined the young nineteen-year-old Lilly when she'd first met Greg.

'He came regularly – at least once or twice a week, while walking Buddy. He loved flowers. He wanted to look, to smell, to draw.' She absently stroked a nearby bouquet of daisies. 'I remember him saying that they calmed him when the world got too loud. They were one of his three most favourite things. Buddy, marine life...' She gazed around the shop. 'And my flowers.'

Once or twice a week. His parents couldn't have known... otherwise, it would have been part of his routine.

'He'd sit in the corner sometimes,' Lilly continued, gesturing to a small nook by the window. Frank could almost picture a young Greg there, hunched over a sketchbook. 'Sketching flowers, or sea creatures. He was talented. Always had a fact to share about marine life or plants. Мил и нежен.'

'What was that?' Frank asked.

'Kind and gentle...' Lilly's smile widened. 'He told me things I knew, but I still found it exciting to hear, because of how enthusiastic *he* sounded. I remember him telling me that some flowers can change colour based on the soil pH. He'd also tell me things I didn't know. Clownfish change gender.' She gazed off into the distance. 'It was the only time I saw him animated when he talked about things he loved.'

There was a genuine affection in her voice when she talked about Greg, a softness that hadn't been there before. Frank felt himself warming to her.

But, even though he was warming to her, he had to remain serious. She'd hidden this relationship... What else might she be hiding? 'It sounds like you got to know him well,' Frank said. 'Why didn't you tell the investigators about this in 1998?'

Lilly's smile faded. 'My uncle, Dimitar, told me I couldn't.' She lowered her head. 'I'm sorry... I was young, and I was indebted to Dimitar for raising me. I *should* have said something.'

Frank nodded. 'Why did your uncle want you to stay quiet?'

Lilly looked over at the picture of her uncle. She had a guilty look on her face. 'Look... please don't think bad of him... he was a good man. *Such* a good man. But it was different back then. My uncle had experienced a lot of racism. Still faced it regularly. People seemed to think it appropriate to challenge us on being immigrants. When Greg went missing, he was terrified. Said that if I told the police about our friendship, we would invite suspicion. That they'd look at us... look at *him*. I was young... he was scared for me... It led to the wrong decision.' She had tears in her eyes. 'I'm sorry.'

Frank nodded, understanding dawning. He'd seen similar situations before, where fear and experiences led people to withhold information, even when they had nothing to hide. 'What was your uncle's relationship with Greg like?'

'Dimitar was kind to him, as he was to everyone, but he was distant. This was normal. Dimitar never really got close to anyone, apart from me, and some other family members who visited over the years.' Lilly's voice held a note of sadness, perhaps regret. 'My uncle let Greg stay and sketch, but it was usually me who talked with him. He also didn't allow dogs as a rule, back then, but he allowed Buddy. He did that for me because he saw that I enjoyed talking to Greg.'

Gerry spoke for the first time in a while. 'How much did Greg tell you about his relationship with his parents?'

'Some. He adored his mother. He said she understood him, knew how to listen to him, help him when he felt over-whelmed... but his relationship with his father wasn't the best. He said his father often made him sad. That he didn't understand him. But I never met his parents myself.'

'Did he ever mention anyone else to you?'

She thought about it. 'His best friend... I remember him saying that he'd a friend who was similar to him – that they had their own treehouse. I said I'd like to meet him, but Greg never brought him along.'

'Did he ever mention church?' Gerry asked.

'Yes... actually... he did. He said the reverend was nice. Reverend Ray Lawson. He still works there. At St Claude's. I remember him saying that Ray understood his challenges.'

Frank pulled out his phone again, this time showing her the message they'd found on Greg's pager. 'Does this mean anything to you?'

Lilly squinted at the screen, then shook her head. 'No, I'm sorry.'

'WA... Whitby Abbey, maybe?' Frank said.

'Maybe... I'm so sorry. It doesn't make a lot of sense.'

'Some of it is missing, we believe,' Frank said.

'How did Greg seem during that last encounter?' Gerry had her pen poised over her notebook.

'He was just like I said back then... distressed. More

than I'd ever seen him. He bought the carnations for his mother, like I said before, but he seemed... really off. Agitated. He said it was because of his father, and what he'd done to his mother. I tried to ask if he was okay, but he just shook his head and left quickly—'

A muffled thump from below cut her off.

Frank noticed Rylan stiffen. His ears twitched.

There was a second, louder thump.

Frank looked at Lilly. Her eyes seemed to stare past him. He turned to look at the counter and the door behind it.

Someone in the cellar?

'What was that, Ms Petrova?' he asked, looking back.

'Happens sometimes,' Lilly said. Frank noticed she was suddenly clutching her hands together. 'Boxes falling over in the cellar. The damp can make containers weak and—'

There came a succession of thumps, growing louder and more insistent. Rylan let out a low whine.

Frank raised an eyebrow. 'Something isn't right.'

Lilly's eyes flicked between Frank and Gerry. 'It really isn't necessary. It's just storage down there. Quite messy, really. I wouldn't want to waste your time.'

'I'm sorry Ms Petrova,' Frank said, his voice gentle but firm. 'I'm concerned. Someone's down there.' He stepped closer, maintaining eye contact. 'Do you know who it is?'

Eyes widening, she shook her head. 'Sorry... I don't... no.'

'Then I'd like to ensure your safety. Can you unlock the door, please?'

Lilly's shoulders sagged. She looked defeated, scared. Her eyes darted to the photo of Dimitar, then back to Frank. 'It will be nothing—'

'Now, please,' Frank insisted. 'Someone could be breaking in.'

With trembling hands, Lilly moved to the door behind the counter. She pulled out a key, fumbling slightly as she unlocked it, opened the door, switched the light on and illuminated a staircase.

There was another thump.

'Shall I call back-up?' Gerry asked.

'Stay here. I'll holler if' – he looked at Lilly – 'there's anything other than falling boxes.'

Falling boxes my arse, he thought, taking a deep breath, slipping past Lilly and descending the steps.

Chapter Thirty-Six

THE SUN CAST long shadows across the quiet street. The crisp air hinted at the approaching winter.

Sharon pulled her coat tighter around herself as she approached the modest semi-detached house.

Reggie had been making awkward small talk for the entire journey, but he'd saved the best for last. 'How's that new fella of yours?'

'Who, Mandy?'

She didn't need to look to know she'd sparked a double take. Besides, the ensuing lingering silence spoke volumes.

When they reached the path to Terry Kane's home, she finally looked.

He looked flustered.

'Sorry, I could have sworn you had a boyfriend.'

'I told you I had a partner, sir. I never mentioned the gender. But you can relax, sir...' She struggled to hold back a grin.

He struggled to meet her eyes. 'Sorry, wrong end of the stick... You know there's nothing in that... I'm fine with people's preferences... don't you?'

His well-meaning but clumsy attempt at inclusivity was oddly endearing. 'Ha! Preferences! Yes, of course I know that.' She smiled at him. 'Believe me, I'm fine with it. Now lighten up.'

When Reggie recovered from her revelation, he'd realise that it was the best icebreaker yet. In a way, she was warming to him. He was nosy, outspoken and rather too jolly in awkward moments, but his heart was in the right place. He wanted everyone to feel happy.

She walked on ahead and knocked on the door.

While they waited, Reggie said, 'So how long have you and Mandy been together?'

'Over a year now,' Sharon said.

'Cool,' he said. 'She's a keeper then.'

The door was opened by a lanky man. His dark hair was combed into a neat, if somewhat greasy, fringe. His eyes darted between the two detectives, never quite making direct contact, instead focusing on a point just past their shoulders or at the ground near their feet.

Reggie showed his identification and introduced themselves. 'Terry Kane?'

'Yes.' He reached up to adjust his greasy fringe. 'Can I help?' His voice was soft and barely audible above the breeze.

'Can we come in and talk please, Mr Kane?' Sharon asked. 'It concerns a friend of yours from a long time ago.'

His eyes focused on Sharon's for the first time. 'Greg?'

Sharon nodded. 'Yes. What made you think of Greg?'

The eyes were down again. 'You said friend.' He stepped back, opening the door wider to allow them entry, his movements precise. 'I've never had many of them. And you said a long time ago...'

Sharon and Reggie entered.

'... back then, I only had one.'

Chapter Thirty Seven

THE LOUNGE WAS IMMACULATELY CLEAN, almost sterile in its tidiness. The air held a faint aroma of lemon-scented cleaning products. There were several abstract paintings around the room. Bold colours and chaotic shapes created an almost jarring contrast against the clinical whiteness of the walls.

'Interesting art.' Reggie pointed at a collection of red and blue swirls, which dominated one wall. He stared for a moment.

Reggie's attempt to comprehend it impressed Sharon. Even though, the way his brow started to crease showed he was failing miserably.

Terry nodded, his hand again moving to adjust his fringe. 'My father's. I've changed nothing since he passed.' His eyes flickered briefly to the painting before returning to a neutral point in the middle distance. 'The body found down by Tate Hill Pier.' He looked up. 'It was Greg, wasn't it?'

'Yes.' Sharon tried to keep her voice warm with compassion. 'I'm sorry... and we really appreciate you taking the time to speak with us today.' She offered a small smile.

A large, grey sectional sofa dominated one side of the lounge, its cushions perfectly aligned and showing no signs of use. A glass coffee table sat in front of it, its surface unmarred by water rings or clutter. Sharon noticed there were no photographs anywhere, or any other signs of personal touches.

The soft hum of the heating system and the muffled ticking of a clock exacerbated the sterile feel.

'I read that the body was inside a fridge,' Terry said. 'Was Greg killed?'

Sharon nodded. 'I'm afraid it looks that way.'

Terry circled the couch twice. His long fingers on one hand adjusted his fringe, while the other plucked at the hem of his shirt, twisting the fabric. His breathing quickened, becoming shallow and rapid.

Reggie stepped forward to assist, but Sharon held up a hand, shook it and creased her forehead, gesturing him to stop.

He did.

'Is everything okay, Terry?' Sharon asked.

After circling the couch a third time, he moved to the window at the rear of the room. He stared outside, his back to the detectives. His shoulders rose and fell with each quick breath.

Reggie looked at Sharon for a cue. 'Give him a moment,' she mouthed.

Silence and space were the best approach here. Terry was finding it difficult to process this hard information.

The ticking of the clock seemed to grow louder in the stillness, marking the passage of time.

Sharon's gaze drifted to the window he was staring out of.

Was something out there drawing Terry's attention?

Eventually, Terry turned. 'I'm sorry about that.' His voice was strained. 'I sometimes need to move, and sometimes I just need to stop. Does that make sense?' His eyes darted between Sharon and Reggie, seeking reassurance.

'Totally,' Reggie said.

'Of course, Terry. Would you prefer if we stood or sat?'

'It doesn't matter.'

'We'll just stay here, okay?' Sharon said.

Terry nodded. 'I'm going to continue to pace.'

'No problem at all, fella,' Reggie said.

'We will take as long as you need,' Sharon added.

His long strides took him back and forth across the room, from the window to the far wall and back again. His eyes rarely went to the detectives, but often ventured over to the window.

'Okay...' Terry said. 'What would you like to ask me?'

Sharon looked at Reggie, who gave her a swift nod. He was happy to leave the baton with her.

'I know it was a long time ago, Terry, but could you tell us about your friendship with Greg? Were you close? How did you meet?' Sharon asked, slipping her notebook from her pocket. She kept her voice calm, a counterpoint to Terry's nervous energy.

Working his fringe as he moved, Terry said, 'We had another friend to begin with. At primary. But he left. Year 1. So, then there were just the two of us. Peas in a pod, Mum said. Not because we were autistic. Although, that helped us understand each other... but our interests.' He paused briefly and nodded. 'Similar. Animals. We both liked them. Still like them.' A ghost of a smile flitted across his face at the memory, gone almost as soon as it appeared. 'Or at least I do. I can take you to my room if you like. I keep my pictures of animals there.'

'That would be nice,' Sharon said. 'Maybe we could do that later?'

He nodded, went to the window again and gazed out. He sighed. The tension in his shoulders seemed to relax momentarily. 'Greg was obsessed with marine life, could talk about fish for hours, whereas I preferred birds. We'd go birdwatching sometimes, and he'd tell me about the seabirds.' His sentences were becoming more complex and less rushed. He turned in profile. The sun highlighted the sharp angles of his face. 'Greg knew everything about the local marine ecosystem. He'd tell me about the migration patterns of different fish species, how changes in water temperature affected their behaviour... and he loved to draw them. He had these sketchbooks full of detailed drawings of fish and seabirds.' His hand moved from his fringe and through the air, as if sketching, tracing invisible lines.

'You used to walk together, is that right?' Sharon prompted gently, guiding the conversation.

'Yes, most days,' Terry confirmed, his pacing slowing as he focused on the memory. His steps seemed to move in time with his words. 'Buddy.' He lowered his head. 'Buddy.' He turned to face them, tears in his eyes. 'Buddy was so soft.' He was rubbing the tips of his fingers with his thumbs as if recalling the touch of the dog. 'Do you know what happened to him?'

'We don't.'

Terry shook his head and paced again.

'We'd always walk. Me, Greg and Buddy. Unless we were on our way to school, then Buddy went home. Most of the time we walked on the weekends and after school.'

'What did you do on these walks?' Sharon asked.

'There were so many. My favourite was to watch the gulls, look for interesting shells on the beach, or throw balls on the beach for Buddy. He loved the ball.' He turned sharply, returned to the window and stared out. 'Loved the ball.'

Sharon's eyes narrowed slightly. Terry had gravitated towards the window many times now. What was out there that held such significance?

'Greg always seemed to take the same route in the morning, before dropping Buddy off and heading to school.'

'Did you ever walk with him, then?' Sharon asked.

'Never.'

Even though he was facing away, Sharon could tell that he was forcing his fringe over his ear.

'He always wanted to be alone with Buddy on those walks... but only those...'

'Why do you think that was?' Sharon asked.

'That was his quiet time. We both have a quiet time. His was in the morning before school and its chaos. For me, it was nighttime, after all the chaos. Then, I'd sit alone, and I'd draw animals.' He pointed out the window. 'I liked to draw out there.'

'In the garden?' Sharon asked.

Terry didn't answer.

Reggie shifted his weight, catching Sharon's eye. He raised an eyebrow. She suspected he'd also sensed that something relevant was in that garden.

'On the day that Greg disappeared—'

'October 14th, 1998,' Terry cut her off, turning sharply.

'Yes. You remember?' Reggie asked.

But of course he remembers, Reggie! Sharon thought. *It*

was one of the worst, if not the worst, moments of this poor man's life.

'I was ill,' Terry said. 'I was sick over breakfast. So, I never went to school.'

'We've a record of that,' Sharon said.

Terry suddenly paced again, at a faster rhythm. 'I would've known earlier that he hadn't come back from his quiet time with Buddy.' He manipulated his fringe with both hands now. 'That he was lost... that he'd fallen...' His breathing was increasing.

'He didn't fall,' Reggie said.

'I'd have known...' Terry was pushing at his fringe aggressively now. 'He could still be here... Greg could still be here...'

'Terry...' Sharon said in a soothing voice.

Terry paced.

They gave him a moment until he slowed, then she tried again. 'Terry... this isn't your fault.'

Terry stopped, head lowered and took control of his breathing. 'His mum was nice. Katie. Always kind to me. I sometimes still see her. She really understood him. Me. Both of us. Katie comes to see me still.' He nodded at the sofa as if she was there. 'She likes to drink tea and talk about animals with me.'

'What about his father?' Reggie prompted.

Terry's face darkened. He paced again, shaking his head. 'No... no... he understood nobody. He made Greg cry. So many times... he made Greg cry.'

'Can you remember why he made him cry?' Reggie asked.

'He always wanted Greg to change. To be different. To grow up. To like football. To be like the other boys.' He was back to rubbing his fringe. 'One time, he told him to stop drawing. To give it up. Told him it was a waste of time.'

He turned and returned to the window, back to look at whatever was offering comfort.

Sharon edged forward. 'Did you know the reverend Ray Lawson?'

'No... Greg liked him though. He was nice. He listened to him. Talked about his problems.'

'Did they spend a lot of time together?' Sharon asked.

'I think so. I think he sometimes met with him during his quiet times. During that morning walk. Greg never talked about him too much. He just said that the reverend was helping him to understand himself more, and that I should speak to him, too.'

'And did you?'

'I thought about it... but then Greg was gone. And everything just went quiet... silent... for a time, and then I didn't see how I could speak to him. I don't go to church, like Greg did. My parents weren't religious. I left it be.'

'How about the florist, Lilly Petrova? He bought flowers from her on the day he disappeared.'

'He said she was nice. He used to tell me about all of her flowers. He said there was nowhere in the world that smelled like it. And she liked his drawings. Greg wanted to talk about his drawings with everyone.'

Sharon knew Frank and Gerry were with Lilly Petrova now. She wondered if they'd gotten her to reveal this truth – that she'd known Greg longer than she'd initially said... that they were close.

How had they not discovered this from Terry in the initial investigation? They should have questioned him at length. This irritated Sharon, and she wondered how equipped they'd been to interview a young autistic boy back then. Still, they should have given it their best shot.

'Did you know about his father's affair with Raven Blackstone?'

'That night... the night *before* he disappeared, he found out about his father and Raven. He phoned me on the landline. He sounded sad. So sad. I didn't know what to say. Do you think if I'd have said the right thing, Greg would still be here?'

Sharon looked at Reggie, who looked back with sadness in his eyes.

'I don't think that would be the case,' Reggie said.

Sharon smiled at Reggie, grateful for his expression of sympathy, and then chanced another step closer to the window.

'What about other friends or acquaintances?' Sharon said. 'Did Greg spend time with anyone else?'

Terry turned from the window. 'Greg found it hard. I found it hard.' He took a deep breath. 'Still do. But we had each other, and we had Buddy.' His fringe swung down. He breathed on his hand and then pounded it back again, flattening it down as best he could. 'Now I have no one. Just people who help me. Bring me food. Walk with me. But they're just doing a job. They aren't my friends, not really. I've a job at McDonald's, but again, they just make me clean, and speak to me like I don't understand them, but I do understand. And I read, and probably have a larger vocabulary than some of them, but no one sees that.'

Sharon said, 'I'm sure there are many people who like you, Terry, you're very likeable.'

He turned back to the window. 'I'm a ticking time bomb. I melt down too often. Everyone tiptoes around me, talks to me like a baby. No one realises that it isn't them that causes the meltdowns.' He pointed at his head. 'It's me...' He stared out the window. 'All the people who understood that have gone. They all need to loosen up. Like you. I like to talk. I like to speak properly with people.'

Sharon's heart ached for Terry. His isolation was palpable. This fascination and connection to looking out the window was linking him to happier times somehow.

'Terry,' she said, 'we found a message on Greg's pager from the day he disappeared. It said "losing control. Meet WA. Bring" Does that mean anything to you?'

Terry worked his hair, thinking. 'WA... could be a person? A place? WA? Whitby Abbey? We walked there sometimes. But he lost nothing. Buddy liked it. He liked to walk the path near the graves. Buddy... Greg... there were good times... wonderful times.' He put his hands to the glass. His breath fogged the glass, creating expanding and contracting circles with each exhalation.

Sharon closed the gap, so she was standing alongside him. She looked out of the window, trying to see what had his attention.

He was looking at a small copse of trees at the bottom of the garden. A tapestry of reds, golds and browns, swaying gently in the breeze. Nestled high in the branches was a dilapidated wooden structure – a weathered and sagging treehouse. Patches of green moss clung to the corners. A rope ladder, frayed and darkened with age, dangled from the entrance, swinging slightly in the wind.

'Terry,' Sharon asked, her voice low and careful, 'what's out there? In that treehouse?'

Reggie had silently moved closer, his presence a steady support at Sharon's back. The air in the room seemed to thicken with anticipation.

Terry worked at his fringe. 'Greg.'

Chapter Thirty-Eight

DOWN IN THE CELLAR, it was damp and musty.

Since reaching the last step, Frank hadn't heard any more thumping sounds.

He saw another door opposite the last step. Slowly, he made his way over to it and pressed his ear against it. He could hear a clattering, and a whistling, which sounded like wind.

Turning his head, he called up the steps to Lilly, 'Is there a door leading out of this room?'

'Yes,' Lilly called down. 'Leads out to a set of iron steps up to ground level. It's locked though. There's a light switch on your left when you go in.'

The key was in the lock. He grabbed a broom from the wall alongside him, turned the key, and opened the door. He called into the room, 'DCI Frank Black. Police. If anyone is in here, I need you on the floor, hands behind your head... Otherwise it's the Taser...' He looked at the broom in his hand. 'I've got it fired up, ready.'

Heart racing, Frank reached in and fumbled for the light switch. His cold fingers were clumsy against the wall.

After finding it, he flooded the room with harsh fluorescent light. He squinted. *That'll do it.*

Before him, the room was chaotic. He noticed a scrunched-up rug just near his feet, and a turned over heater alongside it. In one corner, several stacks of empty terracotta pots teetered precariously. One load had tumbled and smashed, and Frank was certain that was one of the loud noises he'd heard before.

At the far end of the room was a bright slice of daylight. The slice widened and thinned as the door swung outwards, opening and closing. Something was preventing it from slamming shut completely.

He picked his way through the mess, broken pottery crunching beneath his feet. In his hands, he held the broom tensed. He was fairly certain that whoever had been here had gone, but he wasn't taking any chances.

The back door was being wedged open by a watering can on its side. A trickle of water was still seeping from its spout.

He called through the crack. 'Remember the Taser?' Holding his breath, broom in his left hand, Frank pushed on the door and looked outside.

No one was there.

He exhaled and stared up the eight iron steps to street level. Then, still holding the broom, he ascended. He looked up and down the street. Several pedestrians, some shoppers emerging from stores and a couple of dog walkers.

He darted out on the street and moved between them, showing his badge and asking if they'd seen anyone at the back door of the shop. He met shrugs and apologies.

Of course, one of these individuals could have been the very person who'd broken in, but no one stood out to him as particularly suspicious.

He went back down the iron steps, regarded the broken lock on the outside of the back door and then kicked the watering can inside and went in, closing the door behind him.

He sighed. He could imagine Donald with a smug shake of his head and a sly comment: 'A break-in while you were upstairs in the bloody place... and they got away?'

Frank growled as he carefully picked his way through the smashed pottery.

At the foot of the stairs, he asked Lilly and Gerry to join him. He explained that someone had been here.

Lilly's face paled. 'Мамка му.'

'Sorry, what was that?'

'I swore.'

'Aye, fair enough, Ms Petrova.' He made a mental note of the word. It might come in handy on the countless times he wanted to swear around people he shouldn't. 'Has anyone ever advised you to get a security gate?'

'We used to have one. But the hinges rusted too bad, and I had it taken down.'

'Could I suggest another one?'

'Yes...'

'You want to see if they got anything?' He placed the broom back and looked behind himself. 'I mean... what were they after, Ms Petrova? There's an old TV and DVD player, but hardly worth the effort. Are flowers and pots worth stealing?'

'Some rare flowers, but such short life spans... Pots can be expensive.'

Frank sighed. 'Have a look then, please.'

She went inside and looked around.

A few minutes later, she returned. 'It all seems in order. I'll get the door fixed, and a gate put on.'

'When were you last in here?' Gerry asked.

'Yesterday evening. I... I came down to get some extra potting soil for a large order. Everything was fine then. I mean, it hasn't been tidy in a while, but not like this.'

'Okay, we'll call it in. Some uniforms will bob down. Do what they can. At the very least you'll need it for insurance. I'd give them a full inventory of what was down here.' *And I'll look at that list myself, too,* Frank thought.

Upstairs, they concluded the interview quickly. She was very shaken up. Frank asked her again on the way out, 'Ms Petrova, is there anything else you think we should know about you and Greg?'

She paused for a moment, her eyes moving back and forth. Eventually, she shook her head. *Were you considering whether to tell me something?*

'How about the break-in? Any thoughts on why that happened?' he asked.

Again, she shook her head after a pause.

Outside, in the car, Frank turned to Gerry. 'Day break-ins are rare. They're usually desperate robberies. Someone after something valuable in a small window of opportunity.'

'I agree,' Gerry said.

'And I'm not going for pots, or rare flowers. There may be plenty of over-eager gardeners out there, I admit, but that's a step too far. There's something going on here.'

'She was also hiding something at the end.'

'Aye, I noticed that.'

Gerry nodded. 'It was as if she really wanted to tell us something about Greg, but couldn't.'

Frank started the engine. 'Aye. Watch this space, I think.' He looked out the window at the shop. 'One thing I reckon, though.' He looked back at Gerry. 'She didn't kill him.'

'I sensed that too,' Gerry said. 'Kind eyes.'

'I'm not great at assessing the eyes, Gerry,' he said, smiling. 'But she spoke about him with genuine affection. She was almost nurturing. It felt real to me.' He looked at the shop one last time.

So what're you hiding, Lilly?

Chapter Thirty-Nine

After Terry disappeared inside the treehouse, Reggie took hold of the frayed rope ladder.

'What're you doing, sir?' Sharon asked.

He glanced at her and whispered, 'Following Terry into that death trap. What does it look like?'

She pointed up at the childhood relic perched high in the trees. 'You realise that *all* three of us in there will end in disaster?'

'Of course... I never thought you'd be going up.'

'Why not, sir?'

He shrugged. 'Because, as we just said, it isn't safe.'

'That's very gentlemanly of you, sir.'

'It's nothing to do with gender, Sharon, *please.*'

'Well, it's certainly not to do with rank, or you'd send me over the top first.'

He rolled his eyes. 'Am I really to blame for the world's narrow-mindedness? You want the real reason? Anything happens to you, then Frank will roast me, slowly, over a fire.'

Fortunately, Terry was already in the treehouse. Hopefully, he wouldn't hear the whispered bickering. 'He's desperate to do that anyway... Look, sir, I think we both know it would be better with me up there. He's more relaxed around me.'

'Yes, but—'

'Like far more relaxed.'

Reggie let go of the rope ladder, stepped to one side, and gestured toward it. 'Just be careful, okay?'

'I will, sir.' She winked. 'Now give the little girl some independence!'

He looked irritated. 'It was never anything to do with bloody gender! Age, if anything.'

'If it was age, then I should definitely be the one doing this.' She started to climb.

'Ageist. I'll have you know that my stats show that I'm fitter than the average twenty-five-year-old.'

Sharon bit back a retort about having read an article about how regularly smart watches were inaccurate with fitness measurements, and concentrated on taming the weaving rope ladder.

Once she'd pulled herself through the hatch, she lay back on the wood.

It creaked.

'Don't worry,' Terry said. 'It's always creaked... Like I told you before, I still treat the wood. It's not rotten. I check the ropes and trees regularly, too.'

His reassurance didn't help with her palpitations.

She sat up, turned over onto her knees, and looked around. The interior was about two metres by three. She raised herself to her feet, until her head was just touching the peak of the sloped roof. If she moved further in, she'd have to crouch back down. 'This is impressive, Terry.'

'Yes,' Terry said. He pushed his fringe back. 'Greg and I

designed it, and my father helped us build it. It's about five square metres.'

She smiled at Terry as he fidgeted with the hem of his shirt, and then she took another look around.

It was like a time capsule from Greg and Terry's childhood. Piles of comics, Monopoly and some other recognisable board games were stacked in one corner.

The walls had posters of marine life and various bird species pinned to them, the creases through them showing they'd been plucked from magazines.

On the wall, there was even a shelf crammed with dog-eared books on animals and nature. Sharon noticed titles like *The Complete Guide to British Seabirds* and *Whales of the North Sea*. Frequent use had cracked their spines.

There was a handwritten sign on one wall: 'Greg and Terry's Secret Base'.

Sharon's chest tightened as she imagined the two children working together as one. The ultimate team. Unaware that their world would one day be shattered so horribly.

Terry went and sat in the corner and hugged a stuffed octopus. Its long blue tentacles lay against his stomach. 'This is Captain Inkspot. I bought him for Greg for his tenth birthday. We kept him up here to guard the place.'

Sharon smiled. 'Good call. No one is going to mess with an octopus.' Sharon took a careful step forward, trying not to wince as the floorboards groaned beneath her.

'Sharon?' Reggie's voice drifted up. 'Everything okay?'

'We're fine,' she called back, keeping her eyes on Terry.

Terry was rocking as he held Captain Inkspot. The structure felt as if it was swaying. It clearly hadn't been built for fully grown adults.

Terry's voice quavered as he spoke. 'You know, Captain

Inkspot is a good listener. After Greg went, I talked to him often.'

He pressed the soft toy to his mouth. 'I missed him so much. And I missed Buddy. I still do.'

Sharon felt a lump forming in her throat. Terry was thirty-nine. The loss he'd experienced at thirteen had defined two-thirds of his life so far. His parents were gone. She wondered who, apart from the octopus, listened to him, tried to help him. Before, he'd spoken of how people walked on eggshells around him, babying him, not willing to risk his emotional state. But was that compassionate? Supporting someone because of their special educational needs had to go beyond that. Had anyone actually tried to help him deal with his sense of loss?

'When they told me Greg was gone, I couldn't understand. I just kept asking, "Where's Buddy? Where's Buddy?"' His voice cracked. 'Greg would never leave Buddy. *Never.* Yet no one seemed interested in Buddy. And I kind of understand that. But Buddy was so important to him. So, if they cared about him, they needed to care about Buddy too. But they didn't. And nobody listened to me.'

Sharon's gaze fell to a pin board covered in photographs. She moved closer, careful not to disturb Terry. The images told a story of two boys growing up together, always with a golden retriever by their side. Each photo was a window into a world of shared joys and simple pleasures.

She studied each picture carefully, feeling as if she were piecing together a puzzle.

There was Greg and Terry at the beach, watching Buddy bounding through the waves. Sharon could almost hear the laughter and the crash of the surf. Another showed the boys in this very treehouse, poring over a bird identification guide, Buddy's head resting on Greg's lap. Their faces were alight with curiosity and wonder. 'Who took these photographs?'

'My mother,' Terry said.

Sharon nodded and regarded a Christmas day snapshot captured both boys meeting up with one another to exchange gifts. Buddy was nosing at the discarded paper at their feet. The joy on their faces was palpable. A time when the world was full of magic and possibility.

'You three were inseparable,' Sharon said.

Terry nodded, his rocking slowing slightly. 'Buddy understood us. He never thought we were weird or different. I always felt content around him.'

Sharon couldn't help but think of Gerry. Her understanding of her colleague deepened slightly.

'The bond between animals and humans can be so strong,' Sharon said.

Terry's face brightened. 'Yes... it can.'

As she looked around, Sharon noticed a jar filled with seashells on a small table. A crudely made mobile hung from the ceiling, fashioned from driftwood and feathers. It spun gently in the breeze, creating soft sounds.

In one corner, she spotted a stack of composition notebooks. Sharon gently opened the top one, revealing pages filled with Greg's neat handwriting – observations about the local wildlife, sketches of fish and birds, and musings about the sea. It was a glimpse into the mind of a curious, thoughtful boy who saw wonder in the natural world.

'He liked to write and draw,' Sharon said.

Terry's voice was barely above a whisper. 'Yes. Greg had this way of writing things down... explaining things... he said it helped him make sense of things when the world got too loud. He made things clear... to me... in a way no one else has ever done since.'

Sharon realised, in that moment, that this wasn't just a childhood hideout. It was a shrine to a friendship cut tragically short, a testament to the bond between two boys who'd found solace in each other's company and in the natural world around them.

As Sharon shifted her weight, her ankle caught on something solid against the edge. She looked down to see a misshapen threadbare rug. Something was beneath it. She knelt and lifted the corner and saw an old toolbox. 'What's this, Terry?' she asked, taking hold of it.

There was a loud creak as Terry stood. It jarred the treehouse, and Sharon stumbled as she stood holding the box.

She kept her footing and steadied herself against the wall, looking up in time to see Terry quickly coming towards her. He cast Captain Inkspot to one side.

'Terry—'

The words died in her mouth when he aggressively snatched the toolbox from her hands. '*No!* Don't!'

'Terry, stop... What's—'

'You can't have it!' He backed away, clutching the box to his chest like he had done the octopus.

She noticed he was close to the open trapdoor. 'Careful, Terry, behind—'

Again, he cut her off. 'Greg told me to take care of it. Never show anyone. You had no right picking it up.'

Sharon held up her hands. 'It's okay, Terry. I won't touch it. I don't want it. Calm down. I promise.'

Terry stopped an inch from the open trapdoor.

'Everything okay?' Reggie called.

'Yes,' Sharon said. Internally, she was pleading, *Keep quiet, Reggie!*

'I promised. I promised Greg.' Terry's voice was trembling. He held the box against his chest with one arm, and rubbed hard at his fringe.

'I know... and that's fine.' Sharon kept her hands up. 'Take it easy and I'll forget I ever saw it.'

'This is destructive.' He glanced at the box in one hand. 'Greg told me so.' He pounded his fringe. 'I'm *so* stupid.'

The treehouse creaked and moved as Terry shifted his weight. A small model boat tumbled from a nearby shelf, clattering to the floor. Sharon flinched, fearful that Terry would take another step backwards through the open hatch.

Reggie said, 'I want you both to come down.'

Terry's eyes were darting from side to side. He didn't know what to do.

Shut up, Reggie! 'Just relax,' Sharon said, chancing another step, her voice as soothing as she could make it.

'Come down now!' Reggie insisted.

For God's sake, Reggie, Sharon thought, gritting her teeth.

Terry was shaking his hand, rubbing hard at his fringe. 'He's going to take it from me.'

'No he won't! I won't let—'

'Now!' Reggie shouted.

Terry spun, the box was clutched under one arm. He put a foot on the rope ladder.

It was too soon to breathe a sigh of relief. 'Careful,' Sharon said, coming forward. 'You need two hands on that ladder.'

He ignored her and climbed down one handed.

She stared down. Her heart hammered in her chest.

He was swinging back and forth, struggling. She knelt and reached down. 'Please just give me the box, Terry. I won't open it. You've my word. Just give me the box, so you don't fall.'

He looked up at her, wide eyed. He looked as if he was considering it. Then, he shook his head. 'No. You're lying.' He jerked away and spun out from the ladder, holding onto the rope with one hand. The force threw the toolbox from his hand, and he went to grab it with the other, relinquishing his grip.

'Terry!'

Sharon watched in horror as the toolbox clattered to the ground, followed less than a second later by Terry with a sickening thud.

Chapter Forty

As FRANK DROVE BACK towards HQ, he ran through the encounter with Lilly again and again, in case he'd missed something. However, the Audi he'd checked out from HQ was far too quiet to drive, far quieter than Bertha, anyway, and he found the silence unnerving and distracting. He couldn't imagine there were many people in the world who longed for a car that ruptured your eardrums and shook you to the point of a hernia, but he certainly did at the moment.

'I've a question,' Gerry said. 'It's personal.'

Frank's jaw clenched involuntarily.

'Okay?'

'What if I said no?'

'I wouldn't ask.'

He sighed. 'Go on.'

'What do you do for fun and relaxation these days, Frank?'

Seriously?

He regarded her out of the corner of his eye. 'I thought you were happy with Tom. Don't you dare ask me out on a date.'

She creased her brow. 'That would be inappropriate... You're being sarcastic, aren't you?'

Frank laughed. 'I play music, smoke in my garden and sometimes, I get fish and chips. In no particular order.'

'Do you socialise?'

He snorted. 'As in talk to others?'

'Yes.'

'Isn't that what we're doing now? In fact, isn't that what we do, every day?'

'This isn't socialising.'

He smiled. 'If you're sure... then, no, I don't socialise.'

'I thought so.'

He shook his head. 'Why are my social skills that bad? Or... actually, come to think of it... is that Helen's thought transferred into your brain by a phone call... in the same way a lot of her thoughts are being transferred to you these days?'

'Helen said you used to go to the pub often. That you had an active social life.'

'Bloody hell.' He snorted. 'This gets better and better. I knock the booze on the head, and now you want me back in the chuffin' pub! Just brilliant.'

'It's about the fact you went to the pub to see people you liked.'

He shrugged. 'Yes, but I also went to the pub to drink beer I liked ... so...'

'Pubs sell soft drinks.'

He glanced at her. Gerry certainly looked serious. But then, that was nothing new.

'I don't drink soft drinks.'

'You could have water or—'

'You miss the point, Gerry.'

She creased her brow.

'I'm not going to the pub, I'm not drinking soft drinks or water, and if you want me to socialise, then I'll socialise with you. Shall we leave it at that?'

Gerry held up her phone. 'I've found a group called "Souls and Spirits".'

'You what?'

'"Souls and Spirits".'

'Sounds like a religious shoe shop.'

'It's a mental health running club.'

'I'll stop you there. Running? Mental health? I think one will definitely have an effect on the other, but not in the way you may hope...'

'They meet up, run, then go to pubs or cafes afterward.'

'For soft drinks?' Frank rolled his eyes.

'No, to socialise.'

Frank's phone rang. He let out a sigh of relief. He answered, putting it on speaker. 'Sean? What've you got?'

Sean's voice crackled through the speaker. 'Sir, I've been interviewing Kath Lawson. She was very talkative. Most of it was fairly standard. Accounts of daily routines, involvement in various church committees. I've made notes, but I've something significant here that I think you'd want to know. It's about the woman who attacked him in church.'

He looked at Gerry, who already had her notebook out. 'Go on, Sean.'

'She thinks, or rather, she's absolutely adamant that this woman who attacked Ray knew him.'

Frank's eyebrows shot up. 'Really? Now that wasn't what the good reverend said to us, was it now, Gerry?'

'No,' she said, simply.

'She called him by name,' Sean said.

'Could she have got his name elsewhere, though?' Frank asked.

'I suggested that, but she wasn't interested. She was convinced that this woman knew him. She said the way she spoke to him, about believing him, before she clawed at him... it all sounded too familiar.

'Sean, start speaking to the parishioners who witnessed it. Someone might know who this woman is.'

After the call ended, Frank's face hardened. He waited for a break in the traffic and performed a sharp U-turn. 'Will I go to hell for calling a man of the cloth a lying bastard?'

'I can't answer that, Frank. I'm not religious and I don't believe in hell.'

'Really? You don't believe in hell? You've not been alive long enough then, Gerry. This world is a living hell... and you'd hope a clergyman like the good Reverend Lawson would try his hardest to make it less so, rather than lie to our sodding faces.'

And God help you Reverend if you try to lie your way out of this one, he thought.

Chapter Forty One

RAY ENDED THE CALL.

He dabbed at the sweat on his brow with trembling hands.

Time was now of the essence.

After a quick, desperate glass of wine, he reached for his jacket and darted out through the vestry door, almost taking out Pam.

She stumbled back in time, a stack of papers clutched to her chest.

'I'm sorry, Pam...'

'Are you okay?'

'Yes... fine... just late for an appointment.'

'Oh. Look, Reverend, I was just coming to see you about the—'

'I really am late.' Ray slipped past her and headed for the church door.

He heard Pam's shoes clicking on the stone floor as she chased after him. 'But the fete committee is waiting for your approval.'

'It'll have to wait.' He'd failed to keep the edge out of his voice; it would be a noticeable contrast to his usual patient tone.

At the church door, he heard Pam try one last time. 'Reverend, please. Mrs Hodgson is quite insistent about the cake stall placement—'

Ray spun. 'I've more important matters to attend to than bloody cake stalls!'

The words hung in the air between them. Pam's eyes widened, hurt and shock clear on her face. In all the years she'd worked for him, Ray had never raised his voice, never dismissed her in this manner.

Immediately, Ray felt a wave of shame wash over him. He took a deep breath, trying to centre himself. It took another couple before he had enough clarity. 'I'm so sorry, Pam. That was uncalled for. It's just... there's an urgent matter I must attend to. A soul in need. Forgive me.'

Pam lowered her eyes. 'Of course, Reverend. I understand. Shall I reschedule the committee meeting?'

Ray nodded, already turning towards the door. 'Yes, please. We'll talk when I return. And I'll make this up to you.'

He didn't wait for her response, pushing through the heavy wooden doors and out into the crisp autumn air. He hurried across the graveyard to his car, his shirt clinging to his back with cold sweat. He could feel Pam's bewildered gaze on his back.

You fool, he thought. *You fool for losing control.*

After starting the engine, he looked in the rear-view mirror and traced the scratch marks on his face.

I'm coming Megan.

His outreach programmes with troubled youth around North Yorkshire had provided him with many reliable contacts. Ray had acquired Megan's address easier than expected. One of the programmes had helped to house her in Starbeck, which was nestled between Harrogate and Knaresborough. He knew it well enough.

He put the car into gear, thinking of Megan's furious face as she said, 'I believed you. I looked into your eyes, and I believed you.' He reversed, images of Graham on the ground far below him, by the railway track. Then, his wheels squealed on the ground as he accelerated, pictures of Greg in his mind's eye, on that final day, when he'd folded over broken, in the vestry, in despair over his father's betrayals.

Ray's failures.

Not God's.

His.

Lord, guide me. Help me not to fail again.

The familiar streets of Whitby blurred past as he sped towards the motorway. Then, he saw Megan's face again. This time, not as the furious, desperate woman who'd tried to take his eyes, but as the young, frightened girl who'd put her belief in him.

Chapter Forty-Two

Frank and Gerry marched through the graveyard of St Claude's Church. It was a patchwork of weathered headstones and autumn leaves. Frank's eyes were drawn to the marble surface of an ornate headstone gleaming in the late afternoon sun.

He thought of Mary's headstone, the flowers he decorated it with, the updates he gave to her on both his life and the search for their daughter.

Then, for some reason, he thought of Evelyn Wainwright again. That bitter argument by her husband's gravestone.

Rylan was first to the heavy wooden door of St Claude's. His nose twitched as he sniffed at the ancient oak surface, scarred by centuries of use. Frank reached out and touched the door first, then rapped his knuckles against it. The sound echoed hollowly in the quiet churchyard.

Thunk.

The door creaked open. He recognised Pam from their visit the day before.

The church secretary stood in the doorway, her eyes

puffy and red-rimmed, a crumpled tissue clutched in one hand. Her neat appearance from yesterday was no more. She looked as if she'd been running her hands through her hair in distress. 'Hello again...' Her voice wavered.

'Are you okay, Mrs Eastwood?'

'Yes, sorry... just really tired. Can I help?'

'Is Reverend Lawson here?'

She shook her head. 'He left in quite a hurry.'

'Why?'

'I don't know. He said he'd an urgent appointment.'

Frank wondered if this was the reason behind her unease. *What had happened here?* 'Did he say anything about his appointment?'

Pam shook her head.

'We heard that the woman who attacked him may have known him,' Frank said.

She shook her head and looked down. 'I don't know anything about that. I'd never seen her before. She just charged at him and started clawing at him.'

'The reverend's wife told my colleague that she knew his name?'

Pam didn't respond.

'Mrs Eastwood?'

This snapped Pam out of it. She looked up. 'Yes. She did. I don't know who she was, though. It was all too strange.'

'Okay... are you sure everything is all right? You look shaken up.'

Pam shook her head. 'I don't think I am, really. Since she attacked him, he's been different. Distracted. Then, now, he looked like a man... possessed by some kind of evil spirit.' Her eyes widened. 'Sorry about my use of words,' she mumbled.

'No need to be sorry,' Gerry said.

She wasn't apologising to us, Frank thought, glancing in at the church.

'Could you get us a list together of everyone who was in the church on the Saturday, during the attack?'

'Yes. Of course.' Pam nodded. 'I'll get right on it.'

Afterwards, Frank said to Gerry, 'She seems shocked and upset. Let's get a BOLO out on Ray, and his car.'

Gerry nodded, already dialling on her phone to issue the Be On the Lookout.

Something's not right, Frank thought, standing beside the car, staring at the crumbling church. *Something's not right at all.*

First, goth queen Raven Blackstone, and the black hole that was her identity before moving to Whitby. Then, Bulgarian florist, Lilly Petrova, and the mysterious break-in. And now, a popular public figure, a reverend, lying to the police following a vicious attack, out there on urgent business up to God knows what.

None of it was fitting together. Nothing was making sense. The mystery seemed to be branching out in all kinds of directions, constantly raising more questions rather than answering any.

He looked up to the heavens. *Anything else you'd like to throw my way?*

His phone buzzed. *Is this my answer?* he thought.

The call was from Sharon. He walked away from Gerry who was putting in the request for the BOLO on Ray.

Sharon relayed the events of Terry's interview. Frank listened intently, his frown deepening as she described Terry's fall from the treehouse, and the recovery of a mysterious item from a metal toolbox.

Afterwards, he went over to Gerry, and then continued their walk back to the car.

'I just spoke to Sharon.'

'And?'

'Terry Kane broke his ankle falling from a treehouse.'

Gerry looked at him, brow creased.

'I'll explain in the car. It seems he got protective over a VHS tape in an old metal toolbox.'

'A VHS tape,' Gerry said. 'Do we know what's on it?'

'The tape is snapped inside. And the cassette was further damaged by the fall.'

'The slow decline of the VHS started around 1997. It could have something relevant to our period of time.'

Frank nodded. 'It's already off to forensics to see what they can get off it. Now, let's get to HQ before the end of the day, and update that board.' He tapped his head. 'It's like spaghetti junction in here now. Threads of evidence tangling and intersecting, each one potentially leading us to Greg or down another dead end. I need to see it all laid out, to untangle this mess before it completely overwrites my brain.'

Chapter Forty-Three

Lilly sat with Nikolai behind the shop counter, their hands intertwined, voices low.

Nikolai leaned in and kissed her forehead. 'Keep reminding yourself that the children are safe. I've seen Ivana and the other two children with their new families. They'll have good lives. We succeeded. *You* succeeded.'

'I know that but think about how close we came. If we hadn't moved them last night... I can only imagine...'

'But we did. You warned me, I made the call. We accelerated everything and it worked out.'

'Worked out! He broke in to kidnap the kids!'

'And failed.'

'*This* time. You said he was past it? That he wouldn't do anything drastic?'

He shrugged. 'Maybe he was just trying to scare us. Maybe he wouldn't have actually tried to take the children.'

'You do realise that this is all over now, don't you? That this bastard has ended it all?'

He shook his head. 'No... we won't let that happen.'

She could feel her pulse quickening, the weight of their

situation pressing down on her like a physical force. 'How could you be so naïve?'

He chewed his bottom lip.

'Georgi won't let this go,' she continued. 'He'll keep coming back. Checking. He'll have me watched twenty-four hours a day! He won't stop until he's getting a share of the profits.'

'There are no profits, and never will be.'

'He's already made it clear he won't be letting that slide.'

'But—'

'There are no buts!' She shuffled away from him. The space between them felt vast, filled with unspoken fears. 'He'll force himself into the situation like he tried to force himself into it earlier today.'

Nikolai raised his eyes and stared at her for a short time. 'You're forgetting our options. You know there are some.' His eyes narrowed, his tone menacing.

Lilly felt a chill run down her spine, remembering the Nikolai she'd known years ago, before he'd changed. For a moment, she saw a glimpse of the man he used to be, and it terrified her. 'And that makes us no better than them.'

'It could be a means to an end. And it won't be us. Powerful people who want good for these children. They've no time for thugs like Georgi.'

'No,' she hissed. 'No. Okay? I don't want to be part of that.'

'Then we pay him?' Nikolai said.

'But you know it'll never be enough. He'll keep coming back. No. We just stop. We've done what we can. There's nothing we can do.'

They both sat in silence for a short time.

'What're you thinking?' Lilly asked.

He responded with a loud exhalation. 'That I love you.'

She smiled, but that fleeting moment of happiness didn't reach her eyes. The weight of their situation hung heavy in the air between them.

He clucked his tongue for a while and then said, 'I guess then all I can do is talk to him. Try to make him understand that his time is over. Tell him he'll get one final payout.'

'No.' She hit her thigh with her hand. 'He'll keep coming back. Look, I don't want him involved, connected. Eventually, he'll force it into becoming something different. Like it used to be. Like it was for me. He won't be able to help himself. He'll push and he'll push.'

'But if we can still help other children, then we have to try. Even if we're forced to take just a small profit for him?'

'No. That will be a never-ending road. The man consumes.' She crossed her arms. 'He'll consume more and more and then he'll take everything. Promise me you won't offer him anything.'

He didn't speak.

'If you love me, promise me.'

He nodded, but she struggled to see the conviction in his expression.

'What happened with the police earlier, anyway?' he asked. 'You mentioned they were asking about Greg? How much did you tell them?'

'Well, I didn't tell them about Georgi if that's what you're getting at, but I covered everything else. The sketchbooks. His drawings.' She lowered her head. 'They were so good.' She looked back up. 'I admitted he came regularly.'

'And?'

'That was the point he broke in downstairs, so we all became distracted. I don't think it'll be the last I hear from them though. Maybe that's a good thing. Maybe I should just tell them the truth.'

'About Georgi?'

'Yes.'

'Ridiculous. It wasn't him. He didn't kill that boy. And if you get him involved, he'll drag all of us down with him.'

'How do you know it wasn't him?'

'Same reason I knew then. Common sense.'

'Listen.' Her voice was low but intense, filled with a mixture of fear and conviction. 'I was here. I saw the way he looked at Greg that morning. I saw the suspicion in his eyes. You think killing someone is above Georgi?'

'Not a local boy... I can't see him inviting that much trouble on himself.'

She sighed. 'No. He's stupid and capable enough.'

Nikolai shook his head. 'Just don't. Don't speak to them about Georgi. Everything will fall to pieces...'

She glared at him. 'Georgi watched me through the window as I comforted Greg that morning. I can't get it out of my head. I can't shake that paranoid look in his eyes.'

'But you told him it was about his father having an affair!'

'Georgi wouldn't buy it! He saw his tears... my tears. Georgi said his father had cheated on his mother, and it had never reduced him to tears. He was cold. Georgi raged that morning after Greg left. He was too paranoid... he was drinking a lot, back then, too, as you know, and taking God knows what. I remember how swollen his eyes were... how out of it he was. He accused me of sharing secrets about how I came to this country with a kid I barely knew, and I think he genuinely believed it.'

'And if he did, he would've gone away, spoken to someone, and then, surely, his rational thought processes would have kicked in...'

'Rational? Listen to yourself, Nikolai. I think you've forgotten what he's like.'

'Oh, I haven't. I remember well enough.'

'Do you really not think it was too much of a coincidence? I mean, I never saw Greg again. No one did! He vanished. How can I not even suspect he had something to do with it? How can you not?'

'But you made peace with this—'

'Only because I was convinced he'd died from an accident. If the police were convinced, why shouldn't I be? Now we find out he was in a fridge. I'm sorry... come on, Nikolai... a fridge. **Мамка му**!' The Bulgarian curse slipped out. 'And if it was Georgi...'

'You need to stop.' Nikolai took her hands. He leaned in closer.

'If it was him then you know what that means.'

'Stop, Lilly.' She could see him pleading with his eyes, desperate for her not to say what was coming next.

'It'd be my fault. *All* my fault Greg died. I shouldn't have befriended Greg. I should have known I was too dangerous. Like Dimitar always warned me. Never get too close to anyone.'

Nikolai wrapped his arms around her. 'You can't blame yourself. You were a child who struggled, too. Greg needed support, and you offered some. That makes you a good person. Anything else is illogical. Despite that, honestly, I get your concerns, but I really don't believe Georgi would risk everything by murdering a child... it's too far-fetched. He's a nasty bastard, but not a child killer.'

'Just like you were sure that he wouldn't do something silly regarding the other issue?'

'That's different.'

'How?'

'Murdering a local thirteen-year-old? I think you're tired, and not thinking—'

A sharp knock at the door cut him off.

The sound echoed through her bones. Her breath caught in her throat. What if it was him? Georgi?

She stared at Nikolai, wide eyed.

She could tell from his expression that he thought the same thing.

She peered over the counter they knelt behind.

'It's him,' she whispered.

That was why they were kneeling, that was why the cellar door was open beside them. 'Okay, Nikolai, go.'

Nikolai looked at the open cellar door and then back at her.

He hesitated.

There was another heavy knock.

'*Now.*' She raised her voice.

He remained. This was the first time he'd ever refused to do what she'd asked.

'You promised.' She narrowed her eyes.

There was a third heavier knock. She'd be surprised if Georgi got to a fourth without kicking the door in.

'I'm sorry,' Nikolai said. He kissed her. 'I love you but this has to stop.' He stood. 'You'll see this is for the best.'

He darted around the counter.

She jumped up and chased, but by the time she got to him, he was already opening the door.

Lilly sensed that her world was about to burn.

Chapter Forty-Four

FOLLOWING A DAY OF UNSETTLING EVENTS, Bertha's rattles and groans gave Frank comfort and familiarity.

He eased Bertha around two young boys on bikes, wondering why they didn't have lights or helmets on, and cursing their parents.

In the rear-view mirror, he glanced at their laughing faces.

Excitement and impetuousness.

If they didn't meet an unfortunate end on the road, they were starting out on a journey. They had the world at their feet. An adventure to be had.

And then there was Greg Lyle.

Frozen. No journey, no adventure. His world now a fridge. Discarded with no compassion.

He hoped the parents of these young cyclists didn't live to regret not ensuring their children were safe on the road.

Regrets.

He thought of Maddie. Not frozen. Midway through a journey, but it certainly wasn't an adventure. At least not in the positive sense of the word.

In fact, she was completely lost in a world he couldn't understand or even reach.

You're a hypocrite, Frank, he thought. *Cursing the parents of these two young cyclists! Curse yourself!*

Maddie, at thirteen, had been filled with fierce determination for art. Frank had pushed her towards more practical pursuits. He'd dismissed her passion as a passing phase.

It was akin to the day that he sent his child out with no lights and no helmet.

As he pulled up to his house, Frank's eyes instinctively scanned the street for the lurking Ford Cortina. No sign.

He caught the telltale twitch of curtains next door. Henrietta Timber, his ever-vigilant neighbour, was undoubtedly cataloguing his late arrival.

Frank sat in the car for a moment. His house loomed before him, a dark silhouette against the night sky. It always felt so unwelcoming.

Once upon a time, Mary and Maddie had lived there.

Now it was dark and silent.

What made it worse was the fridge full of healthy food and a lack of beer.

For what reason?

To keep him alive longer?

For what purpose?

Frank locked Bertha and made his way to the front door. Henrietta still stared at him. He'd considered getting a video doorbell outside his house recently. In the end, he'd decided there was no point, not while Henrietta was still offering such a dedicated service.

He inserted his door key but couldn't turn it.

The door was already unlocked.

Bloody hell.

He may have been sixty-five years old, but if decades as

a copper had instilled one permanent habit that was in no danger from later life absent-mindedness, it was that you never left your house unlocked.

Never.

Ever.

Heart picking up pace, he picked up 'Grumpy Gus', a gnome that Mary had bought a few years before her passing. Mary had named him, and had referred to Frank as Gus, whenever he was in a bad mood.

For this reason, Frank had grown attached to the gnome. He'd hate to see him broken.

But needs must, and it was a better weapon than that bloody broom from earlier in Lilly's shop.

'Hello?' Frank called out, his voice echoing in the darkened hallway. He moved cautiously through his bungalow, flicking on lights and checking each room, Grumpy Gus ready. The sitting room was undisturbed... two empty bottles of soda water on the table – some soft drinks to keep Gerry and Helen proud. The kitchen was as he'd left it, too.

His own bedroom was untouched and dishevelled.

He cast an eye over Maddie's room, but that looked undisturbed.

He looked at the gnome. 'Well, Gus, seems I'm finally cracking. Donald will be rubbing his hands together. He'll have me out to pasture before the year is out.'

He plucked some soda water from the fridge and a raw carrot, and sat and stared at a blank television screen, crunching on the raw vegetable. Halfway through, he tossed it on the table. 'No wonder I'm cracking up. I've switched to Bugs Bunny's diet!'

Less than a minute later, he stood and pointed at Gus, who he'd placed on the table, and who seemed to scowl down at the half-eaten carrot. 'I'm not having it, Gus. There are a lot of things wrong with this miserable old bastard, granted.' He pointed at his head. 'But this noggin is still firing.'

He headed next door and knocked. Henrietta regarded him from the window and then came to answer. She looked him up and down. Her eighty-year-old stern face was pinched with surprise and mild irritation.

Henrietta used to have a lot of time for Mary and Maddie as a child. Never for Frank. Any man that spent that much time neglecting his wife and daughter was no man in her eyes. These days, he agreed with her, but this was one stubborn mind he was dealing with, and the possibility of trying to convince her he recognised the error of his ways seemed fantastical, and therefore pointless.

He'd need to get to the point quickly. He'd be lucky to get a minute on her doorstep.

'Evening, Henrietta,' Frank said, trying to keep his tone light. 'Sorry to bother you, but my door was unlocked when I got home. Knowing what a good eye you keep on this street, I wondered if you spotted anyone coming by.'

She raised an eyebrow. 'Maybe tell your daughter to lock the door on the way out? She was the last out.'

The world around him suddenly tilted. He stumbled back. If not for the door frame, he'd have gone over.

'Are you okay?' she asked.

Mind suddenly racing, he stared at his hand, white from gripping the doorframe. 'Aye... sorry... I think you're mistaken.'

'I'm not mistaken. More than likely that's you, Frank. After all, you don't look too well...'

'No,' he said, taking control of his breathing. 'My daughter isn't home at the moment... hasn't been in a while.'

'Well, I saw her clear as day. Earlier.'

No words came out of his mouth, just a strangled sound that might have been a question.

'Not alone either... there was a greasy little shite with her.'

Despite feeling like he'd been punched in the gut, he stood up straight, knowing he needed to regain control of himself. 'Maddie? A greasy little shite? Are you sure, Henrietta? This is important...'

'I'm not senile. It was Maddie, clear as day.' Her tone was sharp. 'She opened the bloody door. That unsavoury-looking young pillock was leering at her.'

She still has a key, Frank thought.

'Were they in a blue Ford Cortina? An old one?'

Henrietta nodded. 'That's the one. Battered it was... held together with rust and prayer.' She nodded, gesturing towards Bertha. 'Not unlike your own.'

Frank's heart was like a lead weight.

The mysterious car. The Ford Cortina. It'd been Maddie all along. He'd been so close to seeing her, and he'd missed his chance.

Why didn't I take it more bloody seriously?

Riding a burst of adrenaline, Frank turned and hurried back to his house. He burst into Maddie's old room for the second time that night. He flicked on the light and the sudden brightness made him squint, but he scanned the space desperately. Nothing looked out of place. He looked through the drawers. One wardrobe. He pulled back the bedsheets. He opened the other wardrobe door.

He looked down at the space beneath the clothes.

Something was missing...

He clicked his fingers, trying to remember...

A backpack!

He remembered searching it the day she'd disappeared.

Frank sat on the bed, his legs suddenly weak. Why had she come back for it? There must have been something in it all this time... something she needed... but what?

He thumped the bed. Had he checked it well enough? These backpacks often had inside pockets.

Christ almighty, she'd been here!

He stared around the room, his vision blurring. A matter of hours. She'd been here, and now she was gone again.

He returned to Henrietta's door and pounded.

It opened. 'Frank, what on earth—'

Frank cut her off. 'How did she look? Maddie... How did she look?'

Henrietta's expression softened.

'Tell me!' Frank hissed. He knew she could see the tears in his eyes.

'Tired... she looked tired. And thin. Too thin, if you ask me.'

He rubbed his face and moved the tears away from his eyes. He leaned against the doorframe again.

Henrietta muttered, 'Come inside before you fall over, Frank. But you're not bloody smoking.'

'I should have been here,' Frank muttered, as he followed her in. 'I should have known. I should have...'

'Let me be the judge of that,' Henrietta said. 'Tell me everything and let me be the judge of that.'

Chapter Forty-Five

LILLY'S HEART raced as the two men who'd trafficked her as an eleven-year-old girl faced off.

It was hard not to be frustrated with Nikolai for breaking his promise not to confront Georgi, but she had to give him credit for the way he kept his cool. He didn't seem rattled and was behaving in a calm and reasonable way.

Georgi was in default mode: sneers, wisecracks, punctuated by bursts of aggression.

'You never woke up, Nikolai. Always the dreamer. But being asleep and dreaming doesn't pay any fucking bill I ever received.'

Lilly could see Nikolai clench his jaw as he received the savage words, but again, his voice remained steady when he responded. 'This isn't a dream, Georgi. Those in charge will be happy to pay a small fee on my say.'

Lilly saw a familiar predatory gleam in the depths of Georgi's eyes. 'Those in charge? I'll make the terms.'

Nikolai glanced at Lilly. She sensed his patience was wearing thin and that he was only just realising what she'd tried to tell him – this was going to fail. Nikolai looked back. 'That won't happen, Georgi.'

'Won't it?'

'No. This is the only offer. I'll organise a small fee. Take it or leave it.'

'Leave it.'

'You're being foolish.'

'Sorry.'

'You heard me—'

Georgi grabbed Nikolai's shoulder, cutting him off. 'Here's what's going to happen. You're going to wake up, dreamer, and you're going to listen to how this is going to work.'

Nikolai looked at the hand on his shoulder.

'You need to leave, Georgi, now,' Lilly said.

'It's okay... I'll handle this,' Nikolai said.

'There you go,' Georgi said. 'Dreaming again, Nikolai.'

'Get your hand off me.'

'Or?'

Nikolai's composure was crumbling. Lilly edged forward, deciding it best to come between them—

In a blur of motion, Georgi jabbed his fist into Nikolai's stomach and thrust him against a shelf. Lilly dodged a display of roses that came crashing to the ground. Glass shattered everywhere.

Georgi moved in again. His second blow connected with Nikolai's jaw. There was a sound like a snapping branch, and the force propelled him against another shelf.

Potted plants fell to the floor. Soil spilled across the tiles like dark blood.

'Stop!' she shouted. 'Ще се обадя на полицията!'

'Call the police,' Georgi dared her, backing away

towards the counter, smiling. 'Hopefully, I'll share a cell with the dreamer here. We'd have some fun.'

Nikolai doubled over, heaved and clutched his jaw. Lilly's eyes darted frantically around the wreckage on her floor. She saw a large piece of glass and swooped for it. When she straightened back up, she saw Nikolai launch at Georgi.

Her heart sank.

Nikolai drove his shoulder into the larger man's midsection. Georgi's air came out in a rush. Her boyfriend managed some jabs to the larger man's torso while he was stunned. The cash register was knocked from the counter and clattered to the floor.

'Stop it!' Lilly cried, but the air was thick now with the sounds of grunts, gasps, and the thud of flesh against flesh.

Georgi threw himself over the counter, so it would act as a barrier between them.

Georgi now had time to orientate himself, which made the next part almost inevitable.

Nikolai charged around the counter, and met Georgi's fist in a near-perfect uppercut. With a thud, Nikolai crashed to the floor behind the counter, out of Lilly's line of sight.

Lilly marched forward with the shard of glass in her hand.

Georgi grunted as he repeatedly kicked Nikolai. Veins stood out on his forehead.

When she reached the counter, Georgi stopped and sidled to his left so she wouldn't be able to get to him with the shard over the counter. He smiled.

'Stop it, Georgi. Stop it, or I'll use this.'

Sweat ran down Georgi's ageing face, working its way around creases. He snorted, looked at Nikolai on the floor, and spat on him. 'Glad I kept myself in shape,' he said. 'I missed this.'

Georgi turned to face Lilly, ensuring there was still a suitable distance between them. 'Are you ready to talk properly, now the dreamer is out of the way?'

Lilly could hear Nikolai groaning. Each pained sound made her stomach turn, but at least he was alive. However, she couldn't see him. She didn't know how bad it was.

'Get the hell out of my shop,' Lilly said, her voice trembling despite her attempt at bravery. She proffered her makeshift weapon even though she was too far away.

Georgi was turning his head from side to side, disbelief on his face. 'You just don't learn, do you?'

She saw the crown of Nikolai's head. He was rising, using the wall alongside him for support. He was beside the open cellar door.

Georgi turned to face him and took a side shuffle, so he was standing by the open door. He grinned at Nikolai, who was panting. 'Anything left, big man?'

'Fuck off,' Nikolai said. Blood dribbled down his chin, staining his shirt crimson.

Georgi looked between him and Lilly. 'Really, Lilly, is this the best you could do? You don't fancy a real man? Hey, that's an idea. Me and you together… in business, and otherwise.' He patted Nikolai's face. 'Why don't you take a seat, like a good little dreamer, and let me and Lilly have some quality time together?'

Nikolai's eyes narrowed. Her stomach clenched with dread. *Don't,* she thought. *That's enough.*

Nikolai rose up straighter. Georgi laughed.

'Nikolai,' she said.

He didn't look at her.

'Nikolai, don't—'

But it was too late. Nikolai swung with his left hand, catching Georgi square on the face. It stunned Georgi, and he fell through the open door. As he did so, his hand shot out and grabbed Nikolai's shirt.

There followed a series of grotesque thuds, as the two men fell down the steps together. There were gasps and groans, before there was silence.

Lilly stood there, frozen, hand over her mouth. All she could hear was the pounding of her own heart.

She waited for a sound.

Nothing.

'Nikolai?' she called out.

She waited.

Nothing.

Still holding the shard but feeling unsteady on her feet as waves of nausea crashed into her, Lilly went around the counter.

She hit the switch by the door and the cellar light came to life.

'Nikolai?' she called again, louder this time.

Nothing.

Taking a deep breath, she peered around the corner.

The two men lay sprawled at the bottom of the steps. Neither was moving.

She waited and called again.

When no answer came, she knew she couldn't stay upstairs any longer. Taking a deep breath, she started down the stairs, her hand trailing along the cool stone wall for support.

Lilly blinked, letting her eyes adjust to the dim light. She whispered his name, over and over, her voice barely audible over the pounding of her heart.

From the bottom step she looked down at Nikolai, and gave a small gasp, like a wounded animal.

His eyes were wide and unseeing. They looked like marbles reflecting the flickering light above. A dark pool glimmered as it spread beneath his head.

'Nikolai.' His name caught in her throat as she left the last step and slipped to her knees beside him, his blood dampening her legs. She dropped the shard onto the stone, and then let her trembling hands hover over him. She wanted desperately to touch him but was so afraid of confirming what her eyes were telling her. Eventually, she realised that her sight wasn't deceiving her, and she cradled his face, tears blurring her vision. 'I'm so sorry. Nikolai, I'm—'

A groan made Lilly freeze. Georgi, barely a metre ahead of them, had rolled over and was pulling himself up. He was using the stone wall beside him for support. He glared at her. Blood trickled from a gash on his forehead, a crimson trail snaking down his face. He winced as he straightened up. 'That fucking hurt.' His eyes moved to Nikolai's still form. He edged forward and looked down. 'Fuck,' he muttered, shaking his head. 'Stupid bastard.'

'We have to call an ambulance.' Lilly's voice shook.

'He's dead.'

'No... no... I'm calling them.'

He rubbed the back of his head. 'He should have stayed down. Up there. Stupid prick.' He rubbed harder. 'Shit... let me think... we're going to have to get rid of him.'

'I'm going to phone an ambulance,' she said through a mouthful of tears.

'No. You're talking gibberish. He's dead. Shut the fuck up and let me think... and...'

Her eyes narrowed. A surge of hatred coursed through her. 'How could it be him, and not you? How?'

He shrugged. 'Оцеляване на най-приспособените.'
Survival of the fittest.

She reached for the shard of glass and stood. 'I'm phoning the police.'

Georgi shook his head. 'You need to get control of yourself.'

'I'm going to tell them everything. About the trafficking, the children, me, *you*, all of it.'

'Don't be ridiculous. Everything you worked for... destroyed? You'll lose this shop, your freedom. This doesn't have to be more than a tragic accident. No one has to go to jail.'

She stared at him over Nikolai's body, her voice low and dangerous. A savage grin split her face. 'I don't care if I go to jail. As long as you do, too.'

Georgi lowered his head and sighed.

He rubbed the back of his head a moment longer, then raised his head and shrugged. 'I was afraid you were going to say that.'

In a flash of movement, he lunged.

She swung the shard, but he was too fast for her.

Chapter Forty-Six

On Tom's plate, Gerry placed the salmon fillets, grilled to a light pink, on top of a bed of quinoa. After lining up the steamed asparagus spears alongside, their tips all facing the same direction, she placed a small ramekin of lemon butter precisely two centimetres from the edge.

For herself, she separated the ingredients out onto four plates.

Tom came into the kitchen to assist Gerry in moving the five plates to the table.

He thanked her for mixing his food. He knew it made her uncomfortable.

'And what culinary delight did Rylan get tonight?'

As if on cue, Rylan trotted into the kitchen, his tail wagging. 'Lean ground turkey. It's part of his new diet.'

Tom bent down to scratch behind Rylan's ears. 'Well, buddy, you're certainly smelling a lot better. Mummy really takes good care of you.'

Gerry found his comment jarring. 'I'd prefer it if you didn't say that.'

He stood up, smiling. 'Really...? Sorry, I thought everyone said that.'

'Not to me and Rylan they don't.'

'Okay, message received.'

They sat.

She noticed his glum expression.

'Do you think I'm being ridiculous?' she asked.

'No...'

'I just can't view adopting a dog the same as adopting a human. To me, it implies some cross-species connection in a way that doesn't feel right.'

He shrugged. 'Okay. We used to do it when we had a dog. A habit, I guess. It won't happen again.'

She reached over and touched his hand. 'Thank you.'

Tom immediately dug in, making appreciative noises. 'This is fantastic, Gerry. You've really outdone yourself.'

'It was a recipe,' she said, not wishing to take credit for something as basic as following a recipe.

'I know, but you made a good job of it.'

'I just followed it precisely.' She often wondered how you could make a good job that was already pre-determined. The only element of creativity was the arrangement on the plate.

Tom smiled, then asked, 'So, how was your day? Any exciting cases?'

Gerry put down her fork, her face suddenly serious. 'Tom, is it okay if we don't discuss work?'

'Sorry... I forgot.'

She'd already told him that the main reason she'd sought out a relationship was to have a life outside of work. She didn't believe he'd forgotten. On some issues, Tom was starting to prove persistent. She decided to make it clear that she didn't want to be pushed on the issue. 'I mean, if I talked to you about work, I might as well not be in a relationship, and actually working.'

'I think most people who feel that way just give an overview with no real detail,' Tom said, taking a sip of water.

His determination to change her mind was irritating. 'Is it okay to just tell me about your day?'

He looked disappointed, but quickly launched into a story about a tricky tree removal, occasionally stopping and gauging Gerry's reaction. She'd nod three times a minute to show her engagement.

As they finished their meal, Tom said, 'By the way, I think my parents really liked you.'

She struggled to believe that. 'That seems unlikely, given their behaviour and body language during our dinner.'

Tom laughed. 'Trust me, that's how they are with everyone. Me included. As you saw. But they've asked after you, since, which is a good sign.'

'That's nice,' Gerry said. 'It's good to know. Although I think it's fair to inform you, I didn't like them very much.' She took a mouthful of water. 'At all, actually.'

Tom, who was chewing on his last mouthful of salmon, coughed. His face reddened slightly and then he swallowed. 'You didn't say. You seemed happy... after...'

She recalled their frolics and smiled. 'I was. But at the time, I was being polite. I can be quite skilled with etiquette. That doesn't equate to liking someone. I didn't think they were bad people. Just not to my taste. They were critical of you and taking opportunities to judge me.'

'I'm sorry.'

'Don't be. I want to be honest.'

'In fairness, you've hit the nail on the head. That's exactly what they're like.' Tom took a long sip of water.

'Um, speaking of parents, can you tell me more about yours?'

Having finished her food, Gerry put her knife and fork together on one of her four plates. 'Why? They're dead. You'll never meet them.'

'I know, but...' He put his knife and fork down, too, and looked at her, wide eyed.

She didn't like this expression from Tom – it always made her feel like he was pleading for something.

'I'd like to learn more about you... about your past... If I know about your parents, then I'll know more about you. They must be important to you. That picture on the mantlepiece...'

'It's one picture,' she said.

'It's the only picture in the house.'

'Yes. It was their house. It felt right to have their presence here, somehow.'

'Okay.'

'Although that doesn't mean I didn't adore them... because I did. I'm sure I've told you this before.'

'Yes. You told me they were good people.' Tom smiled. 'You also told me how they died...'

'All good then.' Gerry stood up to clear the table.

'But Gerry,' Tom said. 'Could you tell me more?'

'About what, exactly?'

'About your relationship?'

'Okay.' She sat. 'We played scrabble together. They taught me about etiquette.' She paused to think. 'We sailed a lot.'

Tom nodded, and then his eyes widened again. There was more pleading on the cards.

'I hope you don't mind, Gerry... but I did some research... on how your parents died.'

'I see. But I told you how they died.'

He nodded. 'You didn't tell me you were there.'

She looked down. 'It didn't seem important. I didn't die.'

He sighed. 'I'm sorry, I shouldn't have researched it.'

Realising that she'd have done the same, she confirmed what he'd found out. 'There was a freak storm. They instructed me to put on a life jacket and jump. I did. They didn't. They tried to save the boat. They failed.'

'Gerry, I'm so sorry. That must have been terrible.' Gerry watched Tom's hand coming over the table to hers, and she pulled away.

'Yes, it was terrible. They were very supportive of my... condition. They provided me with a good life, took me on regular yachting holidays, and attempted to aid in my social development. They loved me. A lot.'

Tom nodded encouragingly. 'They sound wonderful, and I'm sure you loved them, too.'

'They were excellent parents... I was very fortunate.'

He leaned forward. 'So tell me more about the yachting holidays?'

Gerry tensed slightly. 'I've already shared quite a bit, Tom. Perhaps we could change the subject?'

'This is a perfect opportunity to get to know you better.' His voice was gentle but that didn't make it any less insistent. 'Okay, if not the yachting – I can understand how that might not be the best subject – what other holidays did you take?'

'We travelled around France one year...' She sat back. 'Can we leave it at that?'

'You rarely open up, Gerry.'

Gerry's fingers tightened around her glass.

Tom couldn't seem to stop himself. 'Gerry, relationships

are about sharing and understanding each other. Don't you think it's important for us to know about each other's pasts?'

Gerry closed her eyes for a moment, taking a deep breath. 'I need a moment of silence to collect my thoughts, please.'

After less than a minute, he said, 'Are you okay? What are you thinking?'

Gerry opened her eyes.

He must have realised that he'd pushed too hard. He stood up and came around to her side. 'Okay, that's enough for now. Already, I feel like I understand you better, like we're closer. I'm fortunate to have you. I'm happy when I'm with you.'

Gerry looked up. 'I'm pleased for you, Tom. But now is a time that I'd like to take a break from our relationship.'

Tom's eyebrows shot up. 'Sorry...?'

'A break.'

'A break when?'

'From this moment.'

His face fell. 'What?' He shook his head. 'Are you breaking up with me?'

'Not as such. I'm requesting a break. After the break, I'll decide whether I wish to continue with our relationship.'

'Why? I don't understand. This seems sudden. Is it because I researched your parents?'

'Not so much that. It's more your persistent nature. Your intense questioning despite my attempts to redirect the conversation.'

'But it's because I really like you!'

'Yes, but this was not one of my expectations for a rela-tionship. Being overwhelmed.' She stood. 'So now I need time to consider whether I can continue with someone who'd persist despite my discomfort.'

'But I was *only* trying to know you better, and you make that *so* hard sometimes,' Tom protested.

'I understand that was your intention,' Gerry replied, standing up. 'However, intentions and actions are separate entities. And now you're blaming me for your actions.'

'Indirectly?' Tom said, raising an eyebrow.

'I think it's best if you leave now. I'll clean.'

She walked to the sink.

When she turned back, he was still there; he looked completely stunned.

She struggled to decide whether that made him endearing or pathetic, but the answer would make no difference. She'd decided.

'Please,' he said.

'Please, what?'

He had to think about this. 'Reconsider?'

'My break is for consideration.'

'Shit.' He lowered his face and puffed out his cheeks. 'How long is this break?'

'I'm not sure.'

He looked up. He looked as if he'd tears in his eyes. 'Could I at least stay tonight?'

She considered. 'But that would slow down the onset of the break.'

'You could start the break tomorrow?'

She took a deep breath. 'I see. And then, now, tonight, we could have sex?'

Tom looked stunned. 'I was going to suggest watching television, but yes, I could do that.'

'Okay, sex tonight, break tomorrow. I'd prefer to let the food digest first though. Fancy Scrabble?'

Tom nodded. 'That would be good, yes.'

Chapter Forty-Seven

STREETLIGHTS FLICKERED, casting sickly pools of yellow light across cracked pavements and overgrown lawns.

Ray pulled up outside a squat, pebble-dashed house. He killed the engine, plunging the street into an eerie silence broken only by the distant bark of a dog and the muffled thump of bass from a nearby house.

He gripped the steering wheel, his knuckles white as he stared at Megan's home.

Then, his phone vibrated in his pocket for the sixth time. It would be Kath. The texts had started an hour ago, growing increasingly frantic. The last one he'd read before silencing his phone echoed in his mind:

> I'm sorry. I know that she recognised you. I had to tell the police when they came. What if this woman comes back? It seemed safer.

He couldn't blame Kath. Not really. That Megan knew him would have come out sooner rather than later, anyway. There was only one way of solving this problem.

He'd have to confront Megan himself.

Ray stepped out of the car, the chilly night air biting at his face. The windows of Megan's home were dark, curtains drawn.

He approached her door, his feet heavy with dread. Her garden was littered with cigarette butts. Paint peeled from the window frames, and a broken gutter sagged above the front door.

He raised his hand to knock, then hesitated. What if she answered the door in that same frenzied state he'd seen her in the other day?

She could be on top of him in seconds, forcing neighbours to intervene, and that would be the fortunate outcome. The other outcome involving her nails and his eyes didn't bear thinking about.

He turned away, clenching and unclenching his fist. But what choice did he have?

The road he was on now only led one way.

Here.

He turned back and knocked.

He waited, and no one answered. After trying a second time, he sighed. *Now what?* Did he wait here, outside in his car, for her to return from wherever she was? Or did he just give it up for the night?

Without really thinking, he tried the door handle. The door opened.

Okay, so this really isn't a good idea.

But maybe this was an opportunity? To learn something about Megan while she was out? Something that could help him? Buy her silence?

It felt so deceitful and horrible, but again, he felt desperate. She was the one who'd come back into his life, threatening everything. If she was hiding something, it may be some kind of way out.

Ray's heart pounded in his chest as he stepped over the threshold.

The hallway smelled of stale cigarettes and something else, something sour and unpleasant. Ray fumbled for a light switch, blinking as harsh fluorescent light flooded the space. Ahead, the door to the kitchen was open. He could see dirty dishes piled high.

A terrifying thought hit him. *What if she's here, after all? Sleeping... drunk on the sofa... or too scared to answer the door? How would she respond if she sees me?*

It suddenly seemed safer to warn her of his presence. 'Megan?' he called softly.

He waited a moment. There was no response.

'Megan, it's Reverend Ray Lawson. I knocked, but I wanted to make sure you were okay... after the other day?'

He spoke louder this time, and there was no response again. He concluded she must be out.

He looked into the living room. It was in chaos. Mismatched furniture and overflowing ashtrays. A half-empty bottle of vodka stood on a coffee table, surrounded by a litter of pill bottles. Ray's stomach churned. Could this all be traced back to his failure? Really? When she'd been young and desperate for his help?

He moved deeper into the house, his footsteps muffled by the threadbare carpet. 'Megan?' he called, still playing it safe. 'It's Reverend Lawson. I just want to talk.'

He turned towards the stairs, his gaze drawn to a door at the top.

The stairs creaked under his weight as he ascended, each sound seeming to announce his presence to the empty house. At the top, he paused, listening intently. Was that breathing he could hear, or just the whisper of wind through poorly sealed windows?

Ray's hand hovered over the doorknob. Maybe it was better just to wait outside.

Except, what if she was in here? Unconscious. Drunk, and on substances of some kind. Desperate for help.

He turned the handle and pushed the door open.

The bedroom was dark, illuminated only by the dim light spilling up from downstairs. Ray could make out the shape of a bed, clothes scattered across the floor. A dressing table stood against one wall, its mirror reflecting the darkness.

At first, he thought he detected movement on the bed. His adrenaline spiked. He took a deep breath. 'I just want to make things right, Megan.' The words sounded hollow, even to his own ears. How could he possibly make things right after all this time? He switched the light on. The bed was empty. He sighed.

Ray turned, reaching out for the switch to turn the light back off—

His heart nearly stopped.

Megan stood in the doorway, her slight frame silhouetted against the hallway light. In her hands, she held a large ceramic vase.

'Megan,' Ray began, raising his hands placatingly. 'Please, I—'

The vase swung in a wide arc. Ray had a split second to register the look of pure hatred in Megan's eyes before pain exploded across his temple.

Ray's vision blurred, darkness reaching in at the edges. He was dimly aware of his body hitting the floor, of Megan looming over him.

Then, blackness.

Chapter Forty-Eight

WHITBY ABBEY WAS a jagged silhouette against dark skies.

Gothic arches, once proud and soaring, now stood broken and exposed.

Shadows played across the weathered stones, and the great east window yawned. Skeletal, hungry, yearning for a soul.

Raven stumbled on through the graveyard. Names worn from the headstones. Beneath her, long-forgotten bones.

Where do all the souls go?

Do they wander?

Like me?

Pausing, certain she could hear the faint echo of long-ago prayers, she tilted her head.

The monks. Voices rising and falling in ancient rhythms.

Maybe centuries of devotion had really seeped into the abbey's stone.

Or was it just the wind whistling through empty arches?

'Hello, Raven!'

She knew the voice, but not where it came from. She spun, heart racing, but saw only the gloom and some figures walking in the distance.

'Lovely evening for a walk, isn't it?' Another voice, this time from behind her.

Raven whirled again, her black dress billowing around her. 'Who's there?'

Graves and ruins.

She pressed her palms against her temples, squeezing her eyes shut, and took some deep breaths.

When she opened her eyes, the abbey seemed to loom even larger. Intricate carvings on the remaining pillars writhed and twisted.

She knew she was drawing closer to the cliff edge. That she was now straying from the path. A warning sign. Bold red against the muted tones of the landscape. She knew if she continued, crossed the fence, she'd join the dead.

And where would my soul go?

Below, the North Sea churned, and the violent waves called. Behind her, the looming abbey judged.

Tommy.

Freckles... gaps between his teeth... steaming hot soup before him.

'Tommy.' She felt the words leaving her mouth.

His eyes were on her. 'Emily. You promised to tell me a story while I eat?'

'Of course. About pirates?'

'No. Tell me a story about monsters.'

'Okay.'

Tommy's eyes lit up. He lifted the spoon to his lips.

'The monsters are here, Tommy,' she said, but she was too late. The boy was gone. The memory over. It was the cliff edge.

And a soul.

A soul with nowhere to go.

Her soul.

'I'm sorry.'

She felt her foot slip on the loose gravel at the cliff's edge—

There was a firm grip on her arm. She realised she wasn't falling, but she was also confused.

There was a man she didn't recognise clutching her. 'Are you all right, lass?'

Was he a lost soul as well?

His hair was white, and his eyes were kind. 'You're too close to the edge.'

She looked down at the hand holding her upper arm.

It looked real... felt real...

'I'm sorry,' the man said. 'I don't want to let go until you step away, okay?'

She looked up, blinking, trying her hardest to focus on him, while behind her the abbey's ruins seemed to shift and change.

'Okay.' She stepped towards him as he backed away.

'It's not safe to be too close to the edge in the dark.'

She kept her eyes on the abbey. Were those windows really empty?

Her eyesight blurred.

'Are you okay? Can I call someone?' the man asked.

She felt the cold on her cheeks and realised she was crying. 'They're dead,' she said.

The words hung in the air between them, heavy with the weight of long-buried guilt. In the distance, the abbey seemed to lean closer. 'Can you hear the abbey? Can you hear the sounds?'

The man's eyes had already widened. 'Who's dead?'

Raven's legs gave way, and she sank to her knees on the cold, damp ground.

'A little boy with freckles and a gap-toothed smile that trusted me and... and...' Her words dissolved into gut-wrenching sobs. 'Others. Children. Small, lost souls. And I let it happen.'

She stared again at the abbey. Its weathered stones held the weight of countless confessions over the centuries.

Stone and sin endure, she thought.

As does my tormented soul.

The abbey remained impassive.

She would never be granted absolution.

Chapter Forty-Nine

THE AIR in Donald's office was thick with the smell of stale biscuits.

Donald asked for a second to finish his email and suggested they grab a biscuit.

'No thank you, sir,' Gerry said.

Frank didn't grace him with a response.

He'd slept badly again. It would be clear in his blood-shot eyes, and further emphasised with his short temper.

He rubbed his temples. The events of last night played on a painful loop.

Maddie.

So close.

So painfully close.

He'd seen that sodding Ford Cortina twice! Why hadn't he chased it down when he'd had the chance?

Unlikely in Bertha, admittedly, but he could have at least tried!

What could have been so important in his house, in that sodding bag, that she'd waited for his absence to grab it?

Imagine if he'd come home early and caught her there. Begged her to listen to him...

He took a sharp breath and sighed.

And who was this chuffing scrote she was hanging about with?

God, what if I never see her again?

What if I missed my last chance?

The thoughts loomed like a dark, cancerous shadow.

'Frank?'

He opened his eyes and stared at Donald.

'You with us?'

'Aye.'

Just about, he thought.

'I'm sorry to call you both in here so early.'

Frank bit back a retort. *Really? Was it so important that you had to make us sit through the end of your email while offering us stale biscuits? Get to the sodding point, Donald... put me out of my misery.*

'Raven Blackstone,' Donald said.

Frank glanced at Gerry, who took a rare opportunity to meet his gaze.

He sat up straight and took a breath. 'We've access to her files?'

'Not exactly.'

'Jesus.' Frank looked at his watch. He did a quick calculation. 'So what've we achieved in twenty-three hours?' He'd been a knife's edge away from saying *you* instead of *we*. Now, that would have charged the atmosphere.

Donald narrowed his eyes. 'Hear me out. We've got enough. She's had an identity change. Thankfully. She'd probably be dead by now if not...' He looked between their faces. 'So that's why we've to be clear here, *clear as day*, that exposing her to the elements at this stage is a complete no-go.'

'Even if she killed Greg Lyle?' Frank asked.

'That would, of course, alter the complexion, as I'll get to shortly.'

Frank sighed. 'Can you just tell us who she is, please...' He paused in a deliberately irritating manner, before adding, 'Sir.'

Donald sat back, linked his hands, and said, 'Emily Thorne.'

The name was familiar. A sense of horror and dread coiled in his gut like a snake as he tried to recall how he knew it. 'Emily Thorne,' Frank repeated to himself, trying to get his conscious mind to catch up with his gut.

'Robert Aldridge's partner,' Gerry said.

The coiled snake struck. 'Jesus. No way.'

Donald nodded.

Frank sat up. '*The* Emily Thorne?'

'Yes. The. Partner of Robert—'

'The Pallister Poisoner?' Frank asked.

Donald nodded.

'Jesus,' Frank said again.

In 1993, primary school teacher, forty-three-year-old Robert Aldridge kidnapped and poisoned five ten-year-old boys in Middlesbrough with aconite. He was caught the same year, and the small bodies recovered from the cellar.

'Five children,' Frank said. He shook his head. 'Senseless. No reason—'

Donald said, 'I recall that the reason he did it—'

'Evil doesn't have a reason.' Frank cut him off and stared at him.

Gerry jumped in. 'Actually, Frank—'

287

'No,' Frank said, turning his stare on to her. 'There's no reason. None you can give me anyway.'

She looked away, and in that moment, he realised that this was the sharpest he'd ever been with her. He felt somewhat guilty and lowered his eyes.

'Okay, then, forget the word *reason*,' Donald said. 'We *know* his pathology came from his own abuse as a child. His experiences as a ten-year-old are well documented by the psychiatrists.'

You always have to have the last word, don't you, Donald?

'How about what I know?' Frank's voice was tight. 'Aldridge used his position as a supply teacher to identify five young boys from different schools whose home lives were under investigation for abuse. He poisoned them and left them underneath his floorboards to spare them the trauma he'd experienced. I can find no reason for any of that.'

'Frank,' Donald said. 'You're tired and shaken up. You know how it works. We ascribe motive.'

'Or, in this case, I ascribe evil.'

'Well, the outcome remains the same. Besides, this isn't about him. He won't ever see the light of day again.'

'He shouldn't be able to breathe air again.'

'So, back to Emily Thorne's involvement,' Donald said. 'We have to be crystal clear on this. She was found not guilty—'

'Yes, but she was still present when all five children were killed.'

'She was fifteen years old, and completely under his spell—'

'I remember it well... that bastard groomed her.' Frank's face darkened.

'And so you understand that she was innocent?' Donald asked.

'Of course, but she was still *there* when it happened.'

'In body, not so much in mind,' Donald said.

'Psychologically speaking, her sense of self likely broke down,' Gerry said. 'She became a passive observer, believing she was helping, fulfilling the greater good, completely under his control. It's not uncommon in cases of extreme manipulation.'

'I'm not disagreeing with either of you. You're missing my point, here! Emily was there. Five children died. How can we just ignore that considering the nature of our investigation?'

'Because it may put her in danger,' Donald said. 'She was fifteen!'

'I get that, but let's not forget that Greg was fourteen. Who is looking out for him if we go down this avenue? I'm going to speak to her... I have to.'

Donald widened his eyes. 'You're a hairsbreadth away from being taken off this case.'

Frank bit his lip and sucked in air through his nostrils. That would be no solution.

Donald looked between them. 'Both of you will stay away from her. Okay? Don't make me do it Frank.'

Frank leaned forward, his voice rising. 'This is the same as being taken off it, anyway.'

'What're you talking about, man?'

'I'm investigating a child-killing, and a once suspected child killer is on our list of last known contacts? You want me to attach my good name to an investigation that ignores the most obvious leads. Better I am off it.'

'Good name,' he snorted.

Frank narrowed his eyes.

'She was suspected, she wasn't guilty, Frank, Jesus, see sense—'

'So she gets a free pass from the investigation?'

'No... of course not... but could you imagine if the truth about her gets out?'

'It won't.'

'But if it did... It would be dangerous for her... very dangerous... but there is no free pass.'

Frank sighed. He closed his eyes, rubbed his temples, and realised now he'd become lost in tiredness, anger and bitterness, which was as much connected to last night and Maddie as this new lead.

'So, how will you proceed?' Frank said, not opening his eyes.

'I'm saying you can't go near her but... if anything else comes to light... *anything*... that suggests her involvement then you speak to me first. Once I have ammunition, then I'll go high again.'

What could I possibly give you, Frank thought, *that trumps the fact she was tried for child-killing?*

'There's something else,' Donald said. 'You won't like this either. I saved it to last because I didn't want you flying from the room until you knew the score with Raven.'

Frank opened his eyes and looked at him. *Flying from the room.* 'This isn't filling me with any confidence.'

'I'm sorry, but you won't like it.'

When do I ever?

'Last night,' Oxley continued, 'Raven—'

'Emily,' Frank interrupted.

'Raven,' Donald continued, 'was seen wandering near the cliff edge up by Whitby Abbey. Malcolm Pearce, retired fireman, offered assistance, concerned she was maybe trying to commit suicide. Turns out, she was drunk and highly distressed. Thing is...' he sighed. 'She told Malcolm she was responsible for a child's death.'

Frank was already on his feet. 'Surely that's the ammunition?'

'Sit down. She wasn't talking about Greg, Frank. She was talking about one of Robert's victims. Tommy Chambers.'

'But she was confessing to murder?' Frank said, still not sitting.

'She wasn't confessing, really.'

'This is unbelievable.'

'Sit down. Now.'

Frank hesitated.

'God help me, Frank. Don't test me.'

Frank gritted his teeth and sat.

'Raven was taken in for questioning last night, but her name obviously triggered the same alarm we triggered,' Donald continued. 'Someone from the UK Protected Person Service jumped in. She was present when Tommy died, as we know, and she was feeling responsible, despite remembering very little of it. Snatches.'

'She was present when they all died,' Frank said.

'Yes... but she can't remember speaking to the others. With Tommy, she remembers snatches of their conversation. He was affectionate with her. Held her hand as she told him stories. The psychiatrists believed it was Tommy that broke through. If not for him, she may not have gone to the police. It could have carried on. She's been spoken to about Greg by someone from the UKPPS. They're convinced that she had nothing to do with Greg.'

'And we're to take their word on that?'

'Yes.'

'And how about my opinion? I'm the SIO.'

'Greg's death shares nothing in common with Aldridge's five victims,' Gerry said. 'The ages are different, the method is different, and—'

Frank turned to her, betrayed, his eyes blazing. 'But how can we just ignore the common denominator? Emily Thorne?'

Donald was rubbing his temples now. 'For fuck's sake.' This was the first time Frank had ever heard Donald swear. 'Frank, pipe down. This cannot get out, or there'll be an emergency relocation. It'll cost a fortune, and the axe will fall on yours truly. Find me some concrete evidence connecting her to Greg's death, and then we'll talk. Is this all clear?'

Frank opened his mouth to argue further but was cut off by the shrill ring of Donald's phone. The chief constable answered, his face growing increasingly pale as he listened.

After a terse, 'I understand,' Donald hung up and fixed Frank and Gerry with a grave look.

'Shit. I have some awful news.' He shook his head. 'Frank, prepare yourself.'

Frank slumped back in his chair, feeling his guts turning over.

Chapter Fifty

THE EARLY MORNING light struggled to penetrate the heavy, acrid smoke.

'Shit,' Frank said. He was standing with Gerry on the opposite side of the road to the blackened skeleton that was, only yesterday, the Seabreeze Flower Shop.

A cacophony of sounds assaulted him: the crackle of dying embers, the hiss of water meeting hot ash, the murmur of shocked onlookers, and the constant chatter of emergency radios.

He couldn't keep his mind from his experience in the cellar yesterday. The door wedged open with a watering can. A broom in his hand.

A break-in.

Had it been an early warning sign that something more devastating was going to happen?

I could have stopped this.

The thought echoed in his mind, relentless and accusing.

A firefighter was winding back his hose on the opposite pavement, shaking his head as he did so. Frank couldn't help but wonder if the man shared his sense of futility, of arriving too late to make a difference.

He recalled the interior of the shop. A vibrant display of life and colour. The memory made the destruction even more stark. The once-quaint storefront had bubbled and peeled, revealing scorched brick beneath. With a partially collapsed roof, the now-gutted interior was exposed to the grey sky above through a gaping maw.

Frank turned back to his vehicle, catching sight of Rylan gazing solemnly from the window at the wreckage.

A firefighter approached them. 'I'm Chief Fire Officer Louise Dawson. We've just finished another sweep. We still can't allow you in.'

Frank nodded. 'I can see that.'

'And it will be a crime scene,' she continued. 'We've found evidence of accelerant.'

'So, the place has been deliberately burned down?' Frank asked.

'It looks that way. There was a lot of accelerant.'

He nodded at the husk. 'So those two people were murdered?'

'Maybe.'

'Is it possible that the arsonists caught themselves up in an accident?' Gerry asked.

'Again, maybe. But both bodies were in the cellar,' Louise said. 'They had an exit route close by. So, probably not, but it is possible.'

'Aye,' Frank said, thinking, *We know all about that exit route. Someone came in through it yesterday.*

'It's difficult at this stage,' Louise said. 'I've seen it all and don't want to call it. Accident, murder, even suicide.'

They were murdered, Frank thought to himself.

'There were two unclaimed vehicles parked to the rear

of the store,' Louise continued. 'We have relayed these details.'

Frank nodded. He already knew about them. The Vauxhall Astra was registered to Lilly Petrova, and a Ford Focus belonged to a Nikolai Volkov.

Frank puffed his cheeks out. That break-in had been lost in the craziness of yesterday. Raven's hidden identity, Terry Kane's fall, and the reverend on the run. But he wished now that he'd pressed harder rather than leaving it to two uniforms to log the break-in.

Two people were dead.

He couldn't speak for Nikolai, but Lilly had seemed a good person. She'd spoken about Greg with sincerity in her voice. Warm compassion. And not forgetting, Gerry had seen the kindness in her eyes.

'Any ideas on how long it will be before we can get a team in?' he asked, knowing already that the answer would deflate him.

'The place is a total loss. The structure's unstable. A complete demolition job. Anyone who goes in will have to be trained. We can stay around and help for now.'

Frank inwardly sighed, nodded and said, 'Thank you.'

As Louise returned to her group, Frank turned to Gerry. 'After yesterday, I didn't think things could get worse. I feel like I'm in a chuffing washing machine.'

Gerry did a full circle, pointing out several CCTV cameras. 'There's got to be something here.'

'Aye. I should have pressed harder to have them pulled yesterday instead of leaving it to others.'

'We weren't to know it'd be this significant,' Gerry said.

'It's our job to know, Gerry. Some bastard just burned two people. How cold blooded?'

Frank made a series of phone calls, setting the investigative wheels in motion. Dr Nasreen Quereshi would start the post-mortems, though a positive ID might take time. He requested uniform to check on Lilly and Nikolai's homes and prepare their families for potential tragedy. He asked Reggie to do a dig into their backgrounds. Who was this Nikolai? He wanted Sharon on the CCTV, but he didn't want Sean distracted from tracking down the peculiar, lying Reverend Lawson.

Even with his assured tone as he coordinated, his team, he felt himself melting inside. They were one step behind everybody who'd been involved with Greg Lyle. Always reacting, never preventing.

He'd had a gutful of it.

He turned to Gerry and pointed at the husk. 'The buck stops with me on this one.'

'It's unfortunate, but I think you're blameless.'

'No.' He plucked his spectacles from his head, so he could run his fingers through his wiry black hair. 'I'm sick of treading lightly, Gerry. Playing by rules set by Donald and co. Rules that these evil bastards don't give a damn about. Think about this, Gerry. Think about how ridiculous this situation has become. About the last four people who saw that poor lad alive that day. The first, Raven Blackstone, a woman tried for child-murder, is protected by top brass. The second person, Lilly Petrova, has just been murdered. The third, the reverend, has disappeared. Then, there was that dog walker, Harold Cross, who died years back. What're we supposed to do... sit here twiddling our thumbs? We either have to get proactive or give up.'

'I'm not sure I understand. We have procedure,' Gerry insisted. 'You heard what Donald said, he'll take you off the case—'

'So? What bloody case is there with all this chuffing procedure?'

She looked away.

'Look.' He nodded at the shop again. 'Procedure hasn't helped Lilly. It's getting us no closer to the truth about Greg. We can't go near someone who was tried for murdering children.' Frank took a deep breath. He turned to his car. 'You go back to the station – take a taxi. Continue coordinating the investigation from there. I need to follow up on something.'

Gerry followed. 'Frank?'

He looked at her. 'I said I want to follow up on something. You grab Rylan and—'

'Frank, no,' Gerry said. 'You can't speak to her.'

'There are two more bodies behind me,' Frank countered. 'No more twiddling thumbs.'

'But we've no proof Raven is involved in this.'

'*Emily's* ex was a child killer. A subsequent boyfriend was the victim's father. Simon. Who isn't coming across all smelling of roses, either, may I add.'

'None of it indicates—'

'All feels fairly indicative to me.' He opened the back door and welcomed Rylan out. He knelt and stroked his ears. 'Comfort her,' he whispered. 'She's going to be pissed off with me...' He handed the lead to Gerry and closed the door. He looked up at her.

'You're tired, frustrated and you're letting your emotions cloud your judgement.'

'Probably,' Frank said. 'But once upon a time, back in the day, that was quite effective. Besides, I'm not long for this job anyway... might as well do some good.'

As Frank climbed into his car, he caught sight of the burned-out husk of the Seabreeze Flower Shop in his rear-view mirror. It stood as a stark reminder of the stakes they were playing for, of the lives that hung in the balance. *Sorry Lilly,* he thought, a lump forming in his throat. *I let you slip through the net.*

The buck stops here.

He started the car.

Donald could piss off. It was time to apply the pressure.

Chapter Fifty-One

RAVEN'S APPEARANCE was a far cry from the flamboyant goth queen Frank had heard about. Simple blue jeans and a T-shirt. No elaborate make-up. Her blue tinted hair was messy and without any style.

There were dark, puffy circles under her eyes which may even give his own a run for their money.

'Ms Blackstone?'

She nodded. He showed his identification and introduced himself.

Her voice was raspy. 'I thought we'd cleared up last night.'

'It's not just about last night, Ms—'

Her forehead creased, and the lines around her eyes seemed to darken. 'It's really not a good time. You probably know I was drunk last night. I've spent most of the morning over the toilet bowl, and I expect to be returning there. I've spoken to the relevant people.'

Frank nodded, lowering his head, so she couldn't see his tightening jaw. *Relevant people trying to protect budgets and self-interests.*

'There's really nothing more to discuss,' she said.

I'll be the judge of that, Frank thought, in no mood to piss about, and holding the most major of cards. He thought of Lilly Petrova, and her kind eyes, being driven away to the mortuary. 'I'm not one of those relevant people, but I'm insisting...' He thought of Greg at the bottom of the ocean for all those years. 'Emily.'

She steadied herself against the doorframe, looking deflated rather than stunned. 'Well, if you know who I am.' Her voice was barely above a whisper. 'Then you should know you shouldn't be here. At my front door. You could put me in danger.'

'It's a chance I have to take,' Frank said. 'Because I'm investigating the murder of Greg Lyle.'

At the mention of Greg's name, Raven deflated further. She was now having to hold herself upright against the frame. 'Please... just leave... you have to leave.'

Seeing her melting with anxiety gave him no pleasure, but Frank kept his voice firm. 'I'm afraid I can't do that.' *If you know anything, Greg's parents have a right to the truth. Greg has a right to the truth.* 'I won't be going until we've talked.'

She shook her head, her eyes full of fear. 'I'm going to close the door.'

Frank leaned his weathered face closer. 'Then I'll stand here all day. Even if you contact my superiors, even if they try to drag me away, I'll shout at the top of my lungs. I'm here about a murdered child, Emily. A boy called Greg... a boy thrown away and forgotten about. If they've to drag me away in pieces, so be it. At least I tried.'

She looked saddened and lost. 'I can't help you with that... but if I could, I would.'

'Let's at least give it a go?' Frank raised an eyebrow, sensing success.

For a long moment, Raven stared at him, her eyes searching his face. Then, with a resigned sigh, she stepped back. 'Come in. It won't matter any more anyway...'

'Why do you say that?'

She led him into a lounge that was heavy with the scent of incense. Black velvet drapes framed the windows, and ornate candelabras stood on antique side tables.

He found the answer to his question in a pile of suitcases stacked neatly by the door.

'You're leaving.'

Raven sank into an elaborate high-backed chair, her fingers tracing the intricate patterns carved into the armrests. 'No choice. The truth is coming anyway. Samantha Wells is threatening to release a true crime podcast. There'll be no stopping her. You think you're driven, DCI, you should see this bitch!'

'So, you're running?' Frank sat on the sofa.

'Not running, no. I'll be moved... again. I told them last night about the podcast. They won't be able to stop it. Freedom of speech. They'll ask her not to. If she goes ahead anyway, they'll move me.'

Frank took a deep breath. He exhaled and said, 'I wasn't aware of this.'

Raven shrugged. 'Obvious really. I'm on borrowed time wherever I go.' Her eyes met his. 'To be honest, I don't really blame Samantha. The truth cannot stay locked away forever. Nature of the beast, I guess.'

No, it can't, Frank thought. *Just like a little boy locked in a fridge.* Frank leaned forward, his voice low and intense. 'But if you were innocent... then isn't that the truth?'

She fixed him with a stare. 'I never actually said I was innocent.'

A chill ran down his spine. He opened his mouth to speak, but stopped when Raven stood and marched to the suitcases. She unzipped a pocket and pulled out a stack of photographs. With trembling hands, she returned to stand before Frank.

'Five,' she said, her voice barely above a whisper. She slammed the first photo down on the coffee table between them.

It was a school portrait of a young boy with fiery red hair. His eyes sparkled with mischief, a lopsided grin revealing a missing front tooth. 'Bruce,' Raven said. 'Over the years, fragments have returned... flashes... Bruce loved to tell jokes. Always had a new one ready. He told me one in the park we took him from. I wish I could remember it.'

Another photo joined the first. This time, a boy with dark skin and close-cropped hair. He wore a football jersey, a look of fierce determination on his young face. 'Marcus,' Raven continued, her voice starting to crack. 'He told me he dreamed of playing for Manchester United when we picked him up in the car. He carried a football with him. I can't remember what happened to it.'

The third photo showed a pair of twins, two boys with matching blond hair and blue eyes. They had their arms around each other, identical grins lighting up their faces.

'Phil and James,' Raven said, her voice growing softer with each name. 'They were inseparable and finished each other's sentences. I recall them arguing over what they were going to watch on television before their last dinner.'

Finally, she placed the last photo on the table. A boy with a mop of brown curls and a gap-toothed grin beamed at the camera. She breathed his name out. 'Tommy.' She stroked the picture. 'He loved stories. I remember him telling me about some of them... Tommy... I remember him the most.' There were tears in her eyes. 'He wanted me to tell him stories. About monsters.' She looked up at Frank. 'But the stories were real, weren't they?'

Frank stared down at the photos, a sick feeling growing in the pit of his stomach. He then looked back up at Raven. She had tears running down her face.

'Five,' she repeated. 'And I was responsible. There's no doubt about that.'

The silence that followed was deafening. Frank felt as if the air had been sucked out of the room. He looked down at the smiling faces of the children, then back up at Raven.

'And I told them that,' she said. 'But they didn't listen.'

Chapter Fifty-Two

RAY'S LUNGS burned as he writhed in the icy water. Panic clawed at his throat, his mind reeling with confusion and terror. Where was he? What was happening? Was he dying?

Eventually, he found air, and he sucked it in, filling himself with both life and hope again.

But then came cold. *Burning cold.*

He saw a figure floating beside him, face down and motionless.

Graham's shoulders. His neck.

My brother.

Bloody and broken.

'Graham... I'm sorry.' Water filled his mouth.

He coughed out water. His skin now felt like it was on fire.

Graham rotated. His eyes were empty.

Blood clouded the water.

He thrashed. He needed to get away. Why was the water so thick around him? Why did his hands and legs feel so trapped?

His brother's empty eyes were on him again, so he closed them.

I should have saved you, Graham.

When he opened them again, Graham was gone, but the icy water was still there, as was the burning... the claustrophobia... the tightness around his arms and legs.

The bathroom came into focus around him – cracked tiles, peeling wallpaper. He looked down. He was in a bath naked. Around him bobbed blocks of ice.

Above, Megan was looking down at him.

She looked different.

Calm.

In one hand, she held a rosary, the beads clicking softly as she moved them between her fingers. In the other hand, she held a blue plastic container.

Ray tried to sit up, to pull himself out of the tub, but his body wouldn't respond. Panic clawed at his throat as he realised his hands and feet were bound, rope biting into his skin.

'Megan,' he sputtered, spitting out water. 'Please.' His voice cracked, a mixture of fear and shame.

The beads clicked in her hand.

Her expression was unaltering.

Ray thrashed in the icy water. The tub seemed to shrink around him, the walls of the bathroom pressing in.

He recognised the container as bleach. It was open.

'Megan... I was telling the truth... I never lied...'

A flash of movement.

His eyes joined his skin in a flaring burn.

He squeezed his eyes closed as she poured more.

'Let us pray,' Megan said. 'Our Father, who art in heaven...'

Chapter Fifty-Three

RAVEN'S FINGERS traced the edge of Tommy's photograph. 'I wish I could explain to you what my time with Robert was really like. But, like I said to you, the memories, although they've partially returned... they remain so fragmented. It's hard to explain. They're like snatches of old dreams, or moments of television programmes you half-remember from childhood. Hazy. Indistinct. Hypnosis has brought some of it out. But what you want, DCI Black, what everybody always wanted, you cannot have. You can't have the entire picture, simply because I can't draw it. I wish I could give you an explanation.' She stroked the photograph again. 'They deserve it...'

The wave of anger and adrenaline from being in the dark that Frank had been riding on the journey had moved towards a sense of unease. He shifted his weight, feeling the tension in his shoulders, wondering what the outcome of this journey into darkness would be.

'There's only one moment that burns.' Her voice caught. 'It is so vivid... it is with me every single second. I think without it, I would've been lost, maybe forever. The least I deserve, you're probably thinking. It is certainly what I think.'

'What was that moment?'

'The moment that Tommy asked me to tell him a story about monsters...' She looked down at the boy in the photo. 'It was a story in which a pirate saved an orphan from a sea monster. I made it up on the spot. He loved it.' She smiled. 'I loved it.' The smile fell away, and she closed her eyes. 'Not long after, he died in my arms.'

Jesus, Frank thought, his knees weakening. He leaned back against the wall, his mind reeling from the stark contrast between such a beautiful, innocent story and its tragic, horrendous aftermath.

She looked off into space. 'Every second of that experience remains vivid. Every moment of his happiness and joy, then his pain, and his death. *Every second.* Clear. Crystal clear.' The raw anguish in her voice was undeniable. She looked up at Frank.

A chill ran down his spine.

'And then I was awake.'

Frank opened his mouth to ask a question, but realised he didn't really have one, so he closed it again.

'For a long time afterwards, my world was silent. Not empty like before with Robert. In a way, that could have been more tolerable. It was like I existed in a muffled patched up place of anxiety, confusion... dread. People were continually asking me for the truth... but I didn't really know what that was. Professionals helped me to claw back my identity. But even now, as I've explained, it only exists in fragments and glimpses. My identity now. Raven Black-stone is more fully formed and recognised. So, the story they wanted, the story Samantha wanted, the story *you* want ... it's not there to have.'

Frank's justice-driven mind struggled against his growing empathy. He didn't believe, *didn't want to believe,* that acts so heinous could simply be forgotten.

He'd always believed that anybody who does such horrendous things should be tortured by them forever.

Still, in a way, she was being tortured every single day. Tortured by the absence of what really happened. Not knowing how much of a part she really played in this grotesque series of events must be a torturous form of guilt, like no other.

She stared at Frank. 'Please understand that I never pleaded innocence. I never asked to be housed and cared for by professionals. I didn't really speak. I didn't speak because I felt lost. I didn't even feel like a person. I sat with my fragments. Then, years later, I was free, here, rebuilding my identity.'

Frank wanted to reconcile the broken woman here with the monster he'd imagined all these years, but he wasn't able to do so. 'How did you meet Robert?'

'Again, fragments, but I know this. He came to me at my most vulnerable.'

Like all monsters do, Frank thought.

'I remember spending most of my time at the local park, away from my parents. My father used to hit me... my mother spent most of her time on drugs and she barely recognised me. I sat on a swing. Every day. I recall him watching me. Then, one day, he approached me. He used to call me his little bird. He said my wings were broken. I recall him promising me, all the time, that he'd fix me. That all little birds will fly again.'

She shrugged. 'And despite what he was, I remember

his small moments of kindness towards me. I also recall his pity for those who were bullied and hurt by those who should know better. I've never seen him again, but I've read about him... He believed himself to be helping those children escape traumatic lives.'

'Do you believe that?'

'What? His sentiment or his claim that this was good?'

'Both?'

'Well, of course, Raven Blackstone doesn't believe that he helped the children. Emily? Well, I can't remember. Him and his sentiment – I don't know. Who knows what a person truly believes? We're all so different. There doesn't seem to be much compassion involved in the way those boys died, despite his claims. But maybe he believed, who knows? He poisoned me, too, you know? Altered my perception with chemicals. Took away my grasp on reality. The drugs may have helped destroy my memory... my former identity. Over the years, professionals have tried to help me decide that I was another of his victims rather than... well... but I never asked for that, and so many times, when I think of them, when I think of Tommy, I struggle to believe I was a victim.'

Frank took a deep breath. He was trying not to feel pity, but was struggling to hold it off. The complexity of Raven's situation – both victim and perpetrator – weighed heavily on him.

'Needless to say, Raven has come with baggage! Dissociative episodes, trauma, PTSD. Suicide attempts. Not an excuse. Five boys. Five. I was there. The pain is warranted. Samantha Wells wants all these fragments. Maybe I should give them to her before I go. Lay them all out. But they're glass shards. Vicious glass shards that come into me every day. And I feel every rip... every tear... It would let everyone know I was suffering... maybe, her listeners deserve that? I don't know.'

'I'm also here about Greg,' Frank said.

Raven stood and went to sit back down on her chair. 'Greg was a nice boy. Smart. Curious. I felt horrendous lying to him about his father's whereabouts that day. Simon was upstairs.'

'We know,' Frank said. 'Simon told us.'

'A mistake. Looking back now. A massive mistake. I cannot hide behind excuses. No fragmented memory on this one. But I think I understand why I did it. I was still young. Twenty. I'd only been Raven for a short time. I was building a sense of self. Simon took advantage of that. He was kind to me. Made me feel that there was still warmth in the world. Obviously, he was doing it for his own benefit, but I wouldn't be the first young person to be suckered into that, would I? In the end, I wanted to help him. He told me it was for the best if I lied to Greg about his presence there... Little bird strikes again... ruining lives everywhere.'

'You could have offered the truth after he went missing?'

'I know. Same weak excuse, I'm afraid. I was a coward. Creating a new identity I was terrified to lose. For a time, I debated it, but then the police announced it was an accident. A fall. I didn't think it would make any difference coming forward... I'm sorry.'

'What happened between you and Simon?' Frank asked.

'Not much. Our relationship was brief. I knew he was married for God's sake – what a bitch I am! I know it means little, but I'd never do that now. No chance. Simon had a nasty streak, too. Not violent, not like my father had been. Never raised a hand to me. But cruel in his words, dismissive of Greg's interests and needs. I remember one time, Simon ranting about how his son's marine biology obsession was "useless" and a "waste of time". Who does that about their own son?'

Frank nodded, encouraging her to continue.

'I ended it after Greg went missing. I told him to be with his wife. Wait for his child to come home. He called me every name under the sun. We never spoke again.'

'And did you ever speak to Greg before that morning?'

'No. I swear. I was new to the town. It was the first time I'd seen him outside a photograph. It was literally that one encounter.'

'Do you think that Simon could have hurt his own child?'

Raven creased her face. 'I wouldn't have thought so. If I'd have thought that, I would've said something. But, as you're now well aware, I can hardly be considered an expert judge of character... It hurt me badly to hear how Greg died. Obviously I, more than anyone, know that such horror exists in the world, but to see it come so close to home again. To think I could have been the last person Greg ever spoke to...' She looked down at Tommy. 'Like Tommy.'

'You weren't.'

She nodded.

Frank watched as Raven's shoulders shook, her composure finally crumbling. He stayed standing, at the wall, conflicted. Part of him wanted to comfort her, but another part recoiled at the thought of what she'd been involved in, even if she couldn't remember it all.

He let her cry for a short time as she became lost in a turmoil of what-ifs and could-have-beens. Frank wondered how different things might have been if someone had recognised the vulnerability and mental instability in Emily as a child. If someone had stepped in to help her, save her from an abusive father, save her before Aldridge got his claws into her.

After a moment's hesitation, he went over and placed a hand on her arm, surprising himself with the gesture.

She looked up at him, her eyes puffy. 'I'm so, so sorry. For all of it. For not being stronger, for not fighting harder, for being that little bird. For Tommy, for Greg, for all of them. I know it doesn't change anything, doesn't bring them back, doesn't erase what happened. But I'm sorry. Do you believe me?'

'Yes,' Frank said simply. And he realised he wasn't lying.

'Will you find who hurt Greg?'

Frank nodded. 'I will.'

'For what it's worth, I don't think it was Simon.'

Everyone I speak to would probably disagree with you, Frank thought. 'I don't think so, either.' Again, he was telling the truth.

His phone buzzed in his pocket. He took it out and saw Gerry's name. 'Excuse me.'

Raven nodded.

Frank stepped outside to take the call.

'How do, Gerry? Before you say owt, don't worry, it's done. I've spoken to her and I doubt there'll be repercussions.'

'It's not about that.'

'Ah... okay...' Although it irritated him constantly, it actually felt rather disconcerting that he wasn't being worried about for once. 'What's it about then?'

'Frank, the video has been restored.'

His heart spiked. 'Fast work. And?'

'Best you just come and see it. It's significant.'

312

Noting the urgency in Gerry's voice, he told her he was on his way; then, he returned to Raven, to bid the broken woman farewell, realising that no matter how old he got, he never failed to be stunned by the complexity of human nature.

Chapter Fifty-Four

THE DOORBELL'S shrill ring cut through the silence of Raven's home, causing her to flinch. She stood frozen, a half-folded black lace dress clutched in her trembling hands. The conversation with DCI Black had left her raw, exposed. Every shadow seemed to hold the ghosts of her past, every reflection a reminder of the lives she'd lived – and lost.

With a deep breath, she approached the door. Through the peephole, she saw Damien's familiar face, a brown paper bag clutched in his hands. The sight of her friend brought a wave of conflicting emotions: relief at seeing a friendly face, guilt at the secrets she'd kept, and a profound sadness knowing this might be the last time she'd ever see him.

She quickly closed the lounge door so he wouldn't see the suitcases if he came in.

She then opened the door, forcing a smile. 'Damien. Good to see you, mate.'

She could tell from his stunned expression that he thought she looked terrible.

'Thought you could use some lunch,' he said, holding up the bag. 'And some company. You've seemed really off recently. And I know Derek has headed off. I've ice cream so we can sit and man bash...'

She considered the suitcases in the lounge. She hesitated, then stepped aside. 'In that case, come in, but sit in the kitchen. I smashed a vase in the lounge. I'll get to it later.'

He nodded, smiling.

As they sat, eating ice cream in the kitchen, Raven felt a curious detachment, as if she were watching herself from afar. She'd changed identity before, but this felt different. Raven Blackstone had been more than just a name – it had been a chance at redemption, a life she'd built from the ashes of her past.

Looking at Damien's concerned face, Raven made a decision. He deserved to know the truth, and it would be better coming from her than from some sensationalised podcast. She'd tell him everything – about Emily Thorne, about Robert Aldridge, about the children. It would be her final act as Raven Blackstone, a confession and a farewell wrapped into one.

As she steeled herself to speak, Raven felt the weight of her impending loss settle over her. Most people feared the end of one life; she was about to lose her second. Yet beneath the fear and sadness, there was a flicker of something else – a grim determination to face whatever came next with dignity.

Outside, the sun broke through the clouds, casting a warm glow through the kitchen window. Raven closed her eyes, savouring the moment. Soon, she'd be someone new, somewhere new. But for now, she was still Raven Blackstone, preparing to tell the truth to a friend, and to face the end of another life.

Chapter Fifty-Five

On the journey back to HQ, Gerry prepared Frank for what he was going to see on the recovered VHS.

Warning him had been kind. He pitied his colleagues for watching that video before knowing what was on it.

Hearing about it now turned his stomach. Raven's revelations had already frayed his nerves, and he knew that viewing this video was going to shred them further.

'Greg had warned Terry that the video should never go out... that it would be destructive. An understatement.' Frank ended the call and, as he drove, lit two pre-rolled cigarettes in quick succession. The nicotine did little to settle his nerves, but it was better than nothing.

At HQ in his office, Gerry awaited him in a chair beside his computer. She'd left his leather swivel chair beside her unoccupied for him.

Rylan was curled up at Gerry's feet. She buried her fingers in her dog's fur.

'You don't have to watch again, Gerry.'

'I want to.' Her tone was flat, but the way she stroked

Rylan suggested a different story. 'I may have missed something.'

'How many times have you seen it? Frank asked, settling into his chair, the worn leather creaking in protest.

'Twice.'

'Good lord, Gerry.'

The glow from the computer screen cast eerie shadows across his cluttered desk.

Gerry's finger hovered over the play button. 'Ready?'

Frank nodded grimly. 'As I'll ever be.'

The video flickered to life. The image was grainy, the lighting poor, but Frank could make out a small figure hunched in a chair. Greg Lyle. He appeared slightly younger than in the photo on the incident room board. His sandy hair fell across his forehead, partially obscuring eyes that darted nervously around the room. Frank recognised the vestry, where they'd sat with Ray yesterday.

'Tell me how you've been feeling, Greg,' Ray said, off camera. His voice was smooth and reassuring.

Greg's fingers twisted the hem of his T-shirt. 'I don't know...'

'Shall we go through it again, then? In the same way that we went through it earlier.'

'I don't know if I can.'

'You can, Greg. Just exactly the same as we did earlier. You don't have to change anything at all.'

'Please, I—'

'Greg... you must. The more times you vocalise it, the greater chance we have of getting these things out. Once they're out, we can eradicate. We're safe... *here*. This is a safe space.'

Frank gripped the arms of his chair. 'Safe space, my arse,' he muttered.

On the video, Greg took a deep breath. 'Yesterday, I felt like I was on the outside... like I do most days. But this was worse than usual. It was as if I was looking in through a window at everyone else, but I couldn't figure out how to get inside. John and Lewis were laughing about *Friends*. I wanted to join in, but just couldn't. I didn't watch it. I didn't know what to say. There was a wall there. The words got all jumbled up in my head, and by the time I figured out how to break through the wall and get involved in the conversation, they'd moved on to something else.'

Frank glanced at Gerry. Her face remained impassive, but she leaned forward while her fingers continued their rhythmic stroking of Rylan's fur.

Greg continued, his words tumbling out faster now. 'Later, Mr Banks, my English teacher, asked me a question. It was about *The Woman in Black*. I knew the answer, but that wall was there again. I broke through the wall, but like last time, it was too late. Someone else had spoken. I could feel my heart... beating too hard... I was desperate for it to stop.'

Frank leaned forward, nearer the screen, drawn into Greg's struggle. It was all too easy to imagine Maddie at that same age, when she'd started wrestling with her own demons.

'Greg,' Ray said. 'I want you to consider something. Something surprising... different... unique to our usual ways of perceiving things. You shouldn't feel so isolated. Teenagers struggle, yes, but not to this extent. These are symptoms of something else.'

Knowing what was coming, Frank clenched his fist.

'There are forces in this world, Greg,' Ray continued. 'Forces that seek to separate us from God's light.'

Frank's fist came down on the desk. The screen trembled. 'Could you just imagine someone speaking to your kid like that? It's like he's being indoctrinated into a cult.'

'It's not too dissimilar,' Gerry said. 'The tactic is to create a problem, then offer the solution.'

With disgust, Frank listened to Ray continue. 'Our world is one born from connection... from understanding. But there's another world that exists, an antithesis to His creation. So, we must look towards this.'

'Hell?' Greg asked. There was a tremble in his voice.

'Not as such,' Ray said. 'Hell is a place of punishment for the wicked. This world doesn't even deserve a name. It's a realm of chaos, of disconnect. It feeds on the energy of our past lives, our unresolved traumas carried through millennia.'

For fuck's sake, Frank thought, pausing the video. He plucked off his glasses, and rubbed his forehead with the back of his hand. 'Do you think Lawson actually believes this stuff?'

'Based on his tone and the consistency of his message across multiple sessions, I'd say yes. He believes it.' Gerry hesitated before adding, 'I found something in Ray Lawson's notes, too, and some old interviews he gave when he discovered his brother's body. After his brother Graham's suicide, he spoke of his brother being under "chaotic control" of "dark souls" which "disconnected him from reality".'

'Shit,' Frank said. 'And this is how he aims to bring someone back to reality... I mean, surely this drives you further from it. So you think this madness started with his brother?'

'I don't know. I can say there are correlations.'

Frank restarted the video. 'Our souls have lived countless times,' Ray continued. 'And each life leaves its mark.

Some souls carry more darkness than others. I've known souls like it. Other souls.'

'How... how do we stop it?' Greg asked.

'There's nothing shocking in what I'm about to say,' Ray said. 'Through prayer, Greg. Through opening yourself to God's love and rejecting the darkness.'

Frank's voice was a low growl. 'There's everything shocking in what you're saying, you bastard! You're manipulating a vulnerable child!'

Ray came into the camera shot for the first time, but it was a rear angle. Unlike now, he had a full head of hair. He knelt opposite Greg and put his hands on his shoulders. There was a moment of silence in which they could hear some faint yapping in the background.

'Buddy?' Frank glanced at Gerry.

'Yes,' Gerry said. 'He comes into the footage later.'

'Are you ready to try, Greg?' Ray asked.

Greg nodded. His eyes were wide. Frank was certain he could see the trust in his expression despite the grainy footage.

'Bow your head.'

Greg did so.

Ray then bowed his own. 'Heavenly Father, we come before you now, asking for your divine protection. Shield this child from the forces that seek to isolate him, to confuse him. In the name of Jesus Christ, we rebuke any spirit of darkness, any lingering energy from past lives that clings to Greg. That break his will. Help us heal him.' Ray's voice rose and fell in a rhythmic cadence. 'We plead the blood of Jesus over Greg's mind, his heart, his very soul. As it is written in Ephesians 6:12, "For we wrestle not against flesh and blood, but against principalities, against powers, against the rulers of the darkness of this world, against spiritual wickedness in high places."'

Greg was squeezing his eyes shut. The poor boy looked in some discomfort.

'By the power vested in me as a servant of the Most High God,' Ray said. 'I command any unclean spirit, any remnant of past life trauma, to depart from this child. In Jesus' name, amen.'

'Amen,' Greg whispered.

Frank paused the video again. 'Sorry. This is too much.' He lifted his glasses again, and squeezed his eyes.

'You should take a break,' Gerry said.

'No... I don't need one. I'm merely stating a fact – that this is too much.' He looked at Gerry; his vision was blurred from rubbing his eyes. 'Who does he think he is? The chuffing exorcist? How many sessions are on this tape?'

'There are eighteen prayer sessions.'

'My word. Eighteen sessions of religious indoctrination. This is horrendous.'

'Actually, there are twenty-one sessions of religious indoctrination,' Gerry said.

Frank stared at Greg's face frozen on the screen, his heart aching for the boy. 'Aye... the water sessions, I'm assuming?'

'Yes,' Gerry said.

'I'm sorry, lad. Having your head stuffed full of such nonsense...' He took a deep breath and slipped his glasses back on. 'Gerry, please go forward to one of the water sessions. You said the last one was the worst.'

Gerry did this.

'It's not as bad as you made it sound, is it?' he asked.

She didn't respond. She merely restarted the video and dropped her hand back into Rylan's fur.

Wearing only a pair of shorts, Greg sat in an old-fashioned metal bathtub filled with water, crossing his arms over his heaving chest, shivering and gasping. Beside him was a bucket full of ice. Ray knelt, and using a plastic measuring jug, he topped up the water with ice. *Bloody monster,* Frank thought.

'Please,' Greg stuttered through chattering teeth. 'I'm cold. I want Buddy.'

'He's waiting outside for you. He's safe.'

'Please.'

Frank wondered how long he could hold on before being forced to grab some air. This was obscene... utterly obscene.

'The cold purifies,' Ray said, his voice maddeningly calm. 'It drives out the darkness. Just as Christ was baptised in the Jordan, we use this icy water to cleanse your soul. The cold sterilises, Greg. It fights off the invaders that cling to your spirit.'

Greg was shivering. He was freezing.

Frank felt bile rising in his throat. He'd seen some sick things in his years on the force, but watching a child being tortured in the name of religion... it made him want to put his fist through the screen.

Ray read, his voice rising above Greg's whimpers. 'Though I walk through the valley of the shadow of death, I'll fear no evil: for thou art with me; thy rod and thy staff, they comfort me.'

Greg's head lolled back, his eyes glassy. He was crying.

'Stay with me, Greg,' Ray urged. 'Fight it.'

Greg suddenly raised himself from the tub. Ray placed his hands on the child's shoulders and pushed him back down. He struggled and writhed.

Frank couldn't understand all of Greg's words. Some of the ones he identified were: 'Burning', 'Buddy', 'Mum'.

Water splashed over the side. Ray continued. 'For God hath not given us the spirit of fear.' He was gasping for air as he chanted, clearly working hard to keep Greg sitting. 'But of power, and of love, and of a sound mind.'

Frank watched in a helpless rage as Greg writhed. His knuckles were white where he now gripped the arms of his chair. Every muscle in his body was tense. His instinct was to leap and somehow intervene.

Eventually, Greg wriggled free of the tiring reverend's arms, and the tub turned over. The water, ice, and the poor lad spilled out onto the vestry floor.

Ray disappeared from view and returned with a towel. He knelt and laid it over the shivering boy, and pulled him close to his chest and rocked him. 'There, Greg, it's over. You did well.' He rubbed his arms briskly. 'The darkness is loosening its hold. I can feel it loosening.'

Greg nodded weakly, his teeth still chattering.

Ray held Greg close in the towel to try and warm him. After a short time, he asked, 'How do those walls feel now?'

'Less thick, Reverend.'

'Like you don't need to break them? That maybe you could walk through them—'

Frank paused it. 'You said there was a final video... a kind of assessment of the treatment?'

'Yes, do you want me to show you?'

'In a moment... first, just go through it with me again.'

'Well, they talk about Greg's main interests. They suddenly seemed more varied... he said he felt less drawn to sea creatures and flowers, and was enjoying some television programmes, and even some sport. Ray relished it, calling it a partial success... that the dark hold of other souls was loosening on him. That his obsessive tendencies were losing their grip.'

'Unless he was merely telling the bastard what he wanted to hear, rather than be subjected to this horror again?'

'Yes... like I said before, these are tactics employed by cults. Physical stress... all designed to break down the victim's sense of self.'

Frank's mind flashed to Raven, recalling her haunted eyes as she explained how Aldridge had stripped away her sense of self with drugs and abuse.

'What a world we live in, Gerry... what a sodding world. Turn it off, please. I've had enough.' Frank slumped back in his chair. 'It's foul and depraved. We need to find Ray and put him away. How are we doing on locating him?'

'I've heard nothing,' Gerry said.

'So, naturally, we're going to think he killed Greg and, having watched some of that video, I think he's going to have a difficult time arguing against it...'

He suddenly noticed something in Gerry's face. There was a tightness around her eyes, which he wasn't used to seeing. There was also a slight downturn of her mouth. 'Are you okay?'

'I don't know,' she said.

It was so unlike Gerry to be uncertain of her feelings.

'Well, it was hard, and you watched it twice through, and then some more with me, so take a moment...'

Gerry nodded. 'It was hard, yes. But I coped well with everything apart from... well...' She stroked Rylan.

'Go on, Gerry?'

'In the last minute or so, Ray got Greg to admit that Buddy was just a dog... nothing more...' Her voice dropped to a whisper. 'And that he didn't actually need him.'

As if on cue, Rylan stood and placed his head on Gerry's lap so she didn't have to lean any more. She scratched behind his ears, her eyes distant.

'I'm sorry, Gerry... I'm sure he didn't really believe it. He was just desperate to escape the sick man. Do we have a timestamp on the video?'

Gerry nodded. 'This last extract was recorded two days before he disappeared.'

Frank stood abruptly, his chair rolling backwards. 'So, if Greg stole the video on that day, and hid it in the treehouse' – he closed his eyes, giving thought to how it could have played out – 'this may have led to some kind of altercation on that final morning. What if "bring" in that pager message on the day he disappeared was referring to this tape? Ray wanted the tape back. This could be because he was "losing control" also in the message. What happened during that confrontation?' He paced the small office, his mind racing. 'I want him found now. This is more than just a BOLO. How many other children has this monster subjected to his twisted secrets over the years?

'I need some fresh air,' Frank muttered, heading for the door.

Chapter Fifty-Six

Raven gripped the edges of the sink. The bathroom mirror reflected a face she barely recognised.

Her intention was to splash some water on her face, gather courage and confess everything to her best friend.

What she hadn't banked on was seeing this coward looking back at her in the reflection.

She didn't have the guts to burden Damien. To taint him with her darkness. Although, it was an inevitability anyway.

It would be best coming from her.

But she was spineless.

A sob escaped. She quickly muffled the next one with her hand. Tears hot and relentless now, she sank to the floor, her back against the cool tile wall.

It was time to claw her way out of her own skin, to shed this identity like a snake shedding its old, tainted scales.

Raven lost track of time, and when she finally pulled herself back to her feet, splashed cold water on her face, and steeled herself to face Damien again, she wondered if he'd even still be there.

Maybe, he'd looked into the lounge, saw the packed suitcases and, feeling betrayed, had left.

When she opened the bathroom door, she saw immediately that Damien was still there. He was by the front door. His face was ashen. His cheeks glistened with tears.

He knew.

'Damien?' Raven's voice came out as a hoarse whisper. It sounded alien to her own ears, as if it belonged to someone else now.

His eyes widened with shock and... *could it be?* Fear.

Her best friend was terrified of her. He held up his phone. 'I can't... I can't...'

'Damien, listen to me—'

'Lizzie texted me...'

'*Listen* to me—'

'She told me about a podcast. There's a podcast.'

The words hit Raven like a physical blow. She staggered, her hand reaching out to steady herself against the wall.

'Tell me it's not true.'

'Damien, please.' She tried to speak assertively, clearly, but she couldn't even be certain the words made it out. 'You have to let me explain—'

'Is it true?'

'Damien—'

'Is it?'

'Yes.'

'My God. No... no... I can't... I just can't.'

She started towards him, but he was already turning, and then he was gone. The door closed behind him with a soft click that echoed like a gunshot in the sudden silence.

For a moment, Raven stood frozen, staring at the closed

door. 'Damien,' she said, knowing with absolute certainty that she'd never see him again.

She went into the lounge, freezing at the sound of the ticking clock on the mantlepiece.

The final ticks of my existence.

She moved mechanically through the room, her fingers trailing over the artefacts of the persona she was leaving behind. The ornate silver candlesticks, the framed prints of Victorian mourning jewellery, the velvet-bound books of gothic poetry.

The sun had set outside her window, casting the room into shadows. In the gathering darkness, she sank to her knees. Far away in the distance, St Mary's church tolled the hour.

Was it ringing out the end of Raven Blackstone and the rebirth of a woman with no name, no past and an uncertain future stretching before her?

Chapter Fifty-Seven

RATHER THAN FRESH AIR, Frank opted for two more cigarettes in his old Volvo's worn driver's seat. It barely took the edge off it all.

But, being in Bertha, on her worn seat with the door closed, always offered him a safe space. Here, time just seemed to stand still, while outside, the world continued its heinous and relentless march.

He rolled another cigarette. His fingers moved with practiced ease, muscle memory taking over where his distracted mind faltered. The rituals of a lifelong smoker, etched into his very being.

He stared up at HQ, wondering if he'd the strength to get back in there, knowing deep down that it wasn't really a question. It was inevitable that he'd be going.

Too many people were relying on him.

Both alive and dead.

He'd lost count of the number of times he'd walked through those doors, carrying the weight of unsolved cases on his shoulders...

How many more times would he be that voice for the voiceless?

Greg in that ice bath, shivering and terrified, flashed before his eyes.

Reverend Ray Lawson.

You were supposed to protect him, you sanctimonious prick!

How many young minds have you warped with your religious bollocks?

Was that woman who raked your face another of your victims?

Frank noticed the smoke coiling around him in the car. He wound down the window and threw out the cigarette.

In the distance, he heard a woman laughing, and his breath caught in his throat.

Maddie.

It was *her* laugh.

He climbed from the car and looked over the vehicles in the car park, and saw two detectives talking and joking together.

It wasn't her.

He closed his eyes and for no discernible reason, thought of the smell of her hair, when she was young. A floral scent.

He climbed back into the car, his attention switching to Lilly in a shop full of similar scents.

Her kind eyes.

What did I miss? Could I have stopped it?

Worse still, did my presence somehow cause your death?

He shook his head, Raven, too, raising herself in his consciousness, revealing her fragments, which connected her to the death of five innocent boys.

When had the world become so dark, so shrouded?

But had it, Frank?

Or are you just losing the ability to push the horrors aside and soldier on?

Are you just getting old?

Going past your best?

The memory of Mary's voice, soft and pleading, cut through him like a knife. What would she think of him now, chain-smoking in his car, chasing forgotten victims, lost souls and monsters?

Sixty-five years of age.

With a daughter lost on the streets.

'I should have listened, Mary. I really should have listened.'

And then, maybe, Nigel would never would have entered the picture.

Maybe?

Who am I kidding?

Most certainly.

His reflection in the rear-view mirror seemed to mock him. Greying hair, lines etched deep around eyes that had seen too much. When had he become this man? A man so intent on torturing himself to despair?

His phone's shrill ring cut through his brooding.

Sean.

'Welcome to Hell, Sean,' he said.

'Eh?'

'Never mind.'

'I got our arsonist. The CCTV footage from near the Seabreeze Flower Shop. It was the same person who broke in yesterday. We have him on the back street, going down the steps to the back door of the shop. Late that night, we have him going into the shop, leaving, then returning with a canister of petrol, and leaving again after setting it alight.'

Frank took a deep breath and closed his eyes. 'I'd been there when the bastard had been there.'

Sean didn't respond.

Am I making mistakes because of my age? Should I have been more vigilant with Lilly and this vulnerability?

'Rather idiotic...' Sean said.

Aye, Frank thought, *I am*.

'... him coming back and forth with the accelerant. I mean isn't it obvious there're cameras everywhere these days?'

'People can be idiotic when running high on adrenaline.' He was wondering how far he might be tempted to go himself before all this was through. 'Who's the killer then?'

'Facial recognition software gave us Georgi Vasilev, fifty-nine, Bulgarian national, been in the country since 1983. He was brought over as a specialist engineer for Ford. For the last ten years, he's had his own workshop – working on car exteriors. I'll arrange an arrest.'

'No. I'll pick him up.'

There was silence.

'What's the address, Sean?'

'Really, sir... you don't have to do that. It's a slam dunk... I'll get some officers to bring him in.'

'Address, Sean?'

Frank started Bertha's engine. The familiar rumble of the engine felt like a call to action.

Another pause. 'He could be dangerous... do you want me to come with you?'

'Why? He's pushing sixty. Two old men? What could go wrong? Give me the bloody address.'

Sean relented. As Frank pulled away, he considered Donald's reaction when he heard about his exploits today, beginning with a visit to Raven, and concluding with a showdown with a murderer that had incriminated himself on camera anyway.

He could almost hear Donald's exasperated sigh, could picture the vein throbbing in his forehead. *Well, sod this,* Frank thought. *If I'm going down, might as well go down swinging.*

As he drove, Lilly, Ray, Greg and his daughter flashed through his mind in a sequence that refused to let up.

Quickly, anger became fury.

The streets of Whitby blurred past, familiar landmarks turned strange and sinister in the grip of his rage. Frank felt something awaken inside him – a primal, righteous anger that burned away the maudlin fog of self-doubt.

Chapter Fifty-Eight

Mind racing, Sharon marched from parishioner Maggie Holland's home to her car, calling Reggie en route. 'Come on... come on...'

The phone seemed to ring endlessly, ratcheting up her frustration.

Shit!

He must have been mid-dialogue with one of the other parishioners.

He didn't pick up.

She left a message which summarised her discoveries.

Maggie had moved to Whitby from Knaresborough in 1997. While in Knaresborough, her reverend had been Ray Lawson. In fact, she'd chosen Whitby as a location for her retirement because she knew about Ray's impending move there. 'Such a fine man...'

Fine.

Maggie had emphasised this several times to Sharon.

Sharon wondered what a sneak peek at the video would do to that impression.

Still, Maggie's adoration for Lawson wasn't the important thing.

The important thing was that she'd recognised the woman who'd attacked him.

Megan Powers.

'I remember her well. From my time in Knaresborough. She was a teenager, rebellious, always in trouble, but her parents got her into church. She always seemed like a lost soul to me, confused and angry whenever I talked to her. I can't believe she just showed up at that church, hurting the reverend like that. He's been nothing but kind with his flock...'

So Megan had been another victim. Another soul Ray had driven his hooks into.

Sharon inquired after Megan Powers' current address.

Her voice was clipped and professional as she made her request, but inside, her mind was churning.

How many others were there?

How many more lives had Ray chewed up?

It was approximately ninety minutes to her home in Starbeck, a village on the doorstep of Ray's old stomping ground.

Twenty-five minutes into the drive, she spoke to Reggie.

'I'll follow, and meet you there.' Reggie's voice crackled through the speaker, concern clear in his tone. 'Just wait for me, okay?'

'I'll be fine,' Sharon said, rolling her eyes.

The motorway stretched out before her, a ribbon of tarmac cutting through the Yorkshire countryside. As the miles ticked by, Sharon's mind raced with possibilities. What would she find when she reached Megan?

She suspected another broken soul, twisted by Ray's manipulation.

Impatient to find out, she pressed her foot down on the accelerator.

Chapter Fifty-Nine

THE INDUSTRIAL ESTATE was a twisted expanse of corrugated metal and concrete. Once thriving, the place was now in disrepair. Many units had their shutters down. Frank's eyes scanned the faded signs: 'Grimshaw's Scrap Metal', 'North Star Mechanics', 'Yorkshire Timber Supplies'. Ghosts of a fading industrial age.

Bertha didn't take to the uneven ground. The rough surface threw the old Volvo from side to side, and the noise was brutal.

He found the unit he was looking for. Simply titled: 'Vasilev's'.

His heart sank. The shutters were down.

Was he chasing another shadow?

He pulled over several units back, smacked his steering wheel twice, closed his eyes and took in some deep breaths.

The dull thud of his hands against the wheel echoed his frustration. He could feel the tension coiled in his shoulders, a spring wound too tight and ready to snap.

He exited the car. The acrid smell of oil and rust hung in the air, mingling with the damp chill of the approaching evening. Beneath his feet, puddles reflected the grey sky, creating a bleak, mirror-world. He smoked another cigarette, realising he'd lost count of how many he'd smoked.

He looked at the shutters of Georgi's workshop up ahead.

The metal gleamed dully in the fading light. It was like a blank, unforgiving face turned towards him, mocking him. Justice? *You're slowing down, Frank. Too long in the tooth, too slow... leave justice to the younger folk—*

The door alongside the shutter opened. The creak of the door's hinges sounded unnaturally loud in the quiet estate.

Frank lowered his glasses and knelt on the driver's side of the car, so he was less obvious.

Georgi emerged like some ageing prize-fighter, his body still holding the memory of past strength and violence. He moved with a swagger... proud of his muscular, threatening physique.

Everything about him was in complete contrast to Frank, who felt every one of his years in that moment, every extra pound, every creak of his joints.

Georgi turned to lock the door, but then he paused, opened it and disappeared inside again.

Forgot something?

The door closed behind the killer.

Frank took a deep breath, and then he realised something.

Beneath the aches and pains, and his insecurities, his old friend still stirred.

Fierce determination.

Age hadn't taken that. *Would never take that.*

And sometimes fierce determination was all it took.

Grabbing his handcuffs from inside Bertha and slipping them in his jacket pocket, he marched to the entrance.

At the door, he fought back the urge to burst in. The cameras around here could still be operational. Georgi himself was in this situation because of such an idiotic approach.

He knocked.

Georgi Vasilev filled the frame. His shoulders were like a bull's and his arms were corded with muscle. His white hair and beard contrasted with the grease-stained overalls he wore. He looked like an ageing WWE wrestler.

'Yeah?' Georgi's voice was a low rumble, tinged with an accent that four decades in England hadn't quite erased.

Frank held up his warrant card. 'Mr Vasilev?'

'Yeah, what?'

'DCI Frank Black. I need to ask you some questions about last night.' He kept his voice steady, professional, even as adrenaline coursed through his veins. 'Like where were you?'

'Eh?' Georgi did his level-best to look confused. 'Home.'

'During the early hours of the morning. Say one o'clock?'

'What the fuck is this about?'

'An arson attack that claimed two lives. We've CCTV—'

'I'd advise you to fuck off, old man.'

Frank took a deep breath. He reached for the handcuffs in the pocket. 'I'd like you to turn around, Mr Vasilev, you're under—'

'Are you deaf?' Georgi clenched his fists.

Frank gestured right and left with his eyes. 'Cameras. Resist, you make things worse for yourself, especially if, as you claim, you were at home and did nothing wrong.

Resisting arrest, assaulting a police officer... they're not minor crimes.'

'What cameras?' He snorted. 'As if they work.'

Frank couldn't resist a grin. 'You made that mistake last night. I'd advise you not to make it again.' He pulled out the handcuffs. 'Now turn around, Mr Vasilev, I am arresting you—'

Georgi moved to close the door.

Frank was ready for this. His hand shot out, stopping the door's progress.

The impact jarred up his arm, but Frank had the adrenaline to cope with the pain.

Georgi retreated into his unit.

Frank followed him in. '—on suspicion of two counts of murder of persons as yet unidentified at the Seabreeze Flower Shop on Church Street, Whitby.'

Georgi disappeared into a pool of darkness.

Shit...

Frank looked around. The light from the open door was limited. He could make out car parts and tools. He could also smell the metal and oil.

Eyes darting around the shadows, he made it three steps in until he was alongside a car in the process of being sprayed, its windows covered in newspaper.

Georgi stepped out. He was holding a large spanner. 'There are no cameras in here, dipshit.'

I know, Frank thought, wondering if he, in fact, wanted a confrontation..

His heart hammered in his chest. 'Even if I screw this up,' Frank said. 'You score three consecutive life sentences instead of two. And life as a cop killer... well... do I need to elaborate?' He clenched his fists. 'Win win.'

Georgi moved closer. 'Win win for me too if I'm already fucked. Might as well enjoy myself.'

Frank narrowed his eyes. Adrenaline coursed through him; he hadn't really imagined it coming to this. Most usually folded when it came to this stage. Stupid of Frank, really... but slamming his knee into the big man's bollocks and punching him in the face might just offer something cathartic.

'Okay, what do you want? Money?' Georgi said. 'I can give you money.'

As expected, Frank thought. *Bottling it*.

'Two people are dead, you piece of shit. Burned alive. I'm not interested.'

'You lot are always interested in money.'

'Are we? Maybe the world's moved on since you were playing in those circles?'

'I didn't mean to kill them. It was their fault. Like you, they got in the way...'

'Turn around and get on your knees.'

'Are you taking payment? I advise you to. This could still end very well for you. For both of us.'

'I'd rather it ended badly for both of us.' Frank held up the handcuffs. 'Turn around now.' He moved towards Georgi. 'You do not have to say anything. But it may harm your defence if you do not mention when questioned something which you later rely on in court. Anything you say may be given in evidence.'

'Coming alone, you must have a death wish,' Georgi said.

The words carried some weight. Frank felt them. Was there truth in what he was saying? I mean, putting himself in this precarious position... was he desperate to be punished? 'Put the spanner down before I have to restrain you.'

The caution felt hollow in this dim, threatening space. Frank took a deep breath. The next move felt almost inevitable.

In that moment, while Frank waited for the bastard to lunge, an inexplicable calm settled over him.

His purpose here was two-fold. He was here for justice and vengeance, but he was also here for whatever fate had in store for him in this shitty, oil-stained corner of the world.

Chapter Sixty

After Raven ended the call with Bryan, her contact in the UKPPS, his instructions replayed in her mind, continuously: 'Do not go out until we've arranged a safehouse and I've contacted you again to arrange your collection. I suspect it will be in a few hours. It will take a while for the information on the podcast to filter through to the public. If anyone comes to your home before us, don't answer the door, just contact the police.'

Raven let out a long, shaky breath.

A few hours until that wave of finality crashed down, and Raven would cease to exist.

Then another life – a *third* life – would begin.

She sat on the edge of her chair, considering the irony of it all.

Nearly everyone else in the world got one shot at life, yet here she was, about to embark on her third.

And after everything she'd been involved in!

To say it was undeserving would be an understatement.

Not that leaving an old life for a new one was anything to shout about.

She'd never see her friends again.

Her last memory of Damien, her closest friend, would be that desperate look of betrayal and anguish in his eyes.

Then, there was Derek. Finally, someone she'd connected with... someone she could have *built* something with...

Her heart ached.

Couldn't she say goodbye? Just once?

Without thinking, she picked up her mobile, sought out Derek's number and phoned him. It rang once, twice, three times before going to voicemail.

Why didn't he pick up?

But then wasn't it obvious?

The podcast was probably all over the place by now.

She imagined Derek sitting there, listening to it with his daughter at university, his face paling, his heart collapsing in his chest.

She left a message. 'Derek, it's me.' She tried to keep control of her voice. 'I'm sorry. For everything. I wish things could have been different.'

After hanging up, she closed her eyes and tried to be positive. She imagined a funeral for Raven Blackstone. She saw Derek there. His face etched with confusion and grief. Damien, too, probably, along with the rest of the goth community she'd built around herself. They'd talk about her, accept that the Raven they knew wasn't the Emily who'd been brainwashed by Robert Aldridge. They *could* forgive her. As they said goodbye, they'd feel some warmth towards her.

A funeral which, of course, would never happen.

Wasn't she allowed something? Some closure?

She hated to defend herself but Raven wasn't Emily. She was a completely different person. Her memories of existence were vague with Emily, but with Raven they were vivid and real. Apart from her one indiscretion with Simon, which had been confusing and misguided, a teething problem that came with a sudden new life, hadn't Raven been a good person? *A very good person?*

But defending herself was futile and, in a way, undeserved, so with heavy steps, Raven moved to her bag and pulled out a blister packet of sleeping tablets. Back in her chair, popping the tablets from the blister packet, she let herself flow back to the funeral scene.

Black roses everywhere, of course.

The Cure's 'Lovesong' playing softly in the background.

There was Damien giving a eulogy, his voice thick with emotion as he recounted their adventures together.

Derek, holding his daughter's hand, whispering in her ear what a good person she'd been, really... at heart.

She filled her mouth with tablets and washed them down with a glass of absinthe sitting alongside her. *One more dance with the green fairy!*

Over the next few minutes, she considered writing a note.

Was it necessary?

Would they think she was seeking out sympathy?

Besides, she'd opened herself up to that detective already. She'd explained that she never doubted her responsibility, didn't want forgiveness... she said their names out loud... 'Bruce, Marcus, Phil, James... and Tommy.' Maybe then the life of Raven Blackstone could be judged and mourned on its own merits.

She closed her eyes, preparing herself, replaying the funeral over and over. Each time, it became more vivid, more real. The faces of her friends, the smell of incense, the sad silences between the words spoken.

But, as her drugged mind began to drift, the funeral changed from Raven's to Emily's. Five boys, forever young, forever innocent, stood around her place of rest.

'I'm sorry,' she whispered, knowing they couldn't hear her.

Tommy looked down into the hole she rested inside. 'Tell me a story.'

'I'm so, so sorry.'

Then, there was a voice from outside the vision.

'What're you sorry for?'

It was a voice she recognised... but it couldn't be?

'What did you do?' There it was again! She opened her eyes.

She was no longer alone in her lounge.

Chapter Sixty-One

Light flooded Georgi's unit.

Two uniformed officers came inside, one wielding a taser. Sean must have called reinforcements.

No hard feelings, Sean lad, Frank thought, raising his hands. *I'd have done the same.*

Out of breath, he was sitting beside the unconscious and cuffed Georgi. He managed a few words between breaths. 'DCI Black... I restrained the suspect...'

The officers looked around as they drew closer.

'Just reaching for my card,' Frank said, feeling his breath return.

'Slowly,' one of the officers said, keeping his taser trained on him.

After they checked his identification, the officer holstered his weapon and groaned as he stood.

'Is that your car outside?' one of them asked. There was a clear tone of surprise in his voice.

'Yeah... why? You have an issue with that?'

'No,' someone said from the door. 'But I'm sure the garage will next time you take it in for an MOT.'

Frank dusted himself off. 'Let me worry about that. Bertha is invincible. Who are you?'

Georgi groaned.

'Jesus...' one of the officers said. 'He's built like a brick shithouse...'

Frank caught the officers moving their eyes between him and the restrained suspect. Frank shook his sore hand. 'I might not look the part... but never underestimate...' He nodded down at Georgi. 'Like this dipshit did.'

'He caught you, though,' one officer said.

Frank touched his swollen lip and looked at the blood on his fingers. 'Think I did that myself, biting my lip.'

The man at the door had joined them. He was in his mid-forties, suited, with a crisp white shirt and a tie knotted with military precision. His shoes gleamed even in the dim light of the storage unit. Everything about him screamed 'career bureaucrat'. He was looking down at Georgi. He squinted at Frank. 'Come on? Really?'

'Never judge an old fat man by his cover.' Frank shrugged. 'But if you must know, boys, for when you reach my grand old age, and potentially, weight, always keep it old fashioned.'

'Old fashioned?'

'Aye. The bollocks first. Once you clobber them, doesn't matter how many dumbbells a man can lift.'

'He's unconscious?' the suited man said, still in disbelief.

'Aye. Another old-fashioned rule. If the bastard is tooled up, you tool up too. You seen the size of the spanner? After I dropped him, he refused to give it up, so I found my own tool.' He tapped a tyre iron on the floor by his foot.

'Rather risky,' the suited man said. 'You could have killed him.'

'You seen the chuffing size of him? Barely made a dint. A lot of adrenaline involved, too. I'm assuming you know what this prick did?'

'I know a lot about this man, DCI Black. I'm Max Riles, Senior Operational Manager for human trafficking in the NCA.'

Frank's stomach twisted. *Another sodding complication,* he thought. *Just what this case needs.*

'I'm assuming you've seen the CCTV footage, too,' Max said. 'We also saw it and were here to take him in...' He sighed. 'Seems you got here... first.'

'I move quickly where cold-blooded murderers are concerned.'

It seems Sean hadn't called it in, after all, Frank thought. *He'd done what he was told. Stupid bastard!*

'Well, Georgi used to be involved with human trafficking years back,' Max said. 'We got a fair number of his colleagues, but he was always the slippery one. He's been off our radar for a while. In fact, we'd been watching Lilly Petrova of late. This was all rather unexpected.'

Frank rubbed his stiff neck. 'Not again. Is Donald Oxley around here, ready to jump out and shout surprise?'

'I'm sorry... I don't follow.'

Frank sighed. 'Am I about to be told that Georgi isn't part of my investigation into Greg Lyle's murder, and that I should politely step away?'

Frank could tell from Max's silence that this was exactly the case. Frank looked at the Bulgarian, who was still face down, but now mumbling and cursing in his own tongue.

'Let's talk outside,' Max said.

'Let's do that,' Frank said.

Outside, Frank took a deep breath, trying to clear his

head. There were another two officers standing beside a vehicle.

Unlike Frank, Max hadn't come without significant back-up.

Old-fashioned Frank. *All good until you get yourself killed, you daft apeth.*

Max continued. 'We wanted Lilly Petrova and Nikolai Volkov for human trafficking.'

'Really? Trafficking? Look, I know sod all about Nikolai, but Lilly was no human trafficker.'

'I'm afraid you're wrong, DCI.'

'Well, then she was being forced into it.'

'Not the case.'

Frank shook his head. The world was a strange place, all right. 'Well, you're not going to get them now... at least, if it is them... they've still to be identified.'

'It's them,' Max said and sighed. 'Look... it's pretty much irrelevant now, but if you want to know, Lilly thought she was doing some good. She wasn't part of the trafficking process to make money, she was just trying to help desperate children, who were in danger back in Bulgaria.'

Frank grunted. 'Christ... it's a shame you never got to throw the book at her.' He rolled his eyes.

'The law's the law... you know how it works.'

'Aye,' Frank said with a sigh. 'Too often without compassion.'

Max sighed, running a hand through his perfectly coiffed hair. For a moment, he looked almost human. 'Anyway, we had enough to move on them. The last three children have been delivered to three families enlisted by our department. It was a set-up. We were ready for an arrest. In fact, you were there when we were ready to move, but then Georgi pops up out of nowhere, breaks in, piques our interest... We didn't realise he was involved. So we held back, because if we could get something on him, too, we could get all three of them.'

'That was a mistake,' Frank said. 'You got greedy. Should have stuck with those two... they'd still be alive.'

'Truth is,' Max said. 'We were watching him before you marched in there—'

'Hey... I didn't sodding well march in. He evaded arrest. Tried to close the door on me.'

Max grinned. 'Well, we came in as quick as we could. I honestly thought I'd walk into a bloodbath.'

'Nah. I went easy on him,' Frank grunted.

Max laughed.

'Too easy... but then I want him intact up here.' Frank pointed at his head. 'I want the truth.'

Max nodded. 'I bet you do. I know what you're investigating... when we saw you in the shop yesterday, we did our research.'

'So, you know how important it is? That man may have killed an innocent child.'

'You think he'd tell you even if he did?'

'It's my job to at least try.'

Max's expression softened slightly. He looked almost apologetic. 'Look, I think you know what's going to happen here. I'm going to apologise up front... but it's going to have to be this way.'

Frank felt the familiar weight of frustration settling on his shoulders. 'Bloody hell.' Another bureaucratic delay on the horizon. How many more obstacles would be thrown in his path before he could get justice for Greg? *You sure Donald isn't going to pop out and say surprise?* He thought it instead of saying it this time.

Max continued, 'We're going to wrap up the trafficking

and charge him with murder. When he knows he's cooked, I'll find out what I can about the kid. If he's involved, I'll get you in the room with him, straight away. And... you've my word. I'll push him hard. If he's anything to do with it... I'll find out.'

'Do I have a choice?'

Max didn't respond.

Frank shook his head. 'For pity's sake. And if he doesn't admit anything to you? Do I get my turn?'

'We'll cross that bridge when we come to it,' Max said. 'But I'll get you the truth. I'm the man who can make the deals. He's facing two life sentences.'

'Well, don't let him off!'

'Right now, this man won't survive long enough to see freedom again. Reduce him to one life sentence and his chances remain slim. It'll be about making him think he's winning when he won't be.'

'You sound so sure of yourself.'

'I've been here before,' Max said.

Frank sighed. 'Well, Billy Big Balls, you sure you can handle him, or do you need me to put him down for you again?'

Max smiled. 'We'll take it from here, Frank.'

'Be my guest,' Frank said, heading to Bertha, wondering if he maybe should have hit the murdering prick harder while he'd had the chance. If he couldn't grill him, then murdering him would have been the next best thing.

Chapter Sixty-Two

GERRY SAT in the dimly lit office at the rear of HQ, far from their incident room and Frank's office.

She'd been here for over an hour, stroking Rylan, using his presence as a comforting anchor in a storm of emotions.

During her childhood, she'd experienced many meltdowns, but since adulthood, she'd nearly always brought herself back from the edge. In fact, she couldn't remember a single breakdown since her career began.

Not even on the day she'd lost her parents.

Although, she had to admit that had been the most challenging day of her life.

In this moment, however, she was struggling. Her mind was stormy. It wasn't so much the image of Greg, vulnerable and trusting, sitting in that bathtub filled with ice, being 'treated' for autism as if it were being 'caused' by a malevolent spirit – although that wasn't helping. It was more the moment that Ray Lawson had attempted to end Greg's dependency on Buddy, and Greg's admission that it may have been happening.

She looked down at Rylan, his warm eyes gazing up at

her. For Gerry, Rylan wasn't just a dog, he was a lifeline, a constant in a world that often felt overwhelming and chaotic.

And it may have been the same for Greg.

Rylan's wet nose pressed against her hand.

She thought of Greg, young and confused, being told that his connection to Buddy was meaningless.

It was cruel.

It wasn't the first time in her career that she'd encountered the inhumane, but it was the first time it'd ever sent her into a spin.

Gerry shuddered at the thought. She knew, with absolute certainty, that she'd fight if anyone tried to separate her from Rylan.

'Over my dead body.'

It was unlike her to use such a phrase. It wasn't literal. It implied purpose and a determination to fight. But she'd heard it many times from colleagues, witnesses and her own parents, and she knew the power of the phrase.

She stroked Rylan again.

And then she thought of Buddy.

What had happened to him? He'd never been found... Had he been taken?

Over my dead body.

Had Greg fought to keep Buddy somehow, and paid with his life?

She felt herself pulling back from the precipice of a meltdown, and her analytical mind kicked in, running through all the evidence so far.

The unfinished message on the pager: *losing myself. Meet WA. Bring*

Bring...

Bring Buddy?

It was a leap, but Gerry was no stranger to the leap that became a lead.

Again, she thought back to her existing knowledge regarding Buddy.

Buddy had been a two-year-old rescue dog.

The simple fact opened up a gaping void in Gerry's mind.

Gerry didn't do voids.

She reached for her phone.

Chapter Sixty-Three

RAVEN TRIED TO HANG ON. She searched for anything. Eventually, she found only the scent of melting candle wax to cling to. It may have been a reminder that the life she'd built was dissolving away, but it kept her grounded. Temporarily.

'Tell me what happened to my son.' Simon's eyes were narrow.

'I don't—'

'Tell me!'

His shouting momentarily cleared her head. No longer reliant on the melting wax, she was suddenly hyperaware of everything. His foot bouncing off her floor in a frantic, uneven cadence, and her own heart, slowed by the onset of the sleeping pills, but still loud and firm in its beats.

'I don't know,' she said. 'But I'm so sorry for what you lost.'

His eyes were bloodshot and wild. 'You know. I've heard the podcast. Emily Thorne... Why did you do all those things?' His eyes bore into her with an intensity that made her flinch even in her growing stupor. 'Why did you kill my son? Greg? How did you do it?'

The room suddenly swung around her. 'I didn't.' The nausea was overwhelming.

'Five children. You lied to me... came into my life... and you took *my* son.'

'I'm sorry—'

'You're sorry!' he roared.

She opened her eyes. He was standing over her now.

'What did you do?'

'I'm sorry.'

'Stop saying you're *fucking* sorry.' His hand moved. She felt pressure on her forehead. He was pinning her head back against the backrest of the chair.

'I am,' she said, the words catching in her throat.

'Say it again and I'll hurt you. Badly.'

'I never touched your son... that's the truth... but I'm sorry all the same. Sorry for everyone I ever hurt.'

He released her and paced. He ran his hands through his hair, pulling at it in clumps as if trying to tear something away.

'But everything you did,' he spat, his voice cracking. 'Everything you *both* did. Those children. How could you? What *are* you? Christ...' He rubbed his hands over his face now. 'My son... my boy. I thought it was me... I thought I'd killed him.'

The raw anguish in his voice cut through the strengthening haze caused by the pills. His guilt was so old, and so familiar to her. Ravenous guilt. Gnawing at his insides for so long.

For a moment, it was like looking in a mirror, seeing her own torment reflected back at her.

'I should have gone to him that day! Instead of hiding upstairs...'

Raven recalled Greg on her doorstep that morning so long ago, his face pinched with worry as he begged to see his father.

'Why didn't you make me go? Why didn't you tell me to go?'

It wasn't fair to blame her for that, but she didn't respond.

'Every minute... every second, I see his face. My son! My boy!' He was crying now. 'They told me he fell from a cliff.' He thumbed his chest. 'What was I supposed to think? What was I supposed to believe?'

'Neither of us killed Greg,' Raven said.

'Bullshit!' Simon roared, his face contorting with fury. He lashed out, his arm sweeping over the mantelpiece. Ornaments crashed to the floor. A vase smashed, spilling water and black flowers across the floor. 'Bullshit!' He yanked ornate candelabras from the walls, flinging them across the room. Wax spattered, flames extinguishing as they clattered to the ground. 'You're a child killer. How did you do it? How did you put the blame completely on someone else? All the time when you were there... licking your *fucking* lips.' He went closer to her, shaking. 'It was all over the news. I remember. No one ever saw your lying little face, did they?'

'Because I was a child.' To her, it sounded hollow, but it was all she had.

His face folded. 'So was he.' He sobbed. 'So was my son.' He sank to his knees. The sound of his despair tore at Raven's heart.

'You cold, heartless bitch...' he murmured between tears. 'You cold, heartless bitch...'

After several more repetitions, he roared with anguish and surged to his feet. She genuinely believed he'd come for her. Instead, he turned, grabbed a framed picture of her and several goth friends in The Elsinore off the wall, and launched it. It exploded against the wall.

Surveying the wreckage, Simon murmured, 'Why did you put him in a fridge? Was he scared? Was my lad scared?' He turned in her direction, pinning his hands together as if praying to her. 'Was he?' His voice had taken on a desperate, pleading quality that was worse than the anger. He shuffled closer. 'He wasn't awake, was he? Oh God, please, Raven, he wasn't awake? Tell me he wasn't awake.' He broke off, choking on the words.

Raven's mind raced, images of Greg's frightened face mingling with memories of the other children. She suddenly felt doubt. Could she have been involved? Could this be another of those dissolved memories? Fragments never to be recovered? She shook her head. *No.* She may not remember everything as Emily, but the feelings, the sense of being there, in some form, were undeniable. She didn't have the same feeling with Greg. Raven shook her head vehemently, instantly regretting the movement as it made the room spin even harder. She couldn't have long left. 'No,' she gasped. 'Believe me... I didn't—' She retched. She tasted bile. She then heaved again, and was surprised she wasn't sick.

She panted, looking up into Simon's wide eyes. 'No... no...' She could feel herself drooling, and parts of her body growing colder.

'What's wrong with you?' Simon asked.

Raven wiped her mouth with the back of her hand. 'It's over... I've finished it...' Her tongue felt too thick for her mouth.

He came closer. She saw his hand move to the side and then he was holding the blister pack in front of her face. 'How many? How many have you taken?'

'I don't want to... start again.'

He shook the packet again. 'How many?'

'I'm tired... no more... this is me... Emily... the *real* me... taking responsibility.'

He knelt, took her by the shoulders and shook her. 'No... no you fucking don't. Tell me what you did.'

'Raven should be remembered... properly...' She retched and tasted bile again. 'She was a good person.'

His hands closed around her arms, fingers digging. He stood and yanked her upwards. She came without resistance. Her body was feeling drained. It must be taking some strength on his part to hold her up. 'No!' he screamed, shaking her. 'You tell me the truth. You tell me the fucking truth!'

Raven's head lolled, her vision blurring in and out of focus.

'Die after you tell me...' He shook her. '*After.*'

Then he released her. She fell backwards. She wondered if she'd sunk back into her chair, but then realised she'd missed it, and was sitting on the floor, her back against it.

'Speak, damn it! Speak!'

Her head lolled forward. 'Sorry...' She closed her eyes—

She felt a tight grip on her throat, then a crushing pressure around her jaw. 'Open... *open*...' She felt his hand in her mouth. His fingers in her throat.

She opened her eyes, gagging. It was painful, overwhelming. She tried to wriggle free, but she had little energy and he had her gripped tight. She gagged several more times, and then he yanked his hand out.

She retched, violently. The vomit burned her throat and mouth before splattering over Simon's hands and down his front. She turned her head to the side, and fell forward, emptying the contents of her stomach on the floor.

'Get it all out,' he growled. 'You think it's that easy... to escape?'

The world was merely a pinpoint of agony and shame to Raven now.

Had she absorbed enough of the drug yet to kill her?

She didn't want to be drawn back now. She was content to go. Content to sleep.

She closed her eyes and lay back. In the distance, she thought she could hear running water.

It was soothing... calm... she felt as if she were bobbing up and down in water, close to a waterfall perhaps, readying herself for freedom and emptiness—

Her cheek stung.

She opened her eyes.

Simon was there again. Slapping her. 'Wake up.'

In his hands, he clutched a bottle of water. He was shaking it up and down. 'I'm going to clean you out.' His voice was oddly calm now, as if trying to be reassuring, as if he was in fact a doctor or a nurse, there to assist.

'Please,' Raven gasped, her voice raw and painful. 'Let me go... I swear... to you—'

The bottle cut her off. The taste was aggressive and salty. She tried not to swallow, but it was impossible. Some spilled out and stung her eyes.

'Drink.'

She tried to turn her head again, but he was now gripping the back of her hair, painfully, keeping her still. She coughed and spluttered. It spilled down the sides of her face. 'Drink!' He forced the bottle in even harder, squeezing, continually filling her mouth until her throat was full too, and then she just went with it for fear of drowning, and she gulped and gulped—

She retched. Her lungs were also burning. It was too much.

He released her, she rolled over and vomited. Acid and salt streamed from her mouth. 'Please...' she begged. She threw up again. 'Please... please...'

'Drink!' he shouted, grabbing her and holding her head steady by her hair again.

She no longer fought it. She gulped what she could and threw up when he released her.

Throughout it she kept her mind on that dinner table in Middlesbrough.

Not on the days in which the children had sat and eaten, but on the days when she'd sat in the darkness, while Robert stood off in the shadows calling to her. *My little bird... my little bird...*

Was this her penance now?

To be here forever?

The peaceful oblivion she'd sought had been a fantasy. No waterfalls for her.

No. She was trapped.

Her wings clipped.

My little bird...

Chapter Sixty-Four

Sharon and Reggie approached the front door together. She took a deep breath and knocked firmly.

For a long moment, there was silence. Then, just as Sharon was about to knock again, the door creaked open.

A woman stood there, her face gaunt and eyes hollow. 'Yes?' she asked, her voice barely above a whisper.

'Megan Powers?' Reggie asked, showing his warrant card.

'Yes...' Although Megan was in her late thirties, there was something in her tortured expression that made her seem far older, as if she'd lived through whole lifetimes of turmoil.

'I'm DS Moyes, this is DC Miller,' Reggie said. 'Is it okay if we come inside and ask you some questions?'

'About what?'

'Reverend Ray Lawson,' Reggie said.

At the mention of Ray's name, Megan's face twisted into a grimace. She backed away.

Irritated at Reggie for being so blunt, Sharon slipped past him into the doorway, and approached Megan with her hand out. 'It's okay, Megan. We're on your side. We're here to help in any way we—'

A moan from upstairs made Sharon's blood run cold.

'Sharon,' Reggie said. 'Step back...'

Sharon eyed Megan up and down. There were no visible weapons. She was grimacing and looked like she was more likely to fold to the floor than attack.

'Megan, who's upstairs?'

'Him,' she said, rubbing at her cheeks now. '*Him.*'

Sharon felt Reggie's hand on her arm. She shrugged him off.

'Megan, are you able to turn and face the wall for me? So we can help you?'

Megan's eyes darted between their faces. 'Help?'

'Yes,' Sharon said. 'We want to help you... so very much.'

Megan nodded and turned to face the wall. Sharon turned to look at Reggie's wide eyes, giving him the nod to go in and restrain her.

As Reggie neared Megan, Sharon said, 'Is it just the reverend upstairs?'

'Yes,' Megan said. She was weeping now. 'It's always been him. But he can't hurt anyone again.'

Sharon took the stairs two at a time, her heart pounding in her ears as she followed the faint moans echoing from above. The sounds led her to a small bathroom at the end of the hallway, its door slightly ajar.

As she pushed it open, a wave of acrid chemicals assaulted her senses.

Ray lay naked in a bathtub filled with ice water, shivering. His wrists and ankles were bound, leaving him struggling to keep his head above the frigid surface. His skin had taken on an ashen pallor, save for his eyelids, which were swollen and an angry, raw red.

The overwhelming stench of bleach made her eyes water. It was now clear as to the cause of Ray's blistered eyes. His moans were weak – hypothermia was probably setting in.

'Reggie, I need you!' she called down the stairs.

'Okay... coming...'

She leaned over and took hold of the binding around his wrists; the stench of bleach was overwhelming.

'Dear God,' Reggie said from behind her, when he came in.

'Megan?' Sharon said.

'Cuffed to the radiator,' Reggie said. 'I called it in... there'll be an ambulance, too.'

'Help me. Get his ankles.'

Together, they lifted the shivering reverend from the water. 'Take him into the hallway,' Reggie said.

Sharon backed out through the door, Ray's head now against her chest as she clutched the rope around his wrists.

They laid him down. 'Towels!' Reggie said, disappearing back into the bathroom. He emerged with towels that Sharon was able to drapeover the quivering man. Reggie then went to grab some duvets from a bedroom.

Ray moaned the entire time. After she wrapped him up, she thought he might be saying something. She leaned in.

'My eyes...' he said. 'My eyes...'

Chapter Sixty-Five

THE TAXI DRIVER's voice broke through Gerry's thoughts. 'Here we go. You want me to wait? This ain't the nicest area.'

She looked out of the window. The estate was a study in urban decay – graffiti-covered walls, boarded-up shops and overflowing bins.

Gerry paid the taxi driver. 'No, thank you.' She knew Scarborough well enough. She'd walk Rylan toward the coast after and they'd find a taxi back en route.

The taxi departed, and she approached a decrepit-looking terrace home with Rylan on his leash. The air hung heavy with the acrid smell of burned rubber and something less identifiable. She dialled Frank's number again and was put straight through to voicemail. She'd already left a message explaining the lead, stating that everyone was occupied, and she'd come alone. She now left a second message, clipped and precise, as was her way. 'I'm outside Ben Rhodes' home in Scarborough. I've chased Clara for a detailed profile on him. When I have it, I'll forward it to you.'

She knew already that Ben Rhodes was fifty-five, unemployed and lived alone.

She also knew that he'd been in serious trouble for abusing his dog, Roland, in 1996.

Gerry's phone buzzed immediately after leaving the recording.

There was yet another text message from Tom, apologising

In a way, it was nice. No one had cared so deeply for her since her parents.

Still, that didn't stop it from irritating her. Constant messages were intrusive.

She'd need to give serious consideration, later, to whether or not the intense nature of his pursuit was benefiting him or not.

Gerry knocked on the door. She expected Frank would criticise her for coming without him, but that was just part of his hypocritical nature. Besides, with Rylan, a steady presence at her side, she didn't really feel alone or vulnerable.

She heard shuffling from inside, then the door swung open, revealing a stocky man wearing oil-stained overalls. He was wiping his hands with a towel.

A patchy beard did little to hide the deep creases around Ben Rhodes' mouth. His face was more worn than the average person of his age, but he had a strong build which suggested he took care of his health.

Gerry struggled with eye contact, but in a professional context, she fared much better. It was a mode she practised, and although it remained awkward for her, it was less painful when it wasn't personal.

Ben didn't even try for eye contact. Instead, his gaze immediately fell to Rylan, and he dropped to his haunches.

'Lab Retriever,' Ben murmured, crouching down. He reached out, but stopped short, clearly recalling the grease on his hands. 'I won't mucky that fine coat.'

Gerry blinked, thrown off balance by his complete disregard for her presence. 'Mr Rhodes, I'm Detective Inspector Gerry Carver. I'm here to ask you some questions about—'

'How old's he?' Ben interrupted, his eyes still firmly on Rylan.

'Three...' Gerry replied. 'Mr Rhodes—'

'What's his name?'

She'd prefer to get to the point, but some kind of etiquette was required, especially considering his atypical behaviour. 'Rylan.'

'Long time since I'd a dog in the house.'

'If you'd prefer Rylan not to enter your home, we can talk outside,' Gerry said.

'Nah,' he said, reaching out again, but drawing his hand back before touching him. 'He's a right bonny lad. Come in.'

Gerry saw Rylan regarding him suspiciously. Rylan was usually very accepting of everyone, but he was also struggling with this sudden focus. 'I'd like a photo of Rylan if I could. When we're inside. Together. Me and him.'

Gerry wasn't sure how to respond to that. She wasn't happy with the suggestion, of course, but she didn't want to get this interview off on a bad footing. 'Shall we discuss that inside?'

He finally stood, continuing to wipe his hands on his towel.

Ben stared down at Rylan, and Gerry was almost certain he was yet to look directly at her. 'Hook him up to the valve on the radiator. It's mucky in here. Break my heart if he got hurt.'

Gerry frowned. 'There's no need for restraint. Rylan is highly trained. He'll remain still if I instruct him to.'

Ben shook his head as he turned. 'Please, now. Hook him up.'

Gerry weighed her options. Rhodes' insistence was an irritation, but it seemed easier to agree than to argue. 'Okay.'

As Gerry crossed the threshold, she tried again to tell him why she was here. 'Mr Rhodes...'

But he'd already disappeared through a door and out of sight.

She followed him.

He'd turned the living room into some kind of workshop. Although there was a single, threadbare sofa, and an old tube television with a rabbit-ear antenna, the coffee table was barely visible beneath a mess of oily rags and screws and bolts. Mechanical pieces were strewn around the floor on oil-stained newspapers. There was also a strong smell of motor oil.

'Are you repairing things?' Gerry asked.

'If I can,' Ben said. 'I like to salvage. There's so much waste, don't you reckon?' He pointed to one mechanical piece. 'A gutted microwave. Fix it up. Sell it on. Good brass in it. And I'm doing my bit, you know, against all the waste.' He pointed to a sturdy-looking radiator. 'For Rylan.'

She went over and looped his lead around the valve. She stroked his head. 'Won't be long, Rylan. Stay still.'

'Tea?' Ben asked from behind her. 'I've Yorkshire?'

'No, thank you,' she declined politely. Gerry never accepted drinks made by others.

'Never known anyone to turn down Yorkshire.'

When she turned from Rylan, she was surprised to see that Ben had gone. 'Mr Rhodes?'

'One tick,' he called from his kitchen.

She sat on the sofa.

He came in holding a photo album and an old-fashioned polaroid camera.

He placed the camera down with the nuts and bolts on the coffee table. 'For the photograph and...' He turned to her and made eye contact with her for the first time. 'Look.' He proffered the photo album. 'You see I'm well-meaning.'

Well-meaning? An odd thing to say.

Gerry opened the album. The first picture was of a younger, leaner Ben with his arm around a sheepdog. On the next page, he was roughly the same age, kneeling beside a pair of Dalmatians. Page after page of photographs. She skipped through to the end. Ben was older in the last one, beginning to grey. He was petting a tiny Chihuahua.

'Nice?'

She nodded. 'Yeah. They're nice. I love dogs.' She was starting to feel impatient. 'But—'

'One tick... I've got more.' He sounded even more eager now. He headed to the other room. 'Wait there!'

Gerry closed the album, setting it aside. Frank always commented on how firm and to the point she was. Overly so, occasionally. That couldn't be further from the truth now. What was it about this man that kept her at arm's length?

'Mr Rhodes, I really need to ask you some questions,' she said when he returned with three albums. 'Could you please sit down?' She used an insistent tone.

He nodded. 'Of course.' He sat down on the other side of the sofa and put the three albums between them. He reached over to the table and started wiping at his greasy hands again. 'Serious, is it?'

'Mr Rhodes. You may have heard about a body recovered from the sea in Whitby on Friday.'

'News to me.'

'Down by Tate Hill Pier.'

'Ah... how awful.'

'The body belonged to a fourteen-year-old called Greg Lyle.'

Ben worked at his fingers with the towel. He looked down at them as he did so. 'Don't know him.' His response was sharper than usual.

'I didn't ask if you knew him,' Gerry said. 'But thank you for volunteering that information.' She took her notebook out.

'What're you doing?' he asked. He glanced sideways, quickly, but then returned his attention to his fingers.

'Just taking some notes, Mr Rhodes. Are you okay with that?'

He looked at Rylan and nodded. 'If you allow me that photo, you can take as many notes as you please.'

Gerry took a deep breath and opened the book. 'Thank you.'

'What do you want to take notes about, anyhow?'

'In 1996, you were charged with abusing your dog.'

Ben put the rag on top of the albums beside him. He rubbed his face. She could hear the bristling of his patchy facial hair. Some of the oil smeared his cheeks. 'Misunderstanding, though, all that... A misunderstanding.' He nodded and smiled at Rylan as if he was addressing her dog and offering reassurances.

Gerry found the photograph on her phone of Greg and Buddy. 'This was your dog. A golden retriever. Roland. He was taken from you.'

He didn't look.

'Do you want to look?'

'I can't...'

'Why?'

'It breaks my heart.'

Gerry nodded. 'The picture shows Roland, your golden retriever and Greg—'

'A neighbour said I was hurting Ro, like.' He looked sadly at Rylan. 'But I wasn't. Rylan can see it.' He winked. 'Can't you, boy? One of them miscarriages of justice.'

'Your neighbour took pictures of you abusing Roland,' Gerry said calmly.

'I never. I loved him. Pictures can be faked, can't they?'

'Yes. Much easier now than back then. Would you like to see the images again?'

'Lies… misunderstandings… miscarriages. Are we ready to take my photograph now?'

'Mr Rhodes, after Roland was taken from you, you received a lifetime ban on owning dogs. You also served three months in prison. I'm wondering, did you ever see him again after—'

'They took Ro from me.' He gave a swift nod at the end to emphasise his perceived injustice.

Gerry nodded. 'Did you ever see him again?' Gerry asked.

He shook his head.

He'd still not looked at the photograph in his hand. She tried again. 'Please could you look at the photo, Mr Rhodes?'

'Whatever.' He turned and gazed down at it. A smile flickered across his face. 'My best lad,' he whispered. He pointed out a distinctive white patch on the retriever's chest. 'Shaped like a crescent moon. That's my best, best lad.'

'And do you recognise this child?'

He shook his head.

'Greg Lyle. The body that was recovered,' Gerry explained. 'Roland was named Buddy following adoption.'

He nodded and looked away again, gazing at Rylan. 'He had a good life then did he? My lad?'

'We don't know,' Gerry said softly. 'Because Buddy disappeared on the same day Greg did in October 1998.'

He rubbed his face again, spreading the oil. 'That's sad.'

She gave him a moment. 'Do you have any idea—'

'Nah...' he murmured again. He stood. 'Just give us a moment. I'm sorry... this is overwhelming.' He left the room.

Gerry looked around the room, trying to get a deeper sense of who Ben was, but all she saw was oil, grime and chaos. A sad man that had cut himself off from reality. Her instincts regarding Buddy's disappearance, earlier, had led her to this man, but she couldn't help but feel now that maybe she'd jumped the gun. She heard the toilet flushing from somewhere in the house.

She reached over and continued to flick through the photo albums.

She stopped dead.

A golden retriever. A distinctive crescent-shaped white patch. Ben, looking proud as punch, kneeling beside him.

She pulled up the picture of Buddy on her phone again. The same crescent-shaped patch. Exactly. At the bottom of the polaroid photograph was scribbled: 8/9/99. It was smudged, but she was almost positive it was the year 1999. A cold feeling settled over her. This had been taken less than a year after Greg and Buddy disappeared. Gerry turned several more pages for further confirmation. The same dog, again... definitely Roland... 6/5/02. As she turned the pages, she noticed that the pictures that included that same golden retriever were becoming more regular, and Ben was ageing in them, becoming greyer and stockier. Then, in some of the later photos, 4/4/06 for example, the retriever looked older, too, more frayed, and losing the lushness in his colour.

So Ben had taken Roland back.

Gerry felt her heart rate picking up. She could hear movement in the house. Her phone buzzed – it was a message from Clara back at HQ. Attached was a PDF titled 'Ben Rhodes' employment history'. She clicked on it and the appropriate app opened it. She scanned the list looking for the most relevant dates.

In 1992-1998, Ben worked for Whitby Appliances.

She took a deep breath.

Whitby Appliances.

WA.

She recalled the pager: *losing control. Meet WA. Bring*

Her eyes moved between the picture of the ageing retriever alongside Ben, and his employment history.

Greg had actually returned Buddy to Ben. Why? Because he was losing control? Did that imply that Ben had then killed Greg?

She felt a chill run down her spine.

The fridge...

Whitby Appliances...

She looked around the scattered mechanical parts.

It could all fit.

She needed to leave. She stood, phone in hand, texting Frank—

An oily hand came out of nowhere, clenched her wrist and snatched the phone from her grasp.

'You shouldn't have come here,' Ben said.

Rylan barked.

Her head suddenly felt like it was on fire. He yanked

her back down onto the sofa. Eyes watering, she reached up to claw at his hand in her hair.

She was dragged along the sofa. She spotted Rylan straining against his leash, barking.

'Don't worry, I'll take good care of him.'

'Get off—'

He yanked her again, sharply and suddenly, over the arm of the sofa, and then she felt a sudden blow to the side of her head.

Everything went black.

Chapter Sixty-Six

SAMANTHA WAS UNDER NO ILLUSIONS. She'd always known that the impact of her podcast was going to be seismic. However, she'd underestimated the speed at which it would go viral. She'd only released it several hours ago, and it was everywhere.

She thought she might have had more time to convince Raven to give up her side of the story.

However, it was now obvious from the online clamour that Raven would have disappeared into the ether before the day was through.

Samantha needed to act immediately before Raven was no more.

Coming to the house of the person you'd exposed – some would argue, destroyed – might seem bold, and somewhat arrogant.

But Samantha didn't flinch.

When it came to the truth, everything else was irrelevant.

She didn't feel overly confident about getting a response from Raven. She'd turned her down flat the other night. But now, with the end nigh, she might relish the opportunity to share her version of the truth to those she'd be leaving behind.

As she knocked on the door several times, she really hoped that she wasn't too late. That they hadn't already moved her.

Could they have swooped for her already... moved her that quickly?

There was no answer.

Feeling heavy with disappointment, she sidled along and tried to see in between the crack in the drawn curtains—

Her hand flew to her mouth.

The room was in disarray. Things were smashed and knocked over. And, in the centre of it all, Raven lay on her back.

Motionless.

She went for the front door handle. It was unlocked. Inside, the stench of vomit was overwhelming. It made her eyes water. She covered her nose with her sleeve as she turned into the room.

Raven was pale, motionless, lying in a pool of vomit.

'Raven?' Samantha knelt beside the prone woman, unconcerned about the sick soaking into her trousers. She shook her gently. 'Can you hear me?'

Nothing.

She touched her pale, cold face, then tried for a pulse. Weak, but there. She spotted a blister pack on the floor. Sleeping tablets.

Her blood froze.

An overdose.

She could feel guilt... rearing its ugly head.

Truth sometimes comes with a cost, she thought to

herself, reaching for her phone. Her beliefs wouldn't be enough long term to stave off the guilt, but they'd give her some strength in the hours ahead.

'You're too late,' a voice said from behind her. 'She's dead.'

Samantha whirled around, her heart leaping into her throat.

Simon Lyle was in the doorway.

'What're you doing here?' Her blood ran cold. Had *he* done this? She glanced around the room, looking for anything that could serve as a weapon...

'I wanted to know if she killed my son.'

'And did she?' Samantha said, rising slowly to her feet.

He shrugged. Then, he turned to his side and walked away.

Chapter Sixty-Seven

OUTSIDE THE HOSPITAL, Frank took a long drag on his roll-up and tried to do a quick calculation in his head of how many he'd smoked today.

He failed miserably.

He looked down at the one in his hand. They had to go.

Last night, when support had come from the most unexpected of places in Henrietta Timber, Frank had remained strong. Despite the near miss of seeing his daughter, he'd fought her offer of a scotch to settle himself.

He sighed. Just thinking about the prospect of fighting alcohol and cigarettes for the rest of his life made him feel exhausted, but it was either that, or he probably wouldn't live long enough to see his daughter again.

And that was inconceivable.

He checked his watch. The doctors had been working on Ray's eyes for quite some time now. There would be damage, but it was still up in the air as to how much.

Megan had also given him a taste of his own medicine with an ice bath, although he'd been left in there for far too long. His organs hadn't reacted too well to that.

Long story short, the man was in no fit state to be interrogated, so the doctors wouldn't let him anywhere near.

This seemed to be the theme of the entire investigation.

With Ray on his mind, he looked up, wondering if someone up there was conspiring against him.

Stay away Frank, thou shalt not speak to any of thy suspects.

He decided against this. After all, he didn't have a religious bone in his body. His final conclusion was that he was just one very bloody unlucky police detective.

Sharon, who was in the hospital at this moment, had told Frank that Ray had been mumbling his brother's name the entire ambulance ride, apologising repeatedly. *Graham.* Reggie had already spoken to Megan in custody. Her story was a similar one to Greg's on those videos. Religious indoctrination which had left her damaged and lost in life.

Frank sighed. He was dreading the truth. How many children had suffered at the hands of this man?

Ray, whether or not he killed Greg, would go away for a very long time.

Having the gumption to steal that video from Ray and hide it away had been a brave and admirable move on Greg's part.

But had it ultimately cost him his life? Had Ray tried to retrieve it?

Had the word *bring* in that pager message been referring to this evidence?

How he wished he could ask!

And then there was Georgi. Max had already called to say that Georgi had admitted to seeing Greg, but was adamant he'd nothing to do with his death. He'd been somewhat concerned over the burgeoning relationship between Lilly and Greg, but his most up to date words on the matter, delivered to Max, were, 'Do you think I'd be so fucking stupid as to confront a local kid, never mind kill them?'

Still, again, Frank would much prefer to do the interrogation himself.

An ambulance cut off his train of thought.

It approached with its sirens blaring.

He watched as the ambulance screeched to a halt near A&E, its lights painting the night in alternating flashes of red and blue.

Paramedics burst from the back, wheeling out a gurney at breakneck speed. Frank wasn't too far away so, as they rushed close by, he dropped his glasses onto his nose, and caught a glimpse of the patient.

Bloody hell... it couldn't be...

Samantha Wells stepped down from the back of the ambulance.

What the hell was going on?

'What happened, Samantha?'

The woman's eyes were wild, her breathing ragged. 'She... she tried to kill herself. Pills. I found her like that.'

'What were you doing there?'

'To offer her an interview.'

'Why? Haven't you been warned off releasing that podcast?'

'Yes... but I released it two hours ago.'

His eyes widened. 'Bloody hell.' He looked at the doors of A&E, still flapping from where she'd been rushed in.

He looked back at Samantha, eyes narrowed.

'I know what you think,' she said.

'You do, do you?'

'Speak your mind if you wish.'

'Would it make any difference?'

'No.'

'I guess we are who we are, eh? No matter the costs.'

'I believe in the truth.'

'Aye, I see. Like I said. No matter the costs.'

She flinched, but then steeled herself and glared back. 'Simon Lyle was there. Greg's father.'

Frank's eyes widened. He stepped forward. 'Why?'

'He said he wanted to ask her about his son. If she killed him?'

Frank nodded. It made sense. He must have heard the podcast. So, why wouldn't he? Earlier, Frank had done exactly the same.

'She didn't,' Frank said.

'How do you know that?'

'I just do.'

'That's not really a decent quotation I can use if—'

'You think I care?'

'Do you think Simon might have done that to her?' Samantha asked, raising an eyebrow.

'Jesus wept. Go home Samantha.'

He turned around. It was a very fair point. He reached for his phone, planning to have Simon picked up.

Shit... he'd left it in the car.

As he approached Bertha, he saw the faint glow of his phone screen through the window. He yanked open the door, grabbing the device. Two missed calls from Gerry, and a voicemail.

After he listened, he started the engine. *Bloody hell, Gerry.*

And you've the nerve to call me a loose cannon.

Chapter Sixty-Eight

FRANK TRIED Gerry four times on the journey with no response. Each time, he grew more and more anxious. Unlike him, she was efficient. She'd answer his calls. By the time he arrived at the dilapidated estate, the sun had set, his heart was pounding and he was damp with sweat all over. *Of all the bloody stupid things,* he thought.

Was this his fault? Was his impulsive approach rubbing off on Gerry?

In all honesty, that made little sense. Influencing Gerry was impossible. She had her own ways and methods.

He killed the engine and looked at the house, hoping that her phone had simply died.

After all, she had Rylan with her.

But as he approached the house, he couldn't keep his paranoid mind from racing. He'd listened to the messages about this Ben Rhodes. It sounded promising. Which meant Gerry could have stumbled across the truth...

And how dangerous could the truth be?

He hurried over the cracked pavement, but each step

felt like a mile. He could hear a dog barking frantically. Rylan?

He shook his head. Right now, to his paranoid mind, every dog would sound like Rylan.

But as he neared the house, the barking grew louder and, as a result, seemed more desperate.

His blood went cold, and he broke into a run.

The light was on in the front room. He went over the garden and dead grass to the grimy front window. His sudden rapid breaths fogged the glass, so he had to wipe it before he got a proper look.

It *was* Rylan!

He was hooked to the radiator, straining against his leash, barking frantically. He turned his attention to Frank at the window, whined several times, and then barked again.

Frank surveyed the interior, which was a chaotic mess of mechanical parts, oil-stained rags and—

His breath caught in his throat.

There was a dark puddle on the floor near the sofa which resembled blood.

Shit! Gerry, shit...

He ran for the front door. It was locked. Heart hammering against his ribs, he considered kicking it in.

As he opted to go round the back, he pulled out his phone and dialled Sharon.

'Sharon... speak to Clara... get response to...' He was gasping for air.

'Sir, are you okay?'

'Ben Rhodes' place now!'

'Sir?'

'You listening? Ben... Rhodes...'

'Yes, sir.'

He hung up.

The back garden, bordered by a low, crumbling wall, stretched out, shrouded in overgrown grass and weeds. There was a large shed at the back in silhouette. He grabbed a loose brick from the wall, its weight reassuring in his hand.

Panting at the kitchen door, he shook his head. *Get a grip, you fat bastard.*

The kitchen door yielded. Frank stepped inside, his nostrils assaulted by oil. Dirty dishes were piled high in the sink. The counter was cluttered with greasy tools and half-eaten tins of beans.

He went into the front room. Rylan whined when he saw him again. 'How do, fella,' His voice was tight with tension. He glanced at the darkened stain again and he felt his stomach turn over. He unhooked the dog's leash from the radiator. 'Where's Gerry?'

With another whine, he tugged Frank back towards the kitchen.

'Outside?' Frank asked, but it was unnecessary. Rylan tugged him *hard*.

Back in the garden, Frank looked at the shed, side-on, in the thickening darkness.

'Okay, wait here,' he whispered, trying to secure Rylan to the door handle. 'Shit, Rylan, hold still—'

With a powerful yank, the Lab broke free and sprinted into the gloom, barking again.

Frank gave chase, remembering the crumbling wall at the last second, and making an awkward little jump. He stumbled. The image of that blood stain flashed through his mind. It inspired him to correct his footing, and propelled him on, despite the fact that his ageing, overweight body was almost spent.

He knew then, in that moment, that if he lost Gerry, he was done with the world.

There was a shout. A man's voice, filled with pain and rage.

Rylan was growling and snarling.

Frank saw that the side-on shed was actually angled slightly away from the house. He was forced to round it to see exactly what was going on.

A man, presumably Ben, was at the entrance on the ground while Rylan had his teeth clamped around the leg of his overalls, tugging and growling.

The bastard was lashing out at Rylan with some heavy-looking metal object.

'Rylan, get away from him!' Frank bellowed, knowing deep down that he'd never give up the fight. He approached them both with the brick. When he could see directly into the shed, his heart almost stopped.

God, no...

There was a torch on the floor which Ben must have dropped when Rylan ambushed him. It was switched on and it pointed directly at Gerry's face.

There was blood smeared on his motionless DI's cheek, and some more glistening on the wood beneath her head.

Rylan cried out.

Frank snapped back in time to see the Lab scurrying back. He was whining.

'I didn't want to do that, lad,' Ben said, who began scrambling to his feet, holding the weapon he'd used on Rylan.

Frank was there in an instant, his arm locking around Rhodes' throat in a vicious headlock. He made a promise he was in no mood to break. 'I'm going to snap your fucking neck.'

Chapter Sixty-Nine

GERRY'S WORLD swam into painful focus. Her head throbbed, each pulse sending waves of nausea through her body. Her thoughts were fragmented, her understanding of what had happened elusive.

But then the memories came in a series of flashes. The photo album, a golden retriever ageing across the pages, the employment history on her phone. WA. Whitby Appliances. Being pulled off the couch. A searing pain in her scalp from his hand, and then from a sudden blow to the side of her head...

The realisation hit her like a physical blow, forcing her to suck in a sudden gulp of air. She groaned, the sound seeming to come from far away. Her hand moved instinctively to the side of her head, fingers coming away sticky with blood. Gerry's analytical mind kicked in, even through the fog of pain. Probable concussion. Possible skull fracture. Uncertain time elapsed since injury...

Rylan!

She gasped. He'd been straining against his leash, desperate to reach her.

'Rylan,' she said out loud.

Immediately, she felt the warm, comforting sensation of his tongue on her face. Her hand found his fur, grounding her in the present.

She blinked against the dim light from the torch beside her. The world tilted and spun as she tried to sit up. Shapes moved, voices echoed, but everything seemed distorted, as if she were under water. Rylan whined softly, pressing closer to her, licking her, convincing her not to move just yet.

Gradually, her vision cleared. From where she was lying, she could see someone's back. Shoulders heaving. A wide man. *Frank?*

'Frank...' Gerry called, her voice barely above a whisper. She swallowed hard, tasting copper, and tried again.

More clarity came. She realised it was Frank and he was hitting someone.

'Stop...' Her voice was too weak. 'Frank.'

Frank was shouting as he swung. He wouldn't hear her.

He didn't look like he was going to stop.

'Frank...'

There was a momentary pause as Frank ceased his attack. Had he heard her? Or was he out of breath?

Did it matter?

'Frank... Frank...'

He turned at the sound of her voice. 'Gerry...'

He stumbled towards her as she tried to sit up again.

'Don't lass,' he said. 'Lie still... lie still...'

'He killed him, Frank... Ben Rhodes killed Greg. Arrest him.'

Frank knelt beside her and took her hand. 'I will... when he wakes.' He touched her cheek with the back of his hand. He had a sorrowful expression on his face that she'd never seen before. 'I'm so glad... I thought... I...'

She felt Rylan licking her other hand.

'Have you hurt him?' Gerry asked.

'I thought—' Frank continued.

'How bad, Frank?'

There was a pause. Her mind analysed. Excessive use of force. Potential manslaughter charges. Career-ending misconduct.

'He'll be fine,' Frank said, but his voice didn't sound sincere.

In the distance, she could hear sirens. She nuzzled Rylan with one hand, closed her other hand around Frank's.

The room swam again.

'Come on Gerry lass, come on now,' Frank said. 'Keep those eyes open.'

She tried to hold on to the sensation of Frank's hand and Rylan's sweeping tongue, but the encroaching darkness was insistent.

Chapter Seventy

Reggie and Sharon sat opposite Ben in the interview room.

His eyes were blackening. He had plasters on his forehead and was holding a tissue to his bloody nose.

Beside him sat his solicitor. She was scribbling in her notebook with a stern expression and pursed lips.

He'd already been checked over at the hospital, patched up and X-rayed. Nothing broken. They had to keep watch on him for twenty-four hours, and it might have been prudent to delay the interview, but he'd insisted they do it now because he wanted to make a complaint. 'That officer went too far.'

Donald was confident the complaint didn't have legs. Gerry's life had been in grave danger, after all. However, as a precaution, the sensible solution was to have Ben interviewed by someone other than Frank.

Frank had told Donald straight. 'Sharon and Reggie, please.'

Donald had granted the request. He was feeling the

stress of the case now and wanted it all wrapped up with no more bother from Frank.

Sharon leaned forward, her voice steady but with an undercurrent of steel. 'You'll be pleased to know that DI Gerry Carver, the officer you assaulted, Ben, will be fine. Concussion, but she'll recover. Like you... we just need to monitor her.'

Ben's eyes moved around the room. They were yet to settle on either detective. 'She fell.'

'You dragged her off your sofa by her hair,' Reggie said.

'Didn't mean for her to bang her head.'

Sharon's gaze was unwavering, her tone deceptively calm. 'So, what were you meaning?'

Ben shrugged. 'There are these moments, see. I come over funny. I'd have called someone.'

'Why did you take her to your shed, then?' Reggie asked.

'I thought...'

The solicitor stopped him with a touch to his shoulder.

'You thought what?' Sharon asked.

'I thought she was already dead.'

The solicitor withdrew her hand. There was a brief shake of her head as she made another note.

Ben dropped the tissue from his nose. His top lip was smeared with blood. It seemed as if the bleeding had stopped, though.

Sharon's voice cut through the silence, crisp and professional. 'Let's talk about Greg Lyle for a moment, Ben.'

There was a moment of silence while he fidgeted with his oil-stained hands. He didn't respond.

The solicitor whispered into his ear and then said, 'My client would—'

Ben's head snapped up, his eyes suddenly focused and on Sharon directly. 'How's the bonny lad? Rylan?'

Sharon fixed him with a stare, then gave a swift nod. 'He'll be fine,' Sharon said.

Ben's voice wavered. 'I didn't mean for that. He was grabbing me. And, sometimes, you know, like I said, sometimes I have these moments...' He broke off.

'I'd like a moment to talk to my client,' the solicitor said.

'I love dogs. I loved Ro. You believe me?' He looked directly at Sharon again.

Sharon nodded. She could see the honesty in his eyes. 'Yes.'

'Good.' He lowered his head, stared at his hands and nodded. 'Greg was a nice lad... I'm sorry for what happened.'

Sharon and Reggie exchanged a glance.

'Ben,' the solicitor said, touching his arm again.

Ben yanked his arm away, his voice rising with a desperate edge. 'It's too late, anyhow.' He looked at Reggie and nodded. 'They know.'

'There's a lot of evidence.' Reggie stared at him with hard eyes.

'Just know it was about Ro... always about Ro. When they took my lad from me, it wasn't just like losing a best friend... Ro was my family. Sometimes I'd get angry with him, things flash. I did things, things out of my control. I never hurt him as badly as they all said. That video the neighbour took, well...' He lowered his head, his voice dropping to a whisper. 'He was a gobshite. That wasn't me, you know, not really. After they took Ro away, I was lost. I wasn't allowed another dog, either, not that it would have made any odds. I wanted Ro back.'

'Ben?' the solicitor said.

'Fuck off!'

She flinched and looked down.

Ben's words started to come faster. 'I saw him one day. My boy, Ro. Walking up near West Cliff, near where I was working at the time. I knew it was my lad. And he recognised me, too. I went closer, and he started calling in my direction.' A ghost of a smile flickered across his bruised, tear-stained face.

Sharon leaned forward, her voice gentle but probing. 'Just to clarify, who were you working for at this time?'

'Whitby Appliances.'

'Thank you.'

He nodded. 'Ro was happy with Greg. I knew it, he really was, honestly. You could tell.' He looked up at Sharon for the first time in a while. 'Couldn't believe my eyes, like... so happy... so well cared for. My lad adored Greg. I was sad, but at the same time, happy, do you know what I mean? Good for Ro.'

Sharon nodded, her expression softening slightly. 'Yes.'

'Nice lad was Greg. Got to know him. All good, you know?' They listened as Ben described a happy few months, his voice rising and falling with the memories. 'He'd walk close to my work every morning, and I always made sure I was there. Course, I couldn't tell him the truth. How could I?' He smiled and closed his eyes. 'But life was peaceful for a while.'

A short time elapsed. Ben's smile fell away, but his eyes stayed closed. He was lost somewhere... and after a couple of minutes, she thought it was time to pull him back. 'What happened?' Sharon asked.

He opened his eyes and locked onto hers. 'I never planned it or anything. That's the truth. Being close to Ro again was what mattered.' He shook his head. 'And I liked the lad, Greg. He was like me, you know? Not the same as everyone. He loved animals, like...' He smiled and stared off again. 'Marine animals. We connected. It weren't just me and Ro; it were me, Ro and Greg. Although, calling him Buddy all the time did hurt my head! We had somewhere to meet too. You see, Mr Faulkes, the owner of WA, was old. He barely came in any more. He'd entrusted me to run that shop. And I was trustworthy, too! People bought their old things in to fix. I love opening things up, seeing how they tick, putting them back together. Anyway, Greg used to come over, and I'd show him these things. He seemed to be interested. He drew. Sketched. Sometimes he sketched the inside of machines for me! Wish I still had them.'

'How long did this go on for?' Sharon asked.

Ben shrugged. 'Months.'

'How many, roughly?'

'I'm not sure... three, four... could be longer... I'm not too good with keeping track of time and shit like that.'

'Did Greg's parents know about these visits?'

Ben shook his head, his voice dropping. 'No. Greg knew it would be our secret. That his parents wouldn't get it. I know how that sounds, but at the time, I didn't want to risk losing both of them... especially, Ro... I finally had him back, you know?'

He closed his eyes again and there was more silence that stretched, and it was Reggie who chose to speed it up this time. 'What happened?'

Ben's face contorted. He shook his head, muttering to himself. He seemed to be in physical pain.

'Ben?' Sharon said, gently.

Ben opened his eyes. 'Greg found out. Morris Nile.

Nosy old prick. I was late to work one morning, and so I ended up behind Buddy and Greg as they went to visit me. I noticed them talking to Morris, up ahead. I hung back. Morris knew the neighbour who'd reported me. But he saw me, didn't he? I started walking the other way. It were too late. The bastard pointed me out to Greg. Old bastard. I shed no tears when I heard he'd snuffed it. Deserved it. That day, I waited until Morris had pissed off, and then I chased after Greg and Ro. Shit. I knew, even before I reached him, that everything was stuffed. Greg was sad... angry... He wouldn't listen to me. He was furious, said he was going to tell his parents, tell the police... and then he was just gone. Vanished. And what was I to think? It was obvious I were going to lose Ro a second time... What if I never saw him again?'

Ben lowered his face.

The solicitor, looking frustrated, continued to scribble down notes.

Sharon said, 'The photographs that DI Carver saw suggest that you did see him again... right into old age.'

Ben looked up, his gaze haunted. He nodded. 'Aye.'

'And you saw Greg again?' Reggie asked.

He nodded. 'One last time.'

'How did that come about?' Reggie asked.

'His pager number. Only his parents ever used it, to get him to ring home, but he'd the number stuck to the back of it on a little white sticker. I'd copied it down one time in the past when I'd seen it. I hadn't seen him over a week. I paged him. Told him to come to the shop the next morning – to bring Buddy. I needed to try. And... well, I told him I was depressed, that I was losing myself... that I was close to the edge. I knew he saw me as a friend. That he'd come.'

'What had you planned to do?'

'Just to beg,' Ben said. 'Cross my heart. Nothing more. Try to convince him that I was a good person... that I loved Ro... Buddy... that I understood that Buddy was his now... That I'd never harm him again. That I was different now, that I could control my temper, but I just wanted to keep seeing him.'

A long silence passed.

'And?' Sharon asked.

'And, when he said that he wouldn't come again...' He looked up at the ceiling. 'That thing happened again.'

More silence.

'What thing?' Reggie asked.

'Same thing that happened with that lass who came to see me today. I lost it, and...'

He broke off.

'Then?' Reggie continued.

'It's a blur... a long blur...' Ben said.

'So do you know what you did?' Sharon asked.

'Aye, I know. I shook him. Shouted at him.' He rubbed his eyes. 'Hit him.' He dropped his hands. 'When I'm like that... I... just keep going until, well...'

'Carry on, please,' Sharon said, feeling her whole body falling in on itself, as Ben recounted the death of a child.

Ben closed his eyes, and put his hands to his temples around the plasters. 'Ro was barking at me, pulling at my leg with his teeth, but all I could feel was rage and loss. They took him off me. And now he was being taken off me again. Why would no one listen to me? Understand me? Help me? Don't I matter? And then... well, and then...'

'Then?' Sharon said.

'He wasn't moving, any more, was he? I'd hit him too hard. Too many times.'

'Was he dead?' Reggie asked.

'It looked that way.'

'But you thought DI Carver was dead today?'

'Aye,' he said, nodding.

'So he could have been alive?' Reggie said.

Oh God, Sharon thought, *please don't let that be the case.*

Ben shrugged. 'I don't know.'

'Did you think about calling an ambulance?' Reggie asked.

'No.'

Sharon looked at Reggie. His face was red. She gave him a gentle nod, trying to communicate to him without speaking.

He seemed to get the message not to lose it. It was horrible, but the confession was everything. He took a deep breath and appeared to steady himself.

'What next?' Reggie asked.

'I had to hide him. There were some old appliances in storage at the back of the shop. Mr Faulkes liked to keep some as memorabilia. Old fridges and ovens and the like. I squeezed him into an old fridge. I knew that if he woke up, he wouldn't be able to get out. I vomited there and then, all over the floor, but what could I do? It was him or me. That night, I lay awake, Ro by my side. I panicked. I imagined Greg banging on the fridge desperate to get out. I imagined Mr Faulkes finding him the next morning.'

Sharon's stomach turned over. She even noticed that the solicitor was grey now, and was probably relieved to just get this full confession out of the way, have him banged up, and get onto a new client.

'I went back that night with the van. There wasn't a sound. I swear he must have already gone, but I couldn't risk it. The fridge was heavy, especially with Greg inside. I used a trolley, got it upstairs by a ramp installed in the shop, loaded it into the van, and took him to the pier. It was dark, no one was about... I dropped the fridge over the side.'

Sharon sat back in her chair. Reggie took another deep breath, still trying to steady himself.

'I'm sure he was already dead, but sometimes, sometimes I wonder if he woke up in there, in the dark, in the cold water,' Ben said, rubbing his face. 'The pain, the nightmares, the agony I've been through over the years... it's been hard...'

Reggie's voice was suddenly louder. 'The agony *you've* been through?'

Sensing he'd snapped, Sharon grabbed his arm.

Reggie's voice trembled with barely contained fury. 'How about his parents? How about Greg?'

She squeezed his arm. 'Sir?'

'How about Buddy? Ro? Losing someone who treated him like royalty?' Reggie's voice was sharp.

Ben's voice was suddenly pitiful, small. 'But I loved Ro.'

'Didn't stop you beating the shit out of the poor animal. Is that what you did again, when you had him back... beat the poor thing?'

Ben shook his head. There was a single, unexpected tear running down his cheek.

The solicitor looked horrified, but didn't speak.

'Sir,' Sharon insisted.

Reggie stood, his body tense with unrestrained anger. 'Could you finish up in here, DC Miller?'

She nodded. 'Yes, sir.'

Reggie left.

Sharon finished up, and afterwards, she stared into

Ben's eyes for a few minutes, trying to find something tangible and solid. Something that really made sense.

But, apart for his love for Roland, there was little to be found.

It felt senseless.

Epilogue

Some time later

THE SHOWER ROOM was thick with steam and the air heavy with the scent of industrial soap. Georgi killed the jets of water. With a towel around his waist, he emerged from the cubicle, suddenly mindful of how quiet it had become.

He'd arrived with eight other inmates, and now he was alone.

He smirked.

It didn't take a genius to work out what was going on.

He peeled off his towel, cleaned the condensation from the mirror and regarded his reflection. Examining his body, he ran his hand through damp, greying hair. He was looking fantastic. Inside, he'd had more time to work out than ever before.

He cracked his back, listened to the steady drip of water from a leaky showerhead for a moment, and then said, 'How long are you going to keep me waiting?'

In the reflection, he watched a younger, naked, stronger man emerge from a cubicle. He held his hands behind his back.

'Mihail!' Georgi gave a swift nod. 'A fellow countryman, too?'

Mihail's hands dropped to his side. There was a rudimentary blade in his right hand. 'Помниш ли ме?'

'Of course I remember you. You were an aggressive little fuck. Bit me, if I remember rightly?'

'Пусна кръв.'

Georgi's face split into a wide grin. 'Yes, you did. I remember. It was pissing out of me. Still got the scar. You think you can manage that again?'

Mihail nodded.

Georgi raised an eyebrow. 'No guilt? After everything I did for you?'

Mihail smiled.

'I brought you to this country, Mihail, gave you a new life—'

'Брей, какъв живот.'

'It wasn't that bad, surely? You're here, which means you made a lot of decisions that had nothing to do with me.'

Mihail narrowed his eyes and spoke English for the first time. 'You gave me to a man who abused me.'

Georgi shrugged and tidied up his damp hair in the reflection, keeping one eye on his would-be assassin. 'You win some, you lose some, I guess. I advise you to be careful with that knife, Mihail... Stronger, younger men than you have failed...'

'I know,' Mihail said. 'Grigor.'

Another man emerged from a cubicle, also well-built, naked and holding a knife.

'Back up. Sensible move, Mihail. So, Grigor... I don't remember you.'

'Don't remember 2005?' Grigor asked.

'As well as I remember 2004 and 2006. Vaguely.'

'My sister, Elena, died on a journey you organised.'

Georgi sighed. 'Shit happens, Grigor. How was Elena's health? You sure it was all down to me?'

'Yes. You wouldn't let her go to a doctor.'

Georgi laughed. 'I'm sorry... maybe I should have checked her into the hospital and sat with her?'

He turned his attention back to his hair. There's been a spike in his adrenaline, but he didn't feel overly concerned. He winked in the mirror. 'I've beaten the odds before.'

Another cubicle door opened. A third man, smaller and even younger this time, lean and wiry, also wielding a knife.

Georgi took in a deep breath. 'Seems like we're having a right little Bulgarian reunion here.' He could feel his heart rate increasing. 'Who are you?'

'Kaloyan.'

'Well, Kaloyan, how did I offend you?'

'This is for Lilly Petrova.'

Georgi's eyes widened. 'Unexpected. How did you know her?'

'She brought my younger sister Rada into the country. Rada now goes to a good school.'

'And you're happy to extend your jail sentence? Considerably. And never see Rada ... again?'

'I'm never getting out anyway,' Kaloyan said.

Mihail said, 'Какви са шансовете сега?'

'The odds? Not great, any more.' Georgi turned, naked, fists clenched. 'Никога не казвай никога.'

Never say never.

The three assassins advanced.

Tessa Bridges breathed the sudden aroma of freshly baked bread as it drifted in from the bakery kitchen.

Heavenly.

The bell above the shop door chimed.

Rose Beevis, the young mother who lived two doors down from her, entered. Her two children, Sam, ten, and Milly, eight, trailed behind her. Both held a book while whispering about pastries.

Rose looked at her. 'You wouldn't have thought going to the library would be such hungry work, would you?'

Tessa laughed. 'This bakery certainly has a way of making you hungry.'

Rose smiled. 'So, how are you settling in? You're getting your free share of pies, I hope?'

'Only two weeks on the job.' She put a hand to her mouth and mock whispered, 'Can you believe they've let me have a go on the ovens?'

Rose laughed. 'All settled in the bungalow?'

'It's finally looking liveable! What're you after?'

Sam pressed his face against the glass, his eyes wide with wonder at the array of treats before him. His sister tugged on her mother's sleeve, pointing excitedly at a tray of colourful cupcakes.

'Two sausage rolls. A chocolate éclair.' She ruffled Sam's hair. 'And a cupcake for this one.' She stroked Milly's face.

As Tessa packaged everything, Rose said, 'I'm having a little get-together this weekend. Just a few neighbours. That counts you in.'

Tessa's stomach turned over. It was all *so* new, still. But it was important to make the effort. To keep up appearances. 'That would be lovely.'

'Great stuff,' Rose said, getting out her phone. 'What's your number?'

Tessa recited it. As she handed over the packages, she noticed Sam looking through his book by the fridge. She smiled at the boy, although he didn't seem to notice. 'I love reading, too, Sam.'

Rose said, 'He's obsessed with reading at the moment. Wish I'd the flipping time for it!'

'What've you got there, sweetie?' Tessa asked.

Sam raised his freckled face. A big gap-toothed smile filled his face.

Tessa took a deep breath.

'It's about monsters!' he exclaimed, holding the book up.

Tessa's hands were trembling, so she kept them at her sides, out of sight. She forced the smile to stay in place.

Rose chuckled. 'All he talks about lately.'

Tessa's voice was barely above a whisper as she asked, 'What's your favourite monster?'

The boy thought for a moment, his brow furrowing in concentration. 'I like the ones that live in the deep ocean,' he said finally. 'Because no one knows what they really look like.'

After the family left, Tessa retreated to the alley behind the bakery for her break. Her hands shook as she lit a cigarette. She leaned against the outside wall, exhaling a shaky stream of smoke. She closed her eyes and saw another gap-toothed, freckle-faced boy.

His eyes were bright with curiosity.

The monsters are here, Tommy.

Tessa squared her shoulders and took a deep breath.

She nodded, accepting, knowing that she'd always carry the weight of her past. It was important she did so. This burden was her penance... her redemption.

And it felt rightly so.

◇

The headache was subsiding, so Ray opened his eyes and, through the haze of his damaged vision, read the letter he'd written and slipped it into an envelope.

The infuriating buzzing sound of the fluorescent lights in the prison corridor broke through his earplugs, so he took them out and slipped in a new pair.

Since his sight had weakened, his hearing had compensated.

He wrote on the front of the envelope but then felt another stab in his temples. He sighed and closed his eyes again. The last thing he wanted was to risk a migraine.

He thought back to his last session with Amelia.

The voice of the prison therapist was calm, non-judgemental, and it echoed in his mind. 'Maybe this isn't your first time in prison, Ray... at least in a figurative sense.'

'What do you mean?'

'Maybe you were trapped in a belief... believing that you could change things that couldn't be changed?'

Over time, Amelia had allowed him to view his memories regarding Graham differently.

Now, with his eyes closed, he saw his brother down by those railway tracks again.

His death hadn't been Ray's fault.

None of this had ever been his to control.

That world of darkness, that realm of chaos he'd conjured to explain away the inexplicable, was dissolving gradually, like mist under the glare of a rising sun. Amelia had made him realise that it was a desperate childhood attempt to make sense of something senseless that had crystalised falsehoods within him.

He opened his eyes and read the name on the front of the envelope: *Megan Powers*.

His fingers, once steady as he delivered sermons, now trembled slightly as they traced the edge of the pile of envelopes. A litany of lives he'd damaged.

It'd been Amelia's idea to write the letters. She warned him that they might never be read. He imagined some would be thrown away. Some might even be burned or spat on.

He could never truly make amends. To suggest so was folly. Words on paper could never heal the wounds he'd inflicted.

Each letter was a confession, an apology, a desperate plea for forgiveness he knew he didn't deserve, but this was his penance.

And it was appropriate that he kept trying.

He could hope that in the trying, he'd find some peace, but he shouldn't expect it.

Ray checked his watch. He had one more letter to write before retiring.

It felt like the hardest one to write.

Outside his cell, the world moved on. But here, in this small space, Ray faced the ghosts of his past, one envelope at a time.

He began the last letter of the evening.

Dear Greg.

The sky was an unbroken blue.

Simon Lyle stood on the doorstep, squinting against the brightness.

He took a deep breath, steeling himself, and knocked.

The door opened, revealing Terry Kane's lanky frame. As a child, his hair had always been unkempt, falling across his forehead in greasy strands. Nothing had changed.

Simon forced a smile, trying to ignore his churning stomach. 'Hello, Terry.'

'Mr Lyle.'

'It's been a long time.'

'Yes,' Terry said, pushing the greasy fringe over his ear. 'A long time.'

'How have you been?'

Terry didn't answer. Instead, an awkward silence fell between them, while Terry played with the hem of his shirt, looking uncomfortable.

Simon cleared his throat. 'Well... I was hoping we could talk.'

Terry considered, his brow furrowed in concentration.

'If you don't mind, that is?' Simon said, trying to keep his tone light. 'It really shouldn't take long.'

'All right.' He worked at his fringe with one hand, and with the other hand twisted his hem. 'Come in.'

Simon followed Terry into a sterile living room. The furniture was sparse and functional. Modern art adorned the walls.

They sat on opposite ends of a rigid sofa, the distance between them palpable. 'So,' Simon said, realising his voice sounded too loud in the quiet room. He took it down a notch. 'What've you been up to these days?'

Terry's eyes darted around the lounge, never settling on Simon for more than a second. 'I work at McDonald's. Cleaning.'

'Fantastic. Well done, you.'

'Ah...' He worked on his hair. 'It's... it's okay, I guess... just okay.'

'I see. Free food, eh? Can't be too bad.'

'I don't like the food.'

Simon smiled. Terry reminded him so much of Greg. 'That's good. It's bad for you! But you know steady work is important.'

'Yes,' Terry agreed. 'And I like it when things are clean. Orderly. I can focus when I'm there.'

'I can see how tidy you are,' Simon said, gesturing around the room. 'Do you have any hobbies? Things you enjoy doing in your free time?'

Simon noticed a spark in Terry's expression.

'I draw animals. Birds, mostly.'

'You always did, if I remember, correctly. Bloody good ones. Excuse my language.'

He blushed. 'I also watch nature documentaries.'

'Just wonderful,' Simon said. 'I remember you and Greg at the dinner table, talking about animals... drawing and drawing.' He looked off into space. 'Greg loved those sea creatures, didn't he? Like you loved those birds?'

'Yes.' Again, Terry looked excited.

They talked for a while. The conversation became more settled, and as long as Simon tailored the conversation around Terry's interests, it flowed and felt as natural as it could.

Eventually, Simon got to the point of why he was here. 'I wasn't a good father, Terry.'

He knew Terry wouldn't respond to this. It would be way too far outside his comfort zone, but he gave him some time to digest it anyway, before following up. 'I was hoping... well, I was wondering if you'd some time...' His voice cracked.

There was a silence while Simon took some breaths. He wanted to get himself back together before making his request again.

He didn't need to.

'I've some time,' Terry said.

Simon smiled. 'You always were a good boy, Terry.' His eyes were filling. He turned away and dabbed at them with his sleeve. He really didn't want to unnerve Terry. When he felt composed, he looked back. 'No one knew him quite like you did.'

Terry's eyes fixed on a point somewhere beyond Simon's shoulder. After a long moment of consideration, he nodded.

'Please tell me about him,' Simon said.

Terry continued to stare. He was maybe thinking of where to begin. It had been a challenging request.

'I'm sorry,' Simon said.

Terry shook his head, stood and walked to the rear window. 'Come with me.'

Simon rose to his feet, followed and stood alongside him. He gazed out over the garden. Nestled among the trees was a treehouse.

Terry raised a trembling hand, pointing. 'Greg and I built it together. It was our favourite place. We could be ourselves.'

Simon could almost see them there – two young boys, unique in the way they viewed the world, different in their wants and needs but, ultimately, happy in the presence of one another. His vision blurred with tears, the treehouse becoming a smudge of brown against the vibrant green of the leaves.

'Tell me about him, Terry. Tell me everything you can remember about my son.'

Gerry sat on a bench on West Cliff, overlooking the North Sea. The waves were calm today, and she could see ships in the distance, their white sails billowing against the horizon. A cargo vessel moved slowly across the water, its dark hull a stark contrast to the sparkling blue sea. Rylan sat at her feet, his tail thumping gently against the wooden slats of the bench.

'Gerry?' Tom suddenly stood before her, bouncing on his toes with nervous energy. He looked like a small child with his eyes sparkling in hope.

'Sit down, Tom please,' Gerry said. 'I've reached my conclusion regarding our relationship.'

Tom sat on the bench beside her, then leaned forward eagerly. 'And?'

'I still recognise the potential for future growth together.'

Tom smiled and nodded.

'Gerry, I—'

'There's something I have to share with you first though.' She reached into the backpack at her feet beside Rylan and pulled out a framed photograph that sat on her mantlepiece at home. 'My parents.' She pointed to the man. 'My father was called Edward. He was adventurous, funny and kind. When I was younger, he brushed my hair every day to get the knots out. He said he wanted to do it because he'd never had knots in his own hair and he wanted to see what the fuss was all about.' A small smile tugged at her lips. 'My mother' – her finger moved to the woman in the

411

photo – 'was called Margaret. The first few times I went swimming, she allowed me to take a stuffed toy in with me as I was nervous...'

As she continued to share stories about her parents, the sun began to set, casting a warm glow over the sea. The distant ships were now silhouettes against the orange sky, their outlines blending with the horizon. Rylan had curled up at their feet.

Tom took her hand and Gerry held his stare for a long time.

It didn't feel awkward in any way.

Frank hung back, shuffling from foot to foot, a bouquet of Bulgarian Zdravets cradled in his arms.

Janet Wainwright put her head into her mother's room and then looked back at Frank and smiled. 'Come in. She's ready for you.'

'Aye, okay.'

Janet came out of the room so Frank could go in. Frank gave her an awkward nod. 'Thank you very much.'

Janet smiled, probably at his nervousness. 'No bother.'

Frank stepped inside the bedroom. The room was bathed in a gentle pink glow, with delicate floral curtains framing the window. A cosy armchair sat beside the bed, a crocheted blanket draped over its back.

Evelyn was lying down. She was smaller, and frailer, than he remembered her from their feisty cemetery encounter a few months back. However, the resilient spark in her fiery gaze remained. 'Frank, I'm glad you came.'

Frank proffered the delicate pink flowers. 'Aye... yes,

well, I got these...' His voice was gruff, betraying his nervousness.

'They're nice. I don't think I've ever seen anything quite like them.' Her fingers reached out so she could brush the petals.

'Bulgarian,' he said. 'But I didn't go all the way over there for them.' He snorted at his own joke.

She smiled and his face glowed.

'Yes, well, where shall I put them?'

'On the side, please, then take a seat.'

Frank placed the flowers on the bedside table, then lowered himself into the armchair, forcing back his usual grunt. He shifted, trying to find a comfortable position. 'Nice place.' He tried not to wince over how forced his small talk must sound.

'My daughter's. Janet has been wonderful while I've been recuperating. I'll be back home as soon as I'm able. She might try and stop me...' A determined glint appeared in Evelyn's eyes as she spoke and she grinned again.

Frank chuckled. 'She won't succeed, I'll bet!'

'Well, you've got first-hand experience of that steel already,' Evelyn said.

They shared a laugh. Frank's posture relaxed slightly. His hands unclenched from their tight grip on the armrests.

'Well,' Frank said. 'About that argument, I'd like to—'

'Please, Frank.' Evelyn cut him off with a wave of her hand. 'That's not why I wanted you to come.'

'Okay... I see...' *Well, if not to address that*, Frank thought, *why are we here?*

'The last thing I wanted was you here apologising for your passion... your loss...'

He nodded.

'We all need our fire, Frank.'

'Aye...' He smirked. 'Best to keep it in check, sometimes, mind.' He thought back to last month when things had got out of hand. He'd been heavy-handed with two suspects; fortunately, their complaints had come to nothing. Unsurprisingly, a human trafficker and a child killer had struggled to gather support. That didn't make it right though. Frank knew that he'd gone too far. There were limits. And now there'd be more eyes on him than ever before.

Evelyn studied him for a moment, seeming to sense the weight of his thoughts. She adjusted herself in the bed, wincing slightly at the movement before settling back against the pillows. 'The reason I spoke to Helen and asked her to get you here may seem strange at first, but please, hear me out.'

Frank nodded, his brow furrowing slightly in curiosity. 'No problem.'

She fixed him with a stare. 'I want to know more about Mary.'

Frank stiffened. His eyes widened slightly. He opened his mouth to reply but had no idea how to respond to that, so simply closed it again.

'I warned you,' she said. 'Strange request, eh?'

Frank nodded. It was all he could manage. His back was ramrod straight against the chair, and aching.

'For whatever reason, Frank, your wife came into my life. I don't want to ignore that. Gloss over it. Truth be told, I can't. And I suspect you feel the same... deep down... You see, I knew everything about Nigel, Frank. *Everything*. Yet I discover I was wrong. There was something else. One thing. And no small thing, either. Mary. A wonderful person, I'm sure. As you told me. By not knowing about her, I feel that

some part of him is missing from me. And I feel empty...
hollow. Regardless of what happened, I loved that man. I
gave my life to him.' Evelyn's voice quavered slightly. 'I
want to know about this special person that came into his
life.'

Frank's throat tightened. He swallowed and looked
down. He could feel the usual irritation within him, threatening, but he could also feel something else. A resigned feeling. He'd neglected Mary in life, potentially caused this
issue, and now she was gone, did he continue to neglect
what Mary would have wanted?

She wouldn't have wanted his irritation... his anger...
she'd want his understanding. 'Aye. She was special. Very.
I'm listening.'

'Just tell me about her.'

Frank's hands clenched and unclenched in his lap, his
gaze dropping to the floor as he wrestled with his emotions.
The world was moving onward, now, in a mysterious way,
and he was not the best person to move with it. But he
had to.

He may have been sixty-five, but he was never too old to
change... to learn...

If he believed that, then he'd be without compassion.

And if he was without compassion, how could he still
do what he did on a daily basis?

He nodded slowly, then added, 'Okay, but listen,
Evelyn, this is important... I'm not ready to talk about Nigel.
And I warn you, I might never be.'

'I understand that.'

He looked down as he spoke. 'Although I suspect he
wasn't the monster I thought he was if he was married to
you all these years...' He chanced a look up at her.

Evelyn's eyes glistened, a sad smile touching her lips 'Frank, I'd never demand that you forgive him. If I choose to forgive him, and Mary, those are my choices... I won't force them on you.'

Frank nodded. He raised an eyebrow. 'You've forgiven him?'

She smiled. 'Yes. Haven't you forgiven Mary?'

'Aye... yes... of course...' He felt his stomach clenching. 'I think... Bloody hell... *sorry*... I don't know, sometimes.'

'You will,' Evelyn said. 'Come to terms.'

He thought about his explosions of anger, his smoking habit. 'I hope so.'

Evelyn leaned forward. 'We're all human, Frank. Your daughter, Maddie... Helen told me she's still not home.'

'No.' His chin quivered. 'I miss her... both of them... I miss *both* of them.'

Evelyn reached over, her frail hand grasping Frank's larger, calloused one. It was an unexpected offer of comfort. He let out a shaky breath.

'We'll both take it one step at a time, slowly,' Evelyn said.

'Aye.' Frank nodded.

'So can we start with Mary, please?'

He nodded. 'Aye, we can.'

'Could you tell me how you met?'

Surrounded by the sweet scent of Zdravets, the two strangers, united by loss, spoke at length as the afternoon light faded.

And although Frank faced the grief burning fiercely within him, he knew that this was a good thing.

For the first time, he didn't run from it, or towards it. Instead, he attempted to accept it.

Join Frank, Gerry and Rylan on their next adventure when the echoes of past crimes lead them down more winding paths in FORGOTTEN GRAVES.

Scan the QR to
Pre-order!

Free and Exclusive read

Delve deeper into the world of Wes Markin with the
FREE and **EXCLUSIVE** read, *A Lesson in Crime*

Scan the QR to
READ NOW!

JOIN DCI EMMA GARDNER AS SHE RELOCATES TO KNARESBOROUGH, HARROGATE IN THE NORTH YORKSHIRE MURDERS ...

Still grieving from the tragic death of her colleague, DCI Emma Gardner continues to blame herself and is struggling to focus. So, when she is seconded to the wilds of Yorkshire, Emma hopes she'll be able to get her mind back on the job, doing what she does best - putting killers behind bars.

But when she is immediately thrown into another violent murder, Emma has no time to rest. Desperate to get answers and find the killer, Emma needs all the help she can. But her new partner, DI Paul Riddick, has demons and issues of his own.

And when this new murder reveals links to an old case Riddick was involved with, Emma fears that history might be about to repeat itself...

Don't miss the brand-new gripping crime series by bestselling British crime author Wes Markin!

~

What people are saying about Wes Markin...

Also by Wes Markin
ONE LAST PRAYER

"An explosive and visceral debut with the most terrifying of killers. Wes Markin is a new name to watch out for in crime fiction, and I can't wait to see more of Detective Yorke." – *Bestselling Crime Author Stephen Booth*

The disappearance of a young boy. An investigation paved with depravity and death. Can DCI Michael Yorke survive with his body and soul intact?

With Yorke's small town in the grip of a destructive snowstorm, the relentless detective uncovers a missing boy's connection to a deranged family whose history is steeped in violence. But when all seems lost, Yorke refuses to give in, and journeys deep into the heart of this sinister family for the truth.

And what he discovers there will tear his world apart.

The Rays are here. It's time to start praying.

The shocking and exhilarating new crime thriller will have you turning the pages late into the night.

"A pool of blood, an abduction, swirling blizzards, a haunting mystery, yes, Wes Markin's One Last Prayer for the Rays has all the makings of an absorbing thriller. I recommend that you give it a go." – *Alan Gibbons, Bestselling Author*

One Last Prayer is a shocking and compulsive crime thriller.

Scan the QR to
READ NOW!

Acknowledgments

Returning to Whitby's atmospheric world for this third instalment has been both challenging and delightful. As Frank and Gerry's story deepens, so does my gratitude for all who've made this series possible.

My family remains my writing cornerstone. Jo, Hugo, and Bea - your ability to weather storms of deadlines and distraction with good humour never ceases to amaze. This book is a testament to your unwavering support.

Heartfelt thanks to the readers who've journeyed with Frank and Gerry from the start. Your enthusiasm has made this series a joy to write.

To the book blogging community - your dedication to championing new series is the lifeblood of authors everywhere.

I owe a special debt to Whitby itself. Its blend of quaint charm and Gothic atmosphere provides endless inspiration. From local historians to sea-worn fishermen, every conversation adds depth to these pages.

I look forward to our next journey, where echoes of past crimes lead us down winding paths...

Review

If you enjoyed reading ***Forgotten Souls***, please take a
few moments to leave a review on
Amazon, Goodreads or BookBub.

Printed in Dunstable, United Kingdom